THE OUTLANDS PENTALOGY
A Touch of Death

Rebecca Crunden

ISBN-10: 154321021X
ISBN-13: 978-1543210217

Edited by Elizabeth Tanner
Cover Design by Heather Maddalozzo
Photo © David Tadevosian - Dreamstime.com

This is a work of fiction. Names,
characters, places, events and incidents
are products of the author's imagination.
Any resemblance to actual persons, living
or dead, is entirely coincidental and not
intended by the author.

For my mother, John and Liz.

The KINGDOM OF CUTTA submits that the outcome of the LAST WAR, otherwise known as the HUMAN-MUTANT WAR or the RECLAMATION OF OUR EARTH, will hold. All ten countries established during the war including CUTTA, REDLAND, THE EASTERN ISLANDS, THE SOUTHERN LANDS, RINLOW, EYRE, CLEARBOW, NITOIB, TALON and MUNTENIA, are presently united, governed and protected underneath the title of KINGDOM OF CUTTA. All countries, joined of their own accord, in part due to the salvation, economic means, protection and might of KING FRANKLIN CROW I, Lord King of Cutta of the House of Auram, First Breath of Our Salvation, do hereby agree to submit, serve, adhere and defer to the might of Crown and Council, hereafter seated in ANAIS, capital city of CUTTA.

Henceforth there is one religion, one language and one ruler as decided within the PROCLAMATION OF UNITY. The sacrifices for this peace being those which are the most insidious and destructive aspects of human nature: FREEDOM and HISTORY. These known forces of destruction and their encompassing evils are hereafter decreed ILLEGAL and REGRESSIVE. The KINGDOM will be ruled in adherence to these beliefs, and maintains that the most important aspects of society will, from this day forth, be CONFORMITY, CONTROL and CONTINUATION.

AR124

INTRODUCTION
The Captain and the Prisoner

The sun's relentless heat had been overwhelming all summer, but it was particularly taxing that morning. Captain Cooper Sikander had been standing in the prison yard for hours watching the inmates do hard labour, their hands bleeding, their backs burnt, their faces grim. He felt infinite pity for the lot of them. He felt infinite pity for himself.

He was thirsty and his flask was dry; lunch time was not for another hour and although he had to relieve himself, he did not leave his post. For some reason, he couldn't. He felt almost in competition with himself at times, arguing that if the prisoners could carry on whilst bleeding, starving, limping, crying and oft-times dying, then surely he could wait it out until lunch time. A silly thing to force himself to endure when there was no reason to do so, but Cooper had maintained the same internal philosophies since he had relocated to Anais, and hardly felt inclined to change now.

He had grown used to it so long ago that now it seemed normal, insignificant and uneventful. The criminals were executed, or if they were rich enough or lucky enough, merely punished and interned for an unknown number of days suiting the Council's whims before securing their release. As they waited for death, the workforce or an expensive reprieve, they worked, they staggered, they bled. It was routine.

The most interesting days were the ones with the rabids. When a rabid – those leftover monstrosities from the Devastation – was found within the borders of Cutta, it was tranquilised and brought to Redwater. One of the few places where complete secrecy was guaranteed. Once, three of them had been trying to bring down a rabid that had broken loose in the yard and only Navi's remarkable aim with a knife had brought it to its knees. The scientists had dissected it in the basement later that evening with glee. Pitiable as much as frightening, at least the rabids were different enough not to give him nightmares the way the treatment of the prisoners often did.

There was few enough that he had not seen, and not much more which he had not done or assisted in, and Cooper had learned over the years that the best way to remain sane was to keep silent, say nothing, and do as he was told. He was nothing, after all. A piece to be moved about at random. Replacing him would be of no urgency or consequence. He was as expendable as the criminals he moved about from cell to yard to infirmary.

The smell of sweat and blood was strong in the air, and something else he could never quite determine. It lingered in his nose for hours after he left the prison, and even after he bathed, he could smell it. The smell of futility. It was worse than fear or hatred or sickness. The constant longing for a quick, quiet death seemed to emanate from most of the prisoners inside the walls.

One of the most boring parts of the job was the waiting. He deliberated on whether working as a guard wasn't a sort of prison in and of itself. He was sworn to service for life and could never work as anything else. His children would be wealthier than he had ever been, and allowed into the best schools because he served the King with his life. Nevertheless, it wasn't a position he greatly enjoyed even if he did see the importance of it. He wouldn't argue with the executions of dissenters or murderers, but the lifelong imprisonment and enslavement of those who stole to feed their families, or accidentally crashed their hovers, or took an extra job on the side to make ends meet, seemed a bit unnecessary to him.

'The new prisoner's arriving soon,' said an amused voice behind him, tearing him from his unspeakable musings.

Blake Navi, one of his fellow guards, sidled up to him, hands behind his back, face expectant. He always seemed close to panting over the arrival of fresh prisoners. A young man who took far too much joy in watching the prisoners toil away, Navi seemed ideally suited for prison work, and Cooper harboured a suspicion that he was not entirely normal.

Cooper nodded perfunctorily and turned back to watch the inmates.

'Aren't you curious who it is?'

He shrugged. 'Does it matter? They're nobody once they're in here.'

'This one was headed for execution,' said Navi. 'Came right close to it as well. I hear he was headed to the gallows when they called him back. Last minute favours. The only reason he isn't dead now is because his family has ties.'

'That's hardly news. Most rich criminals are on bought-off sentences.'

It was too early and too hot to deal with Navi. Sometimes Navi enjoyed his job too much and it bothered Cooper. He wasn't sure why, because so many of the others also liked punishing the inmates – those stupid fools who knowingly committed crimes which would ruin their lives – but Navi bothered him on a level that was almost bone-deep. When they were alone together, he always felt an itch below the surface of his skin to be as far away as possible from the other man.

To Cooper it was a dull job that he spent the day doing so that he could provide for his family; to Navi it seemed to be a calling. Cooper could still remember the morning he'd stepped into the courtyard and found Navi running his fingers over the bleeding wounds of a prisoner's back. He shuddered at the memory.

'Ah, Sikander, you're no fun,' said Navi, wiping his nose with the back of his hand.

Not bothering to reply to him, Cooper began to walk around the edge of the fence. The fence was tall – so tall that Cooper could barely see the tips of the guns of the patrolling guards above – and so thick that sound on the other side was almost entirely blocked out. Being inside the prison was like being sent back in time several decades, and each time he stepped outside to head for home, Cooper had to reassure himself that he was still firmly in the present.

Nothing inside the prison had been changed since it was first built, and the building reeked of decay and mould and damp. The

Hangman said it was to instil fear and maintain order. To that end, it was certainly effective.

It was nearly four in the afternoon when the doors opened and the prisoner was hauled inside. He had a bag over his head and his feet dragged on the ground behind him. He looked unconscious, or at the very least beaten to the point of submission. His clothes had been ripped from him and the bruises on his body were purple, green, yellow and black, displaying the extent and length of his torture. It was clear that whomever he was, the new inmate was not a friend of the Crown whatever his connections may be.

Jack Irving and Marlo Lucius, two of Cooper's fellow guards, hauled the convict across the courtyard and tied his arms above his head to one of the large posts which were erected around the perimeter. The inmates looked up, curious, and Cooper didn't bother to yell at them. He, too, wanted to see who this new criminal was. If he was a son of high society, Cooper would most likely recognise him.

The son of a farmhand, Cooper's parents had risen in society by having twelve children. The grants they received for each child had given them enough money to move out of the Southern Lands and into Clearbow, where his father had opened a shop and had finally been able to put his feet up at night. Cooper had taken the position in the Kingdom's guards to ensure his children rose even higher. And since his binding to Clara, they had had three children and moved to the capital city of the Kingdom, Anais.

His mother had cried with joy, for her own parents had been servants to a lord in Redland and she had never dreamed that her grandchildren might one day dine with the rich. Clara, ever prudent, had made certain that they knew everyone there was to know, and they made as many friends as possible. As a result, they had become regulars at several estate dinners and had even attended a birthday celebration where the King himself was in attendance.

It was expensive and strange living in such a city, but Clara was delighted, and so he said nothing. Clara, to her credit, worked two different jobs to help pay for the taxes and rent, and never complained about his lack of interest in parties and society. It was all for their children.

As he watched, the prisoner was unmasked, his hair dark with sweat and matted with blood. He could not have been much more than twenty, and his soft, un-calloused hands betrayed his wealth and position. No wealthy man had ever worked the fields or dirtied their hands. Cooper frowned as the prisoner leaned against the pole for support, his body shaking. He hadn't turned around, so it was impossible to properly identify him.

'He gave us more than a little trouble on the way in,' said Lucius. 'Spent the weekend in Bernstein for protesting.'

Cooper walked over to them. 'Protesting what? The tax increase?'

'The Crown.'

Cooper's jaw dropped. Now he understood. There had been a small but growing number of dissenters in the cities of late, frustrated by the increasing hunger and the wealth gap. All were shot on sight. Twenty bodies hung from the posts in the city square to remind the citizens of their duty. To even question King Markas' authority was a death sentence.

'Who are his parents?' he asked.

'Friends of the King,' said Irving. 'I think they sold their souls to keep his neck attached to his body. Bastard was headed for the gallows when we were told to stop and turn around. The others that were with him are all dead.'

'You're despicable,' the prisoner croaked, opening a bloodshot eye to glare at them. His lips were swollen, his voice ruined, his eyes caked with dried and crusted blood. 'The Abyss is too good for you.'

Irving punched him hard in the gut and the prisoner slumped against the pole. Irving had been a guard for far longer than Cooper, and seemed to hate the job twice as much. Whilst Cooper wanted only to go home and wrap his arms around his woman and forget the awful grimness of their duties, Irving took out all of his anger and fury on the prisoners themselves. He had no remorse and seemingly negative amounts of patience.

Whether incredibly stupid or incredibly brave, the prisoner rolled a swollen eye in Irving's direction and spat out a wallop of blood. 'Eat me,' he grunted. 'You fucking rat.'

It was perhaps the worst thing the prisoner could have said, and he was rewarded with a series of punches, each one threatening to rid him of all his teeth. He did not cry. He did not beg. Stupid he may have been, Cooper was impressed all the same.

When he was finished, chest heaving, Irving stepped back, shaking his hand to help return sensation. 'Navi, fetch me the lash,' he ordered. 'I want to show the prisoner exactly what happens to malcontents inside these walls.'

Cooper's lip curled. 'Is that necessary?'

'Get back to your patrol, Sikander. You're not needed here.'

With a last look at the prisoner, Cooper walked back to his post and examined the work that the inmates were doing. It was the most pointless task, moving great stones from one side of the courtyard to the other until they fainted with exhaustion. Cooper wondered what was worse, the lash or the stones. Quite frankly, he would have taken death over either.

Too curious about the prisoner to pay attention to the back and forth, back and forth of the stonework, Cooper found his gaze drifting to where the other guards stood gathered around the prisoner. He looked so crippled and defenceless on the ground. A strange feeling of compassion welled inside him. He didn't know what to make of it. He just knew he didn't want the dissenter whipped. He could not have said why.

Navi reappeared a moment later with the large whip in his fist, expression gleeful. He handed it to Irving and stepped aside, hands behind his back as he waited with bloodthirsty anticipation for the prisoner to be beaten. His eyes raked over the man's body in a way that made Cooper frown, stomach twisting with disquiet.

The first crack of the lash sent a shiver down his spine. The inmates cringed and two of them stopped short. Cooper glanced at them. Forcing them to watch such horrors seemed cruel and unnecessary, and he was not in a vindictive mood.

'Inside,' he barked at them.

He led the five inmates back to their cells; none of them looked at him or tried to talk to him the way they sometimes did. All too terrified by the events going on outside. Even so far from the courtyard he could still hear the horrible sound of the lash on the prisoner's skin.

It was another several minutes before the whipping desisted with horrible abruptness. Cooper hoped the prisoner had passed out. It was the only way to endure such pain. He hesitated, knowing he would be expected outside to report to Lucius, but he had no desire to see the man's flayed back. Taking his connecter out of his pocket, he entered Clara's registration and leaned against the wall. She answered a moment later.

'Everything all right?'

'Fine,' he said. 'I just wanted to see how you and the children were getting on.'

Clara laughed. 'Libba's fussing and won't eat. Kieron's asleep. I'm just waiting for Riley to come home at this point so I can start dinner.'

'Good,' he said distractedly. 'What are you making?'

'Not sure yet,' she said. 'Any preferences?'

Cooper frowned to himself. 'Nothing with meat.'

'All right,' she said. 'Enjoy the rest of your day.'

'Yeah.' Somehow that seemed unlikely. Cooper slipped the conn back into his pocket, steeling himself for what he was going to see, and walked back out to the courtyard. Even after seeing it so many times, it was still hard to be greeted with the sight of so much blood running down a man's back, pieces of skin jutting out unnaturally. His stomach threatened to rebel and he tried to remind himself that the man had known the consequences of his actions. He must have known he would be facing death. This was a blessing compared to what could have been done to him.

'Ah, Sikander, good,' said Irving. 'My arm's getting tired.'

'Captain?'

'Finish him,' he said, handing Cooper the bloodied lash. 'Another twenty strokes should do.'

Cooper took the lash but did not raise it. 'Captain, he's not even conscious.'

'Navi's gone to get something to wake him up.'

'If he's hit any harder, his skin will come off,' said Cooper, raising the lash slowly even as he said it. He did not want Irving to think he was questioning his orders. Nothing was more foolish than that. 'Would you not want to leave it until tomorrow when he'll actually be able to feel it properly?'

Irving wiped perspiration from his forehead. 'I don't think he'll be able to move tomorrow. Finish him now.'

Just as he said this, Navi returned carrying a shot of something with blue liquid. He jammed it into the prisoner's arm and a second later the man awoke. He let out a sob of pain as he moved and the blood on his back flowed with renewed vigour.

Irving said, 'Now, Sikander.'

Cooper clenched his jaw and brought the lash down hard on the man's back. Blood sprayed up, coating his face and getting into his mouth. He spat out in disgust and wiped his face before whipping the prisoner again.

He finished it quickly, not wanting to prolong the show any more than he had to, and dropped the lash on the ground the moment he was done. Flesh hung off the man's back, his whole body was soaked in sweat, and the whimpers escaping his mouth should have brought the cruellest of men to their knees. The guards surveyed him with nothing but loathing and turned away, leaving him to bleed against the pole.

Cooper looked to Lucius. 'Should I bring him to the infirmary?'

'I suppose,' said Lucius. 'We can't have him dying on us if the King has gone to so much trouble to keep him alive.'

Relieved, Cooper unbound the man and caught him before he could hit the ground.

The prisoner tried to push him away. 'Go fuck –'

'Don't say anything,' said Cooper, a note of warning in his voice. He lifted the young man easily into his arms, trying not to touch his back. It made for awkward carrying and after five paces he slung him over his back entirely, and walked in carrying the prisoner the way hunters carry their prey.

'Where –'

'Just shut up and I'll see what I can do.'

Cooper carried him into the prison and stepped into the shoot that brought him up three levels to where the bodyman worked. Blood was soaking through his uniform and dripping onto the ground; the strong metallic smell gathered in his nostrils and threatened to set up there permanently. His hands felt sticky and warm, and the whole ordeal turned his stomach.

He had seen many a man beaten, some even to death, but he had never been moved to help one of them before. There was something admirable about a man – a traitor – who did not scream or back down. Even with skin coming off his back, the man did not seem weak. Cooper felt a bizarre sort of admiration towards him.

The bodyman, Faber, was a wizened old man who had been at Redwater Prison since King Markas' coronation and looked well beyond his years. He stood up stiffly when Cooper brought the prisoner in and laid him face down on the bed.

'My, my,' said Faber, voice gravelly and halting. 'What trouble has this young man been up to, hm?'

'A protestor.'

'Goodness,' said Faber. 'And he was spared?'

'Spared?' It was hard not to scoff. 'He lives, barely. I wouldn't deign to call such a fate spared, Faber. Don't let him die. King Markas' orders.'

Faber nodded and turned to attend to his patient.

As Cooper turned to leave, the man reached out and caught him by the arm, his grip surprisingly strong.

'What's your name?' His voice sounded like metal on glass but the lilt was impossible to mask. He was Anaitian.

'Cooper,' he said, startled into informality.

'Cooper,' repeated the man. 'Good to know.'

He said nothing else as Faber injected something into his arm and his eyes rolled back into his head, blissful black sleep overtaking him.

Cooper appraised the prisoner, his stomach queasy. He felt unable to move or walk away or do anything except kneel beside the unconscious figure, watching as Faber set to work on him.

The minutes ticked by with impossible slowness, each one more exhausting than the last. Cooper could not have said why he worried for the young man's fate. He had no reason to. The dissenter had undertaken his actions knowing he was likely to die in the same horrific fashion as his friends.

Deciding that he was more perplexed than empathetic, Cooper sat down in the chair by the bed and thought of all the reasons a rich man would risk his life to protest that which had no effect upon him. Those in Cutta, and especially in Anais, were not in danger of starvation like those in the Southern Lands; nor of the Thinning, which was spreading rapidly through the Eastern Islands. There was no danger of rogue mutants or rabid animals in Cutta as there were in the newly settled places in Eyre and Nitoib. Not to mention the fact that all Anaitians were inoculated from the Plague at birth, so it was not a threat to any of them the way it was for the rest of the Kingdom. Anaitians were the only ones who had nothing to fear.

Anais was a beacon of hope and simplicity, dangling above all other cities in the Kingdom with its wealth and prosperity and ease of life. And so he stared at the copper-haired young man, little more than a boy, and wondered what had changed one of Anais' highest born into a dissenter with welts on his back, pools of his blood staining the floor.

After a long while, Faber finished treating and bandaging the wounds and announced that the prisoner could go. Cooper carried him down the brightly lit corridor towards his cell. It was cold and empty, completely bare. A stark contrast to anything the man would know.

Cooper put him down carefully and nodded to himself, glad that the prisoner had not awoken. He glanced at his timekeeper, and left the cell quickly, making for his post.

It was only when he was back in the yard, all too aware of the bloodstains on his uniform, that he finally realised who the prisoner was.

Shock filled with him dizzying speed. What possible reason could Nate Anteros, eldest son of the King's favourite, have for wanting the Kingdom brought to its knees?

AR127

PART ONE
Infection

MONTH ONE

Away from the harsh glare of artificial light, the constant thrum of human activity and the purr of passing hovers, the world seemed extraordinarily quiet. The sort of quiet where even the softest of footsteps or lightest of breezes could be heard, and every creature was aware of the smallest of sounds.

That said, the two humans who currently joined them were far from quiet. Moonlight illuminated only a fraction of the road and was not bright enough to outline rocks or other sharp objects, and Catherine Taenia found herself tripping and stumbling through the tumbleweeds and gravel which had overtaken the ancient path.

A wild, untouched world, it had been so long since any sort of transport had touched the ground that the old roads had gone to seed. Sticks stuck up in odd places, sinkholes which had once been obvious were now invisible beneath overgrowth, and treacherous water was hidden in shadow and failed to reflect the light of the stars above, threatening to swallow them whole if they stumbled too near the edge of the road. There were no signs to guide the way, only a vague understanding to go northeast towards the adjacent town. It was galling and overwhelming.

The Nitoib Mountain Range was known for being desolate, with endless stretches of valley, lowlands, and dozens of creeks and rivers, each leading in a different direction, some safeguarded, some unknown and treacherous. The mountains themselves stretched the length of Nitoib, from the Uncleared Zone in the southeast, to Muntenia in the north, and kept on until the Outlands beyond Franklin's Wall. Much of the mountains were off-limits due to an increase in rogue rabids and wild animals slipping through cracks in the crumbling Wall, and walking on the roads had been illegal in the fifty years since hovers became the primary means of transportation.

Far from anything and the least populated country in the Kingdom, the patrols in Nitoib were so understaffed that two weeks often went by between fly-bys. It meant they were safe from being seen but in serious trouble if anything went wrong.

It was not merely fear of rabids, mutants and animals which frightened her. Catherine had read about wanderers and vagabonds who drifted to the edges of the Kingdom and died of exposure and frostbite. Diseases were rampant even now, and in spite of her injections, she nursed a constant fear of contracting something. Her father had told her many tales as a child and she could still remember his story about the man who had wandered off, froze to death and had his face eaten by a wild dog with two heads. Whether true or not, it terrified her. She did not relish ending up like that at all, and she was so angry at Nate that she half-heartedly told herself that if the guards managed to catch up to them, she would hand him over in exchange for a lift home.

Renewed anger burned through her chest and she glared around, trying to catch sight of Nate in the darkness. It was impossible.

'Have I told you how much I loathe you?' She heard a snort from somewhere to her right, and turned her head, staring into the murky darkness.

'Shall I apologise again?'

His tone only infuriated her more.

'We might be out here for days,' she snapped. 'My feet are bleeding in these shoes and I've no coat or water or anything that might be of use.'

A huff of exasperation reached her ears. 'We're not going to be out here for days,' he said. 'Two at most.'

'Two days meaning more than one.'

'We'll find something today or tomorrow and we can contact Tommy to come and get us,' he continued. 'Everything will be fine. There's no reason to worry. We both know that you're not the one who's in trouble.'

'Fleeing the guards is completely illegal,' said Catherine. 'I'm in as much trouble as you.'

'None of them are going to accuse you,' said Nate. 'It was entirely my fault.'

'At least we agree on that much.'

An uncomfortable silence filled the space between them for a moment, and then a sudden cracking sound reached her ears and light appeared. Nate face was illuminated by the match's flame. He looked horrible. Blood had dried in five or six miserable rivers down his face from cuts which marred his eyebrows, his nose, his forehead and his lip. His eyes were bloodshot and heavy-lidded. It made him look wild and mad. On anyone else it would have been surprising and a reason to fret. On Nate it was almost normal.

'Here,' he said, after a moment's pause. The flame disappeared and Catherine couldn't make out what he was doing behind the spots now performing in rampant explosions before her eyes. A moment later, he tossed something at her. It landed on the ground and she bent cautiously and picked it up. It was his heavy winter coat, well-worn and a bit wet from sweat, but warm and protective all the same.

'Sorry about your feet,' he added. 'I'll try and find us even ground so it doesn't hurt as much.'

Catherine said nothing as she accepted the coat. It would have been incredibly imprudent not to. She was so cold that her teeth ached from chattering together, and her legs and arms felt like metal poles. The coat went down to her knees and blocked out a fair amount of wind. Suddenly warmer, her anger dissipated just a fraction.

They made their way along the twisting road, alternating between the matches and the dying igniter, only turning it on when they reached a dead-end and had to backtrack onto the road to regain their course.

As they rounded another bend, the sound of rushing water grew louder and louder, to the point of being worrisome, and Nate clicked his igniter once more to see what was ahead of them. Most of the back-roads of Anais were overgrown and rundown, and out here in the mountains it was even worse. Greenwald, the town they were fleeing, and Goodkind, the town they were making for, both had footpaths within town boundaries, for walking, gliding or cycling, but out here the world was wild and desolate.

Where once the road had bridged its way across the raging waterfall, the bridge was now completely destroyed and there was a gap far wider than either of them could jump, directly in front of them. The road leading up to the edge was crumbled and broken, as if angry at being neglected. The empty space dropped down into the river. Catherine could hear water thrashing against the rocks far below. Falling in would mean certain, painful death.

She cursed quietly. Nate, who was holding the igniter out before him like a beacon, appeared only marginally ill at ease. To her fury, he seemed almost amused by their predicament.

'I don't know about you, darling, but I can't swim,' he said, peering cautiously over the edge. 'I suppose we could take the trail.'

'You must be joking.'

'I saw what looked like a proper trail back that way. I reckon it was the one they used to use to get between the towns during the war.'

'How do you even know where those are?'

Nate snorted as if affronted by the question. 'I'm a terrible drunk, darling, not an idiot.'

Catherine raised an eyebrow.

'Funny,' he said. 'I did listen in Cartography. Can't get Tommy to shut up about it.'

'I opted for Architecture.'

'Oh? Any good?'

'It was all right – *Nate*,' she snapped, rolling her eyes. 'Now is not the time.'

He chuckled lowly. 'My point is that I know my way up and over.'

The trails on the side of the road would potentially bypass the waterfall, and they could cut down the mountain when they saw the road pick up again, but it was a dangerous route and not one

Catherine felt inclined to take. She had broken enough laws that night and didn't feel like tempting fate further. She could just imagine the trouble Thom was going through trying to sort everything out for them. Undoubtedly her father and Cecily Anteros were racing to ensure there was no fallout. Catherine did not even want to think about Hamish's reaction. Hamish Anteros made no attempt to hide his hatred of his eldest son.

She stared blindly up at the black mass of the hills and mountains which towered above them dauntingly. 'The trail's been there for an age,' she said. 'It's not been used in decades. I'm not walking up an uncharted mountain in the middle of the night with hardly any light. Let's just think of something else.'

'What if the guards come?'

'Then you'll be thrown in prison again and you'll deserve it,' she hissed through gritted teeth.

Nate tensed visibly. She was sure she could hear his teeth grinding and in the fading light she could see his fingers tapping out an agitated rhythm on the tree branch beside him. 'Kitty,' he said at length, 'I know you're exhausted. I am sorry for that. I know this is all my fault and I'm trying to make it right. I'm not going to wait on the side of the bloody road for men who have an incredible, undeniable urge to torture me. Tommy's going to fix all of this – that's the beautiful thing about money, it can get you anywhere – but it's going to take a while and I'd like to be a figment of their imagination until they are called upon to arrest some other unlucky soul. Can we please walk to the village? Up and over, darling.'

Catherine raised an eyebrow at the enormous cliff beside them. It went straight up and disappeared into the darkness. She wasn't sure how high it was; from where they stood in the middle of the road, it looked near to impossible to traverse and she felt a rising bubble of nausea in the pit of her stomach. She was not about to admit her fear, however.

'There's no path,' she said lamely.

'There is,' said Nate. 'I already told you. Back the way we came there's a turn off that goes straight up and over. Once we're passed the river, we can climb back down. It'll be a detour. It's that or go back.'

He looked at her beseechingly. Going back before everything was sorted out would put him back in the hands of the guards. It would mean going to Redwater before a release was even discussed. It would mean he'd have to go back into a cell. A beating would be a positive outcome.

Much as she detested Nate's entire existence, Catherine was still haunted by the look on Thom's face when he told her that the guards had tortured him. She couldn't let anything happen to Nate for Thom's sake.

It didn't mean she wasn't thoroughly inclined to punch him on the nose.

Wind bit at her already icy legs and she looked down at her feet. They were throbbing badly. Her legs were covered in shiver-lumps. 'I rather hate you,' she said resignedly, and limped past him, back the way they'd come.

It took almost an hour to find the path. She could feel insects happily biting into her flesh and the bites that didn't sting itched terribly. One in particular seemed to have swollen to a great size and she started to worry about infection even though she'd had her bimonthlies only two weeks before. Her body felt more tired and woozy than it ever had, even given the circumstances, and she wondered if she was getting a fever. Most likely she was sobering up and paying the price for it, a by-product of stress and exertion.

When the path began to rise, she was forced to remove her heeled shoes; woefully impractical to begin with, they now proved a hazard. Her feet stung, the ground unforgiving and jagged beneath her toes. Where rocks did not litter the path, the grass was thick, pokey and wet, and soon her feet went numb with a burning cold.

Thunder boomed in the distance, and a *crack* of lightning brought a cold rush of wet wind and a streak of blinding brightness across the horizon, giving her a brief glimpse of the terrain. The last of Catherine's humour left her.

The thick grass suddenly dropped beneath her feet and her ankle slid into a hole. She spun around and hit her back against a rock. Pain shot through her entire body. She cried out, the suddenness of it keeping away the worst of the pain as shock rushed through her and everything seemed to sharpen; all remaining drunkenness left her, chased away by the pain. She felt the warm stickiness of blood beneath her clothes.

'Bloody God,' she cursed, holding her ankle with one hand and clutching at her back with the other. Gold stars were exploding in front of her vision and blood was pounding in her ears.

It took her another minute to realise that Nate was at her side, talking to her.

'... more than just a bruise, hopefully. Darling, you all right?' He lifted the igniter higher, appraising her worriedly. The rain had mixed with the blood and muck on his face, and he was a strange mess of pinks and browns and reds, and the blacks and greens and yellows of forming bruises. His red hair looked black in the darkness. He looked like Thom. She hated him for it.

'Leave me alone,' she said. 'I don't need any of your help.'

'Look, I'm trying –'

'Just go! You've done enough damage already. Why did you even come back?'

He let out a sigh and she wondered if he was offended or simply biting back a snarky retort. Before she had time to gather her own thoughts into any semblance of understanding or maturity, he said simply, 'I apologise. I've said my apologies and I shall repeat them again if you wish. Please hear them. I'm sorry you got hurt and I'm sorry you saw that back there because I can imagine it didn't really do much in my favour. I never thought any of *that* would happen. I never even thought you would be here! You've never opted to come before. I thought Tommy would be alone.'

'That doesn't exactly fix the problem, does it?'

'So my apology means nothing?'

'Not when your actions have turned us both into lawbreakers and disrupters of the peace, no. Yet again your family's cleaning up your mess, lack-brain, and I'm starting to think you've no care at all for anyone in the world except yourself.'

'As you wish.' Nate's face suddenly disappeared as the igniter went out. She could hear him stuffing it into his pocket. He stood and stomped off, all trace of him gone in seconds, swallowed by the vicious night.

Catherine glared after him. Their relationship had always been tempestuous, but when his actions and subsequent arrest lost both her and Thom job opportunities, things had soured even further. No matter their connections, associates of criminals were not trusted. Both of them had had to find a new career path and her annoyance at him had become full blown hatred.

She would have yelled in frustration if she were not so scared. The hunters of Nitoib talked of the animals they encountered. And, as always, there was the small nagging fear of rogue mutants and what an encounter with one could turn into. Catherine had no desire to linger alone, injured and exhausted. It took a long moment and several forced swallows of bitterness for her to quash her pride.

'Nate!' she yelled. 'Nate, come back!'

A pinecone soared out of the darkness and smacked her shoulder. He had not gone very far.

Nate appeared a second later, briefly illuminated by another flash of lightning. He bent down in front of her. The lightning was flashing across the sky often now, and every few seconds she could see his outline moving. It was like a series of sequential captures.

'You're a real charmer,' he said. 'Someone ought to've told you that by now.'

'Will you shut up and help me?'

'Only if you say *please*, darling.'

'Go hang yourself.'

'I'm waiting.'

'Fine. Will you please help me?'

Suddenly, Nate's arms were around her, lifting her into the air. He seemed to have no trouble carrying her, although his lungs were straining from the altitude and cold wet air.

She had broken her ankle a few years before and Thom had had to help her around quite a bit, but he had always struggled to do it, and she had felt guilty asking. Yet it seemed no effort for Nate to lug her straight up the hill towards the switchbacks. She worried immensely about how he had achieved such levels of strength. She didn't know where he had been the last two years but the change was obvious. Gone was the Nate she had grown up with. Gone, too, was the skeleton he had come back from prison as. This new Nate seemed as reckless and criminal as the last, but there was something different.

The anger which once seemed to make him burn was gone. In its place seemed a strange hollowness. A lack of purpose and certainty.

The horizon suddenly turned white, the whole landscape illuminated in an almost black and white setting, like a sudden flare from the sun had passed across the night sky, lighting it only for the blink of an eye. As quickly as it had appeared, it vanished, and Catherine was left blinking rapidly to clear her vision.

'That was different,' said Nate. 'Have you ever seen lightning that close?'

'No,' she said.

'Comforting.'

They said nothing else, and the rain lashed on. Catherine's mood, while suddenly distracted, was still sour. The longer they walked, the colder the night became. Nate slipped downhill several times. At one point, he completely lost his footing as the rocks slid out from under them and they fell a long way down the hill, landing in bushes and brambles. Catherine pushed herself to her feet, cursing and wincing, but she only made a few, limping steps on her swollen feet when Nate reached her and helped her onto his back.

Whether it was because he felt guilty or because he knew that she could not have walked another step, he said nothing about carrying her and she said nothing about how angry she was. It was hard to yell at someone who was attempting to walk up the side of an old mountain trail with another human on their back.

Thunder boomed in the distance, an ominous warning not to keep going. Heedless, Nate trudged on, his large arms holding her easily, even as he descended sharp ravines and jumped over deep puddles. Catherine was so close to Nate's back that his warmth was all around her and she felt herself growing sleepy.

Eventually she drifted off.

Catherine awoke suddenly when Nate lowered her to the ground. It was dawn and they were still on the mountain. She rubbed her eyes and glanced around. The rain was coming down harder than ever. How she managed to sleep as long as she had was a mystery to her. The air was bitter and uncomfortable, and they were both drenched.

Nate was staring at something just down the hill. Sitting up, Catherine followed his line of sight, eyes still heavy with sleep. Her whole body ached from the strange sleeping position. She was also experiencing the bone deep cold which comes from a bad night's sleep without blankets.

There, a short distance ahead, was an abandoned building. The outside had possibly once been white. Now it was an off-grey, ruined by years of neglect and mould and rain. Several sections of the building were missing, but enough of the exterior remained to allude to the year it had been built. The structure was from the early days when people still built buildings reflecting their underground homes. It was hardly suited to an aboveground environment.

'What do you think it was?' she wondered aloud.

Nate shrugged. 'Out here? Could have been anything. Maybe a hospital or prison or school.'

'Those are very different things.'

'Not in terms of architecture.'

Catherine grimaced. 'I can say without hesitation that I've absolutely no inclination to see what's down there.'

'It's ridiculously cold and the storm's getting worse,' said Nate, having to raise his voice over the hammering rain just to be heard.

'I'd rather an old building than open fields. The lightning's struck ground several times and there are too many open stretches of ground without trees to take the brunt of it.'

Catherine glared down at the building. 'How much further do you think it is to the town?'

'Could be hours. The muck is bad and I've twisted my ankle twice now. I don't really relish the hills.' Nate held out his hand and helped her to her feet. 'Shall we see if we can dry off and get some rest and then we'll keep going when the rain lets up?'

'All right,' said Catherine, feeling anything but.

Nate led the way down the hill, slowly picking his way over the sliding mud and tall, prickly grasses. At a few points he stopped and lifted Catherine over areas where water was rising rapidly, heading straight towards the side of the cliff in a deadly makeshift waterfall.

By the time they reached the building the rain was coming down worse than ever and both of them were trembling with cold. Nate kicked the broken and crumbling door in. He lifted Catherine over the sharp pieces of glass and mortar and brick, lowering her carefully onto the ground a few paces away. Here the ground was cold porcelain, and although dirty and slick, there was nothing to trip over or dodge.

Catherine squinted around in the gloom. 'What is this place?'

Nate examined his handful of wet matches, cursed unhappily, and gave the weakening igniter a disheartened click, shining the light around. It looked no less strange and unusual with light, and they exchanged unenthusiastic looks.

'I've not a notion,' he admitted.

'Let's just hope it's empty.'

'Amen.' Nate bent down and examined the debris on the ground. 'It'd be a real mess if there were rabids or wolves in here.'

'Oh wonderful, and here I was feeling so calm and safe.'

'Don't worry, darling. Things out here are more afraid of you than you are of them.'

She raised an eyebrow. 'Are you sure?'

'Not a bit. Was hoping you'd believe me.'

The empty corridors with holes and cracks in the ceiling were eerie and inhospitable. But they made their way resolutely through the building, looking for a place to lie down and wait out the rainstorm.

One corridor led into another, and everywhere they turned there were locked doors of unbreakable iron, impossible to open. They passed through one hallway and then another, taking in the old building with curious, anxious eyes, trying to ascertain what it might have been.

'Here,' said Nate after they crawled under a fallen beam into another room. There was an old dusty sofa in what could have once been a lounge. It was the only open room they had seen thus far. The ground was covered in rubbish and broken things, and Catherine stood on tiptoes, glad that years of dancing had given her the ability to stand at bizarre angles for unwarranted amounts of time.

'I guarantee you there are diseases on that,' she said, nodding to the sofa.

Nate shrugged and sat down. 'I've slept on worse.'

'I highly doubt that.'

'Do you?'

'Your family has more money than half the country put together,' she said. 'Don't pretend elsewise.'

'I was referring to my stayaway in Redwater, actually.'

Catherine peered around the room. 'I'm certain prison has nicer beds than this.'

Nate leaned back, water still running in streams down his face, cleaning some of the grime in places and making it worse in others. 'You're certain of that?'

'Yes,' said Catherine, although she wasn't at all. Redwater terrified her and she had never been inside. Odd, since her father had worked there all her life.

'Sleep on the floor if you wish. Trust me when I say this isn't the worst place to sleep. It's just a bit dirty.'

Catherine sat down unhappily and kicked his shin with her foot. 'Move over.'

'I'm on my half!'

'I can smell your feet through your boots,' she said. 'I don't want that smell in my nose all night.'

'Darling, you just trudged through an inordinate amount of grime and shit in bare feet and you have the audacity to tell me that my feet smell foul?'

Catherine rolled her eyes and dropped her head back against the dusty cushions. She sneezed loudly. Nate smirked, his eyes shut in mock sleep. Catherine turned over and tried to get warm. The room was damp and smelled of mould and earth. Nate began tapping on the ground softly with three of his fingers, a repetitive rhythm that was more relaxing than annoying, although she was loath to admit it. Slowly, the thrum of Nate's tapping fingers became a consistent beat, in tandem with the pounding in her skull, and she drifted off.

She dreamed of nothing. In all her life, Catherine couldn't remember ever having a single dream.

Several hours later, Nate shook her awake. 'Rain's stopped,' he said. 'Let's get moving. I'm starving.'

Catherine nodded wearily, her eyes heavy, and forced herself to her feet. Her vision was blurry and unfocused, and her head was aching from an unhappy mixture of tension, hunger and exhaustion. She took three steps forwards when pain suddenly shot up through her foot. She lifted her foot into the air. Shards of glass were stuck deeply into the ball of her foot. Her stomach twisted at the sight and she swallowed hard, breathing through her nose.

'Shit,' said Nate. He picked her up and carried her back to the sofa, placing her down carefully and examining her foot.

Pain was shooting up through her ankle, her leg, right to her stomach and Catherine clenched her jaw to keep from crying. Or being sick. Nate would never let her live it down if she was sick.

'Don't move,' said Nate. 'Are you good with pain?'

Catherine nodded, teeth gritted.

Nate quickly started to pick the pieces of glass out of her foot. It took a while, but his fingers were deft and gentle, only cutting himself once trying to pull a particularly large piece out of her skin. He cursed and shook his hand hard before continuing; his blood only added to the mess. The rest of the pieces came out without fuss, although her foot was bleeding freely and Nate's hand was stained red.

She leaned back against the dirty cushions, forcing herself to remain calm. It was not the worst injury. Only a bit of glass. 'What was it?' she asked, trying to distract herself.

'I have no idea,' he said, glancing down at the shattered remnants. 'Probably just a glass or something. I think it was full of mouldy water, though. Apologies.' The shards were well and truly crunched, the ground around the pieces stained with liquid, and he winced in sympathy as he examined her foot again.

'Does it look bad?'

'No, you'll be all right. I don't like how it's mixing with the dirt and muck. When was the last time you had your injections?' He wiped his bloody hands on his shirt and ran a hand through his matted hair, brushing it back so that he could see more clearly. 'Tell me Tommy's still a complete guard when it comes to that sort of thing.'

'He is,' said Catherine. The nausea from the pain had subsided a bit. 'I won't get an infection. I just need to get it clean.'

'You can't walk on it.' He made a face. 'Although it's not like you were walking on it much to begin with.'

Catherine glared at him. 'You know this entire thing is your fault?'

'Yes, you've said that,' said Nate. 'Are you going to let me carry you in a clearly vain attempt at trying to make this up to you or are we going to sit here and rot away for the rest of eternity?'

'Just don't talk,' said Catherine.

Nate clapped his mouth shut comically and bent down, lifting her into his arms and carrying her over the broken shards of glass and the blood stains around it, down the crumbling, ominous corridor with its many bolted doors, and out into the late afternoon sun.

'It'll probably take us the rest of the day and night to reach the road,' he said grimly, nodding towards the large incline that would take them up and over the mountain to the road they both hoped was on the other side.

Catherine raised her eyebrows. 'You won't be able to carry me that far.'

'So little faith,' said Nate, adjusting his grip on her. 'It's insulting, honestly.'

'Shut up.'

Whether it was out of pride or sheer determination, Nate managed to carry her for the rest of the day, stopping only twice for a break and to re-examine her foot. His body was soaked in sweat and it was clear that he was exhausted, yet he made not a word of protest and even when Catherine offered to walk, he declined and told her that he was fine, she was barely heavier than a feather. She knew he was lying, but her foot ached and the ground was covered in sharp rocks and potholes, and after offering twice more, she left it alone. He walked until dusk and they stopped near a creek to drink as much water as they could. Catherine was hesitant at first – all water in Cutta was treated, and this appeared clearly stagnant – but it was either risk sickness or dehydration, and she opted for drinking. If she got sick, the bodymen would be able to cure her.

They slept for several hours until, at some point, Nate picked her up again and continued walking.

When she woke up the next time it was morning again, the sun bright and cheery in the sky above, the temperature cool, if slightly humid.

Nate lowered her stiffly and dropped down against a large tree, gasping for breath. Sweat was dripping down his brow and his shirt was soaked through. If possible, he looked even worse than he had the day before. His eyes, which were always dark grey, had a strange amber tint to them. Almost ruddy. His skin was pale and his freckles stuck out noticeably. He was still trying to catch his breath when he doubled over and got sick. He dry-heaved for a short while before dropping onto the ground, his head between his knees. Catherine walked over to him. He looked very close to blacking out. Extreme fatigue, she reckoned.

'You could have taken a break,' she said softly.

He shrugged, wiping his mouth. 'I'm fine. Need food. I always get sick when I don't eat. Strange contradiction, but there you are. How's the foot?'

'Sore,' she said, flexing it. The cut had scabbed over, which was something.

'Your eyes are bloodshot,' he said. 'You all right?'

'Fine. You're rather wrecked yourself.'

Nate chuckled. He spat a wad of bile onto the ground and cracked his neck. 'I probably look a complete disaster.'

'Worse.'

He looked like he might be sick again. 'Where do you think we are?'

Catherine glanced around. This road wasn't as old – and looked like it had been used more recently. She stumbled ahead on swollen feet, and waved for Nate to follow her. He did so slowly, shuffling along with all the enthusiasm of a criminal to the gallows.

She led him down the road until it forked. Another few miles after that and there was a long descent down a hill towards the very clear marking of a flypath.

'Fantastic,' said Nate. He looked down and then back at her. 'You decent to walk down this or you think your feet will give out on you?'

'I'll be fine,' she said, although her foot hurt with every step and she was biting back screams so hard she could taste blood from her cheek, and started to climb down. The pain radiated up from her feet to her shins to her knees to her thighs. Several times she contemplated just rolling down, but with Nate there and her pride at stake, she carried on until they stumbled out onto the flypath and followed the bright white painted markers, eyes peeled for a passing hover.

All the colour had drained from Nate's face when he caught up to her. Catherine wondered how much worse he must be feeling, and felt a small twinge of guilt.

Now that they were on the main path, it was much more likely that they would come across someone. The population of Nitoib wasn't large by any means, but there was a fairly decent chance of someone coming along to meet them.

Nate said very little as they walked and it was apparent he felt worse by the hour. He was sick twice more as the morning dragged on.

Hours later, at last, a hover appeared, banged up and rusting, floating only a few metres above the ground rather than the required ten. A local. The hover came around the bend, sunlight glinting off the solar panels on the roof, blinding both Catherine and Nate. She waved frantically at it, and almost cried with joy as the hover, driven by an old man, flew down to the side of the road. He waved them into the back and they clambered inside.

'Forrest,' he said, extending his arm in greeting.

Nate held up his grubby hands, declining the handshake. Catherine held up her hands as well, smiling apologetically. 'Been walking all night, I'm afraid,' said Nate.

'Good thing I stopped.' Forrest looked back at them with a smile. 'Lost in the mountains?'

'Our campsite was set upon by a bear,' she lied succinctly. 'We had to run.'

'Rotten luck. More good luck than bad if you're both still alive, though. You stay on the trail?'

'Of course,' said Catherine. She quickly wracked her memory for names of places in Nitoib. 'The Gretta Campgrounds, near the East Underground Museum.'

'Ah, very good,' said Forrest. 'I went to the museum myself a few years back. Can't imagine how they lived underground. Did a walking tour and had to leave early I missed fresh air so much.'

Nate nodded in agreement. 'Humans were never meant to live underground.'

'This is what I keep saying, although my Complement disagrees with me.'

'Do you mind taking us to the nearest inn in town, Forrest? We could certainly use a bath.'

The old man laughed and nodded, launching into a mindless discussion about the weather and the wildlife in Nitoib, and how he wondered if the King was going to send settlers down to bolster Nitoib's economy. Food shortages were not as bad in Nitoib as they were in the Southern Lands, but times were certainly getting hard.

There was a pile of maps and books at the ground near her feet and Catherine scanned the titles out of boredom, tuning out the sound of his words, having no urge to speak to him. She was so tired and hungry, all she wanted was to be at the inn.

The titles varied greatly as she nudged the books apart with her toe: *Guide to Farming*; *Map of Nitoib Mountain Range*; *Atlas of the Eastern Countries*; *The Plague*; *Everything You Need to Know About Winter Farming*; *Diseases of War: A Look at the Devastation, the Plague and Mutants*; *The Spread of the New Plague: Are You Safe?*; *Protecting Yourself Against the Bite*; and *The Famine of AR63*, were just the ones Catherine could see.

She wondered if Forrest was a bit mad. He seemed nice enough and talked without a hint of insanity, so perhaps his scattered reading habits weren't anything to concern herself with. Nate, after all, did not seem concerned. Although she would not have trusted Nate's judgement on much, she trusted that he knew enough nefarious and mad people as to know when danger was near.

Catherine was delighted when the town finally came into view. Forrest dropped them at one of the first inns they saw, and Catherine hobbled inside, too tired and sore to wait for Nate, who was thanking Forrest profusely for stopping.

At the front desk, she asked to use the public connector and entered her father's registration, nodding to the man behind the counter who didn't seem even remotely amused by her muddy and bruised appearance. It was a noticeably affluent inn, well used to rich travellers on their stayaways, not dirtied wanderers. Catherine did her best to ignore him, but she felt terribly uncomfortable. She hated when people stared at her.

After a few beeps, her father answered. 'Taenia.'

'Daddy, it's me.'

'There you are. I was conn'd by Cecily Anteros last night. I've spoken to the King. You are not in any trouble.'

Catherine relaxed. 'Thank you, Daddy. And Nate?'

'That young man was better off in prison,' said Mickey darkly. 'How Thomas and Cecily keep working miracles I will never know. He's in no trouble either. There will be no charges.'

Catherine nodded to herself, but didn't say as much. Mickey was not the sort of person who took hyperbole well and tended to overreact to the smallest of infractions. He was a rather forceful man, very used to getting exactly what he wanted. Thom, he approved of. He never had trouble telling Thom what to do. Nate, on the other hand, had not only cut ties with his own father, but had also soured his name and standing in just about every location in the Kingdom. One wrong word would do more harm than good, and Catherine hadn't spent two nights in the mountains evading the guards just to ensure Nate was arrested after all. Instead of agreeing with her father, she made a non-committal noise and changed the subject. 'Will you speak to the manager and assure him that everything will be paid for?'

'Of course. You're not hurt?'

'No, just a bit shaken up and tired is all,' she said. 'Can I put you on?'

'Yes.'

Catherine handed the conn to the clerk and waited patiently as her father finished the transaction. The moment the man heard her father's name, his entire demeanour changed. He looked instantly apologetic and embarrassed, and thanked her father several times before hanging up. She was still smirking when Nate re-joined her.

'All good?'

'If there's one thing my father can do, it's convince people to listen.'

Nate snorted but said nothing.

The clerk handed their keys to the bellhop and they were shown upstairs. It was a gorgeous place, strongly scented from the wide windows open to the large garden in the centre of the building. Splashing water from fountains outside orchestrated their walk. The room was less ostentatious, albeit no less nice, and Catherine thanked the bellhop before closing the door. She left Nate to his own devices and went to the conn by the bed to ring Thom. She had stopped being able to feel her toes a while back and looking down at them, she saw that they were black with dirt and dried blood was caked in several places. She grimaced. Now that the adrenaline was leaving her, she felt more weary than ever.

Thom answered immediately. 'Nasim?'

'It's me,' she said. 'Did you manage to sort everything out with the guards?'

'Where are you? Are you all right? Where's Nate?'

'We've only just got in. It was wretched. I have rocks and muck so deeply ingrained in my skin I think they're going to stay there as permanent residents. I've half a mind to name them and welcome them to the family. I can't move without everything hurting.'

'And Nate?'

'He's in the bathroom, I think. He disappeared a few minutes ago. I wanted to contact you to let you know we're safe.'

'What inn are you at?'

'The Dragonfly. It's just off the main street in Goodkind. It's in the middle of town, not too hard to find. We're checked in under my father's name.'

'I'll be there soon.' He was so full of confident assurance, as he always was, and Catherine felt better already. Thom had never been uncertain of anything, not in his entire life. It was calming to know that someone had faith everything would work out.

Catherine put the conn back on the shelf. She wanted to sleep so badly. First, however, she needed to clean up.

Nate stayed in the bathroom for almost half an hour. When he reappeared, he looked better, although clearly could have done with a meal. He had bathed, and cleaned his cuts and bruises, and his shaggy red mop fell heavily over his eyes, hiding some of the harm done to his face. His entire torso, however, looked like a child's painting canvas. Nevertheless, there didn't look to be any permanent damage, although Catherine could see scars standing out starkly on his wet skin, evidence of just how many fights he had been in over the years.

She wondered why he hadn't visited the bodymen to remove the scars. Everyone else did. 'Thom's on his way,' she said instead.

Nate nodded, his fingers tapping a rhythm on the wooden door for several long seconds before he went to the adjacent bed. 'I'm going to order food,' he said. 'Would you like anything?'

'Yeah,' said Catherine. 'I don't care what.'

Nate sat and picked up the conn. She caught sight of his back and stared, horrified. Thick white lines crisscrossed the surface in an ugly, brutal fashion. It was the worst thing she had ever seen. Doubtless some had cut deep enough in places to be almost life threatening. The thought of such pain made her stomach twist. She turned away, a shiver of empathy passing through her.

Inside the bathroom, she locked the door, stripped, and stepped into the huge shower. It filled instantly with warm mist from the ground, and cleansing bubbles floated onto her skin, eating away the muck and grime. A warm spray descended from the grate overhead, first lightly and then with the strength of a rushing waterfall and then lighter once more. The water that ran off her was brown and pink; the cleanse worked well, and soon she was able to see her skin properly again; light-brown and unblemished. She carefully scrubbed her foot and then rubbed antiseptic into the wound.

When the warm water turned hot, then warm, then hot, then warm again, she finally opened her eyes and began to work out the knots in her long black hair. Small, elegant taps on the wall were filled with soaps, softeners, moisturisers, scents, dyes, delouser, thickeners, straighteners, curlers, and other various puddings, jellies and potions which would do anything desired to the hair or body.

At last, feeling remarkably better despite her throbbing foot, Catherine stepped out of the station and wrapped a thick robe around her body, hobbling over to the large counter to dry her hair and appraise the damage that had been done.

While her skin was raw from scrubbing and sensitive to the touch, she looked infinitely better than she had minutes before.

She tied her hair in a knot above her head and rubbed oil over her body, careful to add extra to the sores. The oil was reparative and could heal a cut within two hours, a scar within two days. It cured eczema, dermatitis, acne and other skin ailments. Had the establishment been less affluent, it likely would not have been on offer. In Anais, it was considered the height of rudeness to display skin inadequacies, and all were expected to restore themselves and be at the peak of composure and health. It was something she and Thom had always adhered to. It was something Nate clearly did not. Surely a few rounds of oil would clear his back up well enough, even with scars that deep. She wondered again why he had not.

When Catherine finally left the bathroom, she found Nate on one of the beds. The food had arrived and Nate's plate was scraped clean, but he wasn't eating. He was staring out the window with an odd expression on his face.

She sat down and grabbed a plate, her stomach growling loudly. She wolfed down the meat and cheese dish, gulping an entire glass of water and then pouring another. Her throat felt two sizes too small.

'It'll be a while before Tommy gets here,' he said at length. 'He's going to have to detour around the mountain which means he won't be here until this evening. Might as well get some sleep while we're waiting.'

'Fine,' said Catherine. 'If you snore, you sleep outside.'

Nate nodded and stood to draw the blankets back, depositing his towel on the ground as he did so, crawling naked into bed.

Catherine followed suit a moment later, the soft, heated blankets kissing her bare skin.

Despite of her exhaustion, she could not fall asleep, and her mind flitted dizzyingly from thought to thought like a trapped butterfly. She tossed and turned, unable to get comfortable.

A low moaning sounded from the bed next to her and she looked over, startled. Nate was deeply asleep, his brow furrowed and his hands balled into fists around the blankets. He seemed to be having a nightmare. His body contorted, his breath coming out in gasps, sweat breaking out on his forehead and chest. She wondered what he could possibly be dreaming out.

He shouted something unintelligible, his voice deep and furious, and sat bolt upright in the bed. He looked at her, a flush of anger and perhaps embarrassment colouring his pale face. Without a word, he rolled over and went back to sleep. Intrigued but not wanting to talk to Nate more than she had to, she turned onto her side and closed her eyes, trying to will her tired mind to shut off.

The knock at the door came several hours later when dusk was starting to fall. Catherine blinked her eyes open tiredly, her body heavy and useless. She turned the light on and looked over at Nate. He was watching her with sharp eyes. Sleep had definitely worked on him. Catherine couldn't say the same for herself. She was so tired and sore that the idea of any movement was ghastly.

It seemed that Nate had no such problem. He stood, wrapped the towel around his waist, and went to the door. Before he opened it, he straightened up noticeably, the worry and tiredness disappearing from his face. All of a sudden he seemed almost well. As if none of it bothered him at all. And when he opened the door, he was able to smile at his little brother as if everything was utterly normal. 'Hallo, Tommy.'

Thom smiled in affectionate exasperation at his older brother. 'Nasim.'

The boyhood names tugged at Catherine's heart and for a moment she forgot to hate him quite as much. When he was around Thom, Nate was almost tolerable.

Thom reached out to embrace him but stopped at the sight of the bruises peppering Nate's pale skin. Furious concern coloured his handsome face. 'What happened? Are you all right?' Thom sounded absolutely shredded. The edge to his voice was one Catherine had not heard since the last time Thom had woken from a nightmare, drenched in sweat, terrified that Nate was hurt or in trouble.

Aside from the few seconds of contact in the inn before the fight, Thom and Nate hadn't seen each other in two years – longer, really, as Nate's stint in prison for almost a year had directly preceded that. Nate left town the morning after his welcome home party. And Thom had barely slept in three years because of it.

Although how much sleep he ever got before that was up for debate. Catherine was well used to the hum of Thom's conn lighting up in the middle of the night as some friend or other of Nate's conn'd to say that he was in hospital, or at their house and in need of medical care, or needed money for bribes, or they simply needed his help and because Nate valued them, Thom always agreed.

Catherine had been delighted when Nate disappeared. Their brotherhood had never made much sense to her. Half the time they simply seemed to *feel* each other.

When they had walked into the inn looking for Nate two nights before, Thom found him instantly in the crowd.

Their reunion was like watching a mirror collide with itself. Nate had stood so quickly he bumped the table, eliciting growls of annoyance from the other gamblers, and embraced his little brother with such intensity that Catherine had winced at the sound of impact. For a long time, it was if no one else in the world existed. And then Nate had spotted her and a strange, thoughtful look crossed over his face. As if he didn't recognise her. But then, three years was a long time. He hadn't even seen her the night he returned from prison.

She wished she could say the same. Nate was the only person she could properly imagine as a skeleton as a result.

Now, however, they were both exhausted, there was too much to say, and neither looked in the mood.

In answer to his question, Nate smiled tiredly at his brother and said, 'I'm upright.'

'You look like death.'

'I feel like it, too.'

'You had me worried.'

'I'm sorry.'

'You're hurt ...' Thom glared at the bruises and cuts on Nate's torso from the fight. 'I got their names.'

Nate stepped aside with a shrug. 'It's nothing.'

Catherine didn't doubt that. Nate wore bruises like a second skin.

Now that they were both assured of each other's safety, the anger brought on by fear returned, and Thom stepped into the room, shoulders tense and face drawn with frustration. His black hair was askew, stuck up in strange directions from hours of stress and worry. Thom had a tendency to pull his hair out when he was anxious. His startlingly blue eyes were narrowed, and it was clear as he slammed the door shut that he was in no mood for games or japes.

'Do you have any idea what we went through trying to sort this one out?'

'He started –'

'And you had to end it, is that it? God's *wrath*, Nasim! You've only just come home! Two years of nothing and now *this*!' Thom stared at his big brother in complete bewilderment.

'Apologies,' said Nate. 'I didn't mean for it to happen.'

Thom deflated. He shook his head at Nate and looked to Catherine. 'Are you all right, my love?'

'Now that you're here,' she said, relief seeping into her bones as she sat up and rubbed the sleep from her eyes. Her head was pounding and her mouth tasted like dried feathers. She desperately needed something to drink. 'How did it go with the King?'

'We took care of it.'

'And Father?' Nate's voice was odd.

Thom stiffened. 'It's none of his concern and he knows that.'

'I'm sure he's pressing for my arrest as we speak.'

'He knows what will happen if he does.'

The brothers regarded each other with weighted looks for several moments before Nate looked away, jaw clenched. There was anguish in Thom's eyes, but he masked it quickly as he turned his attention back to Catherine. It was hard not to resent how close they were.

Not wanting any more dramatics, or to upset Thom further, she held out her hand to him. 'Come here,' she said. 'It's done now. We're both fine, let's just leave it.'

'You're right. I'm sorry.' He moved over to her side and kissed her.

She wrenched back with a cry.

A white-hot agony erupted from where his body touched hers and she scrambled away from Thom, falling onto the floor. Her blood felt like it was curdling, her stomach turned against her and she swallowed hard to keep bile down. Horrible red burns laced their way across her skin and lips where he had touched her.

The pain was consuming, like the very blood in her veins had suddenly gone sour inside of her. Thom moved towards her, alarmed and concerned. She held her hand up desperately not wanting anything to touch her. She wondered if this was what fire felt like. She blinked hard, clutching the carpet between her fingers.

Thom was hovering over her, looking upset and worried, unsure if he should help her or keep his distance. Nate had moved closer at some point. His eyes were wide with baffled concern.

After what felt like eons, Catherine held out a shaking hand to Thom. Her mouth was swollen and burned and it hurt to talk. 'What was that?'

The instant his fingers touched hers, pain ricochet through her hand, up her arm and into her chest, and she doubled over.

This time she *was* sick.

Thom reached out to pull her hair back and the second his hand touched her skin, pain ignited. Nate, who had been watching the entire exchange with a horrified expression on his face, seized Thom's shirt and started to drag him away.

Less than a second later, Nate cried out in shocked, horrified pain. He stared at his skin where his brother had touched him, mesmerised and pained in equal measure. To Catherine's surprise, it was Thom, not Nate, who pulled away first. Nate stared at his skin like it had betrayed him. There were burn marks marring his visible flesh.

He was mystified. 'What the *fuck*?'

Catherine shook her head in complete confusion. Thom was glancing back and forth between them with a horrified look on his face. Nate was gasping hard, surveying the damage that had just been inflicted upon his person.

Thom held up his hands where everyone could see them. 'Somebody? Anybody? Now.'

'It burns,' she said, stunned. It sounded so impossible when uttered aloud. 'When you touched me. It felt like I was on fire.' She appraised her skin. It looked like she'd gone swimming in a deep-fryer. 'You burned me,' she reiterated, touching the skin around the burns in shock. 'How?'

'I don't know.'

'Neither do I.'

Nate looked from one to the other before snorting in derision. 'I'm so glad we've got that covered. Does anyone have any bright ideas for what in God's name is going on?'

'Maybe it was static or something.'

'Static doesn't burn the skin.'

'Really? I had no idea.' She walked over to Thom and held out her hand. He appraised her concernedly before reaching out and touching the tips of his fingers to her palm. It stung worse than anything Catherine had ever felt and she recoiled.

'Perhaps ... perhaps ...' Thom shook his head, thoroughly confused. He ran a hand through his hair, tugging the long black strands hard enough to tear a few out by the roots.

'Why don't I try?' Nate gestured between himself and Catherine.

Thom nodded. 'Might as well.'

Catherine, who could not take her eyes off Thom, nodded, feeling wretched. 'It's worth a try. If we rule that out, then we can narrow it down.'

'Narrow down what? We don't even have a start.' Nate stepped forwards and reached out, taking her hand.

Nothing.

Catherine turned their hands over, staring. It felt normal, almost soothing, and a moment later Catherine realised that the burn on the inside of her hand and the burns on her lips where Thom had touched her were healing. She let go of Nate's hand quickly.

'We need to get to the bodymen,' she said. 'I want to fix this right now.'

'I agree,' said Thom. 'We'll go straight to hospital.'

He seized the blanket off the bed and held it out to her, careful not to brush her fingers. She accepted it gratefully and wrapped it around her shoulders.

'I'm sure you've just picked up an infection from being out in the wilderness. There's a reason you're required to stay on the bloody flypath.'

Fixing problems was what Thom was good at. Thom had fixed all of Nate's problems. Catherine felt a wave of relief knowing that he was in charge.

'There wasn't a whole lot of choice in the dead of night, little brother. We did the best we could.'

'Yes, and now I can't touch you or my Complement,' said Thom. 'You're sick, Nasim. I want this fixed.'

Nate's expression softened.

Catherine cleared her throat. 'Love, can you fetch my clothes? Wearing only a towel isn't doing a whole lot for my ability to think straight.'

'Really? I've always thought thinking in a towel was excellent,' said Nate.

Thom shot his brother a dirty look before nodding to Catherine. 'I'll be right back.'

He left the room and a heavy silence fell between her and Nate. They stared at each other for a few minutes before Nate clapped his hands together.

'Well,' he said. 'This is unexpected.'

'Shut up,' she said. 'This is a nightmare.'

'It's probably just an infection. There's no reason to worry.'

Catherine's lip curled. 'You're a terrible liar, Nate.'

'I'm normally a lot better,' he mused aloud. 'Guess I'm too tired to bother.'

He turned away, staring out the window that had taken up Catherine's attention just a short while ago. Thom returned with their clothing, and both she and Nate got dressed quietly. The oil had done a good job thus far of healing her sores and wounds, and she reckoned she'd look good as new in a day or so. Yanking her silver leggings up her ankles and fastening them to her undergarments, she pulled a clean dress on and slipped her aching feet into the thick boots her father had bought her when she turned nineteen. They hugged her toes and she felt infinitely more confident about walking. Wrapping her thick jumper tightly around her body, she ran a hand through her hair and knotted it on the top of her head haphazardly.

Thom smiled and reached out for her hand, only just remembering, and pulled it back with a sigh. 'Come on. The hover's waiting.'

They walked single file down the corridor. Catherine stopped only to sign the bill on the way out, and then they were on their way. Nate stretched out in the backseat, as if he was going to sleep, and for once said very little. Catherine pulled her legs into her chest and stared out the window as the long stretches of buildings and parks swept by. Although the town was small, and it wouldn't be too hard to determine where exactly the hospital was, none of them had ever been there before and none of them felt inclined to get out and ask for directions.

At last, Thom spotted it and lowered the hover into an empty space. They clambered out and headed inside.

The air smelled chemical and unwelcoming. Nate made a face and crossed his arms, eyes wary and distrusting. He looked ready to bolt.

Leaving Thom to talk to the bodymen, Catherine leaned against the wall. It was strange how the threat of arrest could dissipate in the course of a few hours, but that was how it had always been. Those who had money to buy off arrest only had to fear their brash behaviour momentarily. Others were not so lucky.

The year before several protestors in Anais had been hanged in the square for open disobedience. Catherine and Thom had been able to hear the jeers of the onlookers from their house several streets over.

'If they want to stick anything in me, I'm for the door,' said Nate loudly, eyeing the bodyman. 'No needles, Tommy, d'ya hear?'

The stern look on Thom's face brokered no room for an argument. 'If you have an infection, you'll just have to get over yourself.'

'What kind infection do you think only reacts when someone touches you?' The snort that left Nate echoed throughout the corridor and several people glanced up, eyebrows raised. Nate scowled at the lot of them until they looked away. He turned back to his brother. 'This isn't an infection.'

'It's something.'

'Obviously.'

When the bodyman returned, Catherine and Nate were shown into a large circular room with several empty beds. They were told to change into examination wear and then left alone once more.

Nate looked more unwell than she felt and she eyed him critically. His skin was covered in a light sheen and his hair was damp around his temples and neck. Still, he said nothing about feeling sick as he put the white garments on and sat down opposite her, eyes flicking nervously about the room, one hand balled into a fist, the other tapping out the same rhythm on the wooden desk beside the bed.

Catherine sat down across from him. There were several diseases that had cropped up when King Franklin led the people to the surface. Most of them had been discovered in the first fifty years and the cures were widely available to Anaitians.

The only things which seemed to have no cure were the Plague, the Bite, and the Thinning, and this was noticeably different from that deadly triad.

'Nathanial Anteros?' said a bodyman, returning through a side door and reading the description on the tablet in his hand.

'Yes.'

'Catherine Taenia?'

'Yes.'

'Have either of you been exposed to foreign substances in the last week?'

Catherine glanced at Nate. He shook his head. 'No, we've been only to Nitoib,' he said. 'Well within the Cleared Zone.'

'Were you bitten by any animals?'

'Just the odd insect.'

'Did you drink anything, touch anything or consume anything which could have been contaminated?'

The threat of arrest was never completely assuaged, and Catherine was in no mood to go through yet more bribery on Mickey and Cecily's behalf just because one of them said something stupid. Catherine's lie left her lips before she could even think about it. 'We went swimming in the pools near the Gretta Campgrounds and I stepped on a glass bottle and walked through the muck. That's all.'

There was a glimmer of surprise in Nate's ruddy eyes.

The bodyman nodded. 'Do either of you suffer from skin ailments?'

'No,' said Catherine. 'Just normal dry skin.'

Nate shook his head. 'Acne as a boy, nothing since.'

'No eczema, dermatitis or symptoms of the Thinning?'

55

'No,' they said in unison.

The bodyman nodded, made another note, and then placed the tablet on the table beside him. 'Now, I'm going to have to see what happens personally so that I may be able to make an informed prognosis. If this is uncomfortable for either of you, we can bring in sedatives.'

Nate shook his head, going slightly green at the prospect of needles. 'I'm fine.'

Catherine had no desire to feel the excruciating pain again, but she wanted a clear head, and she wasn't about to take the sedatives if Nate had declined them. She shook her head. 'I'm fine as well.'

The bodyman clapped his hands together. 'Right, now, if you'll both take each other's hands ...'

Nate held out his hand, eyebrow raised. Catherine rolled her eyes and held out her hand to grasp his. Again, nothing unusual happened.

'Good,' said the bodyman. 'Now, Mistress Taenia, would you be so kind as to take my hand?'

'I'll go first,' said Nate quickly.

With no desire to be burned again, Catherine did not argue. She watched as Nate reached out and took the bodyman's hand. His face contorted with pain and he clenched his jaw shut tightly, eyes widening. He wrenched his hand back after a few seconds, the skin on his fingers and palm red and blistered. The bodyman's lips pursed in thought. He leaned down and examined Nate's hand without touching it.

'Would you like some ointment?' he asked kindly.

'I'm fine.'

'Here,' said Catherine, holding out her own hand.

Nate took her hand gratefully. Warmth spread between their fingers and after almost a minute, the burns on Nate's hand started to heal.

The bodyman was stunned. 'How long have you known such a thing was possible?'

'About an hour,' said Nate.

'I've never in my life seen anything like this. And you are both burned if anyone touches you?'

'Yes,' said Catherine. 'Is it an infection?'

'I'm afraid I don't know,' said the bodyman. 'There are cases in the records of skin that burns when touched, but I have no notion why your skin subsequently heals.'

Nate spread his palm out and stared at his skin. 'It's remarkable, really.'

'Indeed,' said the bodyman.

'Are you sure it's not the Plague?' said Catherine. 'Not a new strain?'

The bodyman shook his head. 'It's not. And you are Anaitian, yes?'

'Yes.'

'All Anaitians are inoculated at birth,' he assured them. 'You have nothing to fear.'

Catherine frowned in thought. 'What sort of diseases are known to cause burning skin?'

'I'm afraid that's classified.'

Nate's lip curled and Catherine, fearing that he would say something rash, nodded quickly to the bodyman. 'I understand.'

'I'm going to recommend you see a specialist in Anais. I haven't the resources here and we're instructed to report all foreign infections to the capital.'

'Why can we heal each other?'

'I cannot say for sure,' said the bodyman, lips pursed. 'With the sheer number of new diseases we have been battling since the Devastation, it's possible that this is just another new one. Perhaps you've stumbled across something entirely unheard of.'

Catherine's stomach clenched. 'That's not even remotely comforting.'

'Not necessarily. Some of the greatest discoveries were by accident.'

Nate raised an eyebrow. 'Is there any animal you've ever heard of that can heal another of its kind?'

The bodyman's face darkened, but whether he had or had not, he did not elaborate. Rather, he said, 'It could be any number of various ailments. I wouldn't worry too much about it. Go to the specialist. I will make you two an appointment for tomorrow afternoon. That should give you enough time to take the ferry back.'

'Do you think it's serious?' asked Nate, his fingers tapping on the desk beside him. 'I'd rather like to know if I've to avoid humanity for the rest of my life. Not that I'm complaining, but it would be good to know.'

'I doubt it,' said the bodyman confidently. 'I'm sure it's nothing more than an odd reaction to the strange trees we have down here. Although many hundreds of acres were slashed and burned, spores and germs and pollens drift over the Wall with the wind. It could be anything. Not to worry. Just be at your appointment tomorrow so it can all be sorted out.'

They thanked him, and both Catherine and Nate dressed themselves slowly, dazed by the events of the last few hours.

Garden Port was fairly small, but by the time they reached it there was a steady flow of activity. The trio all deposited their luggage the minute they passed through security and made for one of the least crowded areas of the ferry.

Catherine felt more dreadful by the hour as they waited on the ferry. They sat in one of the restaurants eating dutifully and waiting for their ferry, and she wondered what the strange infection or rash, allergen or pathogen could possibly be. She wracked her mind for anything in the events of the previous few days that might be a clue. Everything from the scratches, bites, mountain water, cuts, and the strange building seemed like it could be the answer. Every direction just led to more questions, more confusion, and her head started to pound.

Nobody said much of anything for the next several hours, all upset and frustrated. Nate bought a book in the shop and spent the entire trip silent and focused on whatever it was he was reading, pointedly ignoring them. He seemed to have something on his mind, for his foot did not stop tapping, and when the food and drinks were brought around, he bought himself a very large glass of whiskey, only meeting Catherine's eyes once, before returning to his book, jaw clenched. Thom wrote furiously in his journal and read from a magazine every time he got too angry at whatever it was that he was writing, evidenced by the fact that his pen went through the paper several times.

His hand kept going to the silver bird which hung around his neck. It was forged from the weapons of the Last War; the silver melted down and recycled into something new. Nate had given it to him years ago, telling him that if the mutants had pulled it from the earth, it must be powerful and would keep him safe. Thom held it whenever he was worried or upset. Where Nate had even bought such a thing, Catherine hadn't a notion, but it was no secret that he would be dead before he bought something from the Perry Mines, so she was inclined to believe him no matter how absurd it sounded.

Catherine sat, staring into space, playing the night over and over in her head, wondering what she could have done differently. Books and stories always had some great moment of chaos and tension when everything began. There had been nothing like that. After Nate's fight, the events had been nothing more than a long, slow peregrination over a mountain.

When the ferry arrived in Anais, they took a hover straight to the clinic for their appointment. Thom was told to wait in the front room and Catherine was taken down the cold white corridor with Nate. They were shown inside a seeing room where the specialist was already waiting for them, studying notes.

The specialist was an aged bodyman with thick blonde hair and an unsettling smirk. He put gloves on and held his hands out to Catherine and Nate.

'Let's first see if fabric rules out anything.'

Catherine looked at Nate uncertainly.

He nodded and together they reached out and touched the doctor's hands. At first, there was no pain, and Catherine almost gasped in relief. And then, slowly, the way petals on a flower unfurl in springtime, discomfort started to grow from where their hands rested on his, and the discomfort burned a bit worse every lingering moment.

Catherine withdrew her hand, holding it protectively. 'It's slower, but the pain's still there,' she said. 'When I was a child I touched a hot iron and didn't let go fast enough. It feels a bit like that. Thermal or nearabouts.'

Nate made a face, brow deeply furrowed.

After asking them a similar series of questions to what the other bodymen had asked in Nitoib, the specialist left to confer with someone, leaving Catherine and Nate alone in the room.

'May I ask you something?' said Nate, gazing at her.

Catherine rubbed her eyes and shrugged. 'What?'

'You said *thermal*.'

'And?'

'I wouldn't say thermal. More of a ... *rotting* burn, if that makes sense. As if the skin wants to bubble and decay down to the bone. It's not just external. I can feel it in my veins, my bones, my chest. Everything feels infected and wrong. As if my whole body wants to collapse in on itself.'

Catherine grimaced but could not disagree.

The specialist returned just then and sat down on the stool between them. He looked at both of them carefully before speaking. 'The two of you are experiencing mirror reactions. When you come into contact with another's flesh, your own rejects it.'

'Great,' said Nate. 'Why?'

'I cannot say,' said the specialist. 'We've requested that your blood samples from Nitoib be sent to the Diseases Department. We should have the results in a few days. I recommend that you both go home, avoid touching people, and rest. That's the best you can do. I will prescribe you both sedatives as well, if you require them.'

'Thank you,' said Catherine, unsurprised by the response but feeling glum and disheartened all the same.

They dressed and met Thom in the hallway, explaining that once again, they had no answers. Thom nodded stiffly at the news, mouth set in a thin line, brow furrowed with worry. It was clear even he had not been harbouring high hopes.

Outside, the late afternoon sunlight warmed their bodies and Nate passed everyone tockers as he waited for his bus to appear. It was clear he still had something on his mind, and he opened his mouth several times to speak, but the words never quite made it out, and Catherine found she cared very little about what he had to say. She just wanted his absence.

Nate glanced at her, clearly not oblivious to her loathing. 'I'll be staying with Blaise,' he said to Thom. 'I suppose I'll come by when we've the test results back.'

It was clear from the look on his face that Thom wanted to invite Nate back to their house. He glanced at her, sighed, and said, 'Conn me later?'

Nate nodded and clapped Thom on the upper arm, winking confidently. Whether it burned him or not, Catherine couldn't tell. His gloves were thick and his expression guarded. 'Don't worry so much, little brother.'

Thom raised an eyebrow and gave Nate such an exasperated look that Nate was still laughing when he stepped into the hoverbus, the tocker between his lips, smoke furling from the tip.

'Come on,' said Thom. He reached a hand out, hesitated, and dropped it again. 'I don't know about you, but I'm more than ready for a hot bath and bed.'

'Thom ...' Catherine wanted desperately to reach out, pull him to her, kiss him, and be reassured that everything would work out.

'We'll fix this,' he promised. 'Don't worry, love. There's always an answer.'

A cab descended in front of them and they climbed inside.

It was a quiet flight home.

Their house was the same as they had left it. For some strange reason, Catherine had expected it to look as bizarrely different as she felt, but it was the same. There were a series of messages waiting for them. Cecily wanted to meet to discuss the Complementation ceremony and other recent events; Raylan Talbot, one of Thom's best friends, wanted to meet up for drinks to celebrate his new position in Marmine Management; Blaise Roman, Nate's best friend and the heir of one of the richest enterprises in Anais, had a proposition he wanted to discuss with Thom; Ciara Khan, Catherine's oldest friend, wanted her to come over for dinner that week. Mickey wanted Catherine to conn him first thing; and at the very end, the deep voice of Hamish Anteros, only just came out when Thom erased the message with a dark look on his face. His blue eyes flashed and his jaw clenched.

Catherine wanted to ask, but the look on his face stopped her. She was well aware of the sour relationship between Nate and Hamish, made only worse in recent years with Nate's arrest and disappearance. At a dinner party several months before, Hamish had told Catherine he was glad Nate was gone and hoped he would never come back.

The look on Thom's normally taciturn and mild face had frightened even her. And when Thom had left without a word, she had followed quietly, not sure she even wanted to know. Thom and Nate had always been *Thom and Nate* and sometimes she wondered if there was even room for her.

She let it go and instead conn'd Ciara to say that she would be over in a few nights as Thom went about unpacking. His shoulders were tensed and the muscles in his jaw seemed to be working overtime as he refrained from saying the many things he evidently wanted to say. Whether or not it was Nate's fault for their mountain trek, it was Thom who had suggested going, despite Catherine's protests, and she knew him well enough to know that he was unhappy with himself more than everyone else. He put her and Nate's happiness before his own at every turn, and now the two people he loved most in the world were sick with an unknown agent, and there was no answer yet, nothing to focus on. Thom craved direction and focus; he was at his very best when life was structured, certain and planned. The chaos of the last few days, and Nate's sudden return, had unbalanced the organisation of his world, and he was doing his best to keep calm and figure out what was to be done next. Thom always had a plan. He was never unprepared or unaware of all of his options. He never acted without thinking it over exhaustively. In that, he was Nate's polar opposite.

Catherine sat down and watched him put everything away until at last he removed his coat, his boots, and sat across from her on the sofa, hands clasped together. His short black hair was stuck up in a messy disarray, and his beard looked like it had been yanked on profusely.

In the nine years since they had been bound together, Assigned by Crown, Council and parents into a match that neither of them had been allowed an opinion on, Catherine and Thom had changed a great deal. It had always been a good match, one that would produce the most well-bred of children, the best of Anaitian bloodlines; future endeavours and fortunes were instantly assured and secured by their binding. Initially baulking at the match, Catherine and Thom had grown from awkward and incompatible around each other, to symbiotic. Even Mickey, who rarely paid attention to his daughter's life, generally far too busy sorting out the King's affairs, had remarked on how very evident it was that Catherine and Thom were the true definition of what Complements ought to be. They seemed to know what the other wanted before asked, what the other needed before prompted, and never grew tired of the other. They could sit in silence for hours on end and know exactly what the other was preoccupied with.

They were best friends.

The quiet, passive avoidance that had suffocated Catherine in her childhood home, and the screaming fights between Nate and Hamish that were the ever-present symphony of Thom's youth, had no place in their home. Theirs was a comradery which few could match, let alone hope to emulate.

Unable to relax, they gathered their books, pads, pens, computers and aught else, and set to work. What it was they were looking for, neither knew, but it seemed better to search aimlessly than to flounder uselessly.

They sat on opposite ends of the sofa, a pillow between them so that Thom wouldn't accidentally touch her, and for the next several hours they read through all of the books they owned, all of the books that Thom could find in the library across the city, and all of the information they found searching through the public archives. They learned more about skin diseases, infections and bacteria than Catherine had ever had any desire to know. She saw captures of rotting flesh, boils, burns, gangrenous infections and worse. One entry in particular stuck out in her mind about an underground building filled with centuries' old nuclear material, which one of the soldiers stumbled across in their pursuit of a mutant. The description of what happened after turned her stomach so badly she set the book aside and return to the relatively boring description of fungi. By early evening her head was pounding, and she leaned back, rubbing her eyes, trying to rid herself of the mental imagery.

'We'll find something, love,' said Thom bracingly. 'This isn't going to be forever.'

Catherine yawned and leaned her head against the cushions. 'Do you really believe that?'

'I do,' he said. 'Nothing is permanent.'

She smiled, somewhat wistful. 'I really want to kiss you right now.'

'I know the feeling.'

Fighting the urge to risk being burned simply for a kiss, Catherine stood and stretched tiredly, cracking her neck. 'Do you want some coffee?'

'I'd love some,' he said. 'Are you hungry?'

'A little. Do we have anything in the house?'

'I think there's some meat in the cooler, although we're out of bread. There might be some stew from before we left.'

Catherine looked over her shoulder, wrinkling her nose in distaste. 'We could order something?'

'You make coffee, I'll order,' he said, winking at her.

Twenty minutes later, they were sitting back down on the sofa, eating out of the paper boxes with their fingers, gulping gratefully at the large mugs of steaming coffee, trying to rouse their brains into proper functionality. Catherine had almost finished the large helping of chicken in yellow sauce when her connector lit up with a private registration. Raising an eyebrow curiously, she leaned over and picked it up.

'This is Catherine Taenia,' she said, holding it to her ear.

'Mistress Taenia, this is Amal Rawling,' said a formal, slightly nasal voice. 'I work for the Diseases Department.'

Catherine mouthed the name to Thom, who frowned. 'Is there something wrong?' she asked, her heart starting to race in anticipation of more problems.

'We were forwarded your bloods this morning and we've tested both yours and Nathanial Anteros'. Would you both be willing to report for inspection first thing in the morning?'

Catherine glanced at Thom who was scrutinising her reaction to what she was hearing, clearly wondering if he had reason to worry. 'Of course,' she said into the conn. 'We'll both be there.'

'Thank you,' said Amal Rawling. 'I will see you then. Please be here by seven.'

'Certainly.' Catherine ended the communication and tossed the conn back onto the table. Her heart was still racing, but as she thought it over, she found herself slightly reassured. After all, if it was an urgent problem, they would have to report immediately; the delay gave her a sense of calm that this was merely going to be another round of tests. She looked up at Thom. 'They want to see us in the Diseases Department in the morning.'

Thom raised an eyebrow. 'What for?'

'To test this thing, I suppose.'

'Only seriously contagious citizens are told to report there. You aren't contagious.'

'I might be,' she mused. 'We don't know for sure.'

'If you were contagious she would have summoned you straight away.'

'That's what I was thinking.'

'Well, I'm perplexed.' Thom scratched the dark stubble on his cheek. 'All I have is more questions.'

'Questions without answers,' she said. 'Perhaps we'll get the latter in the morning.'

'Or perhaps we'll simply have more questions,' he said. 'Did she say anything else?

'Nate's to come as well.'

Thom thought a minute. 'Rawling's the overseer. I wonder why she was the one to contact you.'

'Is that unusual?'

'Highly,' said Thom distractedly. 'I'm going to conn Nate and tell him to come over. He's not going to be happy about this.'

Catherine rolled her eyes in exasperation. 'Whatever for this time?'

Thom reached over and picked up the conn, sighing heavily. 'Nate went through a lot in Redwater. More than you know. The only person who wants Nate back inside that square less than Nate is me.'

An hour later, Nate arrived. Catherine and Thom had been sitting on the front step, smoking morosely in the cool autumn air, when the taxi lowered to the ground and he hopped out, paying the driver and removing the flesh-coloured speakers from his ears, the deafening sounds of music fading as he jammed them into his coat pocket. Nate had once driven a plain black hover which his mother had bought him on his thirteenth birthday, but it had disappeared when he had been arrested and Catherine wasn't sure what had happened to it.

He nodded to them, lit a long black tocker that emitted green smoke, and walked over, his coat flapping in the wind. He looked as ill as he had the last time she'd seen him; he was far too pale, the few freckles on his face standing out noticeably, his red hair a stark contrast to his sickly pallor; his eyes, normally storm-grey, had that strange ruddy hue Catherine had noticed in the mountains, and his hands shook ever-so as he smoked. He seemed close to passing out, and Thom stood automatically, reaching out for him, only remembering at the last second that he could not help, and dropped his hand, jaw clenched in bitter helplessness.

'Any news?' said Nate. His voice, at least, did not tremble.

'We'll tell you inside,' said Thom. 'Come on.'

'I don't like the sound of that.'

In the kitchen, Thom poured them all cups of tea and Catherine hoisted herself onto the countertop, curling her legs beneath her as she drank, her eyes darting between brothers as Thom told Nate their orders.

'We can't go,' said Nate the second Thom stopped talking. He was leaning against the cooler, arms crossed. 'Only those with infectious diseases go inside. You do know that no one who has gone inside ever came back out again? *Died*, they'll say. *Couldn't be saved.*'

Catherine frowned. 'We're not infectious. I'm sure they just want to examine us properly.'

'Don't be a fool.'

'We have to go,' said Catherine. 'We don't have a say in the matter. If we don't show up by morning, we're in violation of the law.'

Nate snorted. 'You're not honestly thinking of going, are you?'

'We have no other choice,' said Thom. 'I'll be there. We can bring Mother as well. Nothing is going to happen to you two.'

'Oh, little brother,' said Nate. 'You have no idea how wrong you are. They don't bring you into the Diseases Department for no reason, Tommy. They bring you in there when you've got something they don't want anyone else to get or know about. It's a place where sick people go to be executed in private!'

'Nasim, we have no other option. You're sick. You need medicine.'

'I'm fine.'

'You're not! Look at yourself.'

Nate smoked angrily for a few seconds, taking pulls from the cone with such ferocity it was a wonder he didn't choke to death on the fumes. After several minutes, he tossed the finished tocker into the sink, took a large gulp of tea, and cleared his throat. 'Listen to me very carefully, little brother,' he said, voice raspy, 'I know more about the things Crown and Council are capable of than you do. We have this, a warning. Let's use it and go.'

'Go? Go where?' said Catherine, completely confused.

'The Outlands.'

Thom sighed and pinched the bridge of his nose. Whilst Catherine was stunned by the suggestion, it was clear that Thom was not. She had a feeling this was not the first time they had spoken of such matters. He said, 'Nasim, what haven't Mother and I been able to get you out of over the years? This, like all the rest, will be sorted as easily as cuttans change hands.'

'An infection isn't something they're going to want to let out. Have you not seen how strange this is? How abnormal? I can touch Kitty's arm and make the burns disappear like *that*!' He snapped his fingers for effect. 'That's not sanctioned, that's not allowed. We oughtn't to have even *shown* it to them.'

'You're acting as if we're somehow the omnipotent ones,' said Thom, exasperated. 'We don't scare Crown and Council. Their power is unparalleled, unmatched. A burn shrinking back into skin isn't going to faze them, Nasim.'

'Won't it?' Nate stared at him. 'If we're infected with something that gives us the ability to heal each other, we're walking targets! Do you really not believe they won't want to study us? To use it to their advantage? Wake up, Tommy!'

Silence fell, and Catherine found herself mulling all of it over. Perhaps it made sense that Nate was scared. After all, he had been to prison, and by the look of his skin, had seen more than his share of pain, but Thom was also right. In all the time they had been alive, there was nothing Cecily could not buy or barter Nate's way out of, and Catherine wasn't even remotely worried about her fate. Her father was the King's favourite; some people called him the Hangman, others called him the Whisperer, as it was said whatever he whispered in the King's ear was done. She had never had anything to fear. Nothing would happen to her because he would not allow it. She had never had reason to doubt it, and even now, even with this strange ailment, she still believed her father would ensure her safety.

At length, Thom sighed. 'Fine, if you won't go without proof that everything's going to be all right, I'll get some.'

Nate raised an eyebrow, but his lips had gone white with fear. '*Get* some?'

'I'll find proof that everything's as it should be,' said Thom. 'I'll go and check the databases and when I come back and everything's fine, we can all go together.'

'Are you trying to give me a heart attack?' Nate's eyes had grown wide with anger, fear and astonishment. He laughed hysterically. 'You are *not* going in there.'

'I go in there all the time on errands for work. I know my way around.'

'Not after dark! Not when it's *completely illegal*.'

'I won't get caught.'

Nate crossed his arms, muscles tense, and shook his head. 'It's too dangerous.'

'It's not a terribly appealing idea, no,' said Thom with equal stubbornness. 'I'm confident, however, that it will be easy enough.'

'No.'

'It's not up to you.'

'Yes, it is,' said Nate. 'I'm not letting you go.'

'I'll be fine.'

'Fine? *Fine*? We have seen men shot in the square; others executed, tortured or starved! We have seen children become orphans because their parents made mistakes or got into accidents. How many people have you seen hanged in the gallows in the square? Were you not paying attention when they brought your class to Redwater? I was! Don't tell me you think accidental crimes or well-meaning curiosity are somehow of a smaller nature than *breaking into a Council building*?'

Thom's expression was unreadable. 'We're not peasants, Nasim. We have more than enough money and influence to avoid such fates.'

Never an arrogant man, the words coming out of his mouth made no sense. His certainty, therefore, gave her pause. Not even she was so certain of her father's reach.

Nate's eyes narrowed. 'That's not a guarantee! I did what I did knowing I might die and knowing it was worth the risk. This is not. This is something we can avoid altogether.'

'I am not letting you go off into the wilderness in the state you're in! You're barely standing! You can't be touched! You could die for all we know! I don't care how frightened you are or how stupid you think it is! If you're not going in there without proof, proof is what I will get you.'

Nate stared at him for a second in complete disbelief. Then, so suddenly it took a second to register, his hand whipped out and hit the lamp as hard as he could. It went flying, shattering into a thousand pieces. He opened and closed his fists several times trying to calm down; the glare he aimed at his younger brother ought to have levelled Thom. Perhaps under different circumstances it would have. Thom was one of the few people that Catherine had never seen Nate direct his anger towards and seeing him so close to it was utterly unnerving. Then, as always, the brothers mended things with one turn of the conversation.

'I'm sorry,' said Thom. 'I'm terrified.'

'It's fine,' said Nate, waving his hand. 'I'm fine.'

'You're not.' Thom smiled reassuringly. Perhaps on someone else it would have worked. 'I know my way around, big brother. I won't be caught.'

Nate made a strangled noise in the back of his throat. 'You cannot know that. I'm telling you now that we must leave. They're not looking for us yet – we have a head start. Gather your things, leave a note for Mother and come with me. I am not going into that building, I don't care what you say.'

Although she was loath to admit it, Catherine felt a tightening in her chest at the thought of Thom doing something so stupid. 'Something could go wrong,' she said. She hated to agree with Nate, but she didn't want Thom doing anything that could potentially land him in trouble. Even if she fully believed that anything he did could be fixed by Cecily or Mickey, she didn't want it to come to that. Thom never got into trouble. Thom never stepped out of line. Doing so for Nate made her overwhelmingly angry. It would obliterate his future.

'I won't be caught,' he repeated. 'And even if I am, I'm in no danger.'

'How do you know that?'

'I just do.'

'That falls short of being an actual answer.'

'I have my reasons. I have my connections.'

Thom knew everyone in Anais, and most likely everyone of merit in Cutta and Redland. He spun words like fine wine and everyone wanted to know him. He was the favourite of all the rich sons in Anais. Yet how he had so many willing to help him, Catherine had never quite figured out. Some part of her wasn't sure she wanted to know.

'Have you ever tried going in there undetected? There's rather a lot of reasons that no one ever does,' said Nate darkly. 'The Diseases Department has been patrolled heavily for years. You'll walk in past dozens of armed guards.'

'It's worth the risk,' said Thom. 'Who will suspect me?'

'What will you use as your excuse? What will you say if you're caught?'

'I won't be. The whole building's empty at night and there's only the security system. I've known how to bypass those for years thanks to you –'

'I taught you how to do that for practical reasons, Tommy, not to break into the bloody Council records –'

'– they keep the database full of all incoming patients or incurables or whatever else. If you're being brought in on charges or brought in for testing or for anything else, it will be listed there.'

Nate snorted. 'I cannot think of a plan with more flaws.'

'Good thing no one's asking you to come.'

'You're not going.'

'Are you going to stop me?'

'Yes.'

The two brothers glared at each other for a long moment, as if assessing the likely outcome of an all-out brawl. Catherine had never seen them so at odds before.

'You know what they will do to you,' said Nate sinisterly. 'Our title and family won't save you if you're caught.'

'My title and family have saved you more times than I can count.'

'For petty crime! Protestations! Perhaps an explosion or three. The odd blunder or rebellion. Not breaking into the Council's private records! Not even I am that foolish.' Nate's eyes suddenly filled with angry tears and his mouth twisted in ugly emotion. 'You know what they do in Redwater, Tommy.'

Thom's handsome face looked old with strain and weary acknowledgement. 'I'll be fine,' he said. There was no fear, no doubt, no uncertainty to him. He talked of breaking the law as if it were too boring to be worth his concern. 'I alone got into Redwater. The *only* one. I can get out, too.'

Catherine stared at him, heart hammering. She knew then that there was something he wasn't saying.

'It's a stupid plan,' said Nate.

'You're the one refusing to go there without information.'

'Exactly,' said Nate. 'I'm saying we get in the hover and go for the coast as fast as possible. I'm saying that we run and don't go near that place. I'm saying that we trust what we know and don't walk straight into the hands of the Council, all of whom would happily put to death any suspected of having a spreadable disease. How many are put to death each year due to the Bite? How many on suspicion of carrying the Plague? I'm not putting your life, Kitty's life, and my life at risk just so you can touch your Complement!'

Catherine bristled.

Thom glared at Nate. 'I'm going to check or I'm going without checking, but I'm not leaving my home with both of you sick. I can't do that.'

'I'd rather be unable to touch anyone for an eternity than walk into that place!'

'I wouldn't,' said Catherine quietly. Both men glanced at her. Thom looked heartbroken, confused and determined; Nate looked sick, fearful and furious.

Thom nodded to her. 'That's settled, then.'

'That's not settled at all!'

'You are *sick*, Nasim! You are ill! Look at your eyes!' Thom's composure slipped and a trace of unsettling hysteria slipped through. It shook Catherine to her core. Thom always knew what to do. He never had any doubts. The terror of what was happening to them seemed to have embedded itself so deeply into his bones not even he could contain the shaking.

Nate's lip curled in a sneer. 'I'm not worth it.'

'Yes, you are,' snapped Thom. 'And so is Cat.'

Nate glanced at her involuntarily. He did not disagree.

'I'll check,' said Thom after a pregnant pause. 'You're right that they have a habit of never letting anyone leave who could potentially risk the populace. Our parents may have clout, but even they cannot buy our freedom if we are a risk to society. If there's any hint of a problem, we'll go. I agree with you there. I won't let you both rot away in isolation – I could never bear that. But I have to try. This is my responsibility, remember?'

The teacup in Nate's hand, which he had picked up a minute before, not likely for drinking but for having something to do with his hands, shattered and blood began to seep from the fresh wounds on his palm. Catherine flinched, staring at the blood dripping down his palm and onto the floor. He hadn't moved or winced or cried aloud when it happened. His hand had simply closed into a fist.

In all her memory, Nate had never been scared of – or reasonable about – anything. The first to jump headlong into any ill-advised situation, Nate never showed any fear. In that moment, on the other side of the room, fear came off him like smoke from a cigarette.

He made no move to stem the flow. He was still staring at his brother. His pale face was flushed an angry scarlet and he looked ready to explode. The muscles in his jaw were clenched and his fingers tapped a repetitive rhythm on the table beside him as he took deep breaths, trying to calm down. He put his uninjured hand to his mouth, as if fighting the urge to be sick. For a long time, no one moved or said anything as he gathered his self-control. Finally, he spoke, and the words came out a heart-wrenching plea. 'Tommy, please. This is a bad idea. Let's just go, now, while we still can.'

'I'm not leaving my home without cause. I'm not leaving you sick if there's a chance of a cure. You are my responsibility and I won't let you die.'

'Better me than you.'

'Don't ever say that again,' sibilated Thom. 'I will go and ascertain that everything is all right – as I'm sure it is. On the off-chance that there is anything wrong, I will be back before dawn and we can leave undetected. That's the best you're going to get.'

'Tommy –'

'*I'm going.*'

'Stubborn fucking boy.' Nate shook his head, finally opening his fist and inspecting the damage. It was hard to look away from him as he picked shards of glass out of his hand with all the urgency of an old man pulling chew off the sole of his shoe. 'I hope to God you prove me wrong,' he muttered, not looking at his brother as he did so. When he had finished examining his ruined hand, he cradled it close to his body.

At length, Thom stood and gestured for Catherine to follow him. In the corridor, he turned and fixed her with a knowing look. 'I know you don't want me to go,' he said. 'I understand why. I'm not exactly jumping with excitement over the prospect, either.'

'I don't want to leave.'

'I'm sure it's nothing,' said Thom bracingly. 'Nate has good reason to fear those buildings. He experienced nothing but cruelty within their walls. Prison will do that to you. If answers will get him to come, then that's enough. When I find out that it's only for a check-up, he'll come with us and get well. I know my brother. He won't go without knowing it's safe.'

'So we'll figure something else out. This plan is going to fail.'

Thom looked slightly offended. 'Do you have so little faith in me?'

'Of course I have faith in you,' she mollified. 'But everyone knows the guards are relentless. Do you remember Emilia's brother in school? He tried to set off a stink bomb in the main building as a joke and was whipped in the square. He was twelve, Thom! You're twenty. They'll shoot you on sight.'

'It's not up to you,' he snapped, his blue eyes darkening with anger. It startled her. Thom had never snapped, not unless someone challenged him on Nate. His brother was always the line. He continued, 'I need to do this. *Me.* If my mother can bribe and donate Nate's transgressions away, why on Earth would I not get the same? I'm not going to get into trouble, and if I do, I will get out of it. That's all I have to say on the matter.'

'Nate's right – his crimes weren't as bad.'

'There's a lot you don't know about my mother's influence and her connections to King Markas,' said Thom. 'There's a reason Nate gets out of everything – look, I can't say more. I know what I'm doing.'

'You don't even look like you believe that. Let's just go in the morning, Nate or no Nate.'

'That's not happening.'

There was nothing she could say that would convince Thom to stay home, and after another ten minutes of trying to sway him, she knew she had lost; Thom donned his coat and pulled his boots on, words falling like water from his mouth, useless assurances that everything would be fine, she only had to wait for him to sort it out.

She crossed her arms as she watched him. 'Please be careful.'

He smiled and held out his hand, hesitated, and dropped it again. 'I love you.'

'I love you, too.'

Catherine's heart was slamming in her chest as she watched him leave. He was gone only a second before Nate darted out the door behind his brother, slamming it shut so that she would never know what was said between them. She wanted to curl into a ball; too many things had happened in such a short space of time, but she was too tired to be upset, too tired to cry or moan. She just leaned against the wall, waiting and wondering.

For a long time, she stood in the corridor, thinking so many things in tandem that not a single thought was actually discernible. Sometime later she heard the sounds of retching from the other side of the door, and a few minutes after that Nate reappeared, face devoid of colour and eyes red. There were burns on his face, neck and arms. Only Nate would embrace his brother knowing it would burn him.

'Stubborn fucking boy,' he said again, more to himself than to her.

'He'll be fine.'

Nate looked at her, his expression plainly saying that he did not believe her, not for a second. They stood staring at each other, Nate breathing angrily through his nose. She wondered if he was going to be sick again. Before she could ask, he cleared his throat and scratched his beard uncomfortably.

'Kitty, can ...?' he began, swallowing hard as if the question tasted foul to him. 'Can I try something?'

Catherine sighed. 'What?'

'You remember what you did for me the other day?'

'Yes.'

'Can I –'

'Just hurry up. I need a drink.'

He reached out and touched her shoulder so lightly she barely felt it. A calming sensation passed slowly through her as he squeezed her arm, and she felt better than she had in days. Her body seemed to refresh, heal and refuel, as if she were made of solar panels and he was made of sunlight. It was the most peculiar feeling.

'It's weird,' he said. 'I feel like I'm in a reel of some kind.'

'I feel cursed.'

'At least I don't smell this time.'

Catherine snorted. 'Small blessings, I suppose.'

'Try not to worry about Tommy, he's never once been in trouble in his entire life. I'm sure –' His voice broke and he clenched his hand a few times trying to control himself. 'I'm sure he'll be fine.'

'You're a terrible liar.'

'Unlike you.'

'You know how well I lie, do you?'

'I've known you since we were both little things, darling,' he replied. 'Only an idiot wouldn't know how well you spin tales on that tongue.'

Catherine glared at him, arms crossed and doing her best not to punch him.

Nate appraised her. 'You hate me for not going with him.'

'I hate you for not coming with both of us without this ridiculous debacle,' she hissed through gritted teeth.

'Do you think I'm doing this for fun? I've been inside the halls of government before and I know exactly how far the Council and good King Markas will go to protect their fragile peace. I'll never go back there. When Tommy realises that I'm right, he'll be helping me pack.'

Catherine shook her head. 'How can you possibly think we're in trouble? My father is Mickey Taenia. Nothing will happen to me.'

'Is that so?'

'Yes, it is.'

Nate shook his head and pulled a cigarette from his pocket, lighting it slowly. He took a long drag and then sneered contemptuously. 'Tell me, darling – have you seen my back?'

Catherine swallowed hard, her throat suddenly feeling tight. 'Why?'

'Don't tell me I don't know what Crown and Council are capable of.' He blew a cloud of smoke towards her, shook his head, and disappeared back into the sitting room without another word.

Catherine stared after him, heart pounding.

The next few hours were the longest of Catherine's life. Neither she nor Nate had much to say to each other. Both were trapped in their own worlds of worry, both wondering what would become of them, of Thom. Being certain before a task is undertaken was one thing, maintaining confidence as it carried on was an entirely different matter. Catherine tried to eat, though it proved impossible as her stomach wouldn't entertain the prospect of food; instead she packed everything away and paced around the kitchen.

Nate spent most of the evening sitting on the window seat, staring out at the backgarden, smoking in agitation. At one point he disappeared into the bedroom. He returned ten minutes later with a bag over his shoulder.

'What's that for?'

'Leaving.'

She rolled her eyes but didn't respond.

His fingers kept tapping out the rhythm she had listened to in the abandoned building, and she wondered if it was a tick of some kind. He smoked, he fidgeted, he tapped, and as the hours passed, Catherine grew less and less certain that everything was going to be all right.

When Nate's conn lit up in his hand, neither of them were expecting it. Nearly dawn, both of them had been glancing at the door every few seconds, hoping Thom would return at any moment. They jumped and Nate read the registration, frowning at whatever he saw. He held the conn to his ear, not saying anything. There was a muffled voice on the other end; Catherine couldn't make out any particular words. Nate's face drained of all colour and he dropped the conn on the floor, stamping on it with all his might.

'Was that Thom?'

Nate didn't answer. He just stared at the smashed pieces on the floor with numb detachment, completely frozen. Catherine moved towards him, her pulse racing, and touched his shoulder.

The change was instant; he snapped into action, darting across the room and into the kitchen, not saying a word.

'Nate? Nate! What's going on?'

He opened a drawer and pulled out Thom's knife. His lips were white with shock, his eyes filled with unshed tears, and she felt, rather than heard, the truth of the matter. She shook her head rapidly, backing away from him, a horrible cold setting in her bones.

Suddenly, there was a pounding on the front door. They whirled around, frozen in place. The booming bark of the Captain of the Private Police turned Catherine's blood to ice.

'This is Captain Tellerman! Open this door or be subject to immediate execution! By order of Crown and Council!'

Catherine hesitated. She did not know where Thom was, did not know what was going on, and yet all her instincts told her that she should obey. Her father would make everything right and she would be in no trouble if she complied. She looked from the door to Nate, wavering.

Nate beckoned to her, eyes wide and pleading.

'Catherine Taenia, by order of Crown and Council, open this door!'

Our parents may have clout, but even they cannot buy our freedom if we are a risk to society. If there's any hint of a problem, we'll go.

She could hear Thom's voice clearly in her head and felt her decision made for her. In the end, she trusted Thom more than she trusted anyone else.

She ran quick as she could across the room on tiptoes, thanking her years of dance classes for giving her such light steps. Nate ushered her in front of him and they slipped into the corridor. A loud banging erupted from the door and Catherine had a sinking suspicion that the guards were breaking it down. They crept hurriedly into the basement as the sound of shattering glass came from upstairs. They darted towards the window and were barely out when the sounds of footsteps on the stairs reached her ears.

Catherine clambered out into the rose bushes, scratching her arms badly. Nate glanced at her once, assessing that she was all right, before waving her along behind him.

The morning was crisp and damp, biting at their ears and sending shivers down their spines as they raced through the backgarden and climbed into the neighbours'.

'Nate, where's Thom?'

He did not answer.

'We ought to wait for him!'

'He was caught, Kitty.'

She stopped dead. 'Who was that on the conn?'

'It doesn't matter who it was,' said Nate hoarsely. 'Tommy's been taken. He was taken into Redwater ...'

The words were so unfathomable, she almost laughed. Thomas Anteros, darling of the capital, favourite son of the King's most beloved family, expected to rise to the highest levels of society, had been arrested. It was not possible.

'No,' she said stupidly.

Nate's face twisted in unguarded grief and he looked away, tears falling from his eyes. Silence was all that was necessary to convey the truth. Everyone knew the stories. The Private Police, the highest level of the Kingdom's guards, were the demons of Kingdom. Even the Anaitians were scared of them. A squad of specialised guards that stole people from their houses in the middle of the day, they were notorious and deadly, and Catherine's father had always told her that if there was only ever one reason to follow the rules, it was them. They'd taken over ten thousand people from their homes over the decades and executed them in the desert, leaving their bodies for the crows.

'What does that mean?' she croaked.

Again, he said nothing, only held out his hand. After a moment, she took it, completely numb.

They reached the end of the road and ducked down off the street into the basement entrance of one of the apartments. They crouched low and Nate gestured around. 'Is there anyone on this street who isn't home?'

Her thoughts still swirling, images of Thom being executed running rampant and cruel in her mind's eye, she didn't answer.

Nate snapped his fingers in front of her face. 'Is there anyone on this street that isn't home? Think *quickly* before we are caught.'

Catherine raised an eyebrow. 'Why?'

'Rich people have spare hovers,' he said. 'There's always a spare.'

She bit her lip, trying to blink the tears from her eyes and focus. She looked around, swallowing hard. 'Ah ... the Abers, just across the road. We were looking after their dogs before they went out of town. We had to hire a walker during the daytime because we got your message and we knew we mightn't be back in town in time. They left a few days ago. They won't be back for a while. I don't think the walker comes until midday.'

'Right,' said Nate. He was looking wildly around, trying to discern their chances. 'I think the guards are still up the street, probably combing the gardens. I don't think they saw us leave. They might even be waiting for us to come home and are hiding themselves. It's a long shot, but it's better than nothing. No one will be down this far yet. Come on.'

He wrapped an arm around her as they crossed the street, their heads bowed inwards, trying to hide their faces. Every fibre of her being inclined her to run, scream, sob, crumple, but Nate's arm kept her from doing any of those things.

Catherine's pulse was hammering loudly in her ears by the time they reached the Abers' front door. The spare key was kept beneath a plank of wood in the outdoor coffee table. She drew it out and opened the door, entering the registration into the codebox before the alarm could sound. Once inside, they bolted the lock and crept into the kitchen.

'All right. If we linger, we're dead,' said Nate. 'If we run, we're *likely* dead.'

'One is slightly better than the other,' said Catherine, wiping the tears from her eyes. 'What – what about Thom?'

Nate ran a hand through his hair. When he looked at her, it was hard to tell who his hatred was directed towards. His anguish could have stopped an army in its tracks. His words, when they finally came, sounded like stones on glass. 'There's nothing we can do for him. Once they catch you, you're taken to interrogation for hours where they torture you. It's always a different location so they can't be found by dissenters. After they torture you to a certain point, they put you in a cell where you wait for them to kill you. Or rape you. If they like your screams, sometimes you live longer. The only chance to live is for low-level convicts and criminals, like hover-crashers and families of the accused, and after a long isolation and torture internment, they're placed in the workforce. He won't be that lucky. He knew that and I knew that –' Nate's voice died. He looked close to being sick.

For a few moments, neither of them moved. Catherine was having trouble processing anything.

Nate's eyes narrowed. He walked over to the wall and picked up the conn, entering a registration he clearly knew off by heart. His fingers tapped on the desk beside him agitatedly. 'Blaise,' he rasped a moment later. 'Tommy's been arrested.'

It sounded so ridiculous even now.

The silence which filled the room as Nate waited for an answer was deafening. Blaise was heir to one of the richest companies in the Kingdom, a brother on the Council, and was one of the few who still publicly associated with Nate after his arrest.

Nate thanked Blaise numbly a minute later and put the conn back. He looked over at Catherine. 'He's the only person after my mother who can help.'

Her throat felt tight. 'What now?'

'Now we hide,' said Nate. 'And we wait for word. Either way, we're not staying in Anais.'

'My father –'

'Your father will be the one passing sentence,' snarled Nate. 'Conn him if you wish. He won't save us. The only people who can now are Blaise and my mother. Not us. If Tommy's just been arrested, so will we. And if we're infected, we're not getting out. I'll be shot on sight.'

Catherine opened her mouth to argue, to say that he was wrong, but the words didn't come. Her father had no tolerance for lawbreakers. He had ordered the executions of friends before. She swallowed hard and nodded.

Nate moved to the cooler and removed a bottle of water, drinking the contents desperately before setting it down with a shaking hand, not looking at her. Catherine ducked into the kitchen closet and began filling bags with food to take with them. Every shop in Cutta had a large entrance where criminals' captures were broadcast to give everyone a reminder of what they looked like so the likelihood of being caught increased a thousand per cent. Nate lit a cigarette and ducked out of the room. When he had returned, it was with a gun.

Catherine shouldered her bag and followed him into the garage. Two spare hovers were parked in the massive enclosure, both close to new and well cleaned. They headed to the nearest one, a dark red vehicle with large solar panels on the roof. Climbing inside, they both sat for a minute, their rapid breathing mimicking each other.

Catherine looked over at him uncertainly. 'Where are we going?'

'Tommy told me that if he couldn't make it back, he would find us in the Outlands. So that's exactly where we're going to go. We find him and then we find a cure.'

'How are we even going to get there? How are we going to get through the minefields?'

'I've done it before. I can do it again.'

Not knowing whether to hope or despair, Catherine nodded. The taste of bitter regret burned her mouth, and with shaking hands, she started the hover and pressed the button to open the gate. If they were two minutes too slow, this whole ordeal would be over very quickly. She glanced around as she pulled out onto the road. It was clear thus far. Lifting the hover into the air, she rose higher than the houses on the street. Hovers were manufactured not to go above a certain speed or height, and pressing them beyond their limits often led to explosions. They were the primary means of transportation, in addition to ships, but they were not very safe.

A brief glance towards her house showed that the entire building was surrounded, men at every corner with guns. She turned the hover around hurriedly and drove as fast as she could without drawing attention. After all, people were allowed to leave their homes. There wasn't a restriction up yet. It would have been broadcast loudly through the streets if there was.

As they flew out of the city, the road turned into one cut between large stretches of grazing land, and the rolling hills felt infinitely more secure than the buildings of the city had.

The day passed into late afternoon and the rhythm of the hover lulled them into a disjointed sense of monotony, Catherine forced herself not to think about Thom. It would have done no good. It felt like someone had punched a hole through her chest and taken half of her away; it did not seem real. It was too horrible to be real. She didn't feel sad. Sad was a conscious, constant emotion. She felt a horrible amount of disconnect and detachment.

How had so much changed in the span of a week?

They drove past Smithville, Indus, Kobul, Xiang and Cinna. All places that had been remade after the war, completely redesigned. Each community was fuelled off their own solar or wind system, each was self-sustaining. In contrast, the spaces between towns and cities were desolate, grim, forgotten places in want of care and tending. The farms in designated areas were tended by convicts of lesser crimes sent to the workforce, or indentured servants, those whose family had been executed or sent to prison; they were gloomy, bitter places and added nothing to the landscape.

Night set in and Catherine and Nate switched places. Exhaustion began to set into her mind, her bones, her heart; she felt sick with despair and every thought she had concerned Thom. It seemed so strange to just have a hole in her future. Where once everything had been so certain, now she had nothing.

Nate cleared his throat and she glanced up, shaking off her fatigue.

'Right, can you talk to me, darling? I'm falling asleep and I need something to keep my hands steady.'

'What do you want me to talk about?'

He shrugged. 'Something funny. Give me something to laugh about. If I don't laugh, I think I'm going to lose my mind.'

She cast her mind around for something funny. Her brain felt completely blank. How could she not remember more? Thom had always made her laugh. She glared into the darkness outside the window, trying to come up with something. She didn't have much success. 'Well … Thom never had a drink before meeting me,' she started stupidly. 'I was shocked, honestly, I'd thought you'd've got him years earlier, but it was obvious from the start that he'd never tasted the stuff in his life. Our first night properly out, we went to one of the dungeon clubs. I think we got lost or something – I can't remember how we got there – but eventually we found ourselves seated on those large cushions they have – those ones that surround the hookahs, you know the ones? We were served these large drinks and then given pipes to smoke from. So your brother, having never done anything in his life, proceeded to down five goblets of wine and smoke an entire serving on his own. I kept waiting for him to get sick. It was so funny. His eyes got so wide and started to roll and he was drooling everywhere – not his most gallant moment, to be sure. He was coughing and swaying the entire walk home but he insisted on walking me. When we got to my house, he stormed in, woke up both my parents and asked my father if he wanted to dance. He grabbed my father by the hand and pulled him out of bed, not giving a single thought to the fact that my father was completely naked.'

Nate chuckled. 'I remember him telling me about that.'

'I don't know if my father liked him, thought it was too bizarre to get annoyed at, or what, but he danced Thom right out the door, down to the kitchen and proceeded to challenge him to a drinking contest. Still naked. My mother couldn't stop laughing. She was crying from it. I don't think I've seen them so confused or bemused since.'

A horrible silence fell between them as both suddenly found themselves remembering Thom.

'Nate,' she whispered, her voice breaking as fresh tears welled up in her eyes, blurring her vision. 'Nate, I feel like I can't breathe.'

His hand left the gearshift and reached out for her in the dark. He found her knee and squeezed tightly.

'I can't believe he's gone,' she said.

'He's not.' The longer he held her knee, the more warmth seemed to spread from his hand through her leg, and up into the rest of her body. She felt herself start to calm down and she sat, hiccoughing and sniffling in depressed silence. Nate eventually removed his hand and reached out, turning on the broadcast.

Henry Gabaldon, the well-known newscaster of Anais, filled the hover with his high, squeaky tone. *'The suspect, whom we have come to identify as a recruit for the Council and previously a well-respected member of society, was apprehended this morning attempting to break into the Building of Historical Records. We mention his status so that all are aware that even the highest in society are not immune to punishment. Even the richest may fall. No one is without reproach and all crimes must be punished. He was tried and executed shortly thereafter with his name to be released to the public in due course once his accomplices are seized. We urge every citizen to stay vigilant and report any suspicious activity to the guards. As always, any fruitful information will be greatly rewarded.*

'The Building of Historical Records is, of course, the most highly guarded building in central Cutta, housing information on the wretched state of society that pre-existed our modern utopia. So terrible was the freedom and chaos which pre-Devastation life allowed that now only a fraction of our once great population remains.

'We are a dying breed, citizens. We must stay ever vigilant. Only through the just rule of the House of Auram have we come so far. His Majesty's shrewdness and grace has enabled those of us that are left to survive and thrive, but we must keep to our code of conduct. We must obey the law. We must not allow dissenters to exist. Any information on the whereabouts of dissenters will be rewarded fully by the Crown. Report suspicion. Report chaos. Stay vigilant ...

'And now for the weather ...'

'The Building of Historical Records?' said Nate, bewildered. 'What was he doing going in there?'

Catherine swallowed hard, forcing her mind not to dwell on the confirmation of Thom's demise. 'Is that near the Diseases Department?'

'Yeah,' said Nate. 'It's directly behind it.'

'Do you think he got lost?'

'Tommy never gets – *got* – lost.' Nate slammed his fist so hard into the window that the hover actually tilted as the glass spider-webbed. '*God* – Tommy.' He covered his mouth with a shaking hand.

Catherine couldn't voice any words of comfort. Her throat seemed to be swelling to twice its normal size and it was impossible to breathe. She let out a strangled choking sound and turned to face the window, tears flooding her eyes.

Grief was something Catherine had seldom had to deal with. Both of her parents were alive and well, and she had never had or lost any siblings. She was the only person she knew who didn't have siblings, much as she had always wanted one.

And where starvation was rampant in some countries, and people contracted new diseases every year from the harsh environment that humankind was still getting used to, Catherine had been lucky. She had never known suffering or woe. She had never had her heart broken or been greatly disappointed by life.

Beside her, Nate had one hand on the wheel, one hand over his mouth. He wasn't making a sound but from the corner of her eye she could see that he was trembling with anguish.

Catherine closed her eyes and tried not to think or feel or be aware of anything.

They flew for hours until they reached the forest and Nate drove down low, flying carefully through the trees until they were well covered. He parked the hover and clambered out, vomiting all over the ground. She heard sounds akin to that of a dying animal, but could not find it within herself to comfort him. She heard him walk a short distance away, and then dull thudding sounds and ragged breathing, and then nothing but silence.

He did not move or speak for a very, very long time.

Too consumed by her own grief, Catherine made no move to help him, sought no comfort herself, and sat motionless in the front of the hover, staring at the forest unseeingly, waiting for someone to tell her what to do.

PART TWO
Effects

Word came from Blaise the following morning. Cutta was crawling with guards. Returning was a suicide mission. There was a price on both their heads. Instead, Nate decided that they would make for the Eastern Islands where a friend of his had been contacted to give them shelter.

The border town of Blue's Cove was small and almost uninhabited. In the late autumn sun, the leaves various shades of red, orange, yellow and purple, it was a beautiful sight, and would have made Catherine cheerful on any other occasion. Right then it just felt wrong. The world did not care that everything had gone terribly sideways for Catherine and Nate; life did not stop no matter how much it felt like it should, and the bright colours and cheerful wind which rustled the leaves made for a strange irony against a town that had clearly seen better days. She had not realised how much the outlying towns had gone to seed until recently. With Thom and her parents, the places and cities she visited were always clean, well-cared for and affluent. The shabby countryside was a bit of a shock.

As they flew over the road towards the coast, the ocean on their left-hand side, the sun glinting off the waves, whitecaps roiling in the distant blue, Catherine felt a strange anticipation flare inside her chest. Aside from the ferrymen, a few aged fishermen and those who came over on the morning ferry from across the sea to run the restaurants, the whole place was deserted. There were many ghost towns after the war, although Catherine had never seen one. Some people said they were haunted and that late at night if you walked the overgrown and unused roads, you could see ghosts of days past with sad, starving, Plague-ruined faces. Their mourning songs were said to break your heart and kill you if you lingered a moment too long, their pain too great to bear. Childish tales, yet they had lingered in Catherine's mind for years.

It was decided that the hover would be dumped on the side of the road. Even if it was found the following morning, it did not matter so long as they were gone. They wiped down their fingerprints as best they could, grabbed their bags and made for the docks.

Blue's Cove had been beautiful once upon a time, Catherine was positive. There was an abandoned lighthouse that had chipping paint and a busted light bulb, but had once clearly been the pride and joy of small town architecture. Many of the outlying buildings were falling down or crumbling, and the footpaths were more weeds and hardy grasses than actual packed dirt. Still, there was a charm to the town which a bustling, busy city could never hope to have, and the smallness of it gave Catherine a sense of comfort. Small places were usually forgotten about. There was safety in that.

The ferry would take them across the bay to Cretan's Valley, a town on one of the smallest of the Eastern Islands. The islands dotted almost two hundred miles of ocean area and it would be easy enough to get lost or disappear. Less than half of them were inhabited, and fewer still had a large enough population to cause actual worry.

The ticket seller handed Catherine change and accidentally brushed her hand as he did so. Pain shot through her body and she had to bite her cheek to stop from screaming. Blistering burns appeared on her flesh instantly. Nate grabbed her, pulling her away from the man without a word.

'Breathe,' he said, holding her close. 'Try not to scream. We can't attract attention.'

Her vision steadied and she leaned against him. 'What's going on?' she said through gritted teeth, feeling better by the second as Nate's touch healed the burns. It was the strangest thing. 'What the fuck is this?'

'I don't know,' he muttered. 'Maybe there's something we missed in the mountains. We'll figure it out once we're safe.'

Catherine sighed. 'I don't think I even care.'

'I promised Tommy I would see you safely to the Outlands and that is exactly what I'm going to do.'

Casting about for a change of subject, Catherine landed on the most pressing problem. 'How are we going to get anywhere if we can't touch people?'

'There have been rumours for years of testing on prisoners. Perhaps they gave me something when I was in custody and it affected you somehow.' Nate made a face, guilt flaring in his eyes. 'Or I brought it back with me from the Outlands.'

Catherine stared at him for a moment, a hysterical laugh escaping her lips. 'That doesn't even sound real.'

'Try shaking that man's hand again.'

Catherine bit her lip. 'Even if we figure it out, we don't have the resources to fix it.'

'If anyone will have an idea of where to start, it'll be the man we're going to meet. Even if he doesn't know, he'll know someone who does. He travels a lot; his hands are in a lot of pockets. We can get information and transportation from him and if we can't figure out what's wrong from him, we'll keep heading north. We'll cross into the Outlands in Eyre. It's the easiest place to cross. Most of the minefields were exploded during the height of the agricultural boom forty years ago and no one bothered to replace them. Eyrites are amongst the least rebellious people in the Kingdom. No one's bothered hopping the Wall there and the Council sends regular contingents of guards to help them bring down stray rabids but there hasn't been an attack in the north for months. They keep showing up in Southern, Nitoib and Redland. The guards will be combing the western countries for us. Across the sea and to the north is our best chance.'

'And your friend won't say anything to the guards?'

Nate smirked. 'He's wanted by the guards, so that's doubtful.'

'I think that phrase would have bothered me more a couple days ago,' she mused. The thought of the Outlands was in no way appealing, but on the off chance that Nate was right, that Thom might, in fact, be alive, kept her from arguing. She wanted Nate to be right more than anything.

It was the first time in her life she had ever felt that way.

The ferry Nate picked out was cheap and had no broadcast. No one aboard would know their faces yet. The ferry finished boarding and a loud horn to signal disembarking sounded. Water shot out from beneath as it propelled them through the calm tides.

Nate stepped away from Catherine and leaned back against the railing. He still looked sick – sicker, actually, than he had in Goodkind. His cheeks were slightly sunken and his eyes seemed deadened. His skin was chapped and dry, and his lips were cracked. At least his cuts all seemed to have faded. Any more dishevelled and he probably wouldn't have been allowed aboard. She surveyed him carefully, trying to be subtle about it, and noted that his fingernails were yellowing, and the ends of his fingers were a slightly darker colour than the rest of his hand. She had a horrible feeling that the infection which tainted them both was killing him faster. Glancing down at her own hands, she wondered just how long it would be before she started to show similar symptoms.

He seemed to be breathing heavily, and Catherine wondered if he was easily seasick. As the boat pulled out onto the waves, shifting up and down with the ocean's mood, Nate turned very green, and Catherine left him alone, walking over to the other side of the ship and staring out into the waters.

The seas hadn't been fished in decades. When the humans first crawled out of the ground, there had been innumerable deaths from eating food and meat harvested above ground. Regulations were rapidly imposed to prevent future deaths. Nowadays there were large fisheries in Eyre and the Eastern Islands which bred fish, crustaceans, roe, molluscs, echinoderms and other types of underwater creatures for eating. The more exotic ones were sometimes bought as pets. No one dared eat the creatures which descended from those who had lived, eaten and died in the radiation soaked seawater for hundreds of years. Mutated fish sightings were not uncommon, and one of the most interesting lectures Catherine had ever sat through had spent an hour showing captures of the strange creatures that lurked below the waves, vastly different from the ones humankind had housed in aquariums below the Earth for decades.

Blue, pink and beige dolphins swam in pods in the distance; jellyfish of all different colours bobbed to and fro near the docks of most ocean towns; and the stories of great sea monsters lurking in the ocean's depths were almost common knowledge, despite how often the Council published leaflets to the contrary. The sun grew brighter the further they sailed, warming her skin, and her mind continued to wander.

Catherine was glad of the time to think. It was the first time she'd been by herself, and she finally allowed the events of the last week to play over in her mind. If she had the energy, she might have blamed the entire thing on Nate, for it was he that had called them out to Nitoib, got into a fight, forced them to walk all night, and then ... chaos. Sickness and pain and fear all blurred together. In truth, it wasn't Nate's fault; he was as heartbroken as she. No matter how stupid, how reckless his actions, blaming him for Thom would not have been fair; blaming him for the curse, problem, mutation, whatever it was that had rendered her incapable of coming into contact with anyone but him, was a different matter altogether. That, she was certain, was entirely his fault.

A man selling drinks, smokes, snacks, chocolates, gambling tickets, books, hats, scarves, cameras, souvenirs and aught else, came around after a while and Catherine bought herself a large glass of whiskey and a tocker, pocketing a small novel for later. She sat near the rear of the ferry and smoked quietly, ignoring the rest of the passengers. A few walked over to her asking if she wanted company, but something in her expression gave them pause, and no one lingered or asked a second time.

The heavy fog of drugs and alcohol numbed her brain and her body, and at last she felt like she could breathe. Staring out over the water where a large pod of whales crashed into the waves as they fled the oncoming ferry, Catherine wept.

Cretan's Valley came into view several hours later. Catherine was so intoxicated that walking in any sort of direction proved difficult. When Nate finally found her as the ferry pulled into port and made for the docks, she was swaying badly, fingers white on the railing where they gripped tightly.

'And here I thought I was drunk,' he observed. He was holding fast to the railing also, trying to stay upright. His eyes were glassy and his mouth slack. They walked unsteadily towards the exit, propelled forwards by the pull of traffic, and twice they almost fell over, grabbing on to each other to stay upright. They were a sorry sight.

Nate glanced at the shoreline, his brow furrowed in forced thought. 'We need to find a hover or something. We won't be able to walk.'

'Where are we going?'

'The other side of the island.'

As the bridge was lowered and passengers were waved off into the moonlight of the beautiful shore town, they stumbled off the ladder and made their way up the docks towards the main street. Near a coffeehouse, they spotted a large white bench, and Catherine dropped down, her head spinning and her legs wobbly.

'Ugh,' she groaned. 'Walking.'

'Are you going to be all right?'

'Momentarily or in general?'

He looked around. 'Wait here,' he said. 'For the love of God please do not get yourself into trouble.'

'Coming from you?'

'Yes, Kitty, coming from me.' Nate dropped his packs and snuck off before she could protest, stumbling over his own feet. Aware enough to know to stay quiet, Catherine pulled her legs into her chest and stared at the flowers in the garden beside the coffeehouse. They were all differently coloured: red, orange, yellow, pink, lavender, white and blends of each with at least two of the others. She hadn't known how pretty the island was going to be. Her mother had always been keen to eradicate anything that wasn't uniform in the garden, and ordered the workers to remove any and all intruding life forms. Catherine had spent much of her childhood watching convicts pull flowers out of the ground because they clashed with the decor. The process always left her melancholy.

After what felt like an age but may have only been ten minutes – she was too drunk to determine the time – Nate returned. He was driving an old hover, the engine humming softly, if slightly strained. Catherine stood, collected the packs, and climbed inside. With a quick glance around, Nate raised them higher and sped off into the night.

Delicious, glorious smells wafted towards Catherine, and she looked around. 'Did you get food?'

'Ah, she can speak, fantastic. I was truly becoming concerned for a minute there. Yes, darling, there's food if you can sit upright and swear to me you won't get sick in this car. There is one thing that you should know about me: I am a sympathy vomiter and it is in both our best interests that we do not trigger such horrors.' He glanced over at her, his face pale and perspired.

'You're more tolerable when you're blurry,' she said stupidly, reaching out and poking his cheek. 'You're not so punchable.'

'You find me punchable?' He seemed amused. 'Why?'

'Not right now,' she said. 'You've been too nice. I can't hate you when you're making it so difficult.'

'I apologise. Shall I be more despicable?'

'Yes. Some things shouldn't change.'

'Here I was thinking that you wanted me to change because you hated me, thus prompting my current take on everything.'

Catherine poked him again. It seemed like such a funny thing to do, although she wasn't sure why. 'So you're making me hate you less by being less obnoxious but you're going to be obnoxious and stay mature even though I'm asking you to become less mature because I'm in a terrible mood and need you to be more you, although I'll probably hate you if you're more you than less you, but less you is very un-punchable. I'll give you that.'

Nate looked over at her, eyebrow raised in amusement. 'That didn't make any sense, darling.'

'It did.'

'Nope.'

'Go hang yourself.'

'Ah, see, I'm more punchable already.'

Catherine rolled her eyes, laughing despite herself. 'Thank you.'

'You are welcome.' Nate reached over and patted her knee.

Heat spread from her knee through her legs and into her bloodstream. She sat up, feeling entirely more aware than she had been three seconds ago. Nate looked at her, the pupils in his eyes suddenly large. They were both stone sober. They stared at each other for several seconds before Nate was forced to look away to keep them from crashing. His hand stayed on her knee until she shoved it off.

'We need to fix this,' she said, glaring at the road in front of them, angling her body away from him. 'This is a nightmare. Thom is *dead*. He's dead and the only person I can touch, the only person I can be near, is the one person I have spent my life hating. Thom spent half his childhood awake, worrying about you, and about whether or not you'd end up in prison or dead. And now he's dead. He's dead and I'm here and you're here and I want to blame it all on you but I can't and I hate you for that.' She was sobbing by this point, her breath coming in sharp gasps as her throat threatened to close. She almost welcomed the choking feeling.

When the hover had stopped moving – had landed, for that matter – she was unsure. Suddenly her door opened and Nate had his arms around her. He pulled her into his chest and held her as she sobbed. It had started raining at some point during the journey, and the warm island rain soaked them to the bone as they clung to each other.

'He doesn't feel dead,' said Nate, his voice barely audible, shaking as he spoke the words. 'He doesn't feel dead and I don't know what to do with that. I can feel him in my bones.'

'He is dead,' said Catherine, her throat closing and her voice thickening as she said it. 'The broadcast said as much. They don't spare anyone. Not for something like that.'

Nate's face twisted horribly. 'I know – I know. I can't make sense of it and I think I'm losing my mind. He doesn't feel dead – *fuck*!'

It was then that Nate began to sob, clinging to her as hard as she held onto him, and Catherine was quite certain that their bodies would have fused together from the pain of it all if such a thing was possible. She wanted to disentangle herself, wanted to push him away, but her body felt solid, as if made of iron, and she could not move. The places where their skin touched warmed in a strangely soothing way, and after a time Catherine found that she had cried herself out.

'Nate,' she said, clearing her throat. 'Should we go?'

'All right.' He stood tiredly and walked back around to his side, slipping into the hover and starting the engine. 'Archie's place isn't far from here.'

'Is that his name?'

'Yes. Archibald Tal.'

'How long have you known this Archie?'

'Years,' said Nate. 'We were both dissenters.'

'Oh,' said Catherine. That didn't make her feel even remotely better.

Nate handed her a carton of still-warm soup. 'Eat up, darling,' he said. 'You're looking peaky.'

'I look fantastic,' she said without feeling, staring into the carton. Pieces of chicken, carrot, parsley, celery, beans, tomatoes and potatoes floated around the top, giving off a heavenly scent. There were small loaves of bread in the package, and two large bottles of fruit juice. 'Where'd you go?'

'A small restaurant a mile from the ferry,' he said. 'It was a bit more expensive, but it's far from where we got off, and if the guards trace us this far, at least nobody near the ferry will recognise a capture of me.'

'It's good,' she said around a mouthful.

Nate set the hover's autopilot on and rotated in his chair to face her, grabbing his own bowl and eating slowly. 'Food is the one thing I'll give this Kingdom. There's great food.'

Dawn was just starting to break when they both finished their meals and Nate took the wheel back, steering off the road and zooming down a cliff. The hover kept a steady two metres above everything, but Catherine was still on edge and she worried about Nate overdoing the drops and turns.

It was illegal to take hovers off the designated roads. Too many people were killed when the first hovers were put out; beheadings and flattenings and squishings. It was nasty business. Catherine could still remember her father telling her stories of the first decade of the hovercars. The roads had been too destroyed in the first years of the King's rule to properly navigate. No one had been able to move much and travel was greatly affected. The King's funding of the hoverprogramme was one of the highlights of his reign.

'Where did you find this anyways?' she said, waving her hand. 'Did you steal it?'

'Would you be annoyed if I had?'

'You shouldn't steal.'

Nate let out a derisive snort. 'I feel no guilt stealing from those with endless wealth.'

'You have endless wealth.'

'If you've not noticed, I am very content with the life I was born into,' he said dryly. 'And I never reported anyone for thievery.'

'Was there a lot of thievery in your highly-guarded manor?'

Nate winked at her. She let the conversation drop, not wanting more details of Nate's lawbreaking. Turning to face the front, she curled her legs beneath her and stared out the window at the beach flashing past.

Archie's house turned out to be a small shack in the middle of a forest, surrounded by potato and marijuana fields; the height of the surrounding mountains loomed in the background. It was a long flight from anywhere that may have people, and so far off the flypath Catherine was rather impressed that Nate hadn't spent hours flying in circles trying to find the hidden hovel. Although the house itself looked as if it had been torn, shredded, crumpled and glued back together again, various different colours of paint thrown into the bizarre mix, the grounds and fields were neatly kept and there was a calming hum of wildlife in the area. Far below, she could see a small herd of farm animals grazing together in harmony. A dog raced around, gleefully scaring the daylights out of a few fat chickens, although the frightened birds managed to escape unscathed.

Nate lowered the hover onto the ground and they got out. It was a muggy, humid day, and Catherine could feel her clothes sticking to her skin. The air felt like a heavy fog weighing her down, and she wiped her cheeks and upper lip, grimacing at the almost instantaneous perspiration.

'I need you to act like you don't hate me,' said Nate as they walked down the path. 'Archie's a bit of a dodgy fellow. He won't trust you if you act sour towards me. He'll suspect something.'

'Why?'

'Because why on Earth would I bring someone who hated me to meet someone who is wanted by the Council? Logic, darling.'

Before Catherine could reply, they had arrived at the house. Nate knocked at the door, his jaw clenched. 'Mind yourself,' he whispered. 'Don't go anywhere without me. He's not a bad man. I just wouldn't trust him to care for my dog, let alone you.'

Catherine raised an eyebrow, ready to question him further, but just then the door opened.

A short, balding man, Archibald Tal was a rough fifty and had thinning hair and several haphazard piercings that didn't seem symmetrical. Catherine's initial impression of him was that he was oily and fidgety.

'Hallo, Archie,' said Nate.

Catherine noticed that Nate had straightened up to his full height, formidable and strong beside her. Although the grief of his brother's death was still visible in his eyes, there was nothing about the way he carried himself that could suggest he was anything less than capable and focused. It was a sudden shift, a noticeable change, and Catherine wondered why he seemed so stiff around a man he called friend. Where his change in demeanour before speaking to Thom at the inn had seemed a show of steadiness, this seemed a show of intimidation.

'Rusty!' Archie's face lit up. 'How good to see you, old boy! How are you? And you've brought a lovely lady with you! How wonderful! How splendid!' Archie reached out to kiss her hand, but she bowed low before he could, forcing him to stop short. 'What is your name, my beautiful girl?'

'Kitty,' said Nate before she could speak. 'Kitty is a dear friend.'

'Not your Complement?' Archie frowned. 'Where's Matilda?'

'Matty did not approve of my prison sentence and has taken another.'

'Oh, dear boy, I'm so sorry.'

'It's all right. She's with a far less handsome man. I'm actually here about some business. May we come in?'

'Of course, my dear boy! Of course! Come in, come in!'

The interior of the house was an assault on all of the senses. Strong odours of food, sweat, old laundry, dishes in need of washing, rubbish stacked high in the corner, flowers overflowing from flowerpots, incense burning happily in several corners, and the smell of dog and cat, all wafted towards Catherine upon entry and she felt almost bowled over. Music came from hidden speakers; a loud, reverberating tune that was somewhat jaunty and entirely overwhelming. The walls were so many colours Catherine felt like she'd fallen into a vat of paint. Drapes, scarves, paintings, lights, posters, captures, paper drawings and paper mouldings were hung, stuck or nailed to the ceiling and walls, creating the illusion that the house was much bigger than it was. It was as if a second-hand shop specialising in the artistry of the addled mind had somehow been cramped inside the tiny house.

'Sit! Sit!' said Archie. 'I'll make some tea.'

'Thank you,' said Nate, sitting easily on the sofa, gesturing for Catherine to do the same. 'How have you been?'

'Oh, fine, fine,' said Archie, messing about in the kitchen, piling things on a plate and pouring three steaming mugs of something that smelled chocolaty. 'It's all a bit lonely out here, you know? Can't go back into the city these days. Can't go more than a mile or so. Have my supplies delivered.'

'Callista still helping you out?'

'She does what she can. It's much too much to do!' Archie returned and passed around the cups. He placed a huge platter of cookies, biscuits, cakes and crackers in front of them. 'Tuck in, tuck in. Now, what was I saying? Oh yes, deliveries. Yes, most of my stuff is brought up from whomever I can sway to bring it to me. It's a bit tedious, honestly; I'm on the connector rather a lot these days trying to bribe and threaten the youths into helping out their exiled elders. No such thing as compassion anymore, Rusty, I'll say!'

Nate inclined his head. 'It's been a hard couple of years, Arch. I think everyone's feeling it. I'm just glad you're managing it all. Most men couldn't make it so long on their own.'

'It is what it is,' said Archie, waving his hand away. 'Now tell me, dear boy, why is it you're lying to me about your friend?'

Nate tensed. 'Pardon me?'

Archie winked, one thick eyebrow raised much higher than the other. 'Dear boy, you've moved closer to that fine woman every time you think you can get away with it.'

Catherine looked at Nate and found that he was in fact sitting closer to her than he had been when they'd both sat down. She raised an eyebrow.

'We've been through a lot,' said Nate dismissively. He made no move to widen the distance. 'My brother, well he's been cursed or infected. We're not sure.'

Archie snorted. 'There's no such thing as curses.'

'Then this will be infinitely easier to narrow down.'

'I'll do my best.'

'My brother,' started Nate, glancing warningly at Catherine, imploring her to follow his lead, 'he was up in Nitoib the other weekend and since then he hasn't been able to touch Kitty here. Every time he does, it's agony. I was hoping you might know something about it. Burns develop. We're not sure why. It hurts her if anyone touches her.'

Catherine wasn't entirely certain why he was being evasive, but she said nothing to correct him. It was impossible to be too careful, even amongst friends. 'Do you have any ideas?'

Archie frowned. 'Nitoib? It's got more rumours and legends than most places, I'll say that much. I know Markas commissioned some programmes that far south in the early years. I think he transported several convoys of prisoners there, labelling it as rehabilitation or exile or some sort of lamb shit. I think they were all killed the minute they stepped off the bloody transport.'

'Is there something in the air down there? Or perhaps something in the water?'

Archie held up his hands. 'I've no idea, old boy, I'm sorry. I could enquire around if you'd like. Nitoib isn't most people's first choice for a stayaway spot. What were you doing down there?'

'Gambling.'

'Ah, makes sense. Fewer restrictions?'

Nate's mouth curled wickedly. 'No restrictions whatsoever.'

'I must visit.'

Catherine leaned back against the comfy pillows and watched them, her eyes heavy and sore. She wanted to sleep. The tea had settled into her bones and she felt more at ease. Allowing herself to doze, she slipped in and out of the conversation, picking up titbits of what they were saying, but not registering much of it. The pillows were too inviting, and her head felt too heavy.

'My dear, would you like to get some sleep?' Archie's voice sounded very far away. She managed a nod. 'You can sleep in the spare room,' he said. 'Come on. I'll show you.'

It was clear from his face that Nate wanted to help her but he stayed put. Stumbling after Archie, Catherine managed not to walk into anything as the pull of sleep became stronger and stronger.

'I'm sorry,' she apologised. 'It's just been an awful week.'

'No worries, dear girl,' he said. 'No worries whatsoever.'

The spare room was cluttered and smelled strongly of mothballs, but the bed she collapsed onto was squishy and warm.

'Let me know if you need anything,' said Archie, turning to leave. 'The window cracks open a bit if you want some fresh air.'

'Thank you,' she murmured, falling easily to sleep a moment later.

That night Catherine dreamed. For the first time in her entire life, she closed her eyes and opened them inside her mind, and found not peaceful darkness, but sunshine on a vibrant green field. She looked around. In every direction there was only more grass. It was a completely flat land with nothing in the distance and nothing to obscure the view. She looked at the bright blue sky. Suddenly, it was raining. The rain made the grass sparkle like emeralds, and she bent down, running her fingers over the blades. The rain wet her skin without leaving her cold.

A great sense of calm security filled her and she forgot her worries completely. She could not even remember why she was so sad. Catherine spread her arms out and danced in a circle. A dance she had learned as a small child and would never forget. Her feet moved without thought, the grass cradling her toes.

'You're going to get sick,' said a familiar voice behind her.

Catherine turned. Nate was walking towards her. He looked different. Rather than sickly, as he'd looked since the mountains, he was strong and healthy, his hair neat and bright in the strange light of the dream, his smile wide. He held out a cloak, produced as if from air.

'You can't get sick in a dream,' she rationalised.

'Of course you can, darling,' he said, his voice echoing in her head. 'Don't be stubborn.'

Catherine took the cloak and wrapped it around her shoulders. 'This is very strange.'

'My cloak? I think it's dashing.'

'No, the dream,' said Catherine. 'I've never had a dream before.'

'You're not having a dream.'

'I'm not?'

'Dreams are in your own head,' said Nate. 'You're in mine.'

Catherine woke with a start. Dawn was glittering happily through the window. She stared at the rising sun, the desire to move having left her. It was a beautiful morning. The sky was clear on the island, clouds dotting the heavens in happy formations, the horizon stained pink and red and orange. Thom used to wake her up early to have a cup of coffee and curl up on the sofa outside to watch the sunrise, soft music emanating from the morning broadcast.

She tried to remember Thom, desperate not to forget his face. His thick, curly black hair, his bright, intelligent eyes, his strong hands and barking laugh. He had been terribly awkward in their youth, covered in pimples and forgetting to brush his teeth. He used too much product in his hair and for three years smelled of strong, choking cologne which threatened to intoxicate her every time they met. Although the Assigning took place when they were twelve and most were bound at sixteen so as to have maximum use of fertile years, the time in between was more or less their own, with parents of both sides encouraging bonding and friendship.

During the first few years they had walked home together after school, spent time together on free days, and went on family stayaways with their parents, Nate and Matilda. Somewhere around sixteen Thom had figured it out, and Catherine could still remember the day she'd first properly noticed that he was handsome, rather than gangly and awkward. Nate had flown him to school in the hammering rain and he'd run into the building, hair plastered to his face, clothes soaked to the bone. She'd fallen in love with him instantly, however she'd been able to come up with nothing eloquent to say on the matter and so she'd simply stared at him, and said, 'Wow.'

'You look nice too,' he had said. He seemed genuinely pleased to see her. His smile had never been so welcoming before that day. 'Did you finish the geometry work by any chance?'

'What? Oh, yes. Do you need to copy it?'

Thom smiled, wiped the hair from his eyes and waved her inside. 'Do you like my haircut?' he'd asked as they walked. 'Nate cut it for me.'

'I like your everything,' she'd said, unable to stop herself.

They had been together from then on. Every day with Thom was so simple, so comfortable. She had felt so certain of life. Until now.

Catherine's breath caught in her throat and she sat bolt upright, gasping for air. Her sobs were silent in that terrible way of true heartbreak. Something so desolating that it had no sound, no cry, no scream. It was emptiness and little else, and emptiness had no sound.

When at last she was all cried out, the sun was fully risen and the room was bright and cheery. Tossing aside the blankets, she crept out of the room and headed for the bathroom. The cold water stung her face, but the cloudiness in front of her eyes and the fog that made her head heavy felt suddenly less consuming. Her hair was a mess, stuck up at all angles and oily, and the pillow had left indentations all over her face.

Archie owned a vast assortment of hair products and face serums and body lotions, and she spent about twenty minutes in the bathroom making herself look less miserable. The mindless actions required no effort, and she was able to keep her dark musings at bay. She sprayed herself with some of his mint mist and, after fetching the bag of stolen clothes, changed into something fresh. Even the illusion of being together was better than nothing. She left the bathroom and headed down the small hallway, packed to the ceiling with all manner of strange items, to the lounge.

Nate looked up at her from where he sat on the sofa. 'Did you sleep well?'

'Well enough,' she said. She had no intention of mentioning the odd dream. 'Anything?'

'Maybe something,' he said, shrugging. He looked a mess, and it was clear he had hardly slept. He was sweating badly, his eyes more bloodshot than she had ever seen on anyone, and there was dried blood in his ear. 'Maybe nothing,' he continued. 'I've printed as much as I could find in the records, but I didn't dare search for too much as I'm sure they're monitoring everything. Archie had some books and old newspapers from years ago. The Nitoib Mountains were common for exiles, supporters of cooperation and mutants who had run in the wrong direction; detention centres were littered all over the place, and other sorts of nasty business was going on out there. Whether that has anything to do with us, I'm not entirely sure, but it's better than nothing. I found this article here –' He held out a file to her. '– that describes a rumour of the programmes King Franklin started during the war. Some are fairly gruesome. Apparently, they tried to see if mutants could still function with the body parts of other prisoners.'

Catherine gagged. 'Why?'

'I haven't a notion. Why does humankind do anything?' His lip curled in disgust. 'Because we can. Morality doesn't hold a candle to curiosity.'

'Did it work?'

'Obviously not,' he said. 'I think it was more an excuse to torture and maim rather than being for any actual scientific merit. But there's another rumour that Franklin was engineering serums to repel the enemy. Perhaps if he created an infection that changed the structure of our bodies or something – I'm not a bloody scientist – but maybe that'll explain it. Aside from those rumours and files though – all missing half their information, might I add – there's not really anything. No one else has taken a gander through the range in decades, so it's unlikely that anyone else will have stumbled across whatever it is we find ourselves cursed with.'

'Sounds about right.'

'At least we've a start.'

'Yeah.'

'Are you all right?'

Catherine frowned. 'How do you mean?'

'Your eyes … are you all right?'

'Fine.'

Nate took the hint and turned back to his research. 'Archie went out to get some food for breakfast. He's also going to ask around and see if he can find anything useful.'

'I thought you said he had people bring the shopping to him.'

'Most days he does, just to be safe. Sometimes he goes in quietly. Certain shops without recordings will mind their own business if he tips well. Some people hold that loyalty to islanders comes before loyalty to Crown and Council. Like in Southern. Country before Kingdom. Not that anyone would ever admit it, but small places like this have their own ways, you know? If he goes a few times a year, no one will remember him, or notice him. He could easily be a passing tourist.'

'But why risk it now? When people are hunting us?'

'It's not exactly like I can,' said Nate. 'And he has to meet a few people to get more information. It made sense for him to go. He's careful – he knows who not to speak to.'

'I suppose.' Catherine picked up a few pieces of paper and leaned back against the pillows to read. It was a half blacked-out document. Although found in the public records, it was clear that much of it was not public access. If it had been easier to read, Catherine might have found something, but as it was, it read: 'STORAGE – BURIED – PAPER – OUTFIT – THE KING ARRIVED – BARN – PLAGUE KILLED HUNDREDS.' Each word or phrase was several lines below the one before it. Catherine put it aside and picked up the next one. It wasn't much better: 'NITOIB MOUNTAINS – MOTORWAY DESIGNATION – PLANNED TO BE THREE YEARS – OPEN GROUND.'

'You've been at this all night?' she said. 'Your head must be killing you.'

'I smoked the rest of the cannabis and got a couple of minutes of sleep,' he said, rubbing his face. His beard was lengthening, darkly aging his face several years. It suited him more than tidiness ever had. He stood and stretched. 'Coffee?' he said. 'Tea?'

Before she could answer, the front door opened and Archie came in. He was carrying a large bag of shopping and a handful of papers. He said, 'Who wants breakfast?'

'Please,' said Nate. 'Want help?'

'I've got it,' said Archie. He smiled at Catherine. 'How'd you sleep, m'dear?'

'All right,' she said. 'The bed was very comfortable. Thank you.'

'Any time, any time. What would you like for breakfast?'

'I'm easy to please,' she said politely.

Archie beamed and disappeared into the kitchen. A few moments later the familiar sounds of cooking and sizzling began, and she looked over at Nate. 'How long have you known him?'

'Archie? He was my Mathematics teacher,' said Nate.

Catherine stared at him. 'He was not.'

'He was,' said Nate, chuckling. 'We got into a slight debate once in class. I think we'd both suspected the other of having dissenting thoughts, but it's not something you just outright ask, is it? That can get you into a world of trouble. So we danced around the subject for a few months during lessons, and then one day he asked Blaise and I to stay after class to discuss a paper. Somehow things progressed and we ended up at meetings down on Wally Street. There's a secret club that meets once every two weeks to discuss politics, revolutionary ideas, idealist passions, that sort of thing. Archie introduced me. I met more than a few radicals in those meetings. We turned it into the Underground Club.'

Catherine gaped at him. The Underground Club made headlines three years before when over a dozen were captured and publicly executed. He was a known member, but this level of authority was news to her. Fascinated, she dropped the leaflet and sat back. 'You *founded* it?'

He grinned proudly. 'Yep. With others including Archie.'

'How many of you were there?'

'In my group? Dozens. Once we started moving into other countries it took on a life of its own. None of us ever knew how many there were, or how other groups functioned. The second largest faction are in Cuzak Square in Muntenia, and I know a few from that group. I stayed with a few of them after prison. Loyalty amongst criminals is no small thing. Long before that, we met up in Burkenz towards the end of my first year with the Club. We blew up the central bank there.'

Catherine gaped at him. 'That was you?'

'And several others,' said Nate. He seemed pleased to have her full attention.

'They said it was a miracle no one died.'

'It wasn't. We waited until the night shift and then dragged the stragglers from the building blindfolded. We put them a good distance away and then blew the building. We wanted to make a statement, not murder anyone.'

'So the meetings were just about discussing the destruction of Crown and Council?'

'No, not at all. Sometimes we sat and discussed things that were outlawed. Sometimes we just smoked and drank and talked the night away. It wasn't just a group of people sitting around and hating everything about our society, our politics. It was a family of people who came together with a shared ideal and could be completely themselves. Do you know what it is to be able to tell a group of people how angry, how scared, how disgusted you are at everything and have them not only listen and understand, but give you words of comfort and wisdom and condolence? For the first time in my life, I felt amongst my own kind. It's a very intoxicating feeling.'

'Did Thom know?'

Nate nodded, a look of anguish flashing across his face before he managed to mask it. 'I tell him everything. More than wanting him to understand, I wanted him to join me. He never did, but I think in his own way he understood that we weren't evil the way Crown and

Council paint us to be. We were – *are* – unhappy. We should be able to say that we're unhappy and not fear the repercussions.'

'Did you go back after you got out of prison?'

'Not to the meetings, no,' said Nate. He had a strange look of faraway bitterness on his face, and he brushed a long strand of red hair from his forehead. The conversation seemed to be an effort for him, and he was sweating profusely. 'Tommy picked me up from prison but it was the welcome party which made me leave. I didn't have the strength to do it. I was so weak from prison and not anywhere near healthy, but being around all of those people, the people I had existed around publicly for most of my life – it just showed me that nothing had changed. It's a very startling thing to go to prison for two hundred days for crimes you've publicly admitted to and return to the detached, gossipy affluence of Anaitian high society. Fake smiles and quick kisses and cold brews. I couldn't bear it. I spent the night drinking with Tommy and come morning I grabbed my bag and left. I went from friend to friend for a while, drifting slowly north. I just kept going until I hit the Wall, and then climbed over.'

'How did you do it? They say it's impossible to survive the Outlands.'

'They say a lot of things,' said Archie, coming into the room with a tray of food. 'A lot of times it's not true. Who's going to check? Most in the Kingdom are too frightened of mutants and rabids to even attempt it.'

'But not you,' she surmised, eyeing Nate thoughtfully. She certainly would never have tried it. Even the idea of leaving the safety of the city was frightening to her. Aside from Nate, she could not think of a single person who would willingly venture that far. Most of her friends dared not even go to the countryside unless it was to a family manor with fences.

'I was,' he admitted. 'At that point I didn't care. I think it's more miracle than skill that I even survived. Most days I walked towards the danger, hoping to die. I wanted it more than anything. I craved death, blackness, the next life.'

'Yet you came back.'

'For Tommy,' said Nate unsteadily. 'I couldn't leave him here.'

Archie handed Nate a cup of tea. 'I'm sure he'll be fine once we figure out what's wrong with him.'

Catherine and Nate said nothing, sipping their tea with shaking hands.

The rest of the day passed without event. They lounged around on various sofas and squishybags, reading over the blacked-out papers, old broadcasts, publications and the few books about diseases, spores, infections and sicknesses that Archie had been able to get his hands on; the small island was not known for its resources. There was plenty of filler information, plenty of interesting factoids about the Thinning, about the Bite, about the Plague, about this, that or the other, but nothing about burns which occurred by touch, nothing about the ability to heal someone else. The whole thing seemed ridiculously impossible even now.

Fruitless as it was, Catherine was glad to have something to focus her thoughts upon. Reading, jotting down notes, drinking copious amounts of tea and smoking continuously gave her something to do, something other than thinking of Thom, and by the time Archie appeared with steaming bowls of thick stew, warm brown bread and cups of pear cider, Catherine realised she'd gone almost the whole day without wanting to cry or be sick, and she almost had an appetite.

For his part, Nate looked terrible but said nothing about feeling ill, and Catherine let the matter go. It wasn't any of her business how Nate was feeling or what he was thinking. He undoubtedly was trying to keep himself from falling to pieces. His fingers tapped softly on the wooden table beside him and he seemed to be murmuring something under his breath. She could not hear it, but his lips moved nonstop when he thought no one was looking.

Suddenly overcome with exhaustion, Catherine bade the pair of them goodnight, closed the book on skin infections she was reading, and walked slowly down the hallway, blinking blearily and thinking of pillows.

She was asleep in seconds.

Acrid smells reached her nose long before any comprehension of awareness did. The horrible stinging smell of paint fumes, cat piss, cleaning solutions and rot, all mixed together with a hearty topping of mould and damp made waking up a truly unpleasant experience. Catherine blinked awake slowly, achingly, the lids of her eyes heavy and hurting. She wasn't in the bedroom, nor was she in the sitting room. Everything was dim, but she could make out the shapes of tools, boxes and junk, and it wasn't hard to deduce that she was in a shed. The reason she was *in* a shed remained to be seen.

Catherine resisted the urge to shout for Nate, and swallowed hard; the sensation was not unlike pouring lemon juice on numerous paper-cuts. It was only as she tried to push herself up right that she realised her hands were bound. The skin on her arms felt badly burned, and though she could not see it, she knew that the flesh was blistered and red from where whomever had bound her had touched skin. She pulled hard a few times but they were bound tight and the tingling feeling of low circulation told her that the ropes had been on for a while. Her legs were also bound, and tied securely to the ground. Heart pounding with confused fear, she blinked painfully several more times, trying to clear her blurred vision and think back to the last thing she remembered: walking into the bedroom, ready to collapse after a fruitless day of studying blacked out texts which made less sense than a five-year-old's attempt at spelling. And then this. What could have possibly happened?

'Nate,' she whispered. Her voice sounded croaked and raspy, and she coughed at the attempt. Had she been strangled? Or beaten? Likely both given the throb of her body and the current state of immobility she found herself in. Where was Nate? Where was Archie? Had the guards somehow managed to find them? A horde of worries reared their heads and she tried to calm down.

It seemed unwise to call out for Nate again, but she was not sure what else to do. She could not stand, nor could she see much beside the dim outline of random flotsam and jetsam, and if he was somewhere in the shed, she wanted to know. Nate had seen her through the mountains, had helped her escape the wrath of the guards; whatever it was that was happening now, she would feel a hundred times better knowing he was there. No matter how much trouble he caused, he was more slippery than a fish at getting out of danger, and right now that seemed incredibly useful. If only she could find him.

'Nate,' she whispered again, swallowing down the cough which threatened to erupt. '*Nate!*'

There was no reply. Giving up for the time being, Catherine felt around as best she could, trying to find something somewhere which might aid her in getting herself free. She succeeded in finding spider webs, pieces of paper, a ball, a roll of twine, and something sticky, but nothing of use.

The hours ticked by with agonising slowness, and all of her extremities began to tingle, aching to move and stretch and regain proper circulation. She needed desperately to relieve herself, but was not yet to the point of breaking where she gave up all sense of dignity and pissed herself. Grinding her teeth and counting the seconds seemed to be the only way to pass the time, and she was well into the high ten thousands before the door opened, flooding the room with light.

'Archie!' she cried. 'Archie, thank God! Untie me!'

The old man looked at her, shook his head, and stepped inside with a smirk. A horrible cold sank into her bones. So it was Archie who had done this to her.

'Why?' she said.

'My dear girl, someone ought to have told you by now that it isn't prudent to ask questions of your captors,' he said, bemused. 'I will say that this is entirely Nate's fault.'

She stared at him. 'Nate would never hurt me.' She knew that much was true. For all his stupid rash behaviour, Nate loved Thom more than anyone in the entire world, and he would care for her to honour Thom. She had no doubt of that.

'Because you are his brother's? My dear girl, that's such a silly thing to rest your trust upon,' he said, leaning against a stack of boxes, appraising her thoughtfully. 'Nate's hurt more people for less.'

'You make him sound like a mutant.'

'He's worse,' said Archie. 'He killed my Complement.'

Catherine froze, mouth open, gaping stupidly at Archie, completely at a loss for words. She could think of a thousand things she disliked about Nate, but she would never have thought him capable of such things. Only the very worst sort of people killed, after all, unless they were doing their duty to Crown and Council.

'Don't know everything about him, do you? No, I didn't think so. Small matter. He'll tell you himself once he wakes up.' Archie glanced towards her left, and in the light of the open door, what had looked like rags in the darkness she could now see was Nate's unconscious form. 'A fiend, yes,' he murmured. 'Not a liar, though. I'll give him that.'

'And me? What am I?'

Archie shrugged. 'Inconvenient. Or very convenient, depending upon your point of view. I have thought about my revenge for many years, dear girl. She was murdered, you see, just weeks before his internment, and I could hardly kill him then. I thought perhaps the guards would do it for me. Slippery bastard somehow wormed his way out of the Hangman's grip thanks to that brother of his. Nate always did have a sickening amount of luck. And then he disappeared, just like that, into the wilderness. I hadn't seen him in years, until you showed up at my doorstep with pleas of help, as if none of it had ever happened. Suddenly I had the opportunity I'd been daydreaming about for years. Suddenly I had the chance at revenge. And,' he said, hungry smile broadening, 'I seem to have much more than that.'

Catherine swallowed hard. 'How do you mean?'

'I don't listen to the broadcast much anymore. It's a horrible thing. Daily reminders of our captivity in this so-called Kingdom. When I went for supplies yesterday, what do you think I happened to hear? Nathanial Anteros, once again wanted, only this time with a reward on his head. Not only that – I've discovered there's one for you as well. How very fortuitous, wouldn't you agree?'

'Seeing as how I'm bound and sitting on a floor, no, I would not agree,' she snapped. 'I'm sure you, however, are delighted.'

'That I am, dear girl. That I am.'

'You'll go to the Abyss for this, Archibald.' The deep, rasping voice made them both glance over at Nate, who was pushing himself into a sitting position, dark eyes fixed malevolently on Archie. There were burns on his arms, face and neck, and Catherine wondered if he'd been dragged unconscious, or if he'd fought Archie and somehow lost. The latter option seemed somehow unlikely, as Nate was twice Archie's size.

'It's nice to know oaths mean nothing to you,' said Nate. He examined his burns as if unbothered by pain.

Archie's face twisted with ugly fury. 'I kept my oath! It never included sheltering the man who murdered the only thing in this world I have ever loved!'

'I didn't murder her,' said Nate. 'She died. It was an accident. Everyone knows it was an accident.'

Archie crossed the room in two strides and smashed his fist into Nate's face. The howls which escaped Nate's throat sounded inhuman, and the place where Archie's flesh had touched his was the colour of cherries, torturous looking burns and blisters forming.

'Handy little infection you've found yourself with,' said Archie. He clapped Nate on the face, causing more burns. Nate yanked his face away, tears of agony filling his eyes, his face contoured with pain. 'I thought you might be sick as well, the way you didn't let me so much as shake your hand when you arrived. At least now I'll get to have some fun until the guards arrive.'

Nate snorted. He was soaked in sweat and trembling with rage, but he didn't look scared, which Catherine found nothing short of admirable given the circumstances.

'You haven't even conn'd them yet, Archie,' he said knowingly. 'You're not going to be here when they arrive.'

'How little you know, dear boy. Of *course* I will be here when they arrive. Turning the two of you in will grant me passage home and a start in Cutta. It's a good deal more than I've ever had.'

'You'd turn in your friend, break your oath, for a change of scenery and a few measly cuttans? You're fucking *pathetic*.'

Archie punched him again. 'You took my life from me, Anteros. I do not forget.'

'It was an accident!' said Nate emphatically. 'It was an accident, Archie. I never meant for any of it to happen. We went because it was what we voted on. The plan was bad and we messed up. Everyone was anxious to get home and we didn't check the secondary locks. There was no way to get her out without the rest of us dying.'

Archie shook his head in disgust and turned to look at Catherine, who had been watching the horrific exchange with wide eyes. 'Nate got us a job a few years back. Sabotaging the railway. Him and Marko, Helene and me. We had it all set and then Helene hears them coming. The guards. She says they're heading straight for us – and then the locks bolted. So what does Nate do? He leaves her and we watch them open the door, easy as you please, and shoot her in the head.'

'I didn't murder her, Archie. What should I have done? Left you there to die? Let Marko die? We ran because we had no other choice.'

Hysterical laughter tore from Archie's lips. 'You should have done something!'

'I did the best I could! We knew what we were getting in to! How many of the Club died during these attacks? How many friends did we lose? Helene wasn't the first, nor was she the last, Archie. It was tragic, yes, no one is denying that. It wasn't murder by my account.

It was murder by the King's. And now you're handing me over to them when you swore an oath to protect your sisters and brothers. Who's the murderer now?'

The two men fixed each other with looks of pure loathing, and it was clear Archie meant to do more damage to Nate before he turned him in. He advanced, drawing a knife from the sheath that was belted to him, and Catherine finally found her voice.

'Stop!' she cried. 'Just, stop it!'

Archie and Nate looked over at her, as if surprised to find that she was still there. Both had been so absorbed in their argument that neither remembered she was listening. Nate's face widened with horror, Archie's contorted with malice. He turned away from Nate and moved towards her.

'When I heard on the broadcast that you were both wanted, I asked myself what possible reason could there be for a woman of such high breeding, the daughter of our very own Hangman, to be travelling with Nate,' said Archie, appraising her as if trying to put together a puzzle. 'Perhaps you both killed Thomas and fled before you were discovered?'

Catherine felt like she'd been punched in the stomach, and the rushing sound of rage drowned out the sound of Nate's reaction. She stared up at Archie, hatred filling her bones, and spat at him, hitting him square in the chest. 'Go hang yourself,' she said, her lip curling. 'You have no idea what you're talking about.'

Archie bent down in front of her and scratched the edge of his beard with the point of the knife. Catherine hoped he'd cut himself. 'If you didn't kill him to run away with his brother, then how come you both are here and he is not?' he enquired. 'It seems to me very suspicious, and if I know Nate, I know how ruthless he can be.'

'Clearly you don't know Nate at all,' she retorted. 'Elsewise you'd never accuse him of such a thing.'

'I know him a fair bit better than you, dear girl,' said Archie.

Catherine laughed, and she hated how terrified she sounded to her own ears. If the guards were coming, they were doomed already. She wished, distantly, that none of this had happened; she wished she was in class right now, thinking about coming home to Thom and curling up beside him, safe and warm, sheltered from the evils of the world she truly had no desire to be a part of. She did not want to know the cruelty of the world; she did not want to know about awful things. She wanted to be safe and sheltered and unaware of it all. Her wants, it seemed, counted for very little.

'You know nothing,' she hissed. 'You're just some madman who's blaming his life's problems on an accident that shouldn't've happened in the first place because it was illegal. If you'd not been so stupid and joined a hopeless cause perhaps your Complement would still be alive.'

Archie lunged at her, his hands wrapping around her throat; burns erupted where his hands touched, and horrible, cold and hot searing pain shot through her, tearing into her body, her heart, her mind, threatening death and promising insanity. She screamed and writhed, trying to pull away, but there was nowhere to go and nowhere to hide, and all she could do was scream and struggle and wish for death until there was nothing, only darkness.

Catherine did not register that he'd let go of her for several minutes. The pain eased to a heavy throbbing and she managed to open a swollen eye. She felt as if someone had rammed a red-hot poker down her throat and made her swallow around the burning metal. Her throat felt like razors. There was a wheezing in her lungs from the exertion and it was impossible to take a full breath. Had she been any more conscious, the strain on her lungs would have sent her into a panic. As it was, she was simply too exhausted and pained to worry.

'Darling? Say something, please.'

Catherine opened her eyes. It seemed very important not to let Nate worry. He was her only way out of this horrible place. He was the only thing that wouldn't hurt. She almost smiled at the thought of hugging him. It would make her feel so much better. If he wasn't so far away, if they weren't bound, then he could heal her skin and make everything better. At least there was a cure to the agony. At least she wasn't alone.

'Please say something.'

He wanted her to talk. She opened her mouth but no sounds came out. It was frustrating. Her body felt like it belonged to someone else. It had belonged to Thom once, just as Thom had belonged to her. Tears filled her eyes as she thought of him and she closed them again.

'Kitty? You've got to give me something. Just say something. Anything. *Please.*'

With a thick, painful swallow and several hard blinks, she managed to clear some of the fuzziness from her head and nod. It hurt, but it was bearable. She thought that was the worst thing about all of it. It was all bearable. It was all surmountable. The only thing truly unbearable was death, and at least in death she knew she would find peace. Nate watched her, his heart pounding so hard that she could see his pulse throbbing in his neck.

It took another five minutes before she was able to muster the strength to speak. 'Y-you look –' She coughed several times. '– l-like shit.'

Nate laughed weakly in relief. 'You had me going mad for a second there, darling. Don't do that again.'

'Where's –'

'He left a while ago. You were out. He said he was going to let the guards know, although I'm not even sure he wants to, so that could be more for scare than anything. He seems to half want to kill me, half want to get a confession. Or he's just completely insane, hasn't a notion what he wants, and is going to torture us until we die. Honestly, darling, none of the options are very good.'

Catherine forced herself into a sitting position. 'Is what he said true?'

'Yes, I suppose.'

'You always were reckless,' she said. 'But if you ask me, it does sound like it was an accident.'

'Thank you.' He dropped his head back against the wall and sighed. 'I tried. God's wrath, I've been teaching Tommy to pick locks since he was a kid and I still couldn't get the door back open. The guards were coming. It was stay and die or run.'

'I believe you.' Catherine examined her ropes. She dearly hoped they would not cut off circulation. Losing an extremity on top of everything was more than she could handle. She rolled her eyes and looked back to him. 'Is there any way out of here?'

'I've been giving that a great deal of thought, actually.'

'And?'

'Nothing.'

'Wonderful.'

Nate's fingers tapped on the floor. 'Why would anyone come up with something like this?'

The door opened and Archie walked in. He had clearly been listening. 'I had a friend who worked for the Council some years back. He was full of stories. Some of them even about buildings in the mountains. They were creating all sorts of things out there. Serums of all kinds. What you've got – my guess is it's a military concoction from Yosef Smith. Now there's a man with a reputation. Mad bastard, but King Franklin wanted more. Newer, better weapons. Newer, better soldiers. Nothing could satisfy that old fart. He funded projects on a whim.'

'Why?' asked Catherine. 'Why did he hate them so much?'

'The devoutness of the mutants bothered him, if the old rumours are anything to go by. Their prophecies contradicted the cult which surrounded him. Hard to spin a tale of us-against-them when the them is welcoming you with open arms and preaching of their God's will. It infuriated him. There were rumours that the mutants even learned our language to try and sway more of our ancestors to their side. Old Franklin couldn't have that, now could he? I think the trials in those mountains killed hundreds of prisoners of war. Many of the volunteers died as well.'

Catherine frowned. It seemed too horrible to fully process. 'What were the trials?'

Archie shrugged. 'Sad to say I'm a bit hazy on that account. Unfortunate, really. I find the whole thing marvellously interesting.'

'How'd we get it?'

'Ah, that one I am able to answer, I believe. The testing facilities were all in Nitoib. That's how he kept them quiet. It's a desolate shithole.' Archie looked at her, his expression changing so suddenly Catherine recoiled. 'Tell me, my dear, what was it you were doing out in the mountains with young Nate?'

Catherine glanced at Nate, before looking back at Archie. 'There was a fight. Thom had gone into the city to collect money to pay off Nate's gambling debt. While he was gone there was a fight. We ran before the guards arrived.'

'Most intriguing,' said Archie. 'And why was there a fight?'

'I don't know,' said Catherine honestly. 'I don't know how it started.'

Archie pursed his lips in thought; the effect made him look rather like an evil gorilla, she noted nastily. He glanced over at Nate. 'She doesn't know why you started the fight,' said Archie, chuckling to himself. 'She doesn't, but I do.'

Confused, Catherine looked from villain to victim, wondering what he was talking about.

'You know,' said Archie, eyes still fixed on Nate. 'The funny thing is I've seen a look similar to the one you wear when you look at her.' His voice caught and he swallowed hard. 'It's the way I used to look at my Helene.'

Catherine raised both eyebrows, and laughed at the ridiculousness of his words. 'You're mad,' she said. 'You're completely mad.'

'Mad, am I?' Archie shook his head. 'No, I don't believe I am. You are young, dear girl, perhaps you cannot yet read faces, but the thing you should know about Nate is that he cannot lie. Ask him. He's madly in love with you. I'm not sure if that makes you incredibly lucky or unlucky.'

Nate said, 'Go fuck yourself, Archie.'

Archie punched him, hard, in the throat, and Nate collapsed in on himself, gagging. Unfazed, Archie looked at Catherine. 'The more I watched you both, the more I realised it was true. How fortunate,

I think, that Nate should bring the woman he loves to my doorstep. It's almost ironic, wouldn't you agree?'

A horrible feeling welled in her stomach as she realised the meaning of Archie's words; it was clear from the way Nate's head snapped up, alert and tense, that he realised Archie's meaning as well.

'Archie –'

Archie didn't look at Nate as he spoke; his eyes were fixed on Catherine. 'Helene was shot. It's a horrible thing to watch. She knew what was coming; she knew I wasn't going to save her. Knowing there was no way at all for her to survive. Can you imagine, dear girl? How truly terrible it would be to die that way? Like an animal in a trap, watching its pack, its mate, flee.'

Fear welled in her throat and Catherine pulled hard at the ropes, trying to break free; do something, anything. She did not want to die. Not yet. She had too much she still wanted to do, too much she still hadn't done. Her eyes fixed on the gun Archie held in his hand. It seemed so small. Insignificant. Not the sort of thing that ought to be able to do much damage.

'How will killing me make it right?' she cried, her voice sounding like it belonged to someone else. 'I haven't done anything wrong!'

'A life for a life,' said Archie. Sweat was dripping down his face, gathering in his beard, soaking through his clothes. His grip on the gun did not seem steady, nor controlled.

'Then take my life!' shouted Nate, his dark eyes wide and horrified as he wrenched at the binds, trying to break free. 'Kill me, Archie, I don't care. You know I've never cared. Kill me and you'll have your justice.'

'How is it justice if you don't care?' Archie wondered aloud. 'No, if I turn you in, alone, then I will have my reward. I will be able to go home. I will be able to see Helene's grave. I will have that, at least. But killing the woman you love – to me, that's a much greater justice than anything I could do to you now that your brother is dead. If I could, I'd've killed him. You always loved him most, after all. Ah well, beggars can't be choosers, now can they?'

Catherine took a deep breath, trying to find some semblance of calm to cling to. Panicking would solve no problems. Clearly Archie wasn't in his right mind, but there might yet be some way to reason with him.

'Listen, all right,' she said carefully, 'I don't know why you think Nate cares about me, but he doesn't. He's with me because we both loved Thom. He doesn't care about me. We hate each other. Anyone can attest to that. Killing me isn't going to do anything to him. It's just going to put blood on both your hands. Please just *listen*. I want no part of this; I've never had any part in this. I'm here because I have no choice. No one gave me a choice. I haven't agreed to be part of any club. I haven't signed on for anything. Your problems, your grief, your revenge, that's your own and none of my business or concern. Hurting me won't bring you peace or justice.'

Archie raised the gun, sweat making his grip unsteady; Nate was shouting, writhing, trying to break free; Catherine stared at the barrel, wondering what it would be like to die.

'What would Helene have done?' she whispered. 'What would she have done if you had been the one to die?'

'She would have burned the world to the ground,' said Archie brokenly. 'She wouldn't have let anyone away with it.'

'Would she have killed an innocent woman?' asked Catherine. She felt nauseated, her whole body vibrating with adrenaline and fright.

'Archie, listen to her! Please!'

'The one who killed Thom,' she continued, not taking her eyes off Archie, 'I want them dead. I want them to know that the only justice for killing is death, but that was cold blooded execution, Archie, not an accident. What happened to Helene *was* an accident. When you're sneaking around in the dark, acting the dissenter, you can't be surprised when things go wrong. They just will. It's inevitable. That's not Nate's fault. He didn't do it on purpose.'

'She's dead because of him!'

'And I'm to die because of you? One bullet and it's over. You won't feel any relief from your pain.'

Archie frowned, glancing at the gun. He lowered it slowly, a thoughtful expression on his pasty features. 'You're right.'

The relief she felt died the second she realised that his words were not what she hoped.

'Killing you would be too quick,' he said. 'I've spent years with my ghosts. Nate oughtn't to be let off so easy.'

'You're not doing anything to Nate! You're doing it to me!'

'Archie, leave her alone, you cowardly fuck!'

Before Catherine could even process what was happening, Archie's hands were on her. Her skin was burning and everything was fire and boiling and *wrong*. She felt wrong. Dying would surely be the better alternative to this. Her vision began to go from white to red to black, and just as she started to lose consciousness, the screams still bursting forth from her ruined throat, she saw Nate wrench himself free.

It was a long while before the pain subsided. When it ebbed to a steady, dull throb, the sort that pounds the head after a night of grinding one's teeth, only this was all over her body, she found that she was being rocked back and forth in Nate's arms. He was holding her tightly, his fingers digging bruises into her skin, whispering words of comfort and solace and fury.

She opened her eyes, blinking away the tears, and looked at him. He was a ruin. His hair was so wet and matted with sweat, it was almost titian. He looked like Thom, and the comparison cut her to the core. She wanted to be dreaming. She wanted to wake up and find herself in bed, safe and beside Thom. She wanted none of this to have happened. Thom, who dealt with those he didn't like through unparalleled cunning and manipulation. Thom, who had never had violence follow him. Thom, who had been so simple and so safe.

'It's all right. You're safe now. I've got you. He's gone. He's gone. You're safe now. You're all right. It's done. It's finished. Everything's fine. Breathe, darling. Just breathe. I've got you. You're safe.' His words of comfort never ceased, his hold on her never loosened, and she realised after a while that he was saying it to himself as much as he was saying it to her. He seemed stuck in a loop.

It was a very long time before either of them got control of themselves. Finally, her head aching, covered in burns and blisters, she was able to sit up. Her body felt like it had been cut into a million pieces, the flesh peeled as one peels the skin from an apple.

'Are you all right?'

'No.'

'I killed him.'

She felt no surprise, no shock or horror. Everything was numb and she didn't care at all. 'You killed him?'

'Yes.'

It was then that Catherine saw. Skin hung off his wrists. The palms of his hands and the tops of his forearms were burned badly. It was a horrific sight and she knew that his arms would be scarred forever, if he even managed to save the use of them. He was missing several fingernails. There was a burst blood vessel in his eye and his lip was broken. Blood stained his teeth as if he'd bit his tongue or cheek. There was a terrified edge to his expression and his grip wasn't relaxing. His eyes couldn't cease roving over her, checking and rechecking that she was together, whole. His hand that was supporting both of them couldn't seem to control its fingers and they tapped out the same rhythm as he stared at her.

She went to work removing the last of their binds. Some were dug so deeply into his skin that when they came away there was hair and flesh ingrained in the rope. Nate said nothing, hardly even flinched, as she removed each piece one by one until his arms were bloody but unbound.

'Thank you,' he said.

'We should get them clean.'

Nate's brow suddenly furrowed. 'Kitty?'

'Yes?'

'Why aren't we healing each other?'

Catherine stared down at where her hands gripped his arms. Her skin was cut and bruised and burned, his a bloody mess. She had completely forgot that they could. In the chaos so many things had slipped her mind. 'I don't know,' she said, confused. 'Do you think we're still infected?'

'Those burns aren't fake.'

'Perhaps we can only do it at certain times.'

'Perhaps,' he muttered, staring at her hand on his arm for a long time before he stood on stiff legs. Holding out his hand, he helped her up. 'Come. Let's get cleaned up and leave as quickly as possible.'

It was unnerving and disorientating being back in Archie's house, knowing that he was dead. Everything felt dirty, as if the bacteria had already taken over the now unowned house. Nate led Catherine to the bathroom and turned the heating on high before he started the shower.

He turned to her, expression uncertain. His hands reached out, rising and falling several times before he said uncertainly, 'Do you – do you want some help getting out of your clothes?'

Catherine, who had been leaning against the counter, too weary, too horrified, too numb to do anything but stare dumbly at him, nodded once, the effort almost taking the last of her reserves. Nate undressed her carefully, and then when he realised that she wasn't moving, he removed his clothes slowly, wincing, and helped her into the warm scented rain of the shower. She leaned against him. It was easier to breathe so close to him. As they stood there, blood pooling on the porcelain below them, Catherine felt a slow spark of heat spring from where her head rested against Nate's shoulder, and she stayed completely still, praying that their bodies would mend themselves back together. How long they stood there, clinging to each other, she wasn't sure, and though it was clear that neither of them was at full strength, the wounds mended themselves ever-so, the skin knitting itself back together timidly, the ripped flesh reattaching with a frailness that seemed at any moment ready to crumple away into red dust.

'Kitty?'

'Yes?'

'I'm so sorry I ever brought you here.'

She said nothing. She doubted very much that Nate was feeling any better about the situation; his apologies weren't necessary.

'Is there anything I can do?'

'No.'

'Do you hate me for killing him?'

'No.'

'Do you think me a horrible person?' Nate leaned away from her, his hair sodden and flat against his forehead, his eyes filled with guilt and sorrow. 'Please give me more than monosyllables, darling. Tell me what you're thinking. Tell me you're still in there somewhere.'

Catherine stared at the blood mixing with the warm water on his wrists, dripping off pink and tainted. She reached out and held up his hand carefully, putting it beneath the gentle spray. The antiseptic tonic on the wall foamed over his wounds, and he huffed in relief as it started to clean his wounds. Between the healing spray and whatever it was they did to mend each other, they were both starting to look more whole. Physically, at least.

'No, I don't think you're a horrible person. Thank you,' she added. 'For saving me. You didn't have to.'

'I did. I brought you here. I thought Archie might've mended in the years since. I thought, if anything, his oath would keep him in line. I never thought he blamed me so much. Our last conversation ended with few words but no anger. I didn't know he was so broken. I didn't realise you could be – not over someone else, someone who wasn't a brother ... not until we were in that shed did I realise how poorly I judged the situation. But then he looked at you – and I knew. I knew the madness had taken over him, had eaten away everything that made him, *him*. I knew that there was no cure, no tonic to his misery. I was so stupid to never realise it until now – how much you can care about someone ... the only person I ever felt that way about was Tommy ... I didn't know you could be so horribly in love with someone.'

'It's all right,' she said. 'I believe you.'

Nate nodded, and stepped back, carefully picking dried blood and skin from beneath the few fingernails he had left. His jaw worked overtime as he mulled something over.

Too tired to care or enquire, Catherine cleaned her hair and then doused herself with another thick layer of soap. She wasn't sure she would feel clean even if she bathed a thousand times.

'Kitty,' he said abruptly, not looking up at her. 'He wasn't delusional about all of it.'

She paused, placing her hands beneath the spray to wash the foam off.

'I am in love with you,' he said, lifting his head to meet her gaze.

Had she been capable of thinking or reacting, she might have done so. As it was, she felt nothing at his words. Not surprise, not confusion, not anger nor reciprocation. She felt blank. A night's sky without stars; an empty abyss. She watched the water drip down the sides of the shower barrier, the condensation leaving long rivulets. All things which came towards her disappeared into nothingness.

'I'm in love with Thom,' she said, not having anything else to say.

'I know,' said Nate. 'I just needed to say it.'

'All right.'

They stood in the centre of the shower for a long time, the hot water and sprays and soaps falling down upon them gently, giving them the feeling of comfort, if only for a while. When there was nothing left to clean, and her hands began to prune, she left the bath, wrapping a thick towel around her body.

She walked out of the bathroom and made her way to the closet. It took a few minutes before she found something to wear. It was a long robe that tied around her waist and fell to her knees. She pulled on tall stockings and ran a hand through her wet hair, sighing slightly. Not a single thought seemed able to form in her head. Thinking of anything at the moment would tear her apart and leave her inconsolable. She couldn't afford to let that happen. She had to keep going.

Catherine bit her lip. She didn't want to keep going. She wanted to set everything on fire. She wanted to tear at her skin and rake it from her bones. Yet she felt unable to feel. It was all so confusing.

She wanted to scream.

'Kitty?' Nate appeared in the doorframe, a towel around him, water dripping from his wet hair. He had thick bandages around his wrists; his knuckles looked painfully swollen. 'Are you all right?'

Catherine shrugged. 'I can't feel anything.'

'Good,' he said. 'You wouldn't want to feel any of this.'

'I want to set everything on fire.'

'You should've just said that, darling. We've got some things for that.'

Catherine raised an eyebrow. 'Where?'

It only took twenty minutes to gather everything they needed and stow it in the hover outside. Nate found gunpowder in one of the storehouses and let the powder fall from his hand as they walked through the house one last time.

He stopped to gaze at a capture of Archie and Helene on the wall. Catherine looked away from the image, unable to take the sight of Archie, and instead focused on Nate's expression. Behind the anger and sadness, there was something wistful in his grey-gone-red eyes which Catherine could not decipher.

Nate reached out and removed the capture from its frame, tucking it into his shirt pocket. He threw a handful of powder at the wall and stepped away, striding towards the door without a word. Catherine followed him.

When the powder was gone, they stepped out of the house. Nate held an igniter out to her.

'Burn the bloody thing down, darling.'

Catherine gazed at the house for another moment before clicking on the igniter and throwing it onto the powder. The house went up in a blast, the sound louder than a thousand shattering mirrors. The heat was overwhelming and even beside the hover, a safe distance away, Catherine could feel it burning her face.

'Time to leave,' said Nate, clambering into the driver's seat and starting the engine.

With a last look, Catherine climbed in and closed the door. They rose into the blackening air and sped down the flypath away from the flames. Whether Archie had conn'd the guards neither of them knew, but there was no reason to linger.

'Will you miss him?' she wondered aloud.

'I miss everyone.'

'I'm sorry.'

'For what?'

'I don't know.'

Nate glanced at her. 'Then don't apologise, darling. You haven't a thing to be sorry for. Nothing that's happened is your doing.'

He reached over and squeezed her hand. Silence fell between them as they left Archie's home far behind with, if possible, even more questions than they had arrived with.

PART THREE
Friends

MONTH THREE

It took more than two months to get out of the Eastern Islands. Initially, they tried to go from Cretan's Valley to Rinlow, but the docks were heavily patrolled and they were almost captured. Forced to detour, they decided to head further east and then double back once they were off the islands. It would take longer but there was nothing else to be done. The western countries were the most heavily patrolled, the eastern countries much less so.

They spent weeks in hiding, sometimes in the jungle, sometimes in the towns, hunting or stealing food, trying their best to remain undetected by the guards sweeping the area. Finding a ship to carry them northeast to Abrage, a relatively small member of the Eastern Islands, proved difficult. Eventually they stowed themselves below deck and managed to disappear into the jostling crowd making for the town centre. From there they made their way east, leaving the Eastern Islands behind; they headed for Talon, the nearest country on the coast, a short boat ride away. A fisherman rowed them from Abrage towards the mainland for three hundred cuttans. It was protected by Franklin's Wall on east side, and Muntenia to the north; just south was Nitoib. For about an hour they entertained the notion of heading south and finding the building where they had waited out the rains, but they nixed that idea fairly quickly.

Eyre, their destination to the northeast, hundreds of leagues away, was where Nate had gone over the Wall. He knew the minefield's layout. It was the best option, and the hope that they would reach the border before they were caught was the only thing keeping them moving, but it wasn't a high hope. They could not get to Rinlow by land, as there was an endless stretch of frozen, barren desert between Talon and Muntenia; thus they had to leave the islands, make for Talon, take a ferry to Rinlow, and from there make for Eyre. It was a long, roundabout, zigzag that would hopefully confuse the guards.

Sneaking around like rats for the last couple of months had done little to improve their tentative friendship and they fought constantly. It had also become increasingly clear that neither of them were dealing with Thom's death very well. Catherine missed him every day, the ache in her chest constant and consuming. She felt like she was walking around with a hole in her torso. The trouble at Archie's had made everything worse, and both were on edge, snappish and angry at everything.

Without fail, Nate awoke every night sweating and shaking, screaming Thom's name. He wouldn't speak of it. Except on one occasion when he awoke, gripping his side, gasping for air, convinced that Thom was hurt. Catherine couldn't convince him otherwise. So she sung softly, filling the night with tremulous tones, until he fell back into a fitful sleep – aided in large part by the three tockers he smoked in quick succession.

Outside of the spell of the night, which always seemed to allow for more honesty than daylight, Nate refused to acknowledge his despair. Instead, he stayed vigilant at her side, paranoid now after what had happened with Archie. He looked more ill by the day, constantly sweating, his nose and ears bleeding, his eyes a deep red, his bones sticking out where once he had been nothing but thick muscle. He wore more layers to cover the damage, but Catherine could tell he was wasting away. She had no notion of what she herself looked like, having no access to a mirror or any desire to seek one out, but she knew she was doing better than him.

They had passed several broadcasts with their faces plastered on the front. There was now not only the reward of a clean slate, but also 70,000 gold cuttans. The average worker barely made a small fraction of that in a year and they'd overheard several discussions calling for their heads, saying they were spreading a disorder that would lead to chaos and unrest. There were whispers of how selfish and thoughtless they were, seizing freedom when it was so expressly outlawed. People feared Crown and Council, but as they feared the unknown more – and no one in the Kingdom had ever tasted freedom – few of them were willing to fight back. The safest place to be was the Outlands.

The pair bought two gliders from a cheapshop and made their way inland, where they were going to try and stay for a few nights in Etten, a small town off the main road through Talon. The plan was to resupply there and buy horses, which were free to ride on all designated roads and weren't tracked like hovers or easily spotted.

Just when Catherine thought her hands were going to fall off from the cold, Nate slowed to a stop and pointed at a sign.

'Etten shouldn't be too far from here,' he said. 'Remember, they're religious in Talon. More so here than some towns, though. In Etten, they're ultimate believers. It's going to be a place devoid of electricity, broadcasts and Council contact. The most they'll have are rumours at this point. It should be safe enough to stop for a few days.'

'Are you sure?'

'Not even a little. It's the best I've got. There's a competition this week. It draws outsiders. No one will question us, no one will notice us. If anyone does recognise us, they'll still have to leave the city and return with the guards for anything to be done. There is no kingly presence in most of Talon. It's a good stopping place. Besides, it's beautiful.'

Before she could say another word, Nate sped several metres ahead, and she was forced to follow him. The moon shone brightly that night, taking up half the sky with its strange orange glow, and everything felt slightly magical. Catherine thought about the stories her nanny had told her as a child. Stories of how the moon had fallen in love with the sun but could never touch her, for she burned far too bright and her brightness could never be shared. The only time the moon could be with the sun were those rare moments when they eclipsed each other in the sky, kissing for a brief moment before separating again for an age. The story had made her so sad as a child, for she could not imagine never being able to touch the one she loved. Now she knew only too well how it felt.

A slow grey dawn was setting in by the time they reached the town limits of Etten. Burning torches every couple of metres lit the way into the holy city. They dismounted the gliders at a check-in desk for out-of-towners and stowed their packs in the back of a horse-drawn carriage. The seats were comfortable enough, and they sat huddled together as the driver set the horses into a brisk trot and made for the centre. It was the most bizarre feeling. Catherine had never been in a vehicle that actually touched the ground before, and feeling it beneath her, she was surprised by how uneven and jarring it felt. She gripped the seat tightly, afraid she was going to bounce right off the back until at last the carriage slowed and the horses halted in front of an inn.

Proudly proclaiming itself the Most Beautiful Inn, the large wooden building did look rather cosy as they disembarked the carriage and retrieved their belongings. The inn was nestled between large trees on a hill that overlooked numerous paddocks and fields. Candlelight flickered from within, and the smell of early breakfast wafted towards them.

'Two cuttans, good master,' said the driver, bowing to Nate.

Nate handed him four. 'Thank you.'

The driver bowed again and left, the *clip-clop* of hooves on rock sounding his departure long after he'd gone. They grabbed their bags and headed up the stairs of the inn. Nate knocked on the door. It opened a second later, and an old woman with a kindly face, who introduced herself as Mistress Kapoor, greeted them.

'How long will you be staying with us for?' she enquired, leading them inside.

'A few nights if possible,' said Nate. 'We're here to watch the game.'

'Ah, now it makes sense.'

'What do you mean?'

'Gamblers always arrive at strange hours, dear,' she said, gesturing to the ornate timekeeper they passed in the hallway. It

134

was four o'clock in the morning. 'How long are you Complemented? It can't be long. Young face like yours, Mistress.'

'Not long at all,' said Catherine, not knowing what else to say. 'Only a couple months.'

'I see they've done away with the branding, then?'

Catherine glanced quickly at Nate, realising then that neither of them bore the facial binding marks all who had been Complemented were inked with. Her parents both had hawk tattoos, Ciara had an oak branch tattoo on her cheek, and Hamish and Cecily were marked with serpents. Each family had a marking to symbolise their skill or trade or prowess, all chosen long ago in generations' past. The Complement who was the most powerful or affluent had their symbol inked upon the other. Adil bore Ciara's, Jaiani bore Mickey's, Hamish bore Cecily's. Thom would have taken the Taenia family's marking upon binding. Cecily was the King's favourite, but Mickey was infinitely more powerful.

'Yes,' said Nate, clearly thinking the same thing. 'As of this summer they've implemented new rules to see if merely swearing an oath of loyalty is enough to keep the bound together.'

'Rightly so,' said Mistress Kapoor. 'Rightly so! Here in Talon we abhor the mutilation of the flesh. Life does enough of that without outside help, wouldn't you agree?'

Nate and Catherine nodded politely.

The stairs seemed unending, and it felt as if they climbed five storeys before they finally came to a stop in front of a heavy oak door. It had '46' stamped out in thick metal on the front. Mistress Kapoor unlocked the door and showed them inside.

'Breakfast is from six to eight, there's a tour of the city that departs at nine should you like to join in, lunch is available from twelve until four, and then dinner is available from seven onwards. We allow no broadcasts, no captures, no televised devices, no hovers and no electricity of any kind. Our home is deeply sacred and we kindly ask all visitors to respect our beliefs and follow the rules.' Mistress Kapoor gave them a wide smile. 'Now, I know that sounds a bit overwhelming, so don't feel as if you can't leave early if you wish. Many do. However, we'd be delighted to have you for as long as you'd like, and can offer many other forms of entertainment.'

Catherine, who had been examining the vast bookshelf of cookbooks, travel books, post-war fiction, holy books, science and astronomy books, and books on farming, planting, building and architecture, looked over at her. 'Your collection is amazing.'

'Thank you, my dear,' she said, bowing her head. 'Our collection isn't what it once was, but we still pride ourselves on our vast resources. We may be without the conveniences of modern chaos, but our resources are the envy of all the Kingdom. King Markas himself sends men down to research in our libraries when he finds himself short on quick-search knowledge.'

A sudden idea hit Catherine like a wallop to the stomach. 'We'd love to see the libraries,' she said eagerly. 'You have one that is over ten storeys, don't you?' She thought she remembered reading that in school once when they were doing projects on the different countries in King Markas' dominion.

'Indeed we do.' Mistress Kapoor's face lit up. 'I shall arrange a tour tomorrow if you would both be interested? We do of course adhere to a code of accompaniment.'

Nate, who had deposited his bags on the bed, walked over to Catherine's side and placed an arm around her shoulders. 'Of course,' he said. 'We'd both love a tour. An extensive one, if possible. I'm beginning classes in the First King's Institute in Anais next term and would love to add more to my repertoire in the meantime.'

No lie had ever delighted someone more. The First King's Institute was the first of four universities that King Franklin had created, dedicating the first three to his children, and the fourth to his own father, Malcolm the Wise. They were elite institutes for the wealthy, influential members of society, and those that attended often endowed libraries, museums, galleries and schools. It was laughable to think someone as reckless and foolhardy as Nate could ever have wormed his way inside the marble halls, but his wealthy childhood had provided him with a pompous enough air to make it seem believable. Talon was hardly a rich place, if the envy of the

Kingdom's academic world, and the prospect of entertaining a future benefactor was more than enough for Mistress Kapoor.

'I shall have a carriage waiting at half nine,' she said, clapping her hands together before departing.

At last alone, Catherine stepped away from Nate and began sorting through their supplies. 'It's a wonder she bought any of that. We look such a mess I didn't think we'd pass for prison escapees.'

'They don't see superficiality here,' said Nate. 'Their people were devastated after the war. They believe that God cursed them for rising up and bearing weaponry, so when peace was declared, they made a deal with King Markas that so long as they maintained their ancient libraries – handing all of the history books over to the Private Police, of course – they should not be forced to join the rest of the Kingdom in its violent way of life. I think Markas was more stunned than anything, but he agreed. The people took their oath to heart, and since then this has been a place without modernity, without materialism, without pride or arrogance or greed. Everything they own they make by hand, and everything they want they build for themselves. They don't see the mud on your face because they work the fields; they don't see how tired you are because they've been tired themselves. If it weren't so religious, I'd be inclined to stay here forever, honestly. But I can't handle the laws of accompaniment, dress, restriction and moderation. I won't even be able to smoke while we're here.' He looked sadly at his pack of cigarettes before tossing them into the backpack. 'God help me.'

A bag holding soap, softener and rinse finally rolled out of the third pack and Catherine snatched it up. It smelled strongly of flowers and spice, a stark contrast to the smell of sweat and musk on her body. 'I'm going to take a bath,' she said. 'Just knock on the door when the food's here.'

'Will do.'

The bedroom, warmed by a large fire, had been gloriously comfortable. The bathroom was large and incredibly cold, with a huge porcelain bathtub and a thick rug waiting to hug her toes the moment she stepped out. A large chandelier of candles hung overhead, with several more littering the windowsill and candelabras on a few tables and flat surfaces, giving the bathroom a cosy glow once she lit them all. Turning the water on as hot as it would go, she stripped and sank into its depths. There were no mirrors in Talon, so the most she could use was her reflection in the bathwater. She thought maybe her cheeks had become slightly sunken, her body in desperate need of several good meals and whole nights of sleep. There was still no sign of the disease which seemed to be killing Nate.

Outside of the burns, there was nothing wrong with her.

She picked up one of the jars she'd brought in and examined it. Handmade in Cretan's Valley, they had stolen it from Archie's cabin. He'd had numerous supplies unopened and unused. It smelled strongly of lavender and helped sooth her dry skin as she scrubbed the deeply ingrained muck from her body. She clipped her fingernails over the side of the tub and forced rinse and softener, strongly smelling of honey and oats, through her hair until it no longer hurt to brush.

A loud knock on the door made her jump.

'Food,' called Nate. 'Want me to wait for you?'

'No, it's all right,' she said, dunking her head back into the murky water to be rid of most of the suds. Feeling around with her toes, she pulled the stopper from the bottom and let the water whirl away down the drain. Grabbing the large pitcher, she filled it with hot water and poured it over herself to get the remnants of grime off her body, and stepped out onto the soft rug. It caressed her toes and she stood for a moment, not wanting to step onto the cold wood. Snatching up a pair of thick woollen leggings, she pulled them on, surprised to find that they didn't have to stretch around her waist. She'd lost more weight than she had realised. Her stomach was the kind of flat that came from too many nights of vomiting and skipping meals, and her ribs, once buried beneath a thick layer of skin and muscle and fat, now stuck out oddly beneath her breasts.

The inn's towels were thick and fluffy, and she spent far too long drying herself off, brushing her hair and teeth, and generally wasting time, before slipping on one of the stolen robes. It fit her well, clinging to her tightly, outlining her thin frame. Her long black hair was now halfway down her back and too long to be anything but a nuisance. Twisting it back into a plait, she rubbed skin butter over her face and neck, and slipped on a pair of thick sheepskin boots that enveloped her sore feet and made walking infinitely easier. When at last she felt somewhat presentable, she opened the door, sighing in pleasure at the warmth of the room.

Morning light was beginning to filter in through the window, the effect lessened by the curtains that lung heavily from metal rods bolted to the ceiling. Catherine pulled the curtains to one side and tied them up, stepping in front of the window to stare out over the fields. Horses were huffing happily as the early risers clambered to their feet to get a drink of water from the trough, a few roosters were making their presence known from the farm further down the road; dogs were shuffling around, anxious for their owners to wake up and feed them. It was startlingly peaceful. Catherine looked over at Nate. He had been staring at her, but caught himself and coughed.

'They brought us coffee, tea, toast, two types of jam, honey, hot porridge and slices of fruit,' he said, gesturing to the assortment of food around him. 'I'm going to take a bath if you want to tuck in.' He stood abruptly and strode across the room to the bathroom, bolting the door shut behind him.

She could hear the sounds of him being sick, but he did not ask for her help and she left him alone.

Catherine opened the other window before curling up on the bed. She sipped eagerly at the tea, wolfed down toast and spread, and had eaten two large bowls of porridge by the time Nate resurfaced. His red hair was brushed back from his face – it was then that Catherine realised how long it had grown. It had been an untidy mop all throughout her memory, but now it hung long and messy. She thought it looked thinner, and there were several places where it seemed to have fallen out. It was clear he had attempted to brush it over the bald patches. His eyes were still bizarrely bloodshot, and the redness around his nose told Catherine that he had stemmed a nosebleed moments before. He had trimmed his beard so that it looked less bushy and matted, now short and neat. He had lost so much weight she was sure that now if they found themselves on a mountain, it would be up to her to carry him. Her insides twisted with concern.

'Get something to eat?' he asked.

'Yeah, it was good.'

'I've always liked this place,' he said. 'I was here a few years ago, although I stayed at the other end of town. Doubtful anyone will remember me.'

'Were you here alone?'

'No, I brought Matty.'

'I'd heard that she was bound to another. For some reason I always thought it was your choice. Thom never spoke of it. I didn't think anyone would have ended a contract with your mother's influences.'

Nate poured himself a cup of tea and leaned against the window. 'We were to be Complemented for years, but her parents decided that I wasn't a good match for her once I was arrested and lost any ability to actually have a future. She was Complemented to another when I was in prison. I found out from my mother when I was released.'

'But you were twenty-one when you were arrested? And you never asked for a study extension? How were you not already together?'

'I kept pushing back the Complementation,' he said. 'Didn't really want to bring children into my mess of a life. In case you haven't noticed, I got away with rather a lot. My mother was always able to pull the strings of society to suit her.'

'I'm surprised you were allowed. I wanted more time at school before we started having children. I was lucky to get as much time as I did, and that was only because of my father.'

'It was because of Tommy, too. He wasn't ready. As for me, I don't think anyone wanted to see me reproduce,' said Nate. 'No one ever pressed the matter. It wasn't a shock to see Matty with another, although I can't say it delighted me.'

'I'm sorry,' said Catherine lamely. 'But your mother supported you completely? You would have had enough money?' A thought suddenly occurred to her. 'Oh, I forgot prisoners aren't allowed to be Complemented upon release. I somehow always forget that.'

'That, and the fact that they sterilise us.' Nate's face darkened for the briefest of seconds before he met her gaze. 'Forgot about that one, didn't you?'

At a complete loss for words, Catherine stared down at the brown liquid in her cup. She had forgotten. They had studied law at school. It had been an intensive programme, but it was required for completion of credit. The King decreed that every citizen know the full extent of the law so that they could not claim ignorance when they disobeyed the rules. One of the modules had focused on criminals and prison life, and how the King attempted to rehabilitate them. All criminals were sterilised on entry, they could not Complement if ever released, and could not adopt children or work an unapproved job. Criminals were indentured servants for the rest of their lives unless their parents were wealthy enough to support them. A few other lucky convicts had a similar deal with their parents, arrested for things like driving whilst intoxicated or getting caught with illegal drugs. It was an unwritten rule that wealthy criminals could buy their way out of prison and avoid the worst of the punishments, so Catherine had always assumed that for Nate it had been the same. She figured that even holding him for so long in custody, they wouldn't do something so vile to him. She had been wrong.

Catherine placed her cup down and stood up. Walking over to Nate, she wrapped an arm around him and gave him a half-hug. 'I'm sorry,' she whispered. 'I didn't know. Well, I did, but I forgot.'

'It's all right.'

'Did you want children?' She sat down beside him on the window seat, feeling wretchedly sorry for him. It was a strange change of dynamic between them.

Nate sighed. 'Abstractly, yes. If I knew that they could live without fear of arrest or disease or death, then I suppose I would.'

'Even without Crown and Council, there would be no guarantee from disease.'

'True,' said Nate. He shrugged. 'I couldn't do it again – lose someone. I've only ever truly loved two people in my entire life. I never loved my parents, nor Matty. Archie was right about that. I'm not a kind person. I would not think twice about defending a stranger or a friend from attack, but that does not mean I love them. It merely means I find it the right thing to do.'

'Only two?'

Nate looked at her. 'Does that surprise you? Thought of me as sentimental, did you?'

'I don't know,' she admitted. 'I just can't fathom why I'm one of them.'

'Do you want to know? You're the reason I'm alive.'

She raised an eyebrow.

'Here I have you,' he continued. 'If – if Tommy is dead, the only thing left that I care about is you.'

'But you don't think he's dead.'

'No.' He swallowed. 'Someday this will all be nothing but a nightmare long forgotten. God be good.'

Catherine looked away. 'Prayer doesn't do anything.'

'You don't have faith in God? How very rebellious of you, darling.'

'I don't have faith in anything I can't touch. I had such conviction in my old life, and now I feel adrift. Completely out of step with the life I once was so certain of. I had faith in my father. I had faith in my King. I had faith in Thom. Now I've lost all those things. I don't know how I feel; I don't know what to feel. I still love my parents and Thom and Ciara. I still think of the life I almost had and it's hard to hate it. Perhaps it was wrong and ignorant, but it was easy, comfortable. Wouldn't I be unusual not to want that?'

'Yes,' said Nate. 'You would be viewed as bizarre, disconnected. Just because our world is wrong doesn't mean people don't enjoy the binds which are holding them in. At least their binds are safe.'

Catherine felt a strange emptiness twisting in her gut and swallowed hard. 'I was safe back in Anais.'

'You were what they wanted you to be,' said Nate. 'Just as Tommy was. Now you are free and they know your name. It's frightening. It frightened me, once. Takes a few years not to care.'

'I'm not doing anything. I'm running away.'

Nate raised an eyebrow at her in disbelief. 'Kitty, how many people do you think would have run away? How many people do you think would have stayed and hoped for the best? So few people have the courage to leave.'

'You did.'

'I left the Kingdom bloodied and broken and scared,' he said. 'I left before dawn, not out of prison two days. I couldn't breathe in Anais. The air tasted like death. Every second threatened to choke me. I saw Tommy and once I knew him to be whole, I fled. I ran for months, years, before I found the strength to return. Even then it was only for Tommy. I would never have come back if it weren't for him. Everything I've ever done – it's all been for him.'

A quiet fell between them, and Catherine poured herself another cup of tea. The sun rose higher in the sky, displaying the true magnificence of the fields and forests which surrounded the town.

'Should we get some sleep before we go?' she said a while later.

'I honestly doubt I could sleep.'

'Same.'

Nate stood and refilled his cup. 'I think the library tour is a good idea. If we can find anything on the experiments, it'd be fantastically helpful. And it might even be possible here because good King Markas doesn't bother censoring the Talonites as much as the rest of us. You don't have to worry about an uprising from people who would rather die than hold a weapon.'

'I think they're right,' said Catherine. 'The world is better without bloodshed.'

'Don't know about that,' said Nate darkly. 'Some people definitely deserve to die.'

'You definitely don't belong here.'

'Told you.'

The library was enormous. Catherine had never seen a building so large. It had clearly existed long before the war, and she wondered for the thousandth time what life had been like then. What they were permitted to know – evolution, the development of society, the evils of mankind and how disease had taken all those who left the sanctuary of their homes – was small, and often abbreviated or summarised. All heavily censored. Catherine knew that humans had existed for thousands of years, but she did not know what they had been like, what had come before. All she had ever been told was that the downfall of mankind had been certain because of the lack of control. Rampant curiosity and too much knowledge had brought disease, ruin and war to every doorstep.

A huge staircase of marble and stone was cut into the side of the hill it rested on, and they were led up the steps into the enormous library. Even Nate let out a laugh of delight at the sight of it. A great table of food and drinks were set up outside, torches burning merrily to keep the flies away.

'They really love food here,' she remarked.

One table was covered in towers of bread, each slice a different colour, all smelling warm and mouth-watering; pitchers of orange, apple, cranberry, mango, cherry, pear and pineapple juice all placed side by side next to great steaming pots of coffee, tea, cider and chocolate. Cakes of every shape, soups of every colour, various meats arranged on large trays; pasta salads, fruit salads, vegetable salads, and potato salads all adorned another table. Catherine snatched up a bowl of pasta salad and a few pieces of bread before following them inside. Nate, she noticed, looked ill at the prospect of eating anything.

'Welcome to the Grand Talon Library,' said a man with large spectacles and a thick white beard. He was immaculately dressed and had an air of sensibility to him that Catherine immediately respected. 'My name is Prosper Jacques. I will be conducting your tour today. Is there any place you'd like to start?'

'The post-war years,' said Nate succinctly. 'I've an upcoming project on the redistribution of medical supplies at the onset of the Markian Era. They're preparing for the anniversary next year, and the First King's Institute is commissioning the top students to conduct research which may be used in the Council's presentation.'

'Of course,' said Prosper. 'Of course. Follow me. You'll be a final year student at the Institute, then?'

'Yes.'

'A good friend of mine teaches at the Institute. Do you know Roger Fields?'

'The psychologist? He taught one of my first courses.'

Prosper laughed. 'That's wonderful. It's always good to meet keen young minds.'

The only person she had ever seen lie so easily aside from herself was Thom. He was the most cunning person she had ever known. He would learn everything about everyone, know all there was to know and befriend even those he could not stand. Sometimes she had the feeling that surely there was no one with more knowledge of the Kingdom than Thom, although he kept most of it from her. His connections were too vast and his connector had lit up with messages at all hours. Apparently some of his tricks had rubbed off on his generally honest and open brother.

Too tired to charm and too distracted to lie effectively, Catherine wasn't up to playing games with people's minds. Instead she opted for silence, moving along quietly in their wake, taking in the columns and stacks and rows and piles of books which lined the walk. Books crowded onto the stairs, overflowing from the shelves and creating their own little formations and buildings. Catherine passed memoirs of the soldiers in the war, books on sickness, disease and especially the Plague, texts on the importance of euthanasia, sterilisation and genetic engineering. Catherine lingered near a copy of one, captivated, before catching up with Nate and Prosper who had walked ahead.

'Pardon me,' she said to Prosper. 'I had a quick question.'

'Certainly, sweet child.'

'Talonites base their entire philosophy on holy actions and perpetual atonement, yes?'

Prosper inclined his head. 'Very true. Why do you enquire?'

She held up the book she'd taken. 'Is it not against the teachings of the temple to do this sort of thing?'

Sadness passed over Prosper's face. 'It is true we find such undertakings to be against the will of God, and we oppose all forms of torture. We are a benevolent, forgiving people. But there is only so much a lowly religious country can do against the might of a Kingdom. We are commanded to take in all the King's required texts and everything academic in the Kingdom must reside here. It is the only way we can carry on as we do.'

'But you agree that it's wrong?'

'We do not question the will of the King,' said Prosper. 'Yet even kings may sometimes be led astray.'

Nate nodded approvingly. It was as close as anyone could come to open dissent without fear of arrest.

They arrived at another, smaller staircase, and he led them up. Here and there were strange objects that Catherine had never seen before. Each looked incredibly old and fragile, all made of wood, gold, silver or ore. She caught Nate's eye and pointed to one that looked like a child's rendering of what the world might look like, only done beautifully with a hundred different colours.

'Excuse the mess,' said Prosper, waving to the items. 'We're cleaning out storage and many of our private collection have found themselves scattered out here.'

'What are they?'

Prosper hesitated. 'Just assorted things the librarians have made over the years in their spare time. We tend to collect the nicer ones. Ah – here we are!'

146

Neither of them called him out on the poor lie.

The room was fairly small in comparison to the rest of the library, but was still big enough to make Catherine's head spin. Prosper spent over an hour showing them how the system worked; which books were his favourites or came highly recommended.

At long last, Prosper announced that he would go and fetch refreshments and lunch. The second he disappeared, Nate ushered her over to the section Prosper had shown them an hour beforehand which contained the medical records from all prisoners during the war.

After a moment's searching she found it: NITOIB DETENTION FACILITY. It was a huge tome with heavy binding and tiny writing. Resting it gingerly on the small reading table in the corner, they began leafing through it, their eyes keen for anything which might help them.

'God's wrath,' said Nate, staring at the headline of the page he had turned to at random.

The title alone was enough to turn Catherine's stomach: SUCCESSFUL LOBOTOMIES TO RECTIFY AGGRESSIVE TENDENCIES. The page had more than a hundred designations and observations. Most also had a date of death noted either on the same day as the lobotomy, or shortly thereafter.

'I hate them,' said Catherine coldly. It was the first time she had ever said it. She wondered how long she'd been feeling it. 'I hate them so much. How could anyone do this?'

Nate turned the page, slightly green. There were drawings of how to perform the procedure, what instruments to use, what areas to avoid, the proper measurements of the tools, and depictions of the mutant head with the organs illustrated. Nate turned the page once more. There was a small pile of captures.

Catherine covered her mouth as bile rose in her throat. Each capture showed a different mutant or human patient. There were some that were taken before, some during, and some after. No patient was recognisable by the end. Some of them had even been children. Catherine wanted to burn the images from her eyes, but even after Nate had put them down, she couldn't stop seeing them.

The stairs squeaked outside the door. Catherine snapped the book shut just as Prosper entered, carrying a towering tray of food. Nate gave her a quick nod and they moved over to him.

Prosper spent the rest of the day showing them around different rooms. By six o'clock, Catherine was certain they hadn't seen more than a fifth of the library, but she was bursting with information and had a piercing headache. They promised Prosper they would come back and climbed into the waiting carriage.

When they were finally back in the bedroom, Nate closed the door and leaned against it heavily. He looked hardly able to stand, and if Catherine was being honest, she felt dizzy and nauseated as well. She reached out and took his hand. At this point, the action was second nature; an act of healing and comfort.

Slowly, like a flame catching, warmth spread from where their hands met. A pleasant, soothing feeling from where their palms touched, up through Catherine's forearm, through her chest and down to her toes. Her body felt like it was healing itself and as she watched Nate, he, too, seemed to be healing ever slightly. Colour returned to his cheeks and where his lips had been cracked and bleeding the skin was now unblemished. There did not seem to be much she could do for his overall health. His eyes looked as if they'd been filled with dye, his bones stuck out, his cheeks sunk in, and his hair continued to fall out.

She met his bloodshot gaze. He did not hide the shame and self-disgust which burned bright in the ruddy depths. She smiled reassuringly at him. Even when she'd hated him, she'd always found him handsome. He could have been Thom's twin after all.

At some point their heads bowed together and before Catherine could register what was happening, Nate was leaning in to kiss her. Her body felt light and relaxed for the first time in a very long time.

Since Thom.

Catherine darted away just before their lips touched. 'That isn't a good idea,' she said. She felt wrong. Horrible. The worst sort of betrayer. One who cannot even honour the dead.

Her skin was crawling.

A look of hurt flashed in his reddening eyes. He said, 'Because it'll feel good?'

'Because I'm in love with Thom,' she cried. '*Fuck*! This is a nightmare.'

Her words seemed to physically hit Nate, and he recoiled. 'You want to discuss horrors, darling? Let me tell you something. Every day my skin feels like it's rotting off. Every day I'm a little bit sicker, a little bit weaker. The only time it doesn't feel like I'm the walking dead is when you're touching me.'

Catherine twisted and untwisted her hair in agitation. She felt like a spectre, a ghost. She didn't feel real. His words didn't process immediately. Everything was distorted. Distant.

A strangled sound escaped her. 'You want to kiss me because you feel like you're dying?'

'I feel dead regardless! This infection *is* killing me. I can feel it. It might not be killing you, thank God, but it's killing me. For whatever reason. We don't know because we don't even know what it is. Every day I'm that much closer to dying. My heart pounds from the slightest exertion. Anything I eat I throw up. I can't sleep, I'm constantly shaking, my head feels like it's being drilled into with a chainsaw day in and day out. I can't breathe without feeling ill. But no, darling, that's not why I want to kiss you. I'm in love with you. Don't play the fool.'

'I can't do this, Nate.'

'Because you hate me?'

'Because I love him! Because of a thousand and one reasons which all conclude that you and I will never be more than two unlucky wanderers who stumbled into an infection that has, subsequently, completely destroyed my life! Your life was hanged already,' she spat. 'All you've lost is Thom. I've lost everything.'

Nate's hand shot out and connected with a clay jug on the table, sending it to the floor with a horrible shattering sound. After a beat, he stormed into the bathroom, slamming the door so hard behind him that the glass cracked and the metal screeched.

Catherine clenched her jaw, trying not to feel guilty.

If only she could control such a thing.

The library's study was a large room on the top floor, its entire ceiling made of glass so that the maximum amount of sunlight could guide the eyes of the students, researchers, professors, scientists, physicians and any who came to spend a day in Etten browsing the gigantic collection. In an attempt to find out more about what had happened at the testing facility, they'd scheduled a full day in the study with access to the library's collection. No books could leave the city, so it wasn't uncommon for students to travel to Talon in the month before their final exams to rent a room and study in the peaceful city. Catherine remembered that Thom's friend Kara had done it one year and was the top in her class come graduation.

As they browsed, she wondered how much bigger it would be if it had history books which predated King Franklin's life. According to the books they were allowed to read, God came to Franklin in the night and bestowed upon him the ability to unite the world and create a better one if only he crawled out of the Belows and seized it from the vicious mutants who had overrun the Earth. Apparently, the new world had only a chance if it was truly fresh, completely cut off from the sins of the past. Any knowledge of past societies, cultures, peoples, was destroyed. And those who remembered died or stopped talking until history became legends and fiction. Catherine wondered just how many had lived lives before them, just how much they didn't know. It made her head hurt.

A large breakfast of skillet cakes with honey, chocolate swirl sticky bread, apple juice and coffee, and a side of toffee rice, had been laid out for them. Nate hardly ate anything, but Catherine managed to eat several helpings of everything before they set out for the library, each glad of the distraction.

Inside the library, Prosper handed them small hand-drawn maps, a journal each and a key to the dining hall where lunch would be served for the studiers and overseers. Thanking him profusely and paying him well, they headed inside and made straight for the shelves.

Neither particularly inclined to talk to the other, they went in different directions and spent hours combing through the books. Catherine's eyes began to cross as she inspected each and every title, taking them down whenever she found something which appeared to be useful, only returning it several minutes later when she found nothing. One book in particular caught her attention and she plucked it off the shelf and sat on a stool, completely side-tracked.

Wantonly superstitious and inclined towards sorcery, it began, *the mutant hordes rigorously attempted to sway the human race into their darkness from the onset. Most were not blinded by the lies, but a few lost souls – and many traitorous deserters – were enticed to betray their own kind and take up with the mutants. Rightly so, most were imprisoned for war crimes upon discovery. By the end of the war, all deserters were accounted for and, if the rehabilitation was unsuccessful, were executed for the heinous crimes.*

Lip curling, Catherine scanned ahead a few pages. The Council's sanctioned tales of the Last War were predictable and liberal with their hatred of the opposing race of humanoids, but that did not mean everything was lies. One line in particular caught her eye: *One deserter, Carrigan Park, claimed that the mutants hoped to mix the races with the ultimate goal of a united world. When interrogated, Park confirmed that the desire was merely speculative and they had not achieved any progress. The rumour was based on a prophecy relayed to him by the so-called mutant Elders. Lies undoubtedly spread by the mutants to brainwash and manipulate weak minded humans into sympathising with their cause. Park later died of unrelated injuries sustained during capture.*

Catherine read and reread the paragraph until she had it memorised. But there was nothing else. She could not say why it bothered her. Undoubtedly, Park had been executed or tortured rather than dying of injuries, but Archie's words still echoed in her head, and she had to wonder what else they did not know of the mutant religion and their intentions. If they were heading for the Outlands, it would be prudent to know more.

Twenty minutes later, still perusing the book and finding nothing of value, Catherine heard Nate eschew a cry of delight from several stacks down, appearing a moment later with two leather-bound tomes which looked exhausting to read. The first was entitled *Yosef Smith, a Madman's Biography*; the second, *Experiments of War: A collection of testimonies from the courageous volunteers during the Last War.*

'Find anything?' he asked, wiping sweat from his face with a trembling hand. He looked close to collapse but was valiantly staying upright.

'*Misfortunes of Traitors,*' she said, holding up the book she had been reading. 'I don't think it's particularly relevant to us, yet it mentioned some of what Archie said to us, so I thought it was worth a longer look.'

'Good idea.'

They carried the books up the winding stairs to the study. The winding turns of the staircase made Catherine dizzy and twice she walked into the railing, her head spinning. At long last, huffing and puffing, they stumbled into the study at the top of the building.

'Sweet son of a mutant,' wheezed Catherine, clutching a pain in her side. 'You'd think we'd be used to this much climbing by now.'

'We're higher in the mountains,' said Nate. 'The altitude, maybe.'

'In the library?'

'Do not rob me of my very thin excuse, darling.'

There was a spare table to the front and they dropped their books down and took a seat on either side. Time passed differently in the library. One minute Catherine would be reading about Smith's childhood, her eyes drifting cautiously to Nate, wanting to make sure he was all right, the next it was three hours later, she'd read about Smith's early experiments which included grisly things like seeing how long a cow could stay alive after being cut open, or trying to create a three-eyed human with stomach churning results. A large number of horrific things were allowed during the war years, most of it unchecked even years later. The man who had done this to them was clearly mad, and it made her feel slightly better to know that no one in their right mind would create such a curse.

By sunset, Catherine had scrawled nearly ten pages of notes, none of them particularly helpful, mostly background information on Smith and mentions of serums concocted during the war but nothing very specific.

Realising they had missed lunch, the pair made their way back to the inn, heads aching and eyes sore.

'I feel like my head is going to bleed out my ears from all the shit I read,' muttered Catherine.

He nodded. 'So we know the prisoners who were part of the experiment were all eventually shot and buried in a mass grave in Nitoib, somewhere in the mountains.'

It was her turn to nod. 'What we need to know is whether or not he had an antidote to this little infection he created, and why everyone was killed. Were they killed because it went wrong and they had no choice – which is something we really need to know – or were they killed because Crown and Council are vile?'

'I'd say the second one.'

'Well, I think so, but we have to be certain.'

'It couldn't have spread by person,' said Nate eventually. 'Elsewise we would have spread it to someone.'

'We could have,' she pointed out. 'We've not been around anyone else for long. Whatever we do, we need to find something soon. You're not looking well.'

Nate shook his head and said nothing. They were at the inn and Mistress Kapoor waved them happily inside. Warm fires lit four grates around the room, and gigantic chandeliers hung from the ceiling, the wax collected in beautiful dishes suspended beneath.

Dinner was a delicious sight: mushroom stuffed pasta, tomato and garlic sauce, soft bread baked in eggs and milk; a steaming salad of carrots, orange sauce, rice, broccoli, peas, onions, chickpeas, potatoes and cheese topping. Catherine tore into her dinner, but Nate ate slowly, as if he wasn't hungry, and only ate a third of his plate. Ordering a bottle of Cisco, the local drink, Catherine snagged a slice of chocolate fudge cake with raspberry sauce and cane powder, and gestured for Nate to follow her back upstairs.

Once the door was shut, she rounded on him. 'What is it?' she asked. 'Something's wrong.'

Nate shrugged. He was looking worse than ever, and in the dark light of the room, he seemed a walking corpse. 'I'm too tired, Kitty. This infection? It's an *infection*. It's not going to get better without treatment. That's how diseases work. I told you last night it was killing me. I wasn't being dramatic.'

'You're not dying,' she said stubbornly. 'I can fix you. I've been fixing you for the last couple of months, haven't I?'

'Yes. No.' Nate slammed his fist into the wall in frustration, the heavy oak doing more damage to his knuckles than anything else. 'I haven't felt right since the mountains. The more time passes, the worse I feel. I'm queasy all the time. I've had a burning fever for weeks now. I'm exhausted and my vision is shit. Everything I read today was blurred. My head hurts so much that just blinking takes effort. I *smell*. It's as if the infection's not just in my body, it's in my fucking soul. People have killed themselves over less, Kitty, but I can't do that because God only knows what would happen to you!'

The bottle opened easily in Catherine's hand and she downed a good deal before allowing herself to speak. 'I don't know what to do,' she said numbly. 'At this point turning ourselves in would be the easiest thing to do. Maybe we won't be shot. They know Thom broke in, but they have no reason to be angry with us except for the fact that we didn't show up to an appointment. We could just say we got scared and ran. Plead stupidity. We might get off.'

'It's not an option,' said Nate firmly.

'Just like that?'

'Yes, just like that. I was in prison before. I'm not going back again. End of discussion.'

Catherine stomped her foot in frustration. 'You need a cure.'

'I need to get you to safety,' he said. 'Once we establish that you're not going to end up imprisoned or dead, we'll worry about me.'

'I'm not agreeing to that.'

'Tough,' he snapped. 'I made a promise.'

'Thom's dead, Nate.' She hated saying it, but she couldn't keep chasing ghosts. They needed medicine not mad hope.

Nate's jaw clenched and agony filled his bloodshot eyes. 'He's not. I can't explain it. I just know.'

Catherine stared at him. Her chest clenched. 'We heard it on the broadcast. He's dead.'

'I know what we heard. I also know what I feel and the only thing I know is that Tommy and I agreed to meet in the Outlands should anything go wrong.' Nate looked at her defiantly. 'I swore to him that I would protect you with my life. I will not let him down. Not again. We're not turning around. If Tommy's out there, he'll meet us on the other side of Franklin's Wall.'

The heartbreak Catherine had been nursing like an open wound since they left Anais now seemed to pale in comparison to Nate's grief. Holding onto the belief that Thom was alive might be the only thing keeping him from killing himself. She couldn't tell him he was wrong. She prayed to God he wasn't.

A loud crack of thunder sounded from outside, and a few minutes later rain began to fall in heavy blankets, soaking the countryside. Nate moved to her side after a time and took the bottle from her, drinking a considerable amount himself. He looked tired and sickly, and his skin had taken on a funny pallor. A body with a slowly rotting soul.

They drank the entire bottle, and then shared the cake. As evening set in, Catherine climbed into the bed, her head heavy and her limbs stiff. Nate fell in beside her, a good distance away. She reached back and took his hand, hoping it would help. He squeezed tightly, and his breathing evened somewhat.

Another three trips to the library yielded little information, although they did find out that Yosef Smith retired to Clearbow, one of the countries that bordered Cutta. Catherine had been there once but barely remembered the place. Not wanting to linger, they bought two packhorses from a farmer down the road and filled their bags to bursting with goods from the local shops. The plan was to ride from Etten to Evre.

There was a sandbar that stretched from the seaside town of Evre to South Brittan, an outlying island, which they could ride across when the tide was out. It was entirely covered when the tide came in, so they had to make sure they got there at the right time or they'd be waiting around in the open for several hours. Fortunately, no one lived on South Brittan. The port was deep enough in the ocean for large ships to bring in supplies, and far enough from Talon that the citizens did not have to deal with the modernity.

Breakfast was a tense affair. Catherine couldn't concentrate on eating, her stomach too full of butterflies to accept much food. She ended up taking a box of biscuits, pasties, tarts and fruit, stuffing the lot into her pack, and nervously drinking her coffee for the rest of the hour.

When at last their horses were ready, they paid their bill and bid farewell to the kindly innkeeper.

'Safe travels,' said Mistress Kapoor. 'You both will be in my prayers. Don't forget to mind each other, now.'

'We will,' promised Catherine. 'Thank you so much for everything.'

Catherine went to her horse's side. The sturdy stallion had cost a good amount, but she was glad to have bought one with years of experience. She had ridden as a child and competed in games for the King two or three times, but it had been years since she'd last been on a horse and she wasn't feeling too confident. Mounting, she gathered the reins and looked over at Nate. He winked at her and nudged his horse forwards with his heels. He rode well, and she thought back to their childhood when riding and running had been for show only, rather than necessity.

The sun was hiding behind the clouds, the day soft and grey, and there was a thin layer of snow upon the ground. Glad of her thick clothes, Catherine nudged Pie forwards. His name had come for his strange habit of snatching food from the hands of whomever was unlucky enough to be close enough. Apparently he'd eaten his last owner's cherry pie whole.

A few hours into their journey, the ocean now on their left, the mountains to their right, Nate suggested they stop for a break. Legs aching and hands sore from holding the reins, she readily agreed.

The ride had warmed them and the day was pleasant enough. Light snow fell from the skies, clinging to their cloaks and hair and eyelashes, and the world seemed calm.

Catherine set about making a fire as Nate pulled out the food supplies, absently wiping blood from his ears. They spread blankets on the ground beside the fire and sat down as the horses nosed around for grasses which might have survived the winter.

It took almost an hour for the fire to be large and hot enough to cook on but eventually the tea kettle was whistling and the soup was bubbling. Catherine wrapped two rolls of bread in cooking paper and put them on the coals to warm up.

'It's amazing how the Talonites do everything without technology,' said Catherine, stirring the soup. 'They have everything they need and it's all set up perfectly.'

'Simple life is usually better than the alternative,' said Nate, feeding a carrot to his horse, a beautiful dapple grey mare with a black tail and three white socks. She huffed contentedly and nuzzled him for more treats. 'When we get to Eyre, it'll be more or less the same. There's no people once you pass the Northern District. Everyone believes the land to be toxic and haunted so no one goes very far.'

Catherine sighed. 'I still think we should find you a cure first. This disease is killing you. Even when I heal you, you're getting worse, not better. Leaving it any longer is too much of a risk.'

'I'm not taking you back.'

'It's not entirely up to you, you know?'

'Kitty,' he said imploringly. 'Don't ask that of me. I cannot risk your life. I won't.'

She glared at him. 'My life is my own to risk and since the only person in the world I can trust at this point is you, I'm hardly going to let you die. We'll find something – let's go to Smith's place in Clearbow – and then double back. If we're careful we can be over the Wall before anyone knows we were even there. The way you're going, you won't make it without medication or treatment. You're getting sicker by the day and you barely sleep. I've never seen someone *look* like death, but that's exactly how you look. I don't even know how you've lasted this long.'

'I do.'

Catherine raised an eyebrow. 'Enlighten me.'

'You're healing me,' he said plainly. 'If you weren't healing me, I'd be far more wasted away than I am. Thus far migraines and nosebleeds and nausea and hair loss are all consistent, but you heal the worst of the disease before it gets any further. It's not killing me as quickly as it elsewise would because you're delaying it.'

'I still don't get why you're sick and I'm not.'

Nate laughed humourlessly. 'I suppose I'm just lucky.'

'Funny.'

'I do try, darling.'

'You're not going to die,' said Catherine fiercely. 'I don't want you to even consider that, all right? Thom died trying to keep you alive and if you think I'm just going to let you rot away, you're mistaken. You have to live. If not for you, then for him.'

The look he gave her was impossible to decipher, but after a few moments he nodded and looked ahead at the road, squinting in the sunlight, his eyes slightly amber – with blood or nearing death, Catherine didn't know – and his skin yellowing; even so, there was something undeniably strong to his posture, as if not even the promise of imminent death frightened him.

The sandbar came into view on the fourth day, a dark stretch of land with sparkling ocean water on either side. The horses were less frisky than they had been when they first began their journey and seemed to have accepted their new owners. Catherine stroked Pie's mane and gazed up as a bird let out a wailing call. It was a bright green bird with long wings and a shiny beak. She smiled at it. Birds were a rare thing in the cities these days. When humankind came up from the ground and began burning everything inside the Kingdom, the birds took flight. The few that remained were the descendants of those who had been kept in the Belows' aviary. The rest of the birds had sought sanctuary in the Outlands and she had only ever seen captures of them in books.

Her mother's father had trained hawks for King Franklin during the war and thus it became their family mark. Taking a piece of bread from her bag, she poured a small amount of water onto it and threw it into the wind. The bird swooped down and caught it before it hit the ground. She laughed loudly, enchanted. Its long wings spread wide and flapped twice before it landed on a tree branch.

'Beautiful,' said Nate.

She glanced over at him. 'I've never seen such a lovely coloured one before.'

'I meant your laugh,' he said, not looking at her. 'You haven't laughed like that in months. It's nice to hear.'

She gave him a small smile. 'I'm glad the mountains are gone. They're nice to look but I prefer the forests.'

'Same,' he agreed. 'I love trees. They're so comforting'

'Do you ever think about what it was like before?'

'Before the war or before the Devastation?'

'Before the Devastation,' she said. 'No place starts with buildings and bridges and trains and houses and such. It was land like the rest of the world. I used to walk around and try and imagine what it looked like before people, or when our ancestors first came up from the Belows and the only ones to touch it were the mutants, the rabids and animals, none of whom made dwellings. Imagine the rolling hills and tall grasses. Imagine no buildings or hovers or people. Such a strange thought.'

'I was a bit nervous at first on the other side of the Wall, I'll be honest. I think it helped that I didn't care if I died, so I didn't bother worrying over it. I just drank.'

'And nothing happened?'

'Nothing happened.'

'And you never saw a mutant?'

'I saw some. I kept to myself and stayed quiet. I slept mostly in the trees or caves and hid whenever I heard anything. If they saw me, they let me live.'

Catherine thought about that as they ate. The Outlands had been so frightening to her when Nate had first suggested it in their kitchen in Anais. Now it did not seem so daunting. So long as he lived to show it to her.

After another hour, they repacked their things, put out the fire and mounted. Even the horses were itching to carry on. The tide had gone out, leaving the sandbar fully exposed and ready for crossing. It was breathtakingly beautiful.

'If we go now the tide will come back in soon enough and cover all trace of us.'

Catherine sighed. 'We're hardly this important.'

'We're not. It's nothing to do with our importance. They'd hunt anyone down, even if they weren't the daughter of the Hangman and the son of the King's closest friend. It's a matter of principle, of law, of order. Any show of failure is a show of weakness. I think that's what the King fears most. The King's control over the Kingdom is fragile, and could fail at any moment. Fear and power are what keeps him where he is. To admit failing to catch two young people would be somewhat laughable, and he cannot abide that. But there's more to it than that, I think. For some reason he doesn't want what we've contracted to be known on the streets. We aren't contagious, we know that much, so why does it matter? Plenty of people are aware that experiments were done during the war on mutants and those who sided with mutants. It's no secret that our population has gone down tremendously over the years. We're not even a third of what we were when we lived underground. That frightens people. So, do you trust the tyrant keeping you safe, or do you trust the unknown which brings almost certain hardship? I've been thinking about it for so long now that I've come up with more than enough to confuse and annoy myself. He won't stop until we're dead or captured.'

'We're going to die anyways if we don't find you a cure.'

Nate looked sharply at her. 'Nothing is going to happen to you.'

It was too exhausting to fight with someone whose mind was so clouded by infection. Instead, Catherine nudged Pie into a canter and headed down the beach towards the sandbar, Nate behind her. They plunged into the shallow water a little early, spray splashing against their legs as they made for the crossing.

Halfway across the sandbar Nate waved a hand at her. She looked over, slowing her horse to a trot.

'What is it?'

'There's someone behind us,' he said. 'Don't turn around. Just keep going.'

Frightened butterflies took flight in her stomach and it took all of her willpower not to turn around. The ocean on either side of them lapped cheerfully against the sides of the sandbar as if to let any passers-by know that it was to return shortly. Catherine eyed the water but felt far less worried about drowning then about being caught. At least one would be quick.

Nate's horse Voyager surged ahead of Pie with a quick burst of energy, covering the remaining distance in ten long strides before leaping up the bank and onto the island. Pie leapt up the bank in a mimic of Voyager, his head shaking with energy, quickening his stride, and Catherine used the opportunity to look around.

Three riders on horseback were galloping over the sandbar straight towards them. She did not look long enough to make out their faces, but she could see that there were two women and a man, dressed in billowing robes of various vibrant colours, the ends of which streamed out behind them in a vivacious dance that would have been bewitching if Catherine weren't so worried. Their clothes did betray them for civilians, however, and for that she was grateful. Anyone was better than the guards.

Not wanting to linger, she clucked at Pie who bucked once on the ascent, throwing her forwards in the saddle. She caught herself on the pommel but managed to keep her seat. Before she knew it, they were on the trail leading away from the ocean. It was a more reassuring place to be than out in the open and, as if reading her thoughts, Nate checked Voyager and made a sharp right.

Catherine steered into the brush with only a hair's width to spare between her foot and the adjacent tree. They whirled around, safely hidden by the thicket, and waited for their followers. Less than two minutes later the trio appeared, their orange, yellow and red robes more noticeable in the forest than a fire at night. The leader was one of the women, her thick black hair halfway down her back, her eyes large and intelligent. The second was the man, with curly black hair just like the leader. The third was far younger than the first two and Catherine guessed her to be a child of one or a sibling.

Catherine wondered if it was foolish to be frightened of them but after a moment's pondering she came to the conclusion that even if they weren't hunting them, there was every chance in the universe that they might turn them in. Avoidance was better.

Catherine and Nate waited nearly an hour, the horses growing restless, before they finally nodded to each other and moved back onto the trail. In the muddy ground it was easy enough to see where the trio had gone and Catherine's heart sank. 'They're making for the ferry.'

'As if there's anything else to make for on this island,' said Nate, glaring at the tracks. 'The ferry won't be here for another two days. I reckon we diverge from the path and camp out on the opposite side of the island until the ferry arrives.'

'We're exposed out here,' she said. 'This place is small and if they're waiting, it's doubtful they'll stay in one place. We'll find them tomorrow if not the next day.'

'They'll have seen us anyways, so they might come looking for us.'

'Or they might want to be left alone as well.'

There were too many options. They kept their voices down, their ears keen and their eyes prone. They remained on the trail for another few hours until evening came and they began searching for a place to sleep. Catherine wondered absently if the trio would prove to be more like the Talonites or more like Archie. A cold chill went through her body as she thought of Archie and it took her a few moments to remember how to swallow properly.

'Kitty?' Nate's voice broke through her fears and she looked over at him. 'Are you all right? You've gone pale. Did you see something?'

She shook her head. 'I'm just hoping they're going to be more like our second host than our first.'

Nate stopped Voyager and looked sharply at her. 'Listen to me, I will never let anything like that happen to you again.'

There was a loud cracking sound up ahead, sticks and twigs snapping underfoot, and the trio appeared about ten paces in front of them. They were spotted instantly. With a wave of her hand, the leader signalled at them to wait.

'Think of a name,' said Nate, barely moving his lips. 'Any name, any place. Anyone but Catherine Taenia.'

Catherine nodded and pulled her scarf over her head, covering her hair which was thankfully pinned out of the way. The broadcasts showed an older capture of her, one that Thom had taken two birthdays ago, and after months on the road, her bones were more obvious, her skin a different shade, her face sunken. There was a chance they would not be recognised. For his part, Nate no longer looked the spitting image of Thom, but a walking skeleton. Once upon a time Catherine had hated their bizarre resemblance. Now she missed it.

'Good evening.' Her accent told Catherine immediately that she was a South-Lander. She had a flower tattooed on the side of her face, the man had a smattering of stars on his. She said, 'We saw you on the sandbar a few hours ago. Myself and my companions are new to these islands and were hoping you could show us the way to the ferry.'

'It's about five miles northeast,' said Nate. 'It dips off a small trail but there's a sign hidden behind some rose bushes. Shouldn't be too hard to find.'

'Excellent,' said the leader. 'I'm Zoe. My companions are Evander and Tove.'

Nate inclined his head. 'Rusty.'

'Ciara,' said Catherine. It was the only name she could think of and somehow she knew that Ciara would be delighted to be part of her deception. There was nothing Ciara had loved more than play-acting. She felt a pang in her chest at the thought of her old friend, and forced the feeling aside before her throat closed.

Zoe's eyes were kind enough and the strange feeling Archie had given off didn't resonate from any of the trio. They seemed like weary travellers, nothing more. All of them were far too thin.

'Shall we share a campsite?' suggested Evander. 'If you could share drink with us, we'd be most grateful. We lost our supply several miles back. The bags split. Terrible craftsmanship.'

'We have plenty of water,' said Nate graciously. 'Do you need some now or should we make camp first?'

Catherine glanced at him. She wondered why he was so readily accepting the proposal but said nothing. Perhaps being in a group would be a better option anyways. The Private Police were looking for two runaways, not a group of five.

'Tove needs a drink,' said Zoe, pointing to the young girl. She couldn't have been more than fourteen or fifteen.

Nate removed his flask and tossed it to Zoe. She caught it and passed it to Tove who drank deeply. Tove looked a bit ill, as if she'd not had a proper meal in days, and Catherine felt a strong urge to show her some kindness. Pulling a chocolate roll from her bag, she tossed it to Tove, who caught it deftly.

They smiled at each other and a surge of desperate hope filled Catherine. She wanted them to be friendly. She wanted them to be good people.

After a few more moments of deciding what to do, the five of them agreed to walk another mile to a grove that Nate knew of which would have some shelter from wind and snow, and they set off.

The trio were from the heart of the Southern Lands where the famine continued and there were only a few thousand people left. They had come north to find work and a new, better life. Migration was common enough in the Kingdom those days and more and more places were having famines. The King owned all of the land and regulated how much went to Cutta, the heart of his Kingdom, and how much was allowed to remain with the laymen, workers, gardeners, ranchers, herders, shepherds, sowers, and all other low level hands who kept the Kingdom afloat. Zoe's stories were full of anger at the King, although she was careful not to say anything that could warrant trouble, and by the time they reached the grove Catherine found that she rather liked them.

They dismounted and unsaddled their somnolent horses. Pie nickered happily once he found the nearby creek, sinking his legs into the low water to drink. Catherine and Evander wound a long rope around the area to keep the horses in as Tove went off to hunt, more energetic now that she'd had something to eat and drink; Nate and Zoe went about setting up the fire and makeshift tents they had brought with them.

Evander's silence was calming rather than off-putting and by the time the horses were secured and brushed, their hooves picked and all sweat stains removed from their thick coats, Catherine felt almost comfortable around their new companions. She had spent so long with just Nate that it was strange being in someone else's company, yet Catherine had always been social, always sought out friends, and it didn't take as long as she thought it might to get Evander to speak.

Just after she'd finished brushing Voyager, the large horse nosed her in the back and sent her sprawling into a pile of thorn bushes. She landed hard and cut her hands badly, but it was too funny not to laugh.

'I like a horse with personality,' said Evander, moving over to help her up.

Catherine managed to stand before he reached her side and examined her hands. They were bleeding a little, and a few tiny thorns stuck into her flesh; it wasn't terrible.

'Personality or vindictiveness?' She glared pointedly at Nate's mare. 'That wasn't nice, fat-arse.'

'I think it's her way of saying "thank you",' said Evander, holding out a handful of brown grass to the horse. 'Cats bring you dead animals to show you they love you; horses push you into bushes.'

'She better be careful or I'm going to push her in,' said Catherine, laughing despite the pain in her hands. 'I've got to wash my hands off. They're stinging like mad.'

Evander nodded. 'Do you have disinfectant?'

'Yes, thank you. Meet you back at camp?'

He inclined his head and disappeared through the trees towards the loud sounds of Zoe and Nate hacking away at firewood. Catherine watched him leave before throwing a dirty look at the dapple and making for the creek. She was almost to it when she caught sight of steam wafting slowly up from a small pond. Curious, she walked to the pond's edge and bent down to touch it. The water was hot to the touch. Delighted, she removed her leggings and coat, folding them in a neat pile before wading into the hot water in only her thin dress. It sent a shockwave through her body.

After a few minutes of splashing around the water began to feel soothing on her skin. Her father had always told her that it was dangerous to bathe in untested waters. The diseases, animals, radiation and bacteria would surely do her in, he always said.

Catherine was starting to wonder if he'd spoken a true word to her in all her life.

'Tove caught two rabbits and a squirrel,' said a voice behind her.

Catherine glanced back at Nate. 'Excellent. I was hoping we'd have something more than soup tonight.'

'Evander said you got cut.' Nate bent down by the water's edge and ran his hands over the glassy surface. 'It nice in there?'

'Yes.'

Nate nodded, though he made no move to join her. 'Your cuts?'

She swam over to the bank and clambered out, wrapping her coat around her shoulders and holding her cut hands out to show him. As he held them, the cuts knit themselves back together as if they had never been there.

'I'm glad I can still do that much, at least,' he said bitterly.

'What do you mean?'

'I mean I don't think I'd be able to heal you if you weren't constantly healing me.' Nate sat down and drew his cloak close around his shoulders. 'I couldn't heal you in Archie's, remember?'

'You did.'

'Not at first.'

'We were both traumatised,' said Catherine. 'I'm sure that's all it was.'

Nate shrugged. 'I don't think we can heal if we're sick. I'm hanging on by a thread. Much longer and I won't be able to heal you at all.'

'Then it's lucky we know about Yosef Smith, isn't it?'

'Darling, no.'

'Yes.'

'I'm not going to Clearbow.'

'What makes you think you have a say in the matter?'

Nate glared at her. 'You can't make me go.'

'So stay. I'll find the cure myself.'

'Must you be so stubborn?'

'Yes,' she said. 'And don't pretend you don't like it because even Thom knew how much you loved fighting with me.'

Nate chuckled. 'We talked about you all the time.'

Not wanting to speak of Thom, Catherine glared down at the moon's reflection in the water and sighed. 'I don't miss it anymore.'

'What? Anais?'

'Yes. I used to hate being away from the city, from the ease and comfort and safety of it. I haven't missed it for a while. I don't even know how long.'

Nate nodded and looked around. 'We may just stay here tomorrow. We're well hidden and the ferry isn't until the day after tomorrow, so it might be prudent to linger. From what I've ascertained of our new friends, they love the King as much as we do, so I'm not sure we've too much to worry about, although I think we should stick with our names. How'd you pick yours? Ciara? Ciara Khan?'

'My best friend.'

'I remember her. Don't remember much. What's she like?'

Catherine raised an eyebrow. 'You want to hear about my best friend?'

'If she was important enough to be your alias, and thus presumably on your mind, clearly she mattered to you,' he surmised. 'I'd like to know more about you. I should know you by your own account. We never talk.'

'We talk every day.'

'About our infection. About food and shelter. About anything but us. I know you're beautiful and strong and pack quite a solid punch; I don't know your favourite colour or if you've ever been to a festival and fallen over because you drank too much or who your first kiss was, although I've gathered it was Tommy. Things you should know about the person you're attached to. I could give you a hundred reasons why I love you already. I want a thousand more.'

Catherine smiled to herself and said, 'Neither my first kiss, nor Thom's, were with each other.'

'I already know about Louis,' said Nate. 'Tommy liked him for years.'

Catherine nodded. She hadn't thought about Louis Jango in years. 'My first kiss was with Ciara,' she said. 'She was my best friend – still is. It seemed sensible.'

Nate raised an eyebrow, his expression amused. 'When was this?'

'We were ten. Ciara's always liked girls and thought I was pretty and wanted her first kiss to be with someone she knew was nice and would give her an honest opinion. I wanted my first kiss to be with someone of my choosing. I remember thinking afterwards that all of my kisses ought to taste like chocolate strawberries.'

'That's adorable.'

'We had talked about it for weeks and wanted it to be perfect,' said Catherine, blushing furiously. It was such a happy memory. She could still picture in her mind's eye the bright, sunny day during the summer when they had decided to do it. It had seemed like such an important moment at the time, something that had to be perfected. Catherine had spent the morning fussing over her outfit, wanting Ciara to think she was pretty enough to kiss, even if it was only for practice. 'She came over – we both made a pact not to eat anything the other one didn't like – and we sat down on my bed and kissed. It lasted at most three seconds and we couldn't stop giggling for almost an hour.'

Nate let out a bark of laughter. In the darkness, he sounded just like Thom.

'What about you?' she asked, chest clenching.

'What about me? First kiss or best friend?'

'Best friend.'

'Tommy.'

'I meant aside from him. You and Blaise Roman were always together.'

He nodded. 'If not Blaise then Jamie, but I spent more time with Blaise than anyone else in the Club. He was always there when I needed him. We work well together. Do you remember Nadia Tam?'

An image of a girl with curly black hair, bright brown eyes and a wicked smile swam into Catherine's mind and she nodded.

'Blaise and Nadia have been in love since he moved to Anais.' This time it was Nate who smiled to himself. It had been so long since she'd seen him do it, she barely breathed for fear she'd break the spell. He continued, 'I never understood it. Blaise and I even fought about it. We were all required to have children. I don't think children should have to grow up thinking their existence is only because they're required, not because they're wanted. Whether it's true or not isn't the point.' He shook his head, lips turning downwards. 'They formed the Club because they wanted to overturn the Law of Complementation. They became rebels for love. I became one because I hated everything.' He snorted. 'And now I know. Now I get it.'

'Get what?'

'Why they cared so much.' He held her gaze intently. 'Nothing has ever been mine, Kitty. Nothing but Tommy. My life, my body, my future – all of that was out of my control from birth. And I raged. God's wrath did I rage. I mean, look at me now. Whatever this is, the Council's had a hand in it.' His face twisted with ugly bitterness. 'But there are things not even Crown and Council can steal and control. Not my mind, not my heart, not my soul.'

His words made her smile with deep, indescribable empathy. More and more she was understanding how so many had flocked to the Underground Club. Even desolate and ravaged, Nate spoke with passion few could emulate. And she knew what he meant. She had never had a choice. Of late it had begun to bother her, too. Like a wound that was slowly festering. Perhaps she never would have known such a feeling if she hadn't run away. If she didn't spend so much time now thinking of what could have been. What ought to have been.

He continued, voice barely more than a whisper, 'My mind is my own. My soul is Tommy's. And darling, whether you ever care or not, my heart is yours.'

Nate glanced over at her and held her gaze.

Not knowing what to say, Catherine smiled tightly and looked away. A silence fell between them then and the only sound was the quiet snowfall.

It was almost ten minutes later when he cleared his throat and said, 'Tell me something else.'

Catherine thought a moment. She had never really given much thought to whether Nate liked milk or dark chocolate, or if he preferred grey skies to clear, or what his favourite book or reel was, or if he was allergic to berries or nuts or fish the way some people seemed cursed to be. She knew every detail of Thom's life and had learned a great deal of it after they'd moved in together. She'd been with Nate for months and knew him distantly, abstractly, the way she knew horses and flowers and the stars in the sky; familiar things that held comfort and continuity, but were not known in the way of actually *knowing*.

After a few minutes of thought she nodded, and leaned back on her elbows. Snow began to drift down slowly, melting when it came near the hot spring. Even with wet hair, the heavy coat kept her warm.

'All right,' she said. 'But I can't think of anything. Just ask.'

'Anything?'

'Within reason.'

'That's hardly so fun,' he bantered. 'Fine. What's your favourite colour?'

'Orange,' she said. 'Like the sunset. You?'

'Yellow. I used to sit for hours as a boy and make sunflower chains for my mother. I spent a whole week once in the countryside with Tommy, teaching him to tie the stems together so that they would hold true. Mother owns a large manor in the Southern Lands. We used to spend summers there as children. There are acres and acres of sunflowers, and Tommy and I would run through them, get completely lost, gather seeds, petals. Our hands would be stained yellow and green and brown for days on end. I made so many that it sort of stuck over the years I suppose. The sunflower gardens of the Belows had been well preserved, and as a result they were some of the first flowers to make it to the surface once the Cleared Zone was slashed and burned. I always saw them as one of the few things our society's done right.'

Catherine smiled at the happy childhood memory. Nate seemed to have so few. She said, 'I think your mother was always your greatest advocate after Thom.'

'She was my only advocate after Tommy,' he said. 'And you were my great detractor after my father.'

'Sorry about that.'

'It's not your fault. I hardly made the greatest of impressions. Favourite instrument?'

'The fiddle. You?'

'Harmonica.'

'Favourite book?'

'*Quiet Mountain*,' he said. 'You?'

'*The Killing Times*,' she said.

'Bold choice.'

She smirked. *The Killing Times* was a book Thom had bought for her a little over a year ago and told a fictional account of the Last War. It had been somewhat salacious and controversial upon publication. For some reason she had fallen in love with it and read the entire novel in less than two days. 'Next question,' she said, thoughts of Thom threatening to darken her mood. 'Favourite time of day?'

'Twilight,' he said. 'It's the most peaceful. How about you?'

'The afternoon. I can never get enough of the sun.'

'I think the sun cannot get enough of you, darling.'

She waved a hand. 'Next question.'

He smirked. 'Favourite animal?'

'Hmm ... otter,' she said. 'I know they're all but extinct, but I saw one once when my father took me north on a business trip of his. There was a small sanctuary there. They're ridiculously soft and cuddly looking. I always wanted one, though I could never put one in a cage. They're meant to roam the seas, aren't they?'

'Once, yes, I think so. I always preferred birds, myself. Any kind, really. I love how much freedom they have. If someone's chasing them, they fly away. If it's cold, they fly south. If they're hungry, they circle above their prey. I've never seen any creature with as much freedom as a bird.'

'That green one this morning was gorgeous.'

'Wasn't it? When I was a child, my father told me that once men used to train birds to hunt for them, find food and such things. He said that the three greatest beasts for a man to befriend are birds, dogs and horses. One to hunt, one to protect, one to carry. It was one of the few times he seemed like a father, you know? We didn't have many good days.'

Catherine cast about for something else to ask. 'Favourite country?'

'The Outlands, although technically that isn't a country,' he said. 'I'm a nemophilist, darling. It's the only place for me. No law, no ruler, no walls. It's the most peaceful place in the world.'

'And you're not worried about rabids or mutants or disease?'

'You can't live your life afraid of everything, Kitty.'

'You do,' she pointed out.

He gave her a half smile. 'My fear pushes me forwards; it does not hold me back. My fear is of what's behind, of what has been done to me. Nothing over the Wall worries me very much. The Devastation was hundreds of years ago, long before Markas and long before Franklin, which is a long time considering their timeline of Cutta since its construction. I mean, Franklin didn't Complement until he was fifty, and Markas is one of the oldest alive in the Kingdom – he's in his seventies, isn't he? Even if you consider the time above ground – which isn't short, mind you – it's over a hundred years, in addition to the two hundred plus years below ground ... Regardless, humans were born in the wild, I'm sure of it. We're meant to return there. The animals are reclaiming their lands, the waters are running clear, and the trees are growing tall. There are dangers in the woods, that's true, but I'd take a mutant or a rabid over the King's men any day.'

Catherine was still mulling that over when she realised Nate was staring at her. 'What?' she asked.

'Can I ask you something?'

'I thought that's what we were doing.'

'Do you still not dream?'

'Why do you ask?'

'I wish I didn't dream. It's not even the nightmares which bother me. Not anymore. Constant fear is something you learn to live with. But ...'

'But?'

'I dreamt of Tommy recently,' he said softly. 'It was unsettling in a way I can't describe. I was having a nightmare and then suddenly I wasn't. I was standing in a valley, staring at the sky, and I saw him. Like a mirage of some kind. He didn't look like Tommy. Not any memory I have of him. His hair was long – Tommy's hair's never been long.'

'And?'

'And nothing,' said Nate, splashing the water with his hand and standing up. 'I woke up.'

'I suppose it's normal to dream about him,' she said. 'I probably would if I was prone to dreaming.'

'It didn't feel like a dream.'

'What did it feel like?'

Nate just shook his head and began skipping rocks across the surface of the water. After a few moments of strained quiet, they both turned and walked back to the trio, each wanting a distraction from their own thoughts.

Tove darted over to Catherine. 'Ciara! Evander's finishing the catch! Want to share a rabbit with me?'

'I'd love to,' said Catherine. 'I've got some vegetables as well, so if you can chop the meat into pieces, I can make a stew.'

The young girl beamed at her and skipped off to ensure that their hare was properly tended to. Zoe gave Catherine a grateful nod. 'She's not been so upbeat in days. It's amazing what chocolate can do.'

'It's the cure for everything,' said Catherine. 'Do you need any help?'

'I've got the fire if you want to start making that stew you mentioned,' said Zoe.

Evander patted his stomach. 'We've not had a proper meal in days. I'm so glad we found you both. How long have you been travelling?'

'A couple of weeks,' said Nate, sitting down and producing a bottle of Cisco from his sack. 'We stopped in Talon on the way to restock, but we're hoping to reach Brine in a few weeks. I've cousins out there who've offered us work on their farm. It's not much, but we figured –'

'Something's better than nothing,' finished Zoe. 'Exactly. We're hoping to get work in Rinlow.'

The fire felt soothing and the crackling of the flames and the distant rushing of water made the grove feel incredibly safe. There was a constant song from the crickets and insects in the surrounding underbrush, and Catherine had long ago learned that so long as the smallest of creatures was singing its song, there were no enemies around.

When Evander had finished gutting and skinning the animals, Tove appeared with a platter of finely chopped pieces of meat. Catherine had a spicy vegetable concoction brewing on the fire, and once the meat was added, the night air smelled delicious. She sat between Nate and Tove, allowing the Cisco to calm her nerves and daze her constant thoughts.

Nate spread thick butter on a loaf of bread and placed it on the rocks near the coals to toast. Zoe handed out heavy cattle skin blankets that they draped over their shoulders and legs to keep out the chill. After Evander had buried the entrails and innards of the animals and washed his hands in the creek, he returned and rummaged around in his bag. He produced a box of cigarettes, cigars, tockers and pipes; along with bags of various different grasses from the south. He pointed out the ones that made you sleep and the ones that made you lively; there were some that made you hungry and others which killed your appetite; a bright pink bag contained grasses that would arouse you, and another silver bag held contents that would cure any head cold or flu. He explained that his father had made his business on the stuff, creating blends that would satisfy any customers. The box was the last of it, although Evander stated proudly that he had at least ten seeds of each plant to start his father's business up again once they found a new home.

Catherine accepted one of the tockers whilst Nate opted for one of his beloved cigarettes; Zoe rolled herself some out of a blue bag that she said would give her a waking sleep so that she could keep watch and rest, and Evander lit one of the fat cigars that smelled strongly of molasses and cacao. Tove took a piece of liquorice from Evander's box and munched on it happily as the others smoked themselves into a state of contented bliss. By the time dinner was ready, the conversation was easy and cheerful and everyone was relaxed.

For the first time in a long time, and certainly since she and Nate had been shoved together in the cruellest of fashions, Catherine felt good. The figurative hole in her chest which had felt like a rotting sore in the wake of Thom's passing now felt like a scar, and in the haze of the pleasant evening, she managed to forget the majority of her troubles, only reminded of them when Nate's ears bled during dinner and he excused himself to go clean up. The evidence of his illness was impossible to ignore and her worry for him increased daily.

They ate bowls of stew and devoured one loaf of bread and then the next, and by the time they finished, the clouds had drifted past the moon and it was once again shining down upon them, the heavens littered with twinkling golden stars.

The conversation turned to tall tales and legends, and Catherine found herself leaning against Nate without meaning to and finding that she wasn't bothered to move. Tove sat beside her, curled up in blankets, and they kept tossing pieces of chocolate at each other from one of the bags Catherine had purchased in Talon.

176

Evander finished his story of a wayward soldier who saved some townsfolk and cast about for some other story.

'Tell the one about the lovers,' said Tove, winking at Catherine as she caught a piece of chocolate easily with her teeth. 'I like that one.'

Nate poured another cup of Cisco for Evander. 'Go on,' he said. 'We've not heard good tales in a long while.'

'Yes, please do,' said Catherine, finishing her cup and holding it drunkenly for Nate to fill. 'Top me up.'

'You're adorable when you're like this,' he whispered, filling her glass and wrapping an arm around her. For once she did not rebuff him and his eyes seemed slightly brighter as he winked. A tocker hung from his lips; he had long ago mastered the art of talking, breathing and smoking all at the same time.

'How long have you been bound?' Zoe gestured between them. 'You're from the North, yes? Your accents give you away.'

'Assigned at twelve, not yet Complemented,' said Catherine, gesturing to her face. 'They let you extend it if you're living together and in school.' She ran her finger over the rim of her cup, her voice sounding not her own when she added: 'Our parents have been planning the ceremony all year.'

Nate glanced at her, expression dark.

Zoe nodded. 'You seem good together. You're lucky. My Complement died two years ago during the first wave of the famine, as did our children. Evander's Complement and daughter followed soon after.'

'To them,' said Nate, holding up his cup.

'To Sylvia,' said Evander. 'And Gretchen.'

'To Mikhail,' said Zoe. 'Joanne. Philip. Foreman. And little Lexa.'

The five of them drank deeply in honour of the dead, and Catherine said a silent prayer for Thom.

'Tell the story, Ev,' said Tove. 'It's too nice a night to be sad.'

'My sister's right,' said Evander. 'Forgive us. Sometimes it's easy to fall into the past. Does everyone want a story, then?'

Shouts of 'Yes!' and 'Go on!' echoed around the grove and everyone settled themselves in for one more story before bed. A few owls hooted, as if in agreement, and the rustling sounds of the horses grazing behind them made the silence feel comfortable rather than ominous.

'A long time ago,' he began, 'in a very distant land, there lived two best friends who had known each other their whole lives. We'll call one Abel and the other Emily. One night, as they are walking to meet their friends, Abel and Emily are kidnapped on the side of the road. No one sees them taken, no one knows where they've gone. A search begins and, after several months, the investigators find that they were taken by a madman. When they arrive at his house, they find that not only is the madman dead, there's no sign of either Abel or Emily. Little do they know that both Abel and Emily are in another land.'

Catherine sniggered. 'That's lucky.'

'Hush,' said Evander good-naturedly. 'It's a story. It doesn't have to make sense.

'Now, Abel and Emily have awoken in a distant world not unlike our own. They speak a language like ours but different, older and more complex. It takes them months to realise that they are in their world, only back in time.'

'Back in time?' said Nate, snorting into his cup. 'I've never heard of such a thing.'

Evander threw a piece of bread at him. 'As time passes, Emily realises that she's pregnant, but it comes at a terrible price, for the child is Abel's but was created under mutual duress. Unable to bear it, Emily abandons Abel in the hope that he will have a better life without her. For years they're separated.

'A great war rages and all the soldiers of the land are called to battle. Emily, having lived in the future, knows a great deal about wounds and infections and the like, and she decides to accompany the men to battle as a physician. Months pass and men die, as they do in every war.

178

'One day, a soldier comes in on a stretcher. He's missing half his face and has no idea who he is. Emily treats him as she's treated a hundred others before him, but she realises that there's something different about him. At night, he screams out for a long lost love but has no memory of it during the day. Desperate to help him, Emily befriends the ruined soldier, pushing his chair through the meadows so that he'll see the daylight, feeding him as he can no longer feed himself, and telling him stories of her daughter who has grown tall and beautiful, her hair the colour of raspberries.

'For months their friendship grows and the soldier's memory slowly returns to him. He finally remembers that he is Abel and she is his lost love, but years of distance and battle have distorted her memories as well, and she has grown to know him only as Patient 300, a man with half a face. But Abel now knows that his daughter is alive and that his friend is grown and more lovely than ever, and he has no intention of letting her go.

'When the war comes to an end and Emily is summoned back to her old life, he asks her to take him on one last walk around the grounds of the hospital. He's scared, for he has everything to lose, unlike her. She has a Complement and a daughter and a life far from the woes of the battlefield, but sometimes, no matter how great the distance or how many years have passed and how much things have changed, those who are meant to be, their fate predetermined by all the laws of nature and rightness, come together even when it shouldn't make sense. Even when it ought to be far too late for any sort of hope.

'And so he tells her of his childhood in a distant land, another world, and tells her of the young girl he had loved since he was five and she was three. The more he talks, the more Emily begins to recognise him and by the day's end, the friends are reunited. Sadly, Emily is still Complemented, and her daughter has never met her true father. Their love for each other might have had the strength to forge through a battle, it could not undo that. Sometimes the things which ought to be the hardest to weather are the easiest, and that which should be bearable tears you to pieces. So Emily tells him that she will return with their daughter one day, to the place where they first came through into this new land, and that he must wait for her.

'In return, she waits until he is able to walk, albeit with a cane and a heavy limp, his face permanently wrapped in a thick cloth to hide his disfigurement, and then she departs, promising him that one day she will return and they will have the life that was taken from them by the madman.

'Abel goes to the beach where they first washed up on shore and waits. He builds a small cabin and grows a garden, counting each day and marking the nights on a large tree that leans over his new home. For three long years he waits, watching the sunrise and the sunset, looking for her in every cave, road, trail and path that he sees. He looks to the sea and the sky, praying that she will return to him. And, just as he begins to lose hope, there she is, her daughter at her side.

'Her Complement died, you see. He caught a sickness in the war that took a very long time to kill him. And no one could leave a dying man for that would be the worst of evils. So she loved her Complement to his dying breath, telling him nothing of their daughter's true father, and giving her daughter time to grieve the only father she had ever known. But, at long last, as the years passed and the scars healed, Emily wanted only Abel, her true soul mate in that life and the one before it.'

'And they all lived happy in the end?' Tove prompted.

'For many years of joy,' he said, winking at her.

Catherine smiled. 'That's a good story.'

'You think so? I've had lots of people tell me it's awful and cruel. My best friend Charles hated it. He wanted me to change the last half. But it's one of the stories I'm always able to remember.'

'No, it's good,' she assured him. 'It's more like life, isn't it? She gave them both time to heal. And since they were meant to be together, they found a way in the end. That's how you know it's real love. They returned to each other.'

Evander handed her another tocker, his handsome face filled with the passion of storytelling. 'My thoughts exactly.'

'Do you know any stories, Zoe?' Catherine looked over at her, lighting the strong-smelling stick with Nate's igniter.

'No,' said Zoe, shaking her head. 'My brother is our resident storyteller.'

'Mine too.'

Everyone looked at Nate, and Catherine reached up, squeezing his hand in comfort.

'When did he die?' asked Evander.

'He didn't die,' said Nate thickly. 'He was brought into Redwater.'

The empathy on Evander's face broke Catherine's heart. 'What was his name?' he murmured, watching Nate.

'Tommy,' he said quietly. 'Thom.'

Evander held up his cup. 'To Thom,' he said sombrely. 'I wish we could have met him.'

Catherine blinked away the tears that filled her eyes and drank the rest of her cup, well and truly drunk now, her mind whirling from smoking so much. She said nothing for fear that her voice would give her away.

'Tell us about him,' said Zoe. 'We talk about our parents most nights. It's important not to forget them.'

And so Nate spoke of Thom. He did it in a roundabout way, telling them of Thom as child, how he'd always loved to build sandcastles and fix up the old hover in the garage; how he'd read their entire library by the time he was fifteen and was top of his class in everything; how he manoeuvred Nate out of all sorts of trouble and never once failed him.

Nate's stories of Thom were so real and vivid in her mind that Catherine was able to think of him clearly, see his face in her mind and even hear his voice. She moved closer to Nate, not wanting to lose the memory of Thom any more than she feared she already had. To hear Nate talk of him, Thom sounded larger than life, an impossibly good dream. It was how she remembered him as well, and she was unsure if it was true, or if they both loved him so much that he was forever golden in their memories.

It was almost dawn before any of them suggested going to sleep. Tove had long since nodded off, lulled by their talking and a full night's meal.

Zoe wanted to keep watch that night and rejected any offer of help. 'I can't sleep much these days,' she said, looking at Tove. 'I worry about something happening when I'm not awake. I'll nap in the morning once everyone's up. Get some rest.'

They thanked her, grateful not to have to keep watch themselves, and Catherine sank heavily onto the pile of blankets inside their tent, her body feeling ten times heavier than normal and her head so full of intoxicants that no real thoughts managed to drift in. It was the most comforting feeling she'd experienced in months.

'I loved that,' she mumbled as Nate settled down on the blankets beside her. 'I loved hearing you talk about Thom. You don't do that much.'

'I'm never drunk enough,' he said honestly.

Catherine searched for his face in the darkness. He did look so like Thom. It never occurred to her that it was strange to be able to see clearly in the dark, she was much too drunk for such details to be apparent; had she been sober, she would have realised that being able to see Nate's face clearly without any source of light, see the colour of his eyes, the length of his eyelashes, the mole on his cheek, was nothing normal.

'I'm terrified I'm going to forget him,' she said, drink making all fears easier to face. 'No matter how much I try, it's like he slips away more and more every second.'

Nate brushed her hair back from her face. 'Can I tell you something?'

'Yes.'

'I can't grieve him,' he whispered. 'I can't. He doesn't feel dead. If I thought him dead, I don't know what I'd do. I'm torn apart by worry and it's eating away at me. I can feel him in my bones and I don't know what to do with that. I think I'm going mad, Kitty.'

Catherine closed her eyes and leaned against his chest, not knowing what to say to that. 'Nate?'

'Yes, darling?'

'Promise me you won't die.'

'I swear I'll do my best.'

'I'm going to hold you to that.'

His grip tightened ever-so.

It felt like a dream being in that grove. Morning dawned bright and beautiful. The winter meant there was little for foraging, but they had more than enough packed food to satisfy and fill them. They ate heartily, hidden from the world and free to laugh. Even the horses seemed at ease, nickering and neighing to each other, picking up a trot every time the wind changed or huddling together comfortably. Though their thick coats were covered with a light layer of snow, they hardly seemed to mind. Catherine had seen horses turn on each other a few times and was pleased that this was not one of those occasions.

As it happened, Zoe was a wonderful singer, and midway through the second day, she began to sing as they lounged around. She sang Southern lullabies, and hearty ballades about the war and the famine and the Plague – the sort of horrible events that always produced the most beautiful of songs. Nate could sing as well, and his sonorous voice was a sharp contrast to Zoe's. Catherine, Evander and Tove asked them to sing until they could sing no longer, and then Evander began to tell stories once more.

The second night passed in a similar manner to the first, although everyone opted out of drinking again. They had to be up at first light to catch the ferry and groggy headaches would have made it nearly impossible.

'You know,' said Evander thoughtfully as they munched on their dinner. 'The road to Brine and Sage is the same for a couple of days' ride once we get off the ferry. Maybe we could all stick together?

There's more safety in numbers and I know we've enjoyed your company.'

Catherine and Nate exchanged a glance. Before she could kindly refuse, Tove voiced her enthusiasm at the prospect. 'Oh yes, please!' she cried. 'I could even show you how to hunt, Ciara. Please come with us. The ride's been so lonely and dreary before we found you. Don't leave us now.'

'Tovy, it's their decision,' said Evander. 'They might have places to stop along the way that they won't want to bring strangers to.'

'No,' said Nate suddenly. 'No, it's fine. We'd love to ride the road with you for a few days.'

'Yes!' Tove pumped her fist into the air.

She was a truly sweet child, still innocent despite the famine that had blighted her childhood, and eyes so harmless and loving that Catherine had half a mind to steal her away and keep her forever.

By the following morning, the sun had retired and it was snowing heavily, the waves of the nearby ocean crashing against the rocks, only adding to the formidable landscape. Catherine was worried about boarding the ferry, but Nate assured her it would be better – less people would be around on a bad day and everyone would be too focused on the weather to notice their faces. Or so he hoped.

It was a short ride from their campsite to the ferry crossing and Catherine rode beside Tove, listening to the girl's excited chatter about the next couple of days and all the things they could do while they had time. Her endless chatter helped banish the fears that plagued Catherine's mind, and she was almost distracted as they arrived at the ferry crossing. Although there was no one living on South Brittan, it was close enough to the mainland that many used it as a transfer dock, and the crowds increased as canoes and boats arrived. The cheaper, more dangerous vessels also rarely checked identification or had working broadcasts.

They paid their tickets and loaded the horses in the cargo hold, one level above the hover park. Voyager baulked at every turn, stubbornly stamping her feet and blowing, but once Pie and the others were settled in the stables, she stormed ahead, not wanting to be left behind.

'Voyager is the worst name for that horse,' said Catherine. 'She's more afraid of a voyage than any of them.'

'Hush,' said Nate, holding a carrot out for her and scratching beneath her forelock. 'She's just nervous.'

'I'm nervous. She's a pain in the arse – undoubtedly literally as well.'

Nate rolled his eyes and turned back to his horse, soothing her with soft words until she managed to settle down, ripping apart the hay with her teeth. 'She'll be fine,' said Nate. 'Come on. Let's go upstairs.'

'Wait,' said Catherine. The others had already gone up to save seats for them, and it was probably the only time she would get Nate alone for a while. 'Why are we riding with them?'

'Isn't that what you wanted?'

'Well, yes, but isn't it a bad idea? We travel with them long enough we'll forget our aliases or they'll burn us and realise that there's something wrong with us.'

Nate sighed. 'I'm inclined to trust them.'

Catherine bit her lip. 'You trusted Archie ...'

It was the wrong thing to say. Nate's body went rigid and his nostrils flared. 'If I could take back everything that happened there I would. You know that. Don't – don't you dare presume I've forgotten. I see him in my sleep every night and every night I kill him.'

'I'm glad we're going with them, it's not that. It's just –'

'You're scared. I get that. *I'm* scared. We're less obvious in a group. We blend. We look like famine fleers heading north for work. As thin and sick as we are, no one's going to doubt it. If anything happens to me, I don't want you to be alone. The longer we're with people, the safer you'll be.'

Catherine grabbed his hand as he made to move past her. 'I was thinking,' she said. 'Rinlow has a huge port. We'll not be noticed when we arrive and we'll not be noticed if we double back.'

'I'm not going to Clearbow.'

'There may be something to find there. Something to help you. We just have to know where to look.'

'We're going to the Outlands,' said Nate firmly. 'We're not going across the ocean towards the very people who are hunting us. I won't do it. We agreed on the Outlands.'

'You agreed. You and Thom. Not me. I never agreed to anything. I'm the one by your side every day watching you die. I'm not just going to do nothing.'

Nate shook his head. 'I can't do it, darling. I can't go back there. We've lost too much. The Outlands are the best chance we have. If there's – if there's even the slightest chance that Tommy might've – that he's – he'll be there.'

It was at this moment that Catherine completely lost her composure. 'Thom's dead, Nate! He's dead and you're dying and I can't lose anyone else. We go to the Outlands with you this sick and we're dead anyways. Stop trying to save me and save yourself! You won't be able to help me if you die and leave me here alone. I can hardly do nothing. Let's just – let's just please do *something*. Please.'

Nate sighed. He leaned back against the wall of the stall and Catherine suddenly realised that it was taking all of his strength to remain standing. She reached out and pulled the cuff of his sleeve up, touching his skin. Warmth spread from where their skin touched and a timid flush of colour appeared in his cheeks as his body valiantly tried to heal itself.

'See,' she said. 'We have to help each other now. We both owe it to Thom to stay alive.'

'What if we're caught?' he asked, although he'd lost some of his conviction.

'Thom died for us,' she said. 'The least we can do is ensure that he didn't die for nothing. If you die as well then what was the point of all of this?'

A loud horn pierced the air, signalling the ferry's departure. Catherine watched him, trying to read his mind. Almost ten minutes passed before Nate spoke again. He reached out and brushed a strand of hair behind her ear. 'May I ask you something?'

Catherine nodded.

'If I go to Clearbow with you, and by the grace of God we find something and we're cured, will you give me a chance?'

'What do you mean?'

Nate's eyes flickered over her face uncertainly, earnest and unsure. She had never known him to waver so, and she could not figure out if it was the disease that had stripped him of his candour and bravado or Thom's death. He reached out, his hand going around her waist, and kissed her. She stayed completely still, wondering if he was going to agree. If he died, she would be all alone, and that thought was terrifying to her. At least with Nate, she felt safe. He was the only thing of Thom she had left. She needed him to live.

He tasted of the spicy mint tea they had drunk that morning, and despite his frail state, held her strongly, no longer leaning against the wall for support, his body moving closer to hers. Where Thom had always been dominant and playful, Nate kissed her like she was the only thing keeping him alive. Which, she realised with a sudden jolt of fear, she was.

Her grip tightened slightly, her chest shuddering, and she gasped against his mouth, pulling away as guilt and confusion burned through her.

Yet Nate seemed almost renewed. 'Give me a chance,' he pleaded, face earnest and vulnerable. 'Do that for me and I'll go to Clearbow.'

'I promise,' she lied.

PART FOUR
Discovery

The siblings had been with Catherine and Nate almost a week while they dallied with whether or not to tell them the truth. At last, fed up with stalling and worried about Nate, Catherine broke the news that they weren't heading for Brine but were instead waiting for the ferry to take them to Clearbow.

'Why?' said Tove. 'What's in Clearbow? I thought you were going to work with your cousins.'

'I'm sick,' said Nate. 'We think the cure might be there.'

They were in Rinlow, at a lodge two days' ride from the ferry. It was a small business with only five or six cabins available, but they'd found one that would house them all, and the night indoors would give them a chance to talk, and offer the horses a chance at a good night's sleep. It had been pissing icy rain ever since they got off the ferry and there was nothing at that point that wasn't completely sodden. All of their gear was piled by the heater in hopes of drying. The horses were in the stables, gleefully devouring the grain they had so long been denied.

Evander, who had been hanging more things up to dry, glanced over his shoulder. 'It's obvious you're sick. I've never seen a corpse upright before. You look like you've seen the wrong end of the famine. What've you got?'

Nate glanced at Catherine. She nodded. She had too many lies in her head to keep track of and constantly remembering to answer to 'Ciara' was driving her mad.

'If you've been near a broadcast in the last few months, you'll know exactly who we are.'

Tove snorted. 'We've known who you were for ages. Evander thought we should wait until you wanted to tell us.'

Catherine's jaw dropped. 'How did you know?'

'Because we've been by a broadcast in the last few months,' said Evander wryly. 'Honestly, you two look different from your captures but not that different. I'm a little insulted that you think we couldn't figure it out.'

Tove leaned forwards eagerly. 'So why are you running?'

'I thought you said you knew?' said Nate.

Zoe shrugged. 'We know what the broadcast says. The same broadcast that said there was going to be no famine and the economy of Southern was on the rise. The same broadcast that listed the deaths of our people in the hundreds, not thousands. We've learned not to listen much to what the broadcasts say.'

And so Catherine and Nate told them. They told them about the fight in Nitoib and the trek that had landed them in so much trouble. They told them about Thom's capture and their escape. They told them about their journey to the Eastern Islands to find safety, hoping for information from Archie. They told them about the library in Talon, Yosef Smith and what they hoped to find in Clearbow. When they finished, nobody said anything for a long time. Zoe busied herself wringing out wet clothes and packing away newly dried ones, and Tove grabbed some bags of tea from their packs. Evander handed them each a cigarette, expression grim and commiserating.

'Thank you for telling us,' he said at length. 'Since you've done that, we might as well return the favour. We're not heading to Rinlow because of the work opportunities. I killed a man in our hometown. It was caught on reel. I'm running because we've lost too many of our family already and we decided running was better than execution. So there you have it. We're all on the run. There's nothing to fear from us.'

Catherine let out a hollow laugh. 'There's something to fear from everyone.'

'Perhaps,' said Evander. 'I'm inclined to trust you regardless. You helped us at great risk to yourselves. That's not something South-Landers forget or take lightly. We have more loyalty than Anaitians.'

'You're not wrong,' said Catherine quietly.

'Save a few,' said Nate, lighting the cigarette and leaning forwards on his elbows, eyes alight with curiosity. 'Why'd you kill him?'

'He tried to take my father's land.' Evander's lip curled. 'I guess we lost it in the end regardless, but still. He was an opportunist and a coward amidst crisis and starvation. The man deserved a worse death than what I gave him.'

'You beat him to death.'

'How did you know?'

'Lucky deduction.'

The men appraised each other a moment, the air between them thick with unsaid appreciation; Catherine could tell that they respected each other a little more now that the truth was out. For her part, she felt slightly less nauseated.

'We'll go with you to Clearbow,' said Evander. Nate opened his mouth to protest but Evander held up a hand, silencing him. 'This is not a world where friends fall out of the skies, Nate. We haven't met anyone worth knowing in a very long time. You've lost weight in the short time we've known you. You're in no shape to protect yourself, let alone Ciar – Catherine, sorry. I know you're the sort who wouldn't near admit it, but it's apparent to everyone. You've grown weak from your sickness. Let us help you. We can cover more ground as five than as two, and once we fix the pair of you we can return here and make our way to the Outlands as you said. It's a better idea than any we've concocted and I'm not ashamed to say that the thought of no more people gives me hope. I'm weary of my own kind but I'd not like to lose you if we can help it.'

Nate eyed him carefully. 'How do I know we can trust you?'

'Why would you tell me so much if you couldn't?'

'I've been foolish before.'

'No time like the present to become smart.'

Catherine exchanged a look with Zoe, who was watching them evenly, if cautiously. And then, as if the tension had never existed, Nate nodded.

After that the decisions came easily. They decided not to head back to the main docks, even if it was unlikely to be spotted. There were smaller, more local places where money was the only question. Nate suspected that there would be a few fishing boats in the area that would happily take them for a hefty fee. The money Nate had stolen from Archie's was enough to cover it, but there wouldn't be much left over afterwards.

The rest of the night passed in distracted chatter, everyone feeling a little uncertain about everyone else. Tove curled up at Catherine's feet, a thick pillow between their skin, and Zoe played the harmonica absently, not much for chitchat.

Catherine's eyes were too heavy to focus on the words in her book, and her mind kept drifting to other things. She thought of her recent promise to Nate and wondered what she was going to do about it. She knew she cared for him, far more than she ever thought she would. It was clear now that they were closer than friends and were of the utmost importance to each other. The friendship Thom had always hope to foster between them now existed undoubtedly. And she could not deny that Nate, when not sick and dying, was handsome. But her thoughts returned to Thom at every turn, and the guilt tasted like ash in her mouth.

She closed her eyes and thought of Thom's face, trying to bring to life the image of him. It was so hard. Certain phrases she could still hear perfectly. She remembered his arms, his back and the indents of his collar bones. Try as she might, she struggled to recall his dimpled smile, always bursting forth to stop her in her tracks, a smile that was far more common when Nate was with them; it was hard to see his face, the face she had loved more than all the rest. She opened her eyes and glanced at Nate, and suddenly she remembered. Close to death, half his normal size and haunted, Nate still looked remarkably like Thom. How brothers not twinned could bear such a resemblance she did not know. They sounded the same, walked the same, laughed and sang the same. It was only the ticks known to those who loved them, the different colour of their hair and eyes, and their completely contradictory personalities which differentiated them.

Catherine's father had once called Nate 'wildfire'. He hadn't meant it as a compliment and at the time she hadn't seen it as one. Yet there was something about his words which rang true. Nate had always been wild and dangerous, burning everything in his path and living with a passion that would only consume him in the end. Thom, on the other hand, was patient, powerful; a polar opposite with ice in his veins and armour made of money and manipulations.

The heat from the radiator was heavy and comforting, and the next thing Catherine knew she was in the bright green field she had now dreamed of a few times. As always, Nate was there. He was sitting on the soft grass, whole and healthy, the sun on his hair making him look like he was on fire. Catherine sat beside him and stared into the distance. There was nothing to obscure the view. Only the endless green of the field and blue of the sky.

When she awoke, it was several hours later and she felt somewhat rested. Their bags were already packed and waiting and she forced herself to her feet and into the bathroom for a wash. This time there were mirrors, and she was able to examine herself more properly than she had in a while. Her olive skin had lost much of its colour and her eyes, once brown and full of life, had deep circles beneath them, giving her an unhealthy appearance. They were a strange, almost maroon shade. Whatever the infection was doing to Nate, it hadn't left her alone entirely.

She turned the water on as hot as it would go. When she finally felt clean and awake, Catherine stepped out of the shower and dried her hair in the hairpress next to the sink. The long black tendrils fell almost to her waist and she grabbed the scissors without thinking. It took her only five minutes to cut several lengths from her hair, leaving it at her shoulders, less heavy and weighed down. She slipped on a bodysuit that was insulated and hugged her comfortably, although her hip bones stuck out through the thin material and if she stretched she could count her ribs. With a grimace, she laced her boots up to her calves and wrapped a coat around her shoulders before leaving the room, feeling only a little bit more satisfied with her appearance.

Outside, rain was hammering against the ground creating a mucky soup of dirt, runoff and faeces from the paddocks. Nate had saddled Voyager and Pie and was waiting inside the shelter of the barn for her, a hood pulled low over his face to keep out the rain. Catherine pulled the hood of her bodysuit up as well and darted through the downpour to meet him.

'Feeling better?' he asked, giving her a leg up.

'A little,' she said. 'Tired.'

'Same.' He swung into his saddle and nudged Voyager towards the trio who were waiting patiently beneath a nearby tree. 'No matter how much sleep I get these days, I'm always tired. Everything feels like such an effort.'

The siblings had changed out of their billowing robes and donned bodysuits like Nate and Catherine. In dark shades of black, grey, blue and red, the five of them looked a formidable lot.

Zoe produced a sharp dagger from her side-pack and handed it to Catherine. 'I thought you might like this,' she said. 'I had an extra one.'

It was a beautiful, handcrafted weapon with a lovely blue stone handle that felt light as a feather in her hand. Catherine strapped it to her side and smiled at Zoe. 'Thank you.'

Evander pointed towards the road. 'I suggest that Zoe and Nate take the lead, Tove in the centre, and Catherine and I will take up the rear. There's no point in you two riding side by side and looking like you've just stepped out of a broadcast.'

Everyone agreed, but before Catherine could join Evander, Nate grabbed her hand and stopped her. 'Kitty,' he said softly. 'You meant what you said, didn't you?'

'Of course,' she fibbed. 'Why do you ask?'

Nate shook his head. 'A queer feeling is all. Never mind.' With that, he nudged Voyager ahead and settled in beside Zoe.

'Are you all right, Catherine?' Evander had appeared at her side, his hair stuck to his forehead from the rain. She realised that he was rather handsome and wondered what he might have been like before the deaths of his family and his people. Handsome faces were unrivalled when they shone with joy, and most heart-breaking when creased in woe.

'Call me Kitty,' she said. 'I like it more.'

'Kitty,' he agreed. 'Is something the matter?'

Catherine bit her lip. She wasn't sure she wanted to confide in Evander, knowing him as short a time as she had. They nudged their horses after the others, picking up a steady pace, and after several minutes, she glanced at him and nodded. 'Are you sure you don't mind?' she asked uncertainly.

Evander winked at her. 'If there's one thing I could never mind, it's lending an ear to a friend. What troubles you? I've been told I'm a good listener.'

She smiled. 'You sound like Thom.'

'I'm sorry you lost him,' said Evander sincerely. 'Trust me when I say I know how it feels. I was not in love with my Complement – we were not so lucky – but she was a good friend. My daughter I loved more than life itself.'

Catherine wanted to reach over and hug him, and felt somewhat useless knowing she couldn't. 'I wish I could have met them,' she said.

'As do I,' said Evander. 'Now tell me what troubles your mind.'

'I can't remember the last time anything made sense. Things keep going from bad to worse. I'm so tired and angry all the time.'

Evander thought about that for a moment, distracted as his steed sidestepped a hare, snorting wildly. Once he had calmed him, Evander turned back to Catherine. 'I don't think it's going to be much consolation for me to say that everything is going to get much, much worse before it improves, but there's two ways to think about it. The first is the easy way, albeit not the optimal one. You could focus on how terrible the events of recent history are, and you could focus on how cruel the world can be and suffocate under its pressures and twists, but that would lead only to a lifetime of suffering for you. Once you settle into a cycle of that sort, there's no recovery.

'The second option, the one I think is the better choice, is akin to a curable illness. Think of it like this – when you're sick, no matter how much you vomit or shake or sweat or cry, no matter how seemingly unendurable the pain, the fact that it's temporary makes it all right. You know you can bear through the pain because you're going to feel whole again soon enough. And even if you're sick months later, it's all right because you know that after that you'll be well once more. Think of your troubles like that. The only unbearable thing is death, Kitty, and you're not dead. There is nothing in this life that can't be lived through save death, so do not allow the darkness to cripple you. It's not worth it. You have your whole life ahead of you, and it's got more adventure than most. You may have lost Thom, but to anyone with eyes it's clear that Nate loves you more than anything. You're not captured or indentured or broken. You have so many things you can still do. And that's not something to throw away or waste.'

She could see the truth in his words easily enough, but they didn't provide her with the epiphany she was hoping for. 'I was meant to bind to Thom and live my life. Do wonderful things like teach mathematics to children and show them that life isn't just about remembering the Devastation and all that came after. Fearing the past as if it's coming straight for you. I know it's stupid and selfish to wish for the life my parents had because I know that they've turned people in and I know my father's said to be horrible and I'm not reconciled with any of that. Even so, I *wanted* that life, Evander. I wanted the ease and the happiness and the comfort. Now Thom is dead and I'm attached to his brother who, consequently, loves me. What am I to do with that? How can that be something I ever make right in my head?'

Evander shrugged unhelpfully. 'I suppose you have to ask yourself if life's worth wasting on lost chances and guilt. Do you think your Thom would want you to live alone for the rest of your life? No caring soul would wish that upon anyone. Do you think he'd hate you for allowing his brother some measure of happiness? Human emotions are for the living, and from everything you've told me, Thom sounds like he loved you and Nate more than anyone in the world. He died to save your life, not to condemn you to a lifetime of misery. Unlike the rest of the Kingdom, you've been given the freedom to see the ills of this world and escape them. For that, for Thom's sacrifice and Nate's enduring devotion to you, I think you should be grateful, not grieving.'

A weighted silence filled the wet air as Evander finished giving his opinion, and Catherine turned her attention forwards, not having the slightest clue as to how to respond.

The hardest part about boarding the ship wasn't parting with most of their money, it was bidding farewell to their horses. Pie nuzzled her hands in search of treats as she sold him to a farmer in the seaside town. He nickered after her as he was led away, his head shaking indignantly as he realised that he was leaving. The only comfort Catherine found in it was the fact that Voyager sold to the same man and both horses would be together. Voyager reared and spooked as she was led away, and Nate watched her leave with a mournful expression on his face.

The trio sold their horses to various people, but seemed melancholy about the arrangement as well. It was with a sombre, thoughtful air that the five of them boarded the ship and watched as their steeds were led off to places unknown.

Once the bags had been stowed and everyone was shown to their rooms, the five of them met back on the deck to watch Rinlow disappear from view. It seemed strange to be moving away from the country they had spent months trying to get to, but Catherine was glad of it. Moving towards a proposed solution gave her the smallest ray of hope that perhaps they'd make it through this entire ordeal. She tried to put thoughts of capture and arrest from her mind as the ship pulled out onto the choppy waters. Trouble was more fixable than rotting flesh and aching bones, after all.

The ship was a medium sized vessel with large sails in turquoise and blue, a figurehead of a mutant on its bow. It seemed half made of wood, half made of metal, but the whole vessel was a powerful display, and Catherine had no fears of it sinking unexpectedly – fears which Nate and Tove seemed to harbour greatly. Within twenty minutes of being on-board, both were slightly green.

Owned by a local fisherman, Marsh Manning, it was normally used for showing tourists around the coast of Rinlow, perhaps to watch the sunset, or see the exotic oceanic life, but more than a few passengers used it to travel undetected.

Marsh Manning was not a foolish man who waited on his thumbs for income, and for a price he could take you anywhere in the sea that you wanted to go. Catherine was wary of him, but he seemed more business man than bitter man, and as the coast of Rinlow disappeared from the horizon and the only thing to see was the great big blue stretches of ocean, Catherine felt a bit more at ease. After all, she now had Nate, Zoe, Evander and Tove on her side, and all Marsh Manning had was a few deckhands who looked like they could do with a meal, and a cook who looked like he could do with far fewer.

Their cabins were located just below the deck; a room of bunk beds that the siblings took, the other a room with a large bed but not much space that she and Nate took. It was weird sharing a bed with him, even now, but whether he was too weak or just had no desire to be rejected again, Nate kept a respectful distance, only touching her on accident when he rolled over in his sleep.

A toilet was located down the corridor near the kitchens, and a lounge filled with books on fishing, sailing, gutting, cooking, the tides, the weather, the winds, how to tie knots, how to repair holes in a ship, and many others besides, all relevant to a life at sea, was located directly across from the siblings' cabin. It was a cosy room, with hammocks instead of sofas, and a huge window that was more often below the water level than above it, and gave off the strange feeling of being inside a tank. Catherine loved it, and over the next few days spent hours staring into the depths of the ocean, wondering what it would be like to live beneath the waves for eternity.

Marsh informed them that it would take him no less than two weeks to reach their destination, not because the distance required it, although it was several hundred miles, but because they had told him they wanted a scenic route and fancied avoiding the last of the year's tourists. The winter festivities would begin soon and most of the Central Countries would be safely tucked away into their homes, too cold to pay attention to fugitives. Catherine spent most of her time bundled up in thick warm clothes, but her ears felt close to falling off from the cold all the time, and her toes could never quite get their sensation back unless she took a hot shower or kept them by the furnace in the lounge.

After weeks on the road, settling in to the confinements of a ship would have made most anyone cagey, but Catherine managed to settle into a routine that she found rather enjoyable. She woke up early – it was impossible to sleep late when the bed roiled with the waves – and went for breakfast with the other four in the kitchens. Isaiah, the cook, seemed annoyed by the extra mouths to feed until Tove expressed a wild interest in learning how to cook and began arriving an hour early each morning to help him prepare. Whether it was the fact that Tove made everyone a bit happier, or because Isaiah finally had someone to share his recipes and prowess with, the meals improved infinitely by the third day.

After breakfast, Catherine would go onto the deck and would watch for an hour or so to see any sea creatures. She usually followed this with reading, wandering about and then lunch. There was a table tennis set in the lounge, and more card games than Catherine knew what to do with, and an old broadcast screen that could just barely play the reels in Marsh's library. After dinner most nights, the five of them gathered in the lounge.

Everyone had a different genre they preferred. Zoe liked the mysteries, Evander the comedies, Tove the romances and Nate the horror flicks; Catherine preferred the information reels on wildlife and landscapes, which meant that every night the theme was different and often they stayed awake later than intended to watch two or three different ones.

On one of her morning watches she saw a few flying fish, and on the fifth day she saw a whale. It was a great blue creature with bumps and fins that seemed half the size of the ship, sending splashes of water metres high. The shock of it made her so happy that she yelled for the others who raced to the deck just in time to see the whale blow a huge jet of water into the air before flipping into the freezing depths. It lifted their spirits for the rest of the day and Catherine joined Tove in the lounge to read up on whales, dolphins, fish, otters, seals, jellyfish, octopuses, squid, sea lions, eels, coral, and all the things that lurked beneath them.

By the end of the first week, a heavy storm set upon them and the ship crashed up and down on the waves for almost five hours, giving them all shaky legs and a pounding headache. Catherine stayed curled in one of the hammocks that seemed to adapt to the roiling sensation better than a chair, the bed or her own two legs; she swayed to and fro as she read, pleased that whomever had designed the hammocks had had the foresight to nail them far enough away from the wall that no amount of swinging would cause her to collide with it.

Nate appeared an hour or so after the storm hit and crawled into the hammock adjacent to hers after three failed attempts and slamming his head against the wall as the ship crashed almost straight down and sent him sprawling.

'I miss land,' he moaned, holding his stomach. 'I miss hovers.'

Catherine offered a sympathetic grimace. 'Sea sick?'

'Ugh.' Nate clutched his stomach as his hammock swung wildly back and forth. It took another twenty minutes before his face returned to its more normal sickly pallor and he sat up.

'Better?' she asked, eyeing him concernedly.

'A little,' he said, breathing through his nose. 'You?'

'I feel like I'm being swung around by a wildly sadistic child at a party,' she said. 'Mostly all right, though.'

Nate gave her a weak smile. 'At least it's only another week.'

'And then there's the trip back,' she teased, winking at him.

'*Hang*,' he groaned, sinking his head back down.

Catherine closed her book. 'Is it just the seasickness or are you feeling worse?'

'Both.'

'I'm sorry.'

'No need to be, darling,' he said. 'There's nothing you can do that you aren't already doing.'

Catherine wanted to argue with him, wanted him to actually admit to how terribly he was feeling, but whether that was because she wanted to feel worse or because she was tired of him trying to shield her from the harsh truth of their situation, she was uncertain.

'Thom was the worst for sea sickness,' she said suddenly, a memory popping into her mind as she cast about for something to fill the silence. 'One time he got so sick that the toilet clogged and overflowed, so he ran back to his seat so no one would know it was him. About ten minutes later the bathroom had flooded and the whole aisle was covered in vomit. He felt so bad he bought the entire group drinks upon arrival.'

Nate chuckled. 'When was this?'

'My seventeenth birthday trip,' she said. 'We were meant to go skiing but at the last minute we decided that another trip wasn't going to be the best idea for him. We ended up staying at a hotel in the city when we landed and spent the whole week exploring the local areas and sightseeing. It was great, actually.'

Nate arched an eyebrow. 'Wait, when is your birthday? It's soon, isn't it?'

Catherine pursed her lips in thought. She hadn't kept track of time in a very long while. There was a calendar on the wall and after a moment's scrutiny, she said, 'Less than two weeks, apparently.'

'We should do something when we land,' he said. 'Anything you fancy?'

'I haven't given it any thought,' she said honestly. 'I was supposed to ... well, old plans.'

As clear as a summer's day, she could remember the discussion she'd had with Thom about how she wanted to spend her birthday. They had planned to be Complemented a few days beforehand in Anais, and would celebrate her birthday on a stayaway to one of the new resorts in the mountains. She smiled sadly at the memory of how easy and comfortable her old life had been. Something on her face must have given it away, because Nate's expression darkened and he looked down at his hands.

'You and Tommy were going to be Complemented.'

'Yeah.'

Nate frowned a moment before clapping his hands together. 'Evander and I were looking over maps of Clearbow the other day. There's a ski place a few hours out of town. Maybe if we find something on Yosef Smith before your birthday, we could go up there.'

'And risk being seen?'

Nate gave her a crooked smile, his eyes filled with genuine affection. 'You should have a proper birthday, darling. After everything we've been through, it's the least we could do. The broadcasts are saying we're in the Southern Lands, although I've no notion as to why. No one's looking for us in the Central Countries.'

That piqued her interest. 'You've been listening to the broadcasts?'

'Every day since we left home when it's available,' he admitted. 'I usually wait until you're asleep.'

'Why?'

He shrugged. 'I don't think I could take seeing your face look the way it did after we heard the first one.'

'Oh.'

'Kitty?'

'Yeah?'

'How are you?'

Catherine thought a moment about his meaning. 'I suppose I'm better,' she said after a time, and for once it felt true. The longer Thom was gone, the easier it became to deal with. Like losing an arm and having to master life with just one. Noticeable and hard, but manageable after a long period of time.

'It's been so long that now it feels real,' she mused aloud. 'I can focus again, which I didn't think I'd be able to do once. I miss him, and he's in my thoughts every day, but I spoke to Evander and I think he's right – Thom would want me to be happy. He would want me to enjoy life as far as I'm able. That was something he always seemed to want. Whenever there was a moment of uncertainty between us, he would always insist that I did what made me happy. I'm not saying I'm dancing with joy, but I can breathe a bit better, and that's enough for now.'

A comfortable silence descended between them and Catherine returned to reading *A War on Two Fronts* and Nate focused on quelling his queasy stomach. The waves eventually calmed and when the hammock had gone more than five minutes without swinging, Catherine braved standing. She gestured to Nate and they walked down the corridor towards the kitchens.

'Evening, Isaiah,' she said, nodding to the chef. 'Got anything left over from dinner?'

'There's a few cakes in the press,' he said, waving a ladle at the large wooden cabinet in the corner, secured by a heavy metal beam. 'Help yourselves.'

Catherine unlatched the beam and found the box of chocolate cakes that Isaiah had baked earlier in the day. She sat down at the table and handed the box to Nate, munching on one and getting icing all over her fingers.

'How's Tove getting on with the cooking?' she asked, looking around to see if the young girl was still about.

Isaiah grunted. 'Good enough. She's better than the last apprentice I had.'

'Oh yeah?' said Nate. 'What happened?'

'Almost blew up my ship.'

'You're joking!'

Isaiah seemed the sort of man who had never once told a joke in his entire life, but he nodded gravely and pointed at the corner where a new cooker was placed in front of a wall covered in black stains. 'Three years ago and it still stinks like a rubbish heap when the cooking doesn't mask it.'

Nate raised an eyebrow. 'What happened to her?'

'She almost blew up my ship trying to cook,' said Isaiah grimly. 'Take a gander.'

Catherine swallowed hard and looked over at the cooker. 'She died?'

'Aye. Took me almost a week to scrape the bits of her off the wall.'

Nate, who had been about to eat, put the cake down. 'Yeah, that's me done with eating for a while.'

Neither of them knew what to say next so they excused themselves, feeling infinitely less hungry than they had been moments before, and trudged back to their room. It was well past midnight but all the lights in the ship were still on and the constant crashing of the waves against the sides of the ship made all sense of time a little off.

Catherine locked the door behind them and began to undress, suddenly bone-tired. 'I can't wait until this whole thing is over,' she said, removing her leggings and searching the pile of clothes on the floor for something to sleep in. She found a long shirt under a pair of dirty boots and wrinkled her nose as she pulled it on. 'And we have clean clothes.'

'You realise that in the Outlands we're not going to have a cleaner, yes?'

'One can dream,' she said.

As she changed, Nate followed suit, and began to remove his many layers. Without meaning to, Catherine found herself staring at him as he changed. Once muscular and thick, Nate was now ruined skin and bones, his ribs sticking out and bruises covering a good two-thirds of his body. The arch of his spine stuck out like a jagged rock and she could count the vertebrae without needing to be near. Blood was crusted in his ears and there were remnants of dried blood down the back of his neck. His skin had a horrible yellow tint to it. He looked like he'd just escaped from an emergency ward.

Nate looked up as he fastened a pair of sleeping trousers around his waist and caught her staring. His face fell and he quickly pulled on a jumper, his wide shoulders giving the appearance that he was larger than he actually was.

'Apologies,' he muttered.

Catherine frowned. 'For what? It's not your fault. I feel terrible because there's nothing I can do to help.'

'I look disgusting.'

'You look ill – there's a difference.'

Nate crossed his arms over his chest self-consciously. 'This isn't how I want you to see me. How I was – who I was – that's what I want you to think of me as.'

She had no answer for that and sat down on the bed, drawing the blankets around her. 'Do you want to sleep or read or ...'

'I can't sleep much these days,' he said. 'Fancy reading to me?'

'Are you serious?'

'Why not? Everything I see is blurry anyways.'

Catherine pondered that a moment before pulling out her book and gesturing for him to sit. 'It's terribly dry,' she warned. 'I keep falling asleep reading it.'

'All the better.' Nate sat down beside her and wrapped one of the blankets around his shoulders, shivering with cold and sickness.

After a minute's deliberation, Catherine flipped *A War on Two Fronts* open and began to read. '"The Famine of AR63 was one of the worst Cutta had ever seen. It was most devastating in the outer regions where the remnants of radiation still clung to the soil and water, preventing proper growth and agriculture. Despite these terrible times, a great many advances were made in the Central Countries of Cutta, Clearbow and Redland. Cutta, the stronghold of the King's military and a burgeoning metropolis, made great strides in the scientific fields and often outsourced work to its neighbouring lands as progress was made."'

'You're right,' said Nate, scratching his chin absently. 'It is dry.'

'Told you.'

'What are the two fronts?'

Catherine pursed her lips in thought. 'The first is the actual disease aspect I presume, and all the problems which ensued. The other is the political one, perhaps. I can't say I've been paying much attention, although it does have more information than most of the books in Cutta on the subject. King Franklin was such a powerful leader, but the war lost him a lot of the fanaticism which followed him out of the ground. I think he was in his seventies by this point. He made it clear that all knowledge of life before the Devastation was disallowed and he would kill anyone who challenged his orders. The Belows were raided and all the information stored there was locked away or burned. Whether true or hyperbolic, it says he personally killed something like a hundred thousand people and gave the orders to kill nearly five million.'

'Five *million*?' Nate looked ill.

She nodded. 'It's close to that. You know something? I think life would be so much better without government. Maybe we need some sort of community to form bonds and such, but that doesn't mean we should have someone ruling over us.'

'Those are dangerous words,' said Nate, his eyes alight with mischief and admiration. 'I like you like this.'

'Contemplative?'

'Rebellious. I always knew you were a fighter. Seeing it ... I like it. Don't ever let them tell you what to think.'

Catherine frowned. 'I never knew there was anything to know.'

'Therein lies the problem.'

'How did you?'

'What do you mean?'

'We all grew up together, experienced the same things. I understand for Evander and the others. They grew up with hunger and confusion and no help. We grew up with everything. How could you tell anything was wrong?'

A dark shadow passed over Nate's face. 'I tended to think anything my father valued was inherently wrong. That belief has not proved faulty thus far.'

Several memories reared their head in Catherine's mind and she put the book down, leaning forwards. 'Before we were Assigned, I remember you two together. Thom. He was different back then. More open. We were schoolyard friends in the way that I'd share a biscuit with him or loan him a pen. But I remember him. Odd things other children didn't do. There so were many times when we were in class and he'd suddenly raise his hand, ask to leave, and not return for hours. He always said he was needed at home.'

Nate's jaw clenched and he shrugged. 'Tommy always knew.'

'Knew what?'

'When I needed him.'

She could tell there was something else on his mind, but she decided not to press the matter. Instead, she took the conversation in a different direction. 'He always knew my mind before I did,' she said, smiling sadly. 'Even when we were first brought together and hardly got along at all. Somehow he could always look at me and know what I was thinking. I think he found me boring.'

Nate laughed wryly. 'Yes, he did always like a challenge. I think he found you too agreeable at first.'

'Until we were about sixteen. I don't know what changed. One day everything was different. We went home as little more than friends and the next day he wanted to hold my hand.'

'I remember that day,' murmured Nate. 'He came to my place afterwards and told me you smelled nice. Which is true – if you wanted a second opinion. You smell like autumn.'

Catherine blushed. 'What else did he say?'

'Ah, darling, that's between brothers,' he said, winking at her.

'Did he talk about me often?'

Nate nodded. 'Tommy and I had no secrets. Even when he did not agree with something I did or said, he would never let anyone know it. Only me.'

'He defended you at every turn.'

'I know.'

'I've never seen anyone bring out that side of Thom,' she admitted, recalling many occasions when stoic, unflappable Thom would tear his hair out and pace frantically over the state of his brother. The day he had returned from his visit to Redwater to see Nate, after months of bribery and failed attempts, he had gone straight to the bathroom and been sick. He had said nothing the rest of the night. Catherine still did not know what had happened. 'Not even me,' she added, saddened by the realisation. 'We never even fought. Everything was so quiet and still in our home. I miss it.'

'Really?' said Nate, eyebrows raised. 'Now that, darling, sounds terribly boring. Life needs excitement.'

Catherine glared at him. 'It was wonderful.'

'You're telling me that you – fiery, quick-tongued, harsh and analytical, and one of the most intelligent people I've ever met – enjoyed a life without confrontation?'

'Yes.'

Nate snorted.

'What?'

'Nothing.'

'What?' she pressed. 'You don't get to make that sort of stupid noise and then say nothing.'

'I was just wondering if your ability to lie extends to lying to yourself.'

'Don't talk about things you have no understanding of,' she hissed, suddenly feeling defensive. 'My relationship with Thom has absolutely nothing to do with you.'

For a walking skeleton, Nate was suddenly filled with vehemence. 'Your relationship might have nothing to do with me, but darling, ever since the mountains your life has had everything to do with me. I know you better than anyone. I mightn't know your favourite fruit or what your marks in school were, but I know you to the bone. Better even than Tommy; don't doubt that. What, did you think me deaf since you were a child? I've listened to Tommy talk about you since you were Assigned each other. I've listened to everything you've ever said since you started coming by our house. You may have loved him and tolerated me, but I know you. You weren't happy, you were just comfortable. You liked the idea of Tommy and he grew to like the idea of you.'

Without thinking, Catherine punched him. Her fist collided with his jaw and sent him sprawling, pain spiralling up her wrist to her elbow. She scrambled off the bed, seething. 'What gives you the right?'

Nate wiped blood from his lips and chuckled darkly, the blood staining his teeth and giving him a truly vicious air. 'I know a little bit more about life than you do.'

'That's a fierce amount of horse shit,' she spat. 'You know what you know and I know what I know, but it's not more or less than the other. I've lost my family, my friends, my future and my Complement. How can you have the audacity to say that when you know exactly what it is that I have lost?'

'And I've lost all of that and my brother!' he shouted, spit and blood flying from his ruined lips. 'He was mine! Don't be so arrogant as to think you know *anything* of what I feel. I'm simply not blinded enough by grief to paint everything a stupid sunshiny capture of a life that wasn't real.'

'It was real!'

'It was by *law*! Nothing in that world is real!' Nate's chest was heaving. His nose was bleeding freely, and his eyes were reddening with thin, angry veins. He looked like he was boiling from the inside. It was incredibly upsetting to watch and Catherine's eyes burned just looking at him, yet he did not back down, and she refused to ask him to.

'You were a child when you were told that you had to be with him forever. In what world is that love?'

'How *dare* you!'

'Truth hurts, doesn't it, darling?'

Catherine felt hot with rage and wanted to hit him all over again. She had never been so angry with him and there was a small part of her that knew he wasn't saying any of it to hurt her. He was saying it because he believed it to be true, and that made her even angrier.

'I *loved* Thom,' she said emphatically.

'And I don't? Let's not forget that you believe him dead and I still feel him alive. I love Tommy more than anything in this world, the next or any other. He's *my* brother. There's nothing I won't do for him. I came back for him. The place that beat me, imprisoned me and –' He stopped short, deflating. He looked away, panting hard, his fingers reaching out automatically and tapping their rhythm on the shelf beside him. He took several deep breaths before he continued. 'The place I fear more than any other – and I went back. For *him*. He is the one person in this universe that I would go to prison for and only he will ever know the meaning of *that*. You two made the best of a required agreement and that's admirable. Of *course* you love him. He's amazing, Kitty. But there is a stark difference between falling madly in love with someone and loving someone because you have to.'

'Well you don't have to love me,' she retorted. 'You're being forced to by this infection.'

Nate frowned, taken aback. 'That's not true. I loved you before I even knew we were sick.'

Catherine didn't believe him. 'Oh, it's not? You're only here because you have to be, same as myself. We're both here for Thom because he would want us to stick together. To stay alive. That is why we're doing all of this.'

The look of horror on his face almost levelled her. His nearly maroon eyes narrowed shrewdly. 'You have no intention of keeping your word.'

'I'm trying to save your life.'

Nate shook his head as if trying to shake away the truth. Without another word, he stormed out of the room, slamming the door behind him. The silence in his wake was the most deafening sound Catherine had ever heard. She sat down on the bed and stared at the wall, suddenly sorry for having said anything at all. She had too much pride to go and apologise, but she felt wretchedly contrite.

The expression on Nate's face was one she had never wanted to be the cause of, not even when she hated him. Heartbreak was not a feeling she would have wished on her worst enemy, let alone the man who had, amazingly, surprisingly, become her closest friend.

They arrived in Clearbow a week later without much trouble. The place was covered in a fine layer of snow, and only the footpaths near shops were disturbed. Hovers floated above the city of Bridgetown with a gentle hum, and everything was a white, crystalline paradise. It was pretty even if it wasn't real.

Bowans were far more relaxed than the Cuttish crowd yet far less friendly than the Talonites. They kept to themselves, which suited Catherine and her friends wonderfully. No one bothered them as they walked away from the docks towards the inner city.

Evander and Nate found a room in the cheapest, dirtiest location Catherine had ever seen. It was remote and well hidden, and none of them felt much concern at being found. It helped that the innkeeper was so old she was almost blind.

The inn was downtown near Yosef Smith's old residence. A renowned – albeit widely considered mad – scientist, it was not terribly difficult to find his old house and the laboratory he had used after leaving Nitoib decades earlier.

Nate hadn't said more than a few words to her since their fight and more than once Catherine had overheard him getting sick or waking up wheezing, his chest wracked with wet coughs, blood coating his hand where he'd tried to cover his mouth. She wanted to speak with him, and from the corner of her eye, she saw him open his mouth as if to speak to her, but they were both too stubborn and too angry to make the first move.

After two days in Bridgetown everyone decided that a change of appearance was a good idea. Hearing hovers and gliders all night, broadcasts at full volume every time there was news from Cutta, and seeing their faces in shop windows alongside other wanted criminals was incredibly disconcerting. Tove, the least conspicuous, bought dye and makeup, and they spent the next day changing their appearance as much as they could.

Catherine dyed her black hair and eyebrows a shocking shade of white and gritted her teeth as Tove injected her eyes with green to mask the dark maroon they had become. It was a horrible feeling, one that Catherine had never had the desire to undergo despite its popularity, but when she looked in the mirror after, she saw a very different Catherine staring back at her. The light colours changed the entire look of her face, and with small amounts of makeup, Catherine had a feeling that not even her own mother would have recognised her without a closer look.

Nate shaved his head but they didn't dare touch his eyes, which were so bloodshot and watery that everyone worried the slightest change would blind him. Tove and Zoe weren't wanted by any law or authority, nor were their captures in any windows, but after they saw Evander's capture in a shop, wanted for murder in the Southern Lands, Evander agreed to dye his hair and change his eye colour also. Small changes, but most people weren't looking for a group of starving travellers.

Zoe arranged a tour of Smith's old laboratory and they were scheduled to visit the place later that day.

Everyone dressed warmly for the walk, wrapping their heads in scarves and hats, pleased that the cold weather gave them an excuse to hide even more of themselves than they would have been able to in the summertime. It was strange being back in a proper city after so long away. Catherine had grown used to the wild, and she missed the quietude more than she ever thought she would.

Known as Eastwind Research Museum, Yosef Smith's laboratory stood at the edge of town beside the River Calling, which snaked its way through Bridgetown. It was a large, lovely building that was clearly older than any other on the street. The caretaker showed them and fifteen curious visitors inside at precisely three in the afternoon. The siblings were to keep everyone busy downstairs whilst Catherine and Nate snuck up to Smith's old study and see if they could find any helpful information. Catherine had a lock pick and Nate a bolt cutter, but they hoped they wouldn't have to use them. Either would be laughably obvious upon discovery.

It took almost ten minutes of walking through the second storey, examining old pieces of equipment and studying charts, listening to the guide explain Smith's more famous work before they were able to break away, moving as soundlessly as they could through the kitchen.

The layout of the building kept to the same format as every other built in that year, and Nate had spent enough time sneaking out of parties and functions with Blaise, Nadia and Matilda to know the layout like the back of his hand. The dumbwaiter was located beside the large central spinner and was, like so many other places presumed uninteresting, unlocked. Catherine shoved the door open and crawled inside.

Nate pulled her up as quickly as he could and she scrambled out three storeys up. Catherine lowered it from her end and waited until a heavy weight dragged against the rope before using all of her strength to lift Nate up to meet her. As Nate was half his healthy weight, she was able to do it easily enough. He crawled out a few seconds later and they darted through what appeared to be an old bedroom towards the door.

'Where do you think the study is?'

'This floor or upstairs,' he whispered, cracking the door open and squinting into the corridor to make sure there was no one about. 'I'll take upstairs. You go across the hall.'

Catherine nodded. They waited another moment before bracing themselves and hurrying out.

The door to the room across the hall was locked and her heart slammed in her chest as she tried to force it open. It took her a minute to remember the lock pick.

Once inside, Catherine bolted it behind her and turned around. Not daring to turn the light on for fear of being seen, she was still able to find the journals and notebooks and a large computer that looked newer than she would have thought given that Smith had been dead for years.

Creeping across the room, Catherine sat down at the desk, frowning. She touched the mouse and the computer sprang to life, a bright blue box appearing on the screen, awaiting a password.

'Hang,' she cursed. She scratched her cheek, trying to think of a password. The small amount of information she had on Smith would not give her enough to attempt cracking it in the two tries which were allotted on any Council protected system.

The registration was listed as Eastwind Research Museum, but there was a downward facing arrow beside it. Biting her fingernail, she clicked the arrow and scanned the other registrations. Overseer, Summons Medical Centre, Administrator, and then at the very bottom, Redwater Administration Access. She clicked it and with Redwater Administration Access now at the top, a new password was requested.

She drummed her fingers, trying to think of what it could be. Her father worked at Redwater. He was the head of security, the King's advisor and one of the highest ranked members of the Council. The only thing her father cared about aside from Crown and Council was his dog, a small fluffy creature who was almost fifteen years old, Compass was an aging creature who spent most of his days with Mickey at Redwater. Catherine had always been frightened of him. Holding her breath, she typed 'Compass' into the system. It shook and then turned red.

'Fuck. All right.' She ran a hand through her hair, thinking quickly. Her father had given her a passcode once – years ago – for a school project. Gritting her teeth and praying to God that he'd never taken it off, she typed it in with her eyes half-closed.

The page brightened suddenly and she opened her eyes fully. She was on the home screen.

Catherine pumped her fist into the air in delight and quickly went to the system database. She found the index after a quick search and typed in the first thing that came to her mind: *Nitoib*. It came up with almost three hundred results. Biting her lip, she typed *Nitoib – Research Facility*. That came up with just over two hundred results. *Nitoib – War – Facility* yielded fewer, but still too many to work through. She wracked her brain for the names they had found vaguely referenced in Talon and typed *Nitoib – Prisoner – Experiment – Serum*. It produced five results.

Catherine almost yelped in delight. She clicked the first link and skimmed the page. It was an old journal entry from Smith's logs:

> *Entry 36,*
>
> *King Franklin has determined that all courses of upfront warfare have been exhausted and the loss of the Great Kingdom is close at hand. The Radiant Project is our last hope. Crichton's team are focusing on engineering a weapon which we hope will cause mass elimination of the enemy. My own team are tasked with perfecting the prototype of Serum 23.*
>
> *My hope is that Serum 23 will be my legacy, our one true course of winning this Last War. The Serum is in its early stages and will not be ready for warfare for many months – if not years – to come, but the King has given his complete support and funding, and my hope is that there will be no further delays.*
>
> *The first patients will soon be administered with Serum 23.*
>
> *I pray that it goes as planned.*
> *YS*

Catherine clicked on 'Serum 23' and found several dozen more links. Her eyes rapidly searched each one until she found one dated several months later.

Entry 48,

A group of mutants laid waste to one of the facilities this week. Fifty of our subjects were taken and their fates remain unknown.

YS

Intrigued, Catherine clicked on another one.

Entry 62,

It has been eight months since the testing began in Nitoib, a truly desolate landscape that I cannot wait to abandon. Crichton's team were unable to create a toxin for widespread elimination of the mutants. They hoped to magnify the radiation like burns which present themselves upon the skin of the enemy when their flesh touches human flesh. Alas the project came to nothing and has been abandoned.

I have little hope that Serum 23 will prove more fruitful.

There is no life here, no hope. I watch my patients die by the day, and it is becoming harder to convince myself that this is to be my legacy.

From a large selection of five hundred to experiment upon, there are less than a dozen left. Most last no more than two months, some make it three, few enough have made it to four. None have made it longer.

Three of my own scientists have been infected accidentally and we have been forced to research an antidote. As of yet there are no answers, and I fear we may never have any.

We have started to burn the bodies, but I fear it is too late. Word has been sent to the King asking grievous pardon, and for permission to abolish the problem.

I cannot believe the extent of my failure.

YS

Catherine swallowed hard and clicked back to the results page and typed *Serum 23 Antidote* into the search. There was one result. Hands shaking, Catherine clicked the link and read:

Entry 98,

For a few weeks I had hope for Carmilla and Shai. The last of the northern sympathisers who fought for the failed peace talks and were captured amongst a group of mutants. They have been imprisoned nearly five years, and were on the last transport to the facility.

All of the mutant prisoners have died out as a result of the Radiant Project. Carmilla and Shai are the last of the human sympathisers. I don't know if this is a reward or punishment for their sympathy, for the results are not what I expected at all.

I have created no airborne pathogen to rid us all of the mutants, nor have I created super-humans who might battle them. In truth, I hoped for at least one or the other. I have made nothing more than a half-life which neither of them will be allowed to endure under His Majesty's rule.

Carmilla was the first who displayed signs that the mutant infusion had taken hold. I do not know what made her different from all the rest of the failures. We made a few adjustments to the Serum before injecting her, but ten others died from the same infusion, so I cannot say what the difference is. Perhaps if I had more time to study her, I could ascertain the difference, but time is no longer on my side.

Just as we discovered with the mutants when we first brought them here, her skin too now rejects all human touch.

It was during an examination that we realised the very skin under my fingers could almost cook her skin. Her arm blistered and she seemed in excruciating pain for a long time after I released her. Shai, who had been in the corner of the room, ran to her side instantly.

My second anomaly, Shai, survived only because we engineered a vaccine with Carmilla's blood. It took months to engineer, and he had only a few days left before we knew he would rot away like the others.

Just barely, he survived. If one could call it that. They are humans no longer; they are not mutant, either. Some strange mixture of the two who belong in neither world.

It appears they discovered in their bunks that their skin could heal each other. Again, this is a mutant trait.

We have ended the project. A complete disaster. All my mutants are dead; all of my humans either died from the injections or, with a mere two, they adapted the mutant traits to suit their human bodies, but with a high price. Our hope for super-humans came to nothing. We have made half-humans.

All the research will be sent to Anais for further study. What will be known of Serum 23 is unclear, and perhaps someday another, more brilliant scientist will further the research I have undertaken for years now, but I am done. I have seen too much and science tastes like ash in my mouth.

The King has ordered their execution despite the antidote. They know too much. They were sympathisers from the first.

We are to return home disgraced.

Still the war rages on.

YS

Catherine stared at the screen for so long she felt herself going cross-eyed. It was mutant. They had been infected with mutant genes. Catherine looked down at her hands. She held them out in front of her face as if she would suddenly be able to tell the difference. She saw nothing so terribly different, and then a sudden thought struck her. She could see perfectly in the dark. Her stomach twisted into knots as her mind whirled with conclusions and questions that she had never wished to consider.

She felt suddenly violated, wrong. There was something inside of her that should not be there and it was no infection or curse or illness. It was another species.

She wanted to vomit.

Her mind back to that day in Nitoib, after they stumbled out of the mountains, the building that they now knew to be Yosef Smith's testing facility, when she'd noticed the strange hue in Nate's eyes which had never left. Dark grey and piercing, Nate's eyes had been reddish and strange ever since.

Mutants were known to have amber coloured eyes, no sclera or iris visible. They could see perfectly at night-time and seemed more inclined to nocturnal habits than humans. It seemed so obvious now, she wondered why it had never occurred to them before. Her own eyes were no longer brown and had adopted an almost bay tint. She was not dying like Nate, at least not yet, but the changes were obvious.

Catherine reread the passage. As she was not sick, she wondered if that meant she was like Carmilla. If the disease had simply spared her for no other reason than biological randomness. Nate, like the majority of the test subjects, was rejecting the serum and slowly dying as a result, only kept alive because she was continuously healing him. At least there was an explanation.

Four months.

They were cutting it very close. Catherine read the passage once more before wiping the system's memory and slipping from the room. If there was any hope for a cure, it would be in Anais with the rest of Smith's research. It was the only chance they had.

In the corridor outside, Catherine almost ran headlong into Nate. He was breathless and looked close to fainting from sickness, but his face was flushed with adrenaline and there was an air of excitement to him that not even imminent death could expunge.

'It was in Anais the entire time,' he whispered. 'There is an antidote.'

Catherine's heart leapt. 'I read that as well. The journal I found said they used blood to make it.'

He grabbed her hand and pulled her to the side of the corridor, just in case someone wandered up and surprised them. 'I found references to Smith's work at the facility. He concocted an antiviral from the one who was immune to the sickness. It was an add-in to an antiviral they were already testing. She was the missing ingredient, or something to that effect. Copies of all the medications were sent to Anais for checking and referencing and whatnot. There's most likely half a cure waiting in the Diseases Department. We only need to add in you.'

She stared at him, digesting his words.

Nate met her gaze in the darkness, and she was once again reminded that the reason she could see him so clearly was not because her eyesight was impeccable; it was because she had mutant genes melding with her core. It shook her to the bone, but not nearly as much as the realisation they were both silently coming to.

'*Thom.*' Her voice sounded like breaking glass.

Nate pulled her into his chest, his arms wrapping around her.

They stood there in the corner of the corridor, the weight of all that they knew and all they could have done differently threatening to suffocate them.

So many simple moments in life, once looked back upon, seem so very important. And Catherine could not help thinking, even as the guilt of such notions poisoned her soul, that if Nate had simply agreed to go with them that day in Anais, so long ago now it felt more dreamlike than real, then perhaps Thom would still be alive. Perhaps they would never have had to leave. Perhaps none of this would ever have happened.

'Let's get out of here,' he said after what seemed a small eternity.

Catherine followed him quickly into the room, down the dumbwaiter, and back the way they had come. She was so distracted that it was impossible to be aware of much besides the swirling thoughts and images in her head and she was glad that Nate at least seemed to be thinking on his feet.

By the time they were back in the relative comforts of their temporary home, Catherine was shaky and nauseated. She had no desire to speak to anyone, let alone Nate. Excusing herself, she left the group, crawled beneath the large pile of blankets on the sofa, and pulled them over her head. It was reminiscent of a child's thinking that all was safe beneath blankets, but Catherine felt comforted all the same. For the moment, just this one moment, she was going to pretend that so long as she didn't see anything, none of it was real.

When Catherine awoke, it was midmorning and pale winter light was filtering in through the windows. The smell of brewing coffee and hot breakfast was enough to entice her out of her blankets, and she sat up wearily, wiping the strange white strands away from her face and tying her hair into a knot so as not to have to deal with it. She wiped crust from her eyes and squinted tiredly at the kitchen.

Tove and Evander were cooking, Nate was sitting at the table, drinking a cup of coffee and checking the broadcasts on a tablet he had bought from Marsh for a few dozen cuttans; Zoe was staring out the window moodily, her brow furrowed as always.

'Good morning,' said Tove. 'We're making skillet cakes and eggs. You want?'

'Yes to the former, no to the latter,' said Catherine. 'I don't think my stomach could handle eggs with any degree of dignity this morning.'

'Coffee?' said Evander.

'Bless you.' Catherine stood and stretched, cracking her back and glancing out the window. Bridgetown was much quieter than Anais, but after Talon and the ocean, it seemed an alarming ruckus.

She walked to the sink and washed her face thoroughly, rinsing her mouth out with the icy water. Evander handed her a cup of coffee, and she sat down beside Nate at the table, yawning and sniffling in the cold morning.

'Did you find anything of merit last night?' Tove sat down, folding her thin legs beneath her, eyes bright and expectant. 'You still haven't said what happened.'

Catherine nodded. 'We think there may be something in Cutta.'

Tove's face lit up. 'That's wonderful! That's not far from here.'

Evander, who had started doling out the cakes, raised an eyebrow. 'You're going back?'

'Have to,' said Catherine. 'Elsewise Nate will die.'

Nate's eyes darted to her, but she couldn't hold his gaze.

'How much do we all have between us?' asked Evander. He handed her a plate of steaming cakes and placed a jar of honey on the table.

Tove and Nate accepted their breakfasts, and Zoe left her watch by the window to join them. Once everyone was seated around the rickety table, discussion of the next few days began with fervour.

'I have a few thousand left,' said Nate. 'Archie's.'

'We have a little less than that,' said Evander. 'Most of it stolen as well.' He winked at Nate. 'We could buy a hover and make our way to Cutta. Whereabouts are we heading?'

Nate grimaced. 'City centre, Anais. Right near Redwater. We haven't much choice, regrettably.'

'I was hoping you wouldn't say that,' said Zoe.

'As was I,' said Nate. 'There we are.'

Evander pointed a fork at him. 'Explain.'

Nate lit a tocker and gulped down coffee before he began. 'We discovered that we're not sick. Not exactly. It seems that when we were in Nitoib, the place we slept in for the night was an old experimental facility used by King Franklin's scientists during the war. Kitty wasn't wearing shoes, so that's likely what happened. She stepped on a vial that contained the serum and because it went straight through her foot, she was infected. I got cut cleaning out the wound, so that's that determined.

'It seems initially they wanted to see different things; ways to win the war that circumvented battle. Cheating, if we're being blunt. They discovered at some point that mutant skin was sensitive to human touch. That any contact with us would burn their flesh. Like radiation burns. Somehow, over the years when the rest of our kind were hiding underground after the Devastation, the mutants evolved differently. They're not quite human, not quite anything else. We don't know how or why they evolved like that, but they did. Our touch harmed them, which really ought to have been enough. It wasn't. Still they were faster, keener of sight. They could heal each other. All of this and potentially more.

'I don't think anyone ever discovered the full extent of their abilities because harnessing their visible ones was more beneficial to humans.' Here Nate snorted in disgust. 'Yosef Smith, the leader of this facility, pitched to good King Franklin that he could harness the mutants' abilities for humans. Could enhance humanity, if you will. Only mutant genes aren't meant to mesh with humans', so the bodies of the patients started to rot from the inside out. They were incompatible with each other. The human hosts were poison to the mutant genes and started attacking them. Almost everyone died.

'Towards the end of the experiment, Smith noticed two things. First, it took – maximum – four months for the disease to kill the host; second, one of his test subjects was immune. I don't think he ever knew why. Just one of those things, I suppose. The way some people never died of Plague even when their whole family's infected; how some people never get cancer, no matter how much they smoke. Lucky. If you could call it that. One woman, Carmilla, managed to withstand the injections and they realised that her touch was a temporary cure for their only other surviving patient, who was dying of the disease and was almost out of time. They created an antibiotic of sorts with her blood, and something in her system not only inhibited the development of the mutant pathogen, it cured them both of the burning and saved his life. Whether it got rid of the healing abilities or the eye-sight or whatever else, is unclear. They never bothered to continue testing.

'Smith presented the results to the King. He had saved two of his hundreds. But Franklin wasn't impressed and there was not enough to warrant continuing the programme, so everything – including Carmilla and Shai, the other patient – was destroyed. They never bothered to see what else had been achieved. If anything else could have been achieved. It was all tossed.'

Nate finished his story, his thin face drawn tight with anger and contemplation.

'Humans really are a blight on creation,' said Evander, lip curling.

Nate nodded and slowly, without much enthusiasm, ate his cakes. His nose had started bleeding again and every few seconds he had to wipe his face with a napkin that was steadily becoming the colour of rust. Catherine reached out and put a hand on his shoulder. After a minute, his nose stopped bleeding and the tiniest flushes of colour returned to his flesh. She left her hand protectively on his shoulder as he returned to eating.

'So you've how long left?' said Zoe.

'A few weeks,' said Nate. 'Not long.'

'But you'll be fine!' cried Tove. 'We're not going to let you die.'

Nate gave her a grateful smile. 'You sure about that, darling?'

Tove nodded without a trace of uncertainty. 'I know it.'

Catherine wished she had Tove's conviction.

'So that means,' said Evander, looking to Catherine, 'you're the one who's immune.'

'I suppose. Haven't a notion why.'

'It's curious. Both were women. Perhaps there's something to that.'

Catherine shrugged. 'I'm still trying not to get sick knowing I've mutant inside of me.'

Nate arched an eyebrow. 'Why?'

'Mutants are disgusting,' she said. 'Rabid creatures who attack anyone and everything.'

'That's hardly true,' he argued. 'How can you think that?'

'Given the evidence we've been presented with, it's true. Did you sleep through school? What am I saying, of course you did.'

'Given the evidence we've been presented with, King Markas could do no ill and I ought to be beaten to death,' said Nate acidly. 'Or have you forgotten that everything you've ever been taught is a blatant lie spewed by those who wish to keep you complacent and passive in your plush little cage?'

Whether it was the burning violation that had ignited within her upon reading what it was, exactly, that had happened, or because of the realisation that Thom had died for nothing, or simply because she was exhausted and bitter and angry and scared, Catherine found herself arguing the point, never mind the fact that she completely agreed with Nate.

'Not everything they've said is a lie,' she said. 'Some of it is true.'

'Like what?'

'It's not as if we've been beaten into a life we didn't want. We allowed for these things to happen to us. We allowed King Franklin to seize control. We allowed King Markas to take his place. We stood by and watched it all happen. If someone wanted to disagree with him, they ought to've done it then.'

'I think the several million who died as a result of Plague and war and assassination and genocide are certain to agree with you.'

'Two men, Nate. *Two*. How hard do you think it could be to get rid of them?'

'Clearly it's very hard as no one's been able to thus far!'

'Well maybe someone ought to try if they're so unhappy!'

'Why the fuck do you think I was arrested? What do you think I was doing all those months with the Underground? Tap dancing?'

'It's not my fault you were so inept that you got nothing accomplished. Perhaps someone with more intelligence would've been able to get something done!'

'And perhaps the rest of the Kingdom is infected with the same useless stupidity that you so happily coat yourself in!'

'Go hang yourself, Nate!'

'I've tried that already, darling. Clearly God wants me to stick around and annoy you for eternity.'

'No, just another couple of weeks.' She regretted the words the second she said them. 'Nate –'

He was already shoving back from the table. The hurt on his face made her chest constrict. Without a word, he stormed out the front door, slamming it so hard behind him that everyone at the table flinched.

'I'll go,' said Evander, jumping to his feet and grabbing Nate's coat, disappearing out the door after him.

Catherine grabbed a cigarette from Nate's box on the table and rubbed her eyes tiredly. 'I didn't mean it,' she muttered. 'I'm just so angry at everything.'

'I know,' said Zoe. 'We all say stupid things.'

Unhappy with herself and feeling sick with guilt and fury, Catherine left the table, returning to her corner of the small room, hoping Evander would find Nate quickly and bring him back. He was so weak that walking around without a coat could surely kill him.

It was over an hour before Nate and Evander returned. Nate was shaking badly and his ears were bleeding, but it was his hands that drew her attention. His knuckles were an ode to his anger, and had clearly borne the brunt of his rage. He ignored her and instead walked directly towards the bathroom, closing the door behind him. The sound of running water followed a minute later.

'He's all right,' said Evander. He looked pointedly at Catherine. 'That wasn't kind.'

'I know,' she said, chastised.

Evander nodded and walked over to his siblings.

Catherine stood and went to the bathroom door. She knocked once and opened it slowly. 'May I come in?'

'Go away.'

She walked inside and closed the door. Nate was standing in front of the mirror, his hands on either side of the sink. He had taken his shirt off and she could see just how much of a skeleton he was becoming. His skin was completely covered in bruises and there were sores like a butterfly's spots all over him, infected and crusty. His bones were sticking out and his veins looked like a map of rivers. It was a miracle he was standing at all.

'I was an arsehole,' she said without preamble. 'I didn't mean it. I was angry.'

'And I'm not? You think I'm having fun? All of this – all of this is torture. This disease. You. Tommy. Fuck, Tommy.' Nate was gripping the sink so tightly she heard his knuckles crack. 'I want to die, Kitty. All I want is to die. I'm so tired.'

His words terrified her. 'I'm sorry, all right? I'm sorry. It wasn't fair. I apologise. Truly.' She stepped closer and reached out. He cringed at her touch but did not move away. She took one of his ruined hands in her own and held it carefully. Slowly, the way a kettle boils, warmth spread from her hand into his, and the skin on his knuckles started to mend.

Nate let out a sigh and looked at her. His eyes were full of unshed tears, and his jaw was clenched.

'I don't want you to die,' she said softly.

'Don't you?' he croaked. 'It's what I deserve, isn't it? If Tommy's dead, then I – then I killed him. I'm the reason he's gone. I let my fear take over everything. None of this would have happened if I'd've just gone to that bloody appointment. Even if they put me in the worst sort of prison – put me in the darkness forever – it'd be all right because Tommy would be alive and *here*.'

His face was contorted with anguish and he let out a strangled sob. Catherine stepped closer and wrapped her arms around him.

It was then she realised that she was stronger than him. Nate had withered away before her eyes. Since she was twelve years old, Catherine had always seen Nate as hulking, impossible to hold back or hinder. He had always been larger than life – obnoxiously so. Something to fight that would always fight back.

She had relied so heavily on that assumption.

Nate clung to her as he sobbed, his entire body racked and trembling. How long they stood there in the centre of the bathroom, clinging to each other, Catherine didn't know. All she knew was that she could not leave him. She held him as he cried, hoping that his skin would soak up as much from her proximity as it could.

Sometime later, when Nate had cried himself out and all the superficial cuts and wounds on his body had healed from her touch, they finally broke apart. He still looked like walking death, albeit somewhat better, and was able to step into the bath without help, his eyes hooded and red-rimmed, blood dribbling from his nose, ears, and from around the fingernails that seemed to be close to rotting off and falling away.

Catherine sat on the floor beside the bath, gazing at the wall as he washed. They didn't speak for a long time. Sometimes, when there are too many things to say, the best way to say everything is to say nothing at all.

She watched him, he watched her, and when they returned to the siblings, both felt infinitely better about the other.

Two days later, they were packed and on their way to Anais. It was strange to be returning to a place they had fled from, and the closer they flew, the more Catherine's stomach twisted and turned. She sat beside Nate in the front, the three siblings in the back.

A strange calm had settled between Catherine and Nate following their argument and subsequent reconciliation. She had forced all thoughts of Thom from her mind. There was nothing else to be done. Thom was dead and Nate was all she had left of him. Holding onto what could have been would only drive her to madness.

Thus, with as much resolution as she could muster, Catherine reaffirmed her loyalty to Nate inside her own mind and determined that the next few days would see him cured and the five of them on their way to the Wall and the Outlands beyond.

Far below them, the countryside of Cutta stretched wide and uninhabited. There was nothing very old to see. Catherine assumed that whatever had existed before the Devastation had looked similar, but she could only guess what life was like in the Outlands. Hundreds of years of growth following the Devastation; it could look like anything.

Suddenly curious, she posed the question to Nate, turning the music from the broadcast down as she did so.

'Definitely different,' he said. 'Standing on top of the Wall and looking at both sides is the strangest feeling. You can *see* the difference.'

'How so?'

'Well, the grass is only green in some places in the Outlands,' he said. 'Some places it's red, others it's white. There are flowers of brown and black, not just red or pink or yellow or blue. The animals don't look like the animals we have here. I mean, some do. Some are completely normal. But others are much different. Everything's changed, evolved. Nothing's been hampered by humanity or stopped by industry. It's a world where evolution was forced to adapt very quickly. The dogs and cats and horses and whatever else that hid beneath the ground with us and stayed the same did not do so above ground amidst the radiation and destruction. Some things died out in the wild, others adapted and became completely different. The plants, the animals, the smells. It's hard to believe it until you see it, but it's all new.' He smiled at some memory. 'It's all free.'

'Sounds wonderful,' said Tove, sitting forwards. 'Are there any green animals?'

Nate grinned at her. 'Haven't seen any.'

'You wouldn't, would you? Green animals would blend into the grass.'

'Not if the grass was red.'

She said, 'I really want a green pony.'

Everyone laughed.

'I'm glad we met you guys,' she added, beaming at them. 'I wanted my parents back, but I got a new brother and sister instead. It's almost as good.'

Catherine was stunned. She searched for words and found that she had none adequate enough. 'I always wanted a sister too,' she murmured. 'And now I've got two and a brother.'

Evander leaned forwards. 'How can you not have siblings? It's the law.'

'My father was groomed by King Franklin for the position he holds now,' she explained. 'He fought in the last of the war; he helped make Redwater what it is. He was never going to have a child at all but King Markas wanted everyone to set an example. So he and my mother had me. They never wanted another.'

'Because you're more than enough,' said Nate, winking at her.

Catherine snorted.

'And your parents?' said Evander, glancing at Nate. 'Only two?'

'There was a girl,' said Nate softly. 'Long before I was born. Alicia. She died after only a year. My mother had a stillborn after that. And then me. And then Tommy. She and the King are friends enough that he told her she had done her duty.'

'We had two other siblings,' said Evander. 'Life has a way of doing things we cannot expect or understand.'

A thoughtful silence fell in the hover and the next few hours passed quietly, only broken when a well-known favourite song came over the broadcast and Tove turned it up, insisting everyone sing along.

By nightfall they had travelled through most of Cutta and were near enough to Anais to carry on, but as no one felt like creeping around in the dark, they all agreed to camp.

Nate landed the hover in the wilderness a half hour's flight from the city. Under the protection of dense foliage, they started a fire and curled up around its warmth for the night.

They all slept badly, too full of anxiety and questions about the following day. Zoe, for instance, wanted to know exactly how they planned on getting the antidote without being caught and having no way of accessing the Diseases Department.

'I have an idea as to how to get the antidote,' said Nate. 'I'm not too sure about the mixing aspect, however.'

Catherine raised an eyebrow. 'How are we getting in?'

'We're not,' said Nate.

'Oh, thank God. What are we doing?'

'I know someone who may help. I'll contact him when we reach the city.'

Evander looked surprised. 'Who?'

'An old friend,' said Nate. 'He tipped me off about the guards coming to snatch us, so it's not outside the realm of reason to think he'll help with this as well. He won't want me dead. He's kept me alive this long.'

That piqued Catherine's interest. In the wake of Thom's death, she had been too overcome with grief and horror to enquire further as to the mysterious conn which saved them.

'As for the rest of it,' said Nate before anyone could ask any more questions, 'I've a thought to that as well.'

'What?' she asked.

'My mother,' he said, lip curling. 'She knows almost as many people in the bloody Kingdom as good King Markas. As irritated and disappointed in me as she may be, she hasn't wanted me dead yet. It's worth a try.'

Zoe sat forwards. 'Do you trust her?'

'I trust that she doesn't want me to die,' said Nate. 'Past that …
I'm not too sure of anything.'

'She did used to get you out of all kinds of trouble with Crown
and Council,' said Catherine.

'Exactly.'

'What if she goes to the King?' said Zoe.

'She won't,' said Nate. 'My father, on the other hand, would make
the executioner his first stop.'

'That's awful,' said Evander quietly.

'Hamish Anteros never did enjoy my presence,' said Nate,
shrugging. He lit a tocker and smoked nonchalantly. 'After twenty-
four years, I don't mind.'

'You've never been close?'

'As close as a wolf is with a rabbit.'

Evander's expression darkened. 'You're nothing like him.'

'No,' said Nate, handing him the smoking tocker. 'Many thanks
to God for that.'

'What about you, Kit?' said Tove, smiling uncertainly at
Catherine. 'Are you close with your parents?'

Catherine shrugged, her lips pursed. 'My father was never
around much. I used to be so much like my mother, and I suppose
we were close once, but now that I think about it, she was always
away. Most of my youth was spent either at Nate and Thom's house,
at school, or with minders or nannies.'

'One of the benefits of a life of poverty is that your parents can't
afford to bring someone else in, I suppose,' said Evander. 'It's a pity
there seems to be very little middle ground between the two.'

'Amen,' said Nate. 'I can't wait to get out of this godforsaken
Kingdom once and for all.'

'Will you miss it?' said Tove.

'No,' he said. 'Not even a little bit.'

Anais looked the same as always, which surprised Catherine. For
some reason she had expected everything to change in her absence.

The light-coloured houses, all carved from stone; the clean streets with clean shops displaying the most current in fashion, technology and the arts; the crystalline river which flowed through the centre, cutting the city in two; the hovers high above the streets, humming softly as the citizens walked below. None of it had changed.

Nate parked on the edge of town near an abandoned house and they all climbed out. With Nate bald and thin, a shadow of his former self; Catherine blonde and green-eyed, looking more like one of the Reddish dancers than her normal dark coloured self; and the siblings in varying degrees of disguise, they wouldn't be instantly recognisable on the street. Nonetheless, they kept a low profile and took the streets less travelled by, hoping it would keep them safe.

The further they walked, the more anxious Nate became, until he reached out tentatively and took her hand. He glanced at her, his eyes uncertain and worried. Catherine squeezed his hand in solidarity and he seemed to find renewed strength.

A fierce wind picked up as they reached the river, and they all drew up their hoods. A public conn by the boardwalk stood empty, only a few people braving the icy weather, and Nate approached it after a quick glance around. His fingers tapped in a code and he gave Catherine a tight smile as he waited. All communications were monitored by the Council and there were reels everywhere, recording their every move.

'Captain Sikander,' he said a moment later. 'Tell him it's Nate ... Thank you.' There was a long silence and Nate's fingers tapped on the wooden pole in an old practised rhythm of anxiety. When he stopped, she knew that someone had answered. 'Hallo, Cooper ... Would you meet me for a drink this evening? I have a few things to discuss ... Of course ... Excellent ... Goodbye, Captain.' Nate ended the conversation and turned the conn off. He grabbed Catherine's hand and led her down the boardwalk at a brisk but controlled pace.

'Is he meeting you?'

'Tonight at Dark Corners,' said Nate. 'Let's get out of this bloody cold.'

'Where are we going?' asked Evander, falling into step beside them. Zoe was holding Tove's hand a few steps behind them.

'My mother hasn't changed the code to her second house in ten years,' said Nate. 'We'll go there.'

A dozen ugly worries reared their heads and Catherine glanced at him, brows knitting together with nerves. 'Are you sure?'

'No,' he said bluntly.

They made their way through the streets, eyes on the ground when they passed near enough to other people that their faces might be recognised. Twice Catherine saw people she used to know and drew her hood down lower, hoping to disguise herself.

It took them about twenty minutes to reach Cecily's second house; a beautiful, expensive home on a street with bright flowers, kept alive despite the harsh winter weather by gardeners paid more than the businessmen of any other country. The pulchritude of the bright flowers was strangely fitting against the untouched snow.

Nate typed in the code carefully and pushed the door open.

Catherine's heart was hammering as Nate told them to wait and he walked around the house first to make sure that no one was home. He returned a minute later with a satisfied nod.

'Who's hungry?'

'Me,' said Evander. 'Should I make us something?'

Nate nodded. 'That would be wonderful. I'm going to change into something a little less ill-fitted. I can hardly go into an Anaitian pub looking like this. Ladies, you can have whatever you fancy from my mother's closet.'

Buoyed by the prospect of wearing decent clothing that was both clean and sized correctly, Catherine followed Nate up the winding stairs. While Zoe declined, Tove brightened at the opportunity to don rich clothing and raced up the stairs after her. Nate excused himself into one of the bedrooms and bolted the door, pointing down the corridor towards another bedroom.

It was slightly smaller than Catherine's childhood room, albeit very grand, and from Tove's expression, the nicest place the girl had ever set her eyes upon. They both took turns in the heavenly bath before removing various items from Cecily's wardrobe and trying on different outfits.

Tove pulled a bright green dress on and held up her arms. 'What do you think?'

'You're a vision,' said Catherine. She had donned a black bodysuit with a low neckline. Cecily had always been thin, and months ago Catherine would never have been able to fit into any of her garments, but life on the road had left her tiny and Cecily's clothing was now almost too big for her. The bodysuit fit well, however, and she pulled on soft leather boots that went up to her knees, leaving her feeling secure and stable. She tied the odd white hair out of her eyes and made a face at her reflection. It was certainly not a shade which suited her dark features.

Upon closer examination, she saw that the amber colour was beginning to overtake the green dye, as if the mutant genes were determined to make themselves known. Not sure what to make of that, Catherine looked away.

Something caught her eye on the mantle as she appraised her reflection, and she stepped forwards, picking up a capture of Thom and Nate. They could not have been more than twenty and sixteen respectively, both boyish and handsome, their smiles broad and untarnished. Nate's arm was around his little brother, and he was smiling at Thom rather than at the capturist.

'They really do look alike,' said Tove, walking up behind her.

'I thought they were twins as a child,' said Catherine.

Tove picked up another capture. This one was of Thom with the King. 'Nate told me that he started hating the King when he was a child but Thom never did,' she said. Her fingers traced over Thom's face as she spoke. 'I wonder why. Why him and not Thom? Or you?'

'I wonder as well. I've been wondering for months, actually.'

'Have you come to any conclusions?'

'A few,' she said. 'None of them particularly conclusive. Hamish hated Nate from the first, yet he doted on Thom. I haven't a notion as to why; usually firstborns are the favourite. Isn't that always the case? I never wanted to ask Thom specifics. Perhaps it was because

Thom looked most like Hamish, whereas Nate only looked like Thom, if that makes sense. You could see the father in Thom, but only the brother in Nate. Genetics are fickle. For whatever reason, Hamish chose Thom to love and Nate to loathe, and they became the product of contrasting childhoods. When you've been rejected by nothing, I suppose it's easy to enjoy life. I had no reason to doubt my father until I left home and realised how many things had been adjusted to my own worldview. Nate was never sheltered as Thom and I were. When Thom did something wrong he was merely reprimanded and would never do it again. Whenever Nate did something wrong, he was rebuked. If Hamish wanted to dampen Nate's spirit, his abuse certainly had the opposite effect.'

'Do you think Nate would have rebelled if his father had liked him more?'

Catherine nodded, smiling fondly at the capture. 'I think Nate was always destined to rebel. Perhaps if Hamish had loved him more, it would not have been in the same manner, but I don't think Nate was ever destined to a life that would be approved of by Crown and Council.'

'Why?'

Catherine shrugged. 'Thom and I always took everything at face value. We were easy to please. The only person who ever brought out extremes in us was Nate. He enjoyed it; being the only person who could. I think he loved that he could do that when no one else could. My love for Thom was the product of years of affection, loyalty and togetherness. A love grown from care and tending. I loved him as anyone would love someone so good, so handsome, so pure and kind. There's a lot to be said about consistency. But I never felt anything truly extreme for Thom until his death. Now I don't really know what or how I feel. It's all so muddled with everything else that's going on. And Nate – Nate's always loved extremes. He feels things to the bone. He loves few enough because when he loves it's consuming, violent, unending. I think he hates his feelings as much as he needs them to carry on. It's impossible to feel so strongly about things without them being the death of you.'

Tove pursed her lips, nodding, and returned the capture to where it was. 'I think it's good, though. It suits him.'

'It does. It also ensured that he would never suit this Kingdom. This is not a society for extremes.'

'No,' said Tove. 'I suppose not.'

'Come on,' said Catherine. 'Let's see if Evander's finished making food.'

Downstairs, Evander had set to work, and there was a large assortment of food awaiting them. All of it smelled wonderful. Catherine piled her plate high with lamb, buttered bread, steamed vegetables with spicy sauce, and a large glass of Cecily's finest wine. She had just tucked in when Nate appeared.

'You look amazing,' said Tove, coughing on her lamb, staring at him with wide eyes.

Evander nodded in agreement, and even Zoe looked surprised.

Catherine turned around and swallowed hard, trying not to choke on her wine. Nate was wearing a dark suit that was likely Hamish's. He had a black hat on that covered up his baldness, and had darkened his eyebrows to black. He could easily have been Thom. He caught Catherine's eye and smirked.

'That good?' he said.

'Better,' said Tove. 'If I liked men, I would fall in love with you.'

'Well, that's the best compliment I could have received. Thank you, my darling.'

Tove beamed at him.

'You look handsome,' said Catherine at length.

'Thank you,' said Nate. He seemed to take her words to heart and walked over to them, pouring himself a glass of wine.

'How are you feeling?' said Evander. 'I thought I heard you getting sick.'

Nate waved his hand. 'I'm fine. It's only a touch of death.'

'Come here,' said Catherine, holding out her hand.

'It doesn't help for long. What's the point?'

'It helps a little,' she argued. 'It's better than nothing. You can't go out there if you're barely standing.'

'Rotten apples still roll,' he said, although he took her hand gratefully, and sighed as colour started to fill his death-white cheeks, warmth spreading from her touch.

The siblings watched as Nate was returned to somewhat decent shape. His skin felt fragile, paper thin, as if it would rip with the slightest pull, and she could see veins snaking their way up his neck, barely hidden by his high collar.

'You're going to be fine,' she said with conviction. 'We're so close.'

Nate winked tiredly at her. 'I'm the only one who kills me, darling.'

'Good,' she said. 'I'm holding you to that.'

It seemed to take an age for the evening to arrive and by the time it did Catherine almost wished it had taken longer still. She didn't like Nate disappearing into the night with no protection or backup, but he refused to let anyone come.

'Cooper's saved my life,' he said. 'He's not going to turn me in.'

Curious to know what that meant but not having the time to ask, Catherine watched him go with trepidation. Evander stood beside her in the doorway.

'Do you think he knows what he's doing?' she wondered aloud.

'I think he'll do whatever he can to keep you safe,' said Evander. 'And he doesn't trust anyone but himself to keep you alive. So yes, I think he knows what he's doing.'

Only somewhat reassured, Catherine sat in the window, watching the street outside and smoking neurotically as she waited for Nate to return. It felt far too much like waiting for Thom not to make her want to be sick everywhere. As she watched, all the lights in the house off so that no one would see them inside, Catherine glimpsed fragments of the life she had left behind so recently. Mothers with their children, students with their bags, Complements walking side by side down the street. This was a world without poverty, without fear or hunger. It was a lie, she knew that now, but watching it unfold once again made her wistful for the life that had been snatched from her by complete accident.

Evening melted into night and night crept into dawn, and still Nate did not return. Tove joined Catherine at her perch, her youthful face drawn tight with unspoken worry. Catherine desperately wanted to reach out and hold her hand.

By morning, Evander sat on the ground at their feet, his foot tapping in agitation. Zoe picked up a pacing routine and kept it up for more than an hour.

It was nearly noon when Nate's form appeared at the top of the street. He made for the front door quickly, and Catherine wrenched it open before he even raised his hand, ushering him inside.

'I'm sorry it took so long,' he said without preamble. 'We decided not to delay.'

'What does that mean?' said Catherine and Evander at the same time.

Nate held up a small box, a triumphant grin on his face. 'Cooper had his morning shift and managed to get it from a friend who works in the stockroom and owed him a favour.'

'My God,' said Catherine, completely stunned. 'We've got it.'

'Almost,' said Nate. 'Now I've to conn my mother and see if she'll help.'

'She will,' said Catherine. 'I know she will.'

Nate's ruddy eyes were bright with hope and excitement, and suddenly he was embracing her, his depleted energy heightened by the recent success. Catherine wrapped her arms around him and hugged him tightly, so delighted that he'd returned safely that, at least for a moment, all worry was forgotten.

'I'm exhausted,' said Nate. 'Don't know if I could sleep, though.'

'I'll make coffee,' said Evander. 'We've been up all night waiting for you. We could do with some as well.'

'Thank you.' Nate cocked his head up the stairs, indicating that Catherine follow him, and they headed up to one of the bedrooms. Nate sat down on the edge of the bed and gazed tiredly up at her. 'I didn't think that would work,' he admitted.

Catherine sat beside him. 'Your friend, Cooper ...'

'What about him?'

'How do you know him?'

'He worked in Redwater,' said Nate. 'He kept an eye on me.'

'Family friend?'

'No ...' Nate sighed and rubbed his neck. His ears were bleeding again and there was an ugly patch of sores at the base of his neck.

She reached out and touched the blisters. They receded hesitantly under her fingers. 'What then?' she asked, hoping to distract him.

'He's one of the King's men, but he's not evil. He saw a young man brought in and almost whipped to death and I think he took pity on me. He visited me in the infirmary to see that I was alive. After that, every few days, he would bring me an extra bit of food or something to read. For months that was all. Nothing more or less, just little fragments of kindness. I clung to those with every fibre of my being.' Nate rested his chin on his hands and shrugged. 'One day, a few of the guards decided that I was owed more punishment. Anyone else in my position would have been killed on the spot. They saw me as a rich bastard who thought he could get away with everything. Perhaps I did. I don't really remember.

'After,' he continued, croaking slightly on the words, 'I strung myself up. It wasn't even hard. Bedsheets are remarkably strong, you know? I don't know whether Cooper was going to check on me because he knew what happened or if he simply happened to be passing by, but he found me. Cut me down and saved my life. I think he stayed the whole night. I sat in a corner and waited for death. He never left me. He changed to the night shift and came by my cell every hour. More than once I heard him call them off. I heard him almost start a fight defending me. When I say that I trust him, I mean that with more conviction than you could ever imagine.'

'No,' said Catherine, taking his hand. 'I know exactly that kind of trust. I have that much in you.'

They sat, holding hands, until Evander called up that the coffee was ready, and Nate changed into more comfortable garments and followed Catherine down the stairs slowly, each step an effort for his weakening bones.

After the coffee, Nate smoked about ten cigarettes in quick, stressed succession before he finally picked up the conn on the wall and entered his mother's registration. His fingers tapped the counter nervously as he waited. Catherine could tell the moment Cecily answered, for Nate's entire body stiffened, and his voice, so deep and sarcastic most of the time, was suddenly softer, audibly worried.

'It's me,' he murmured. 'I need to see you … Your house.' He said nothing else and ended the conversation abruptly. 'She'll be here in a few minutes,' he said to the rest of them. 'Ev, Zoe, Tovy – if you three could make yourselves scarce, it might be for the best. She'll know I'm with Kitty; there's no need to expose the rest of you.'

The siblings wished them luck and disappeared up the stairs to wait. Catherine sipped her fifth cup of coffee nervously. She had not seen Cecily since a few days before she and Thom went to Nitoib. They had been discussing the binding. It seemed so long ago now; another lifetime. Too much had happened in so short a time.

Catherine barely had time to contemplate her feelings of guilt when the door opened and in walked Cecily.

A tall, fearsome woman in her day, Cecily Anteros was still a sight to behold even now in her mid-sixties. She commanded the attention of anyone who watched, and although not necessarily pretty, she was striking and attractive, even after the loss of a son. Her hair, once as black as Thom's, was now dark violet, her eyes the same slate grey as Nate's had been, her chin pointed and defined, her eyebrows thick and well groomed. Even entering her twilight years, Cecily commanded the attention of everyone in the room when she entered. It was no wonder Nate had managed to get away with as much as he had. Anyone coming up against Cecily was either very brave or very stupid.

She surveyed them both the moment she entered, her gaze taking in the sight of their dyed hair, their malnourished bodies; Nate's thin and crumbling frame. She let out a small gasp and walked straight to her son as if no time had passed. Hamish's relationship with his son was bizarre in contrast.

'Nathanial!' she cried, reaching out to touch his bony face, the dried blood in his nostrils and the corners of his eyes giving him a truly corpselike appearance, only to stop when Nate recoiled. 'What have you done to yourself?'

'Hallo, Mother,' he said. 'Thank you for coming.'

'It's wonderful to see you, Mistress Anteros,' said Catherine uncomfortably.

Cecily looked at her. 'Oh, Catherine, darling. You look so different!'

'Mother,' said Nate. 'I don't have a lot of time.'

'What do you mean? What is going on?'

'I'm sick – dying, as it happens.'

Cecily's perfect, well-composed face fell. 'Dying?'

'It's the reason we ran,' said Nate matter-of-factly. It did not seem to touch him that his mother cared whether he lived or died. 'We were infected in the mountains. I've managed to find a way to reverse the infection. We need help.'

Nothing could surprise her after a lifetime of fixing the errors of the men in her life. Cecily nodded, poured herself a large glass of wine, and listened to Nate's abridged version of everything that had happened. It was a well spun story, with enough truth to make the lie sound believable. Catherine was impressed.

'I've only a week or so left,' he finished, and the edge to his voice told Catherine that now he was putting on no airs. 'We need help.'

Cecily stood and brushed her hands together in thought. 'All right. I will see what can be done.' She looked from Nate to Catherine. 'You should know that I've come from the King's palace and he questions me frequently as to whether or not I've heard from you. I have never been a good liar.'

'Then don't see him,' said Nate. 'Help us and then tell him if you must. We'll be gone before there's any chance of capture.'

'Catherine, might I have a minute with my son?'

'Of course.' Catherine stood, giving Nate a small smile, and went to sit on the sofa in the adjacent room. She heard the low murmur of conversation begin anew betwixt mother and son, but she forced herself not to listen. Cecily hadn't seen Nate since before Thom's death. There were likely a thousand private things she wanted to say to him.

Catherine twisted and untwisted her hands as she waited. When the tension became too much, she lit one of Nate's cigarettes and smoked anxiously until Nate and Cecily appeared in the doorway.

'I will see you in a few hours,' said Cecily, nodding to her. She glanced one more time at her only remaining son before she pulled up the hood of her cloak and walked gracefully out the front door.

Nate sat down beside Catherine. 'She's going to help.'

'It's a wonder how everyone just does what you want,' said Catherine, although she was insanely relieved to hear that Cecily was aiding them.

'Trust me, darling, hardly anyone does what I want,' he said.

Catherine raised an eyebrow. 'Is that so?'

'True enough, but I would hate it if you did as I said.'

She couldn't help the smirk that twitched her lips. 'Why is that?'

He said, smile wicked, 'Fighting with you is one of the greatest parts of my life.'

Catherine laughed and leaned back against the cushions. 'I just want all of this to be over with. I want to be able to touch people again, I want to be able to brush against someone without having burns coat my body. I want you to be healthy and whole. It breaks my heart every time I look at you.'

Nate leaned back beside her. 'I am utterly irresistible on a good day, aren't I?'

'Good to see death hasn't humbled you,' she said wryly, her heart relaxing at his banter. It reassured her to see him acting more like his old self.

He chuckled. There was a wheezing edge to his laugh. She didn't know when that had started, let alone become normal. 'Seeing my mother is certainly strange. Last time I saw her was the day I was released from Redwater. She held a party in my honour. As if cakes and wine made up for prison.'

A bubble of blood appeared in Nate's nose, and suddenly his nose was bleeding profusely. He doubled over, coughing and spluttering, his hands clutching his head in agony. He forced himself to his feet and staggered into the kitchen. He turned on the water and rinsed out his mouth, washing the blood from his colourless face.

Catherine stepped up behind him and placed her hand on the back of his neck. As ever, he seemed to heal somewhat, but the deep purple bruises did not recede and his lips were stained with blood. He was so thin and skeletal looking, even his eyelashes seemed to be falling out.

'Is there anything I can do?'

He was gripping tightly to the sink; his body convulsing. 'I'm fine,' he grunted. 'It's nothing.'

'Nate, it's clearly not nothing.'

'I've heard that it's in bad taste to argue with the dying.'

'You're not dying. Stop that. What do you need?'

'Just don't go anywhere.'

'I won't,' she promised. 'I'm not going anywhere.'

Nate let go of the sink and turned around. She wanted to look away; the mere sight of him stung her eyes and brought a lump to her throat, but she forced herself to show none of this. Instead, she reached out and touched his face. As she watched, the smallest of flushes spread from beneath her hand, across his cheek and down his neck. The sudden appearance of colour was startling.

'I love you,' he whispered.

'I know you do.'

He nodded and closed his eyes. They stood there until Nate's heart stopped slamming, and she helped him back to the sofa. It seemed that the night with Cooper and the conversation with Cecily had taken the last of his reserves from him. He collapsed on the cushions, breath coming in ragged gasps. Catherine pulled a blanket over him and went to retrieve the siblings still hiding upstairs.

It was early evening when Cecily returned with a short, balding man. He carried a heavy case with him, and had a shrewd, ratty face. Catherine didn't trust him for a second.

'This is Mister Grigory,' said Cecily. 'He will help.'

'Good evening,' said Grigory. He surveyed the lot of them before his eyes quickly found Nate. 'I take it you are the one that is dying.'

Nate raised an eyebrow. 'What gave it away?'

'May I see the antidote that you have?' he asked, sitting pompously on an adjacent chair.

Catherine took the vial from Nate and handed it over carefully.

Grigory appraised her. 'Are you the one who is also infected?'

'Yes,' she said.

'All right,' said Grigory. 'I will need some time to study this.'

Nate fixed him with a curious look. 'Where do you work?'

'The Diseases Department,' he answered. 'I am one of the leading scientists. I have been researching Smith's creations since I finished school. He was very close to succeeding and in the years since we have made a great deal of progress in recreating his work. We have merely lacked the subjects to test it.'

Catherine and Nate exchanged a worried look.

'Would anyone like a drink?' said Evander, clapping his hands together. It was clear that he felt uncomfortable in the man's presence.

None of the trio opted to hide this time; all were worried about Nate, and neither Evander nor Zoe believed that he was capable of defending himself, and told him that under no uncertain terms were they hiding.

'Yes,' said Nate. 'A very large one.'

Evander looked at Catherine.

'Yes, please,' she said.

Grateful to have an excuse to leave, Evander disappear into the kitchen, beckoning to Tove to follow him. Zoe stood in the corner, a watchful guard. Her eyes never left Grigory.

The scientist began to set out instruments and pieces of equipment on the table, not sharing with them what he was doing.

Everyone watched him as he worked, studying the contents of the vial and then making notes on a sheet of paper beside him. He hummed to himself as he worked, selecting different items every few minutes to study or read or use. After an hour or so, he asked Catherine if he could draw some of her blood.

Nate sat up abruptly. 'I'll do it.'

Grigory raised a fluffy eyebrow. 'Do you know how?'

'I know how,' said Nate tersely. He stood with far more authority than he had, and took the syringe and vial from Grigory. He walked back over to Catherine and kneeled in front of her. 'Needles again, darling.'

'You must be so excited,' she teased.

'It's not my blood I'm drawing, now is it?' he retorted. 'Hold still.'

Catherine bit her lip as he cleaned her skin with disinfectant and pressed the needle gently into the crook of her elbow. It pinched a little, but Nate's hands were deft and careful, and almost instantly the vial began to fill with dark blood.

'I think I need that drink now,' said Catherine, her stomach protesting at the sight of it.

'You and me both, darling.' Nate finished and wiped her skin before standing and placing the vial down in front of Grigory. 'There you are.'

Nate returned to Catherine's side, sitting down heavily on the cushions. She knew that the effort had taken a good deal of strength on his part, but it was hard to tell just how taxing it had been on him.

They sat in silence as Grigory continued to work, his humming orchestrating the tense atmosphere of the house. Cecily sat in the chair opposite them, sipping nervously at a glass of wine, her eyes frequently darting to Nate. Although Evander did bring them all drinks, it was evident that he had no desire to be around a government official and for the next few hours, Catherine saw very little of him or Tove. Zoe, for her part, did not move.

Catherine fell asleep beside Nate, exhausted from the stress. She dreamed of nothing, only blackness, and when Nate shook her awake, it was midmorning and Grigory was holding two syringes.

'I do hope this will work,' he was saying. 'From Smith's old files and the studies that were done in the years following the closure of the programme several strides were made – none of them very fruitful. If we'd had test subjects, that may have been different, but ...'

Nate sat up. 'Let's give it a try, shall we?'

'Indeed,' said Grigory. He had the intense, anxious air to him that one who finally gets a break in their field always exudes when a breakthrough is realised. It wasn't an air Catherine trusted. 'Would you like to administer it yourself or shall I?'

'I don't fancy burning more than I already have,' said Nate dryly. 'Kitty can do it.'

'Does she know how?'

Catherine, who was not fully awake, rubbed her eyes and stood. 'I went through the same courses as everyone else. I know how to administer injections.'

'Fine,' said Grigory. 'Here you are.' He handed her the one in his right hand. 'This one is for Nathanial. The other is for you.'

'It'll stop the burns?'

Grigory nodded. 'I believe so. I have replicated it as best I can from Smith's notes. We won't know for certain until we try, however.'

Cecily stood up nervously. 'It's not going to harm either of them, will it?'

'I don't believe so.' Grigory gestured to his table. 'I have an extra vial in case we need to try something else.'

'There's an arse-load of conviction in all of these assurances,' said Nate, but he was holding out his arm to Catherine. 'Might as well give it a chance.'

She cleaned a spot in the crook of his arm, all-too aware of how purple and protruding his veins looked, and how fragile and papery his skin was. 'Ready?' she asked, holding her breath.

Nate met her gaze. 'No.'

'Excellent,' she said, pressing it into his vein, her heart pounding so hard she could hear the hammering rhythm in her ears.

The serum disappeared into Nate's vein and she placed the syringe on the ground. Nate held out his hand to Grigory, who handed him the other syringe.

'Your turn, darling,' said Nate stiffly.

It was then over so quickly that both of them sat, staring at each other, as if waiting for an explosion to occur.

'How will we know?' she whispered.

Nate said nothing. He was gripping her hands tightly, his eyes fixed on her face. Each second seemed to last an eternity. And then, all of sudden, it was as if time started to reverse itself.

The minor healing that Catherine had been doing for him for months suddenly seemed laughably inadequate. A flush of strong heat spread from where their skin touched, and whether it was the injection, her touch, or the two of them combined, the veins standing out on Nate's forearms slowly calmed, returning to their normal place, the colour disappearing until his skin was unmarred. The death-white colour that had him looking like spoiled milk for months started to darken; his eyes became less bloodshot, although the grey did not return, and it seemed clear that his eyes were now permanently amber; the circles beneath his eyes disappeared; the flaky, chapped look of his lips, that for so long had looking like rotting peel, evened, and suddenly he was himself as he had always been, albeit thin and bald.

'My God,' said Catherine, too ecstatic and relieved to say anything more eloquent.

Nate looked down at his body. He let out a bark of surprised laughter and sat forwards, wrapping his arm around her joyously. He no longer smelled of death and rotting flesh. Catherine hadn't realised how much she missed his previous smell until that moment, and her fingers dug into his skin, clinging to him as tightly as he was to her. Nate had always smelled of forest and earth, spice and herbs, tockers and coffee. The smell was heady and overwhelming, and she felt tears spring to her eyes as they clung to each other.

For a long time neither of them moved. It was only Cecily's voice that broke them apart. Nate let go of Catherine, kissed her cheek, and stood, walking over to his mother. He held out a hand. 'Shall we?'

Cecily held out her hand tentatively. Grigory, who looked delighted by his success, tensed for this second test. Zoe moved to Catherine's side, sitting close enough to touch, holding back. Tove and Evander appeared in the doorway, watching with clenched jaws and closed fists.

Nate grasped his mother's hand carefully, and then, after a beat, hugged her briefly before stepping back. They nodded to each other but said nothing else.

Catherine's breath caught in her throat and she reached out, taking Zoe's hand.

There was no pain. No burning. Nothing. Only flesh upon flesh and the normal warmth of human contact.

It was then that the explosion both Catherine and Nate had been waiting for occurred, but in a very different sense. Tove squealed and raced from the doorway, colliding with Catherine and hugging her enthusiastically.

Evander stepped up and embraced Nate like a brother. 'Looking well, my friend,' he said, clapping him on the back.

'I can't believe it,' said Tove. 'I'm so happy!'

Catherine was at a loss for words. She felt stunned, elated, terrified, pleased, confused, surprised and, after all of that, exceptionally calm. When Tove and Zoe finally ceased hugging her, she stood and walked over, embracing Evander first, and then Cecily.

When she turned to Grigory and held out her hand, he pumped it enthusiastically, chatting all the while about how he knew the whole time that it was going to work, how it was just a matter of reading the notes and scripts of the previous scientists and doctors who had studied Serum 23 before him. Humble in a very un-humble way.

'Thank you,' said Catherine. 'Truly.'

Nate stepped up beside her, his hand placed protectively on her lower back as he shook Grigory's hand. 'Thank you,' he echoed. 'You've no idea what you've done for us.'

'All in the name of progress, dear boy,' said Grigory.

A chill shot through Catherine at his words, and she instinctively moved closer to Nate. Those words would never again sound anything but oleaginous and evil. Nate's hand moved from her back to around her waist.

'We will of course pay you well,' said Nate, voice oddly diplomatic. 'That said, I must insist that you leave everything you brought with you in our care.'

Grigory's fluffy eyebrows shot up. 'I'm afraid I don't understand.'

'All of the name of progress, indeed, but not in this Kingdom,' said Nate. 'What it is you have done is wonderful, and we are grateful, but none of it will ever leave this house.'

'My dear boy –'

'You will be compensated accordingly,' said Nate, glancing to his mother, who nodded and stepped forwards. 'Thank you for your help, Mister Grigory.'

A red flush of anger distorted the man's face, and he opened his mouth to argue, but Cecily grasped his hand and he quieted himself.

'We will never forget your efforts,' said Cecily smoothly. 'You will of course join myself and my Complement at the King's feast this week, won't you?'

Somewhat placated, albeit clearly displeased, Grigory allowed himself to be led from the room by Cecily.

Nate glanced at Catherine. 'Are you all right?'

'Fine,' she muttered. 'I just don't trust anyone anymore.'

'I can't say I disagree,' he agreed. 'Zoe?'

Zoe stepped forward, expression unreadable.

'Burn the lot of it,' he said. 'I don't want anyone to have it.'

'Happily,' said Zoe, stepping away and gathering up all of the items left scattered on the desk and floor.

Something caught her eye and Catherine stepped over. 'What is that?'

Beside the spare vial of the cure was another vial. Its contents did not look like anything that should ever be injected into a body. Dark, unnatural gold.

She moved towards the table. After pocketing the extra vial of cure for safe keeping – she was becoming as diligent as Thom as regards planning ahead – she lifted the gold one. Somehow she doubted it was as charming as it appeared. 'What is this?'

The others shook their head, equally confused. Nate stepped forwards and examined the vial over her shoulder. 'I dunno, darling. I wouldn't trust anything with strange labels, though.'

'I agree,' said Zoe. 'Whatever you do, don't break it.'

'We did that once,' said Nate. 'Don't recommend it.'

Slightly curious, and unable to explain why all her annoyances at thievery had suddenly left her mind, Catherine wrapped the vial in a scarf and pocketed it, too, before handing the box back to the Zoe, who chucked it in with the rest. She then piled everything into Grigory's case and left the room, calling to Tove to help her. Catherine hoped all of it would burn, never to be remembered or used again.

'Ev,' said Nate, glancing at the other man. 'We're leaving.'

'Finally,' said Evander. 'I can't wait to see the last of this bloody city.'

When they were alone, Nate turned and appraised Catherine, his eyes bright and happy. 'Are you ready?'

'More than I ever was before,' she said.

'Good. I'm going to bid farewell to my mother. I want to leave as soon as possible.'

'Nate?'

'Yes, darling?'

'You're not dying.'

He smiled. 'I've certainly had worse days.'

Catherine squeezed his hand once more before she followed Evander from the room and began to gather up their few things.

Nate bid farewell privately to his mother, and what was said between them Catherine never knew, but she was glad not to have to say anything to Cecily. She had no words to express how sorry she was about Thom, and nothing would ever be adequate enough.

The streets were busy and bustling in light of the better weather, and everyone agreed to leave the moment it was visibly deserted and they wouldn't feel too greatly exposed. In the meantime, bursting with adrenaline and the joy which comes at the realisation that death has been postponed, everyone was in the mood to relax and enjoy the reprieve.

The celebrations lasted the rest of the afternoon. It seemed too wonderful, too unlikely to be true, and every few minutes, as if to double-check, Catherine or Nate would touch one of the siblings, delighting each time there was no burn or pain.

An hour or so before they determined to go, the siblings disappeared into the kitchen to make one final meal for the road, and Catherine found herself on the sofa, content for the first time in a long time. She was wrapped in a thick blanket, a cup of Cisco infused coffee in her lap.

Nate walked in, eating a sandwich heartily. He looked reborn.

'How do you feel?' she enquired, smiling at him.

'Odd,' he said, taking a seat beside her.

Catherine shrugged. 'Maybe that's normal. It'd probably be weirder if you didn't feel a bit strange. I do.'

He shook his head after a moment. 'I feel like my whole body is different.'

'Well, it is. For one thing, it's not rotting anymore. Feeling healthy will likely feel strange for a time.'

'That's not what I mean. I feel as if I've been drowned and blended and spat back out again with pieces of me all scrambled about. Nothing feels the way it used to. Everything feels hollow and misused.'

Catherine frowned. 'Maybe it just takes some time to get back into your old rhythm?'

'Or maybe once you've been infected there's no real cure,' he said. 'It's not just that, though.'

'How do you mean?'

'Death would be so easy,' he said quietly. 'It's all I think of for hours at a time. So many times on the road I stared at my knife and wondered. I think the only thing I'm not afraid of is death. Perhaps that makes sense. I'm afraid of everything else.' He looked at her with raw intensity. 'I love Tommy with every beat of my heart and every piece of my soul, and I never knew there was enough in me to love someone else. You're the only reason I'm here.'

Catherine gazed at him. 'Why do you love me?'

'Well you've always been so lovely to me.'

She laughed. 'I'm curious. Have you always and just never said?'

'The mountain,' he said simply. 'Or perhaps before. I always noticed you. Always thought you were forthright and vibrant. You were like the first breath of air after being underwater for too long. I would probably have loved you sooner if you'd come around every time Tommy did.'

She stuck her tongue out. 'I made every single excuse never to go and deal with you. After that day in Market Square, do you remember? I wanted nothing to do with you after that.'

'Ah, mystery solved.' He laughed ruefully. 'I don't think I ever really explained what happened in Nitoib, did I? I had planned to go there that weekend with Marko and Diana. I hadn't seen them in years and wanted to see if they were interested in leaving. I planned on meeting Tommy in the next couple of weeks and slowly get him around to the idea. I knew it would take time, but I've always been able to convince him to do things even if he doesn't like the idea at all in the first place.'

'This I know.'

Nate nodded, lips curving into a bitter smile. 'I was in such high spirits – for the first time since prison, I was actually laughing. So I conn'd Tommy to come out.'

It felt like it had happened yesterday; it felt like it had happened to someone else.

'I still remember what you were wearing. You looked so beautiful. I've been with a few in my life, darling, and I've even liked a couple of them, but that night … I could barely talk to Tommy, I was so distracted by you. You just started yelling at me and all I could do was smile because I thought anger sounded all right coming from you. Most people yell at me. I'm used to it. I've never liked it before.'

'I thought you were mocking me.'

Nate grinned. 'Perhaps a little. Mostly I just wanted to see how much passion and fury one person could hold within them. You seemed filled with both. More than anything, I noticed how I was the only one who could ignite it. I think I liked that far too much. Still do.

'When Tommy left to get the money and you elected to look after me, I can't say I wasn't delighted. I wanted to see how much you'd changed since my arrest. I wanted to see if you were still as unlived as I remembered. I wanted to see if life had changed you. I remember thinking how much I would have wanted someone like you to protest with. I wanted someone with your fire to scream about the cruelty of Crown and Council. I wanted someone like you to be with me. But you were Tommy's, and I knew that if we continued to debate, I would never want to stop, so I left to get a drink.' He scratched his face and raised his eyebrows at her. 'I've hated many people in my life, darling, and I hate more now than I ever have.

'When I saw that man put something in your drink – I don't think anything prior to that ever made me feel such rage. I believed, however foolishly, that you were mine. Not many ever raised a hand to Tommy. He was too good, too wonderful and driven. Tommy was never told off a day in his life and his few enemies were schoolyard bullies which I disposed of quickly enough. But you were his and he was mine, and the only thing I knew in that moment was that I wanted to shove that bottle into the man's eyes. For your sake, for

Tommy's, for mine. I've always known that anything Tommy loved, I would love as well. It frightened me how very true that turned out to be.

'Afterwards, when we were on that road, and then the trail and the facility ... I carried you for hours and I never got tired of it. You fit perfectly in my arms and I hated putting you down. How foolish and silly must that sound to actually say aloud?' He flushed. 'We were stumbling towards that flypath, just before Forrest came along – do you remember him? Bless his heart, he was a kind soul – and your eyes were slightly amber-coloured, which of course I know now is because you were just as infected as I was, and I remember suddenly everything just fit. This thing that brought us together, that kept us from other people, that made us leave – I know I should hate it and hate everything it's done, and believe me when I say there is no limit to what I would do to bring Tommy back – but I don't regret this. *Us.* I don't hate that we had to leave together and I certainly don't hate that you were the only person I could touch. You're the only one I want to touch.'

Catherine found that she had no words for him. She had loved Thom, and she had hated Nate, and there had been few chances in all the chaos for her to grieve one and learn to love the other. The few moments of joy didn't seem enough to fully know Nate as she had known Thom after years by his side, learning what every smile, every sigh and every insinuation meant. It was all so amalgamated and confusing and she just wanted everything to stop for a while. In the end, unable to bear the look on Nate's face, she said, 'I do care. Please don't doubt that.'

The snow outside the window was thick on the streets and the glass was crusted with snowflakes and ice. It seemed far too beautiful and pure to be in such a wretched place. She remembered so clearly the stayaways with her parents.

'I miss my parents,' she said suddenly, still thinking of her childhood. 'I haven't really let myself think about them in months. It's easier not to miss people if you put them out of your mind. But seeing your mother ... I miss them. Whether they're good or bad people, they're still my parents.'

'I doubt your father ever broke your arm because you annoyed him,' said Nate mildly. 'It makes more sense for you to miss them.'

Catherine gaped at him. 'Hamish did that?'

'A couple of times.'

'God's wrath.'

Nate shrugged. 'It is what it is. I have no ties holding me back from leaving, so perhaps it's almost better.'

'I keep thinking about contacting my dad,' she admitted.

'Kitty, he helped build this Kingdom beside King Markas. He's hardly going to go against the express rules of his leader. I know you say he loves you, but I don't think that means much to people like that.'

Catherine swallowed hard. 'People like what?'

'People who kill innocents,' he said frankly. 'Your parents have as much death on their hands as mine do. Can you really forgive them that?'

To that she had no answer, and she sipped at her coffee until the cup was drained and her exhaustion from the day's events caught up to her.

'When do you think we're going to leave?' she asked.

Nate glanced over her shoulder towards the kitchen. 'Probably an hour. Perhaps sooner. You want to try and get some sleep before we go?'

'Yeah,' she said. 'Might help.'

He nodded. 'I'll wake you when it's time to leave.'

'Thank you,' she said, closing her eyes. 'And Nate?'

'Yeah, darling?'

'I'm really, really glad you're going to be all right.'

She could almost hear his smile.

Catherine awoke to the sound of smashing wood and shouting. She felt herself dragged into the air before she had even opened her eyes fully, and bright lights were being shined in her face. Fear laced through her body and she looked wildly around for Nate and the others. It took a moment for her eyes to stop seeing stars. He was a metre or so away from her, pinned to the ground.

It was complete chaos; everyone was screaming at once.

'What's going on?'

'I don't know – *ouch*! Get off me, you piece of shit!'

'Kitty!'

'Tove!'

'Help me! Kit, help!'

'Get down!'

'Nate! Ow! Fuck – *get off me!*'

'Get off of her!'

'Zoe, behind you!'

'Leave her alone!'

'Zoe, duck!'

'Leave him alone!'

'*Zoe!*'

'You mutant bastard!'

'I said – get the *fuck* off of her!' Nate was wrenching against the grip of the guards with all the strength he could muster, violently trying to get away from them. His eyes never left Catherine's, his gaze filled with fear and fury. Had he been as large and strong as he once was, he may have succeeded, but the sickness had eaten away at his muscles and reserves of energy, and no matter how hard he tried, he could not rip himself free.

Chaotic sound echoed from all sides as they were hauled out of the house and into the snow. A bitter wind bit into Catherine's skin, waking her rapidly, and as sleep finally cleared from her eyes, she could see what was happening. Several hovers were parked in front of the house, and no less than thirty armed guards were aiming guns and electrifiers at them.

'I think Grigory is a rat,' said Nate through gritted teeth.

One of the guards responded by smashing the butt of his gun into Nate's face. The force of the blow caused him to double over, spitting blood. He raised his head and spat at the man defiantly, splattering blood all over his face and getting some directly in his eye. The guard shrank away, howling with fear. Blood was a known carrier of the Plague and everyone in the Kingdom feared coming into contact with another's blood. No matter how brave or stupid the move, Catherine wanted to applaud him for it until another guard kicked him in the stomach.

'Leave him alone!' she yelled with all the courage she had, wiggling away from her guard long enough to drive her shoulder into the stomach of the guard who had hit Nate. They fell over, landing heavily on hard frozen ground.

Catherine was dragged to her feet, a hand closing around her throat.

'Don't fucking touch her!' Nate kicked out and connected with the shin of the man clutching her. The man lost his grip and she fell against Nate. His fingers gripped tightly to her coat. Before she could get her bearings, another guard seized her, and she could feel the cold press of metal against her neck.

'Enough!' The guard pressed the device harder into her neck. 'One more move from any of you and she's the first to lose her head. You ever see what a ripper does to a girl's neck? I'll tell you, it isn't pretty. The wall back there's going to be a whole new shade of red if you don't stop.'

Nate, Evander, and Zoe, who had been trying to rip free of their captors, stilled instantly. Tove was curled into a ball, sobbing, and didn't seem to have registered any of it.

'Fine,' said Nate, holding up his bound hands. 'Fine, you win. Just let her go. We'll behave. I promise. We all promise. Just let her go.'

'Good,' said the guard. He shoved Catherine hard to the ground and she scrambled to Nate's side.

The guard surveyed the lot of them with loathing. 'By order of His Majesty, King of Man and Ruler of the Land, Markas I of the House of Auram, you are all under arrest for crimes against Crown and Council.' The booming voice of the guard almost levelled Catherine as he read out their sentencing. 'Catherine Jaiani Taenia, you are charged with conspiring against the Crown, thievery, breaking and entering, breach of public propriety, attempting to circumvent the wishes of the Crown, evading arrest and aiding known dissenters, for which you are hereby sentenced to death by hanging.'

Cold terror swept through her body. It was too shocking to frighten her. In her hysteria, she almost laughed.

'Nathanial Asim Anteros, you are charged with repeated vagrancy, thievery, breaking and entering, conspiring against the Crown, fugitive status, breach of public propriety, previous charges of indecency, lewdness and criminal actions such as fighting, spreading falsehoods, speaking against His Majesty, conspiring with spies and enemies, and leaving the Kingdom for the Outlands, home of the Kingdom's greatest enemies, for which you are sentenced to death by firing squad.'

Nate rolled his eyes.

'Evander Brayford Ray,' continued the guard. 'You are charged with murder and evading arrest, and for this you are sentenced to death by firing squad. Zoe Louise Ray, you are charged with aiding and abetting known fugitives, and for this you are sentenced to death by hanging. Tovelyn Green Ray, you are charged with association and aiding and abetting, and for this you are sentenced to life of hard labour in service of the Crown. You will be relocated to Muntenia shortly. May God have mercy on all your souls.'

Catherine wasn't even aware of being hauled to her feet and shoved in the back of one of the hovers. Everything felt horribly numb and far away. She was secured in place with metal bindings that nearly cut off the circulation to her wrists and ankles. When Nate was locked in beside her, she almost cried with relief. At least she would not be alone.

Nate's fingers inched across the seat as far as they could go and curled around her own frozen ones. He leaned his head close to hers and pressed their foreheads together. 'Don't let them see you cry,' he said sharply. 'Don't let them see your fear. Whatever you do, darling. Don't ever give them that.'

'I won't,' she said. 'I swear.'

And then Nate kissed her. He kissed her slowly, softly, his mouth lingering against hers as if he was trying to memorise the feeling. He still tasted of tea and cigarettes, and the hope of the last few hours. He kissed her like the world was ending, and Catherine wanted to scream that this wasn't the end, that they would get out of this, that they would not end up in the cement pit where Thom's bones likely lay. But she couldn't form the words. So she kissed Nate even harder, hoping to forget, just for one second, that they were going to the very worst place in the Kingdom.

The hover began to move but the windows were completely blacked out and she had no idea who was driving or what direction they were going. Her eyes still seemed keenly adapted to the dark, and she wondered how long that would last before the antidote removed the benefits as well as the drawbacks. Perhaps it was a lingering gift of sorts.

'I don't want to die, Nate.'

His only response was to kiss her again.

She wanted, absurdly, for him to make everything better, to fix this somehow, as he had fixed everything else. He had always known what to do, when to run, where to go. He had been her rock for so long she wished furiously that he would brace against this new storm and hold her steady. She squeezed his fingers as tight as she could, her hand unable to move closer no matter how much she willed it to.

'Will we live?' she whispered.

'Tommy did.'

Catherine didn't know what to say to that. She couldn't strip Nate of that one small bit of baseless faith. She buried her face in the crook of his neck and wished that the person she believed in the most wasn't sitting right beside her, as captured as she.

PART FIVE
Bargaining

It seemed hours, but was probably much less, until they were hauled out of the hover and marched across the frozen grounds, their feet and hands shackled together to prevent bolting. It was a pointless precaution. They had been unloaded inside the prison and the several metre-high walls, electrocuted and spiked, guards walking between the huge points, deterred any thought of escaping.

Redwater Prison was a relic of the old days and an ominous reminder of what happened to anyone who disagreed with the Council's laws. It was one of the first prisons erected during the Last War and the first to become infamous throughout the battling lands. Located in the centre of Anais, on the banks of the River Crow, where a thousand birds would take to the skies in an ominous flight at the end and onset of each day, the prison sprawled over several acres.

Even fifty years later, the place still felt cursed and screams could be heard whenever the winds howled. It wasn't unheard of to see spectres out of the corner of one's eye, or feel a chill pass through if walking down the wrong empty corridor.

The five fugitives were marched into the entrance hall, its light so bright and blinding Catherine baulked instinctively. The dark red and black colours, the cold marble, the invading lights and stone-faced guards were enough to make even the bravest man lose control of his bowls. A few steps behind her, Tove was openly sobbing and she heard Evander vomit, retching up the tea and sandwiches from earlier.

Before them stood the Captain of the Private Police, the same man who had stormed her home months before, his uniform declaring him recognisably as thus, his face one that could haunt children for generations.

There were large binders in his hands, each one several hundred pages thick, and it took Catherine a minute to realise that each binder was a file on each of the five of them.

'Bring Taenia to the holding chamber,' said the Captain. 'Put the rest in their cells for examination.'

The holding chamber was where prisoners awaited imminent execution. Catherine looked at Nate in horror.

The moment the Captain had spoken, he'd started struggling in his bonds. He managed to elbow one the guards in the crotch and head-butt a second. There was a horrible *thunk* of metal against bone as one of the guards clubbed him over the head.

Two guards unchained her from the others and she was shoved forwards through the large entryway behind the Captain.

'Nate!' she screamed, hauling against their hold. '*Nate! Evander!*'

Evander was struggling against his own bonds; Zoe slammed her forehead into the face of the guard holding her down, but ceased when one of the guards smashed his fist into Tove's face.

Nate, who had rallied himself valiantly, blood flowing from a wound on the side of his head, kept screaming and struggling. '*Kitty!*'

'*Nate!*'

'KITTY!'

'NATE!'

As the door closed, the very last thing she heard was Nate screaming her name.

The sudden silence that descended as the thick door slammed shut and she was marched down the corridor chilled her to the bone, and she had to work hard to keep herself standing. Nate's words rang in her mind.

Don't let them see your fear … don't let them see you cry … don't let them see your fear … don't let them see you cry …

Catherine lost all hope as she was led down the cold passage, but she didn't lose her anger, and months of fear had the adrenaline pumping so violently through her veins that she was able to kick and bite and scratch to what small extent she could, mostly tiring herself out but getting in several gouges and cuts on the guards holding her, and gaining some small level of satisfaction from that.

Thom's death had seemed so pointless, so causeless, but as she was led around one turn and then the next, going further and further from her friends, Nate slipping from her grasp, she felt a new level of senselessness. Thom had died so that she and Nate could live, and now that was ruined too. It was so horribly unfair.

The guard in front of her opened a large metal door with the King's crest stamped in with great care, and Catherine suddenly found herself in a crimson room with a cheerful fire, her father standing in the centre of the room. His office.

Not the holding chamber at all.

'Daddy!' She tried to run for him but the shackles tripped her and she fell gracelessly to the floor.

'Untie her this instant!' Mickey Taenia was a formidable man at the best of times and now his voice sent shivers down even her spine as the guards hastily unlocked her cuffs. Her father helped her to her feet, brushing the matted white hair from her eyes. 'What's this?' he said, eyebrow arched. 'White hair? When was the last time you even ate? You look half starved. Gillett, fetch us some food and drink and send for a blanket. My daughter is freezing.'

The guard bowed low and disappeared, his feet *tap-tap-tapp*ing down the corridor as he hurried away.

Catherine gaped at her father. 'I thought I was going to be hanged?'

Mickey wiped snot from her nose that she hadn't even realised was there. 'You're in an awful lot of trouble, but no, you're not going to be hanged. Did you really think I would let that happen? Family loyalty comes first, Catherine Jaiani. Come, tell me what happened over these last months.'

'But my friends –'

'Your friends are being dealt with accordingly. Their crimes are their own.'

'Daddy –'

'Sit, Catherine Jaiani.'

So Catherine sat in the comfortable chair by the fire, the feeling slowly returning to her body, and she forced herself to breathe, focus; the gift she had been born with suddenly returning to her, and the lies spilled free.

She told him of the infection and how scared they had all been and how Nate had saved her because she had been Thom's Complement and he felt he owed it to his brother. She left out the parts about Nate's criminal activities and Archie's betrayal and how much they had started to hate the King and everything he stood for. She told him about how amazing the siblings were and how they had saved her life, too. Each detail she spun carefully, painting them all as terrified, confused, good-hearted youngsters who had had such an awful run of luck.

By the time the food had come, her father was visibly relieved, his greatest fears of his daughter's radical leanings assuaged for the time being.

'You're well now?' he enquired, drinking deeply from a glass, filled halfway with amber whiskey and smelling almost as strongly as the large cigar he was smoking. It was once the most comforting sight in the world, and a lifetime of curling up beside her father in front of the fire, talking to him about school or work or Thom and hearing him tell story after story, the puffs of smoke making them seem all the more fascinating, came rushing back to her. 'And Nate? He was good to you?'

'Yes, Daddy,' she said, cradling her mug of steaming tea. 'He kept me safe. He kept me alive.'

Her father sighed. 'I'm glad you're better. You say a scientist helped you?'

'He works for the Diseases Department.'

'Not anymore.'

She didn't want to ask what that meant.

'Why did you not come to me at the start?'

'Everyone that's taken to the Diseases Department is euthanised, Daddy,' she reasoned. 'And Thom was killed. We thought we were next. We panicked. We wanted to find a cure first and then come back once we wouldn't be executed for having a disease. That's why we went to Grigory! I was going to contact you first thing in the morning. Ask to come home. Apologise to the King. I'm so sorry, Daddy.'

Mickey nodded thoughtfully.

'Please don't let them kill my friends,' she whispered, her voice breaking just so and tears welling in her eyes. It had been years since she'd cried on command, but she hadn't forgotten how. She prayed she was convincing enough.

Maybe there were some parents who could tell when their children lied, but hers were not those parents, and her father had always been susceptible to her tears. A hard, unyielding man in life, Mickey had no ability to deal with upset and woe, and tended to avoid it at all costs.

'We weren't trying to be criminals or anything of that sort. I would never, Daddy. You know that. I was just so upset over Thom and nothing made sense and it all happened so fast. Isn't there something you can do for them? *Please.*'

'Nate was a criminal long before you two were infected,' said Mickey, puffing on his cigar. 'Hamish is pressing for the ultimate sentence. I think he just wants to be rid of the burden. Cecily, on the other hand, wants him alive. She found out you were being arrested a few minutes after the decision was made and went directly to the King. I think he might change his mind for her sake.'

Catherine clung to that small nugget of hope. The next words which left her mouth tasted vile, but she said them regardless. 'Nate wasn't the one who broke into the Council records! His only crime this time was keeping me alive. It was Thom who broke the law.' She hated herself for the words but swallowed the guilt and kept her face earnest and pleading.

'He has a history of crimes, sugar.' Mickey's lip curled. 'Let's be blunt – he has a history of madness. That boy was born broken.'

She felt like throwing something at him. It took all her willpower to stay still and earnest. 'Daddy, he's never going to be able to work or bind or have children. Isn't that enough? He was only trying to save me. He didn't know what Thom was doing – neither of us knew. Thom went off on his own. We panicked when the guards showed up, and ran. We were sick and scared is all. We weren't thinking. Please, Daddy, he didn't know, I swear.'

It felt awful to lie about Thom in such a way, to paint him as the orchestrator and villain, yet she knew he would understand. For Nate, he would understand. Thom always was what everyone needed him to be.

Mickey stood and walked over to the fire, leaning against the mantle. The King's crest stood large and ominous above him: a mutant lion with two heads sat arched and powerful, a weapon of the Devastation in the jaws of each head; a bomb in one, a vial to represent the Plague in the other. Above the lion heads was a large tree, its limbs withered and dead; above that, a smattering of stars. It had been on every building, every paper, every broadcast in all of Catherine's memories. She had been frightened of the heads once, frightened of their meaning and their power. Now she found them ominous and distasteful.

'I'll see what I can do for Nate,' he said at last. 'I'm making no promises.'

Catherine wanted to faint with relief. 'And the Rays?'

'You say the girls knew nothing of their brother's crimes?'

'No, nothing. But I'm sure Evander only killed the man because they were starving. It was undoubtedly self-defence! Things in the Southern Lands are terrible. Everyone's sick and starving; half are dead. Surely that's a good enough reason. The King can't expect everyone to roll over and die, can he? The man he killed was a criminal! And Tove and Zoe thought they were going north for food and work. They're completely innocent. Can't that be forgiven? The population is dwindling, Daddy. Survival is paramount.'

Mickey pursed his lips in thought and tossed the end of his cigar into the fire. 'Let me see what I can do. Wait here. There's a bathroom in there, take a shower. I'll have one of the guards bring you clothes. You smell like death and I can't abide that colour on you. Fix yourself up and eat and wait for me here. I'll be back as soon as I'm done.'

Catherine stood on shaking legs. 'Where are you going?'

'To talk to King Markas,' he said. 'He always did have a soft spot for Cecily, perhaps that will be enough.'

Catherine's heart was pounding. 'What if it takes too long? What if they're killed before you get back?'

'Nothing is going to happen at this prison if I'm not here,' he said plainly, as if this was information she should already have known. 'I run the place. I've been running it for over forty years. Nothing happens here that I do not oversee or delegate. No guard does anything I do not know about. They won't be touched until I return.'

Catherine stared at him, suddenly remembering Nate's story of the guards. 'Nothing?' she said, voice croaking. 'Guards don't ever act of their own volition?'

'Guards do not have volition. Everything they do I have approved.'

She wanted to be sick. Face blank, she nodded and smiled. 'Of course, Daddy.'

'Always my innocent dove,' he said, walking over to her and touching her cheek. She had to work every muscle in her body not to flinch away from him, horror sinking into her bones. She swallowed the vomit that rose in her throat.

'Wait here. I'll return soon.'

Catherine stood in the centre of the room for a long time, staring at the door where he'd walked out. At last, from sheer want of something to do and needing desperately not to think about where her friends were, she headed into the great marble bathroom and stripped. Her coat fell to the floor with a *clink*. Frowning, Catherine bent down and rifled through the pockets. The two small vials rolled into her hand.

She turned the golden one over several times, wracking her memory for answers, hoping to distract herself, but nothing came to her. Stowing them back in the pocket, she made a mental note to research the gold as soon as she could, and turned on the tap. A screen on the side of the bath beeped quietly, waiting for commands, and Catherine typed in 'dye remover' and stuck her head into the circular hole in the wall beside it.

When at last she was clean, she stepped out, wrapping a thick robe around her small frame. For the longest time she had missed her old body, her soft stomach and larger breasts and full thighs. Now she was all angles and points; sunken, gaunt and hard. As she stared at her reflection, the woman in the mirror staring back at her, she felt glad of the change. The old soft Catherine had been ignorant, gullible, an Anaitian with no understanding of truth. The woman in the mirror was nothing like her.

'Kitty,' she whispered. 'Just Kitty.'

A knock on the door startled her, and a moment later one of the guards stepped in, holding a pile of clothes. 'Your food is waiting outside, Mistress Taenia,' he said coldly. 'Here are your clothes.'

'Get out.'

The guard seemed delighted to leave and tossed the clothes on the ground before departing. He clearly did not share her father's sympathies, though it hardly mattered. If her father was the one in charge of this wretched place, there would be no trouble. She had never known the extent of her father's power, but she'd seen him break more than a couple bones throughout her childhood. The guards had undoubtedly seen even worse. Her father was a monster, but he was the monster in front of the King, and the monster fighting her corner. She told herself to be patient.

They had to live first.

The clothes brought to her were prison clothes, a crimson bodysuit, a black coat and black boots, but they were soft and warm and she did her best to ignore the writing on the back that declared her PROPERTY OF REDWATER PRISON. By the time she had dressed and dried her hair, the food had gone a bit cold, but she hadn't much appetite anyways, and it was purely for something to do with her hands that she ate a few bites of the goat stew. Her father's decanter of whiskey was still out and she filled a large glass, drinking it in one swallow and filling it again, the heat radiating through her body and giving her some sense of strength. By the time her father returned, almost three hours had passed and she was feeling rather drunk; the haze escaped her the moment he entered. She shot to her feet.

'What did the King say?'

Mickey waved at her to sit down, which she did obediently, mouth clamped shut as she waited.

He eyed his half empty bottle of whiskey, said nothing, and filled a glass for himself. He sat across from her on the other sofa and said, 'The King's angry. It's a great offence to run from the guards and on top of that you both evaded arrest for months and wasted valuable resources and manpower in the search for you. However, our King is a generous man and not without a heart – which I beg you to remember when next you see him.'

Kitty nodded rapidly, her heart pounding. 'Of course,' she lied. 'Of course he is. Our King has always had a kind and loving heart.' The words tasted like acid and she was grateful that her father was staring at his drink, rather than at her face. She wasn't sure she could lie effectively at the minute. She was too tired and drunk and worried. 'I'll do anything,' she added. 'Anything he wants.'

'I'm glad to hear it,' said Mickey. 'He has agreed to lessen Nate's sentence to five years of hard labour in the west. They're building a new city out there and he'll be part of the workforce. He will bear the mark of a criminal his entire life, but he'll live.'

Kitty almost fainted with relief. 'Thank you, Daddy. Truly. Thank you so much.'

'There are conditions.'

'What are they?'

'The King's nephew, Lord Gabriel, is recently widowed. His Complement died of the Bite and he's been without a companion for nearly a year now. Markas is sympathetic to your loss and believes that you are without fault, but he cannot let you wander about unattended after so much chaos. If you Complement Lord Gabriel, he will expunge your record and allow Nate to keep his life.'

Kitty choked on the whiskey she'd been sipping. Of all the punishments she'd been expecting, that was one which had never occurred to her.

Lord Gabriel, several people down in line to the throne, was the son of the King's sister and had been in high society for as long as she could remember. He was incredibly affluent, and she had always found him repulsive, although in truth she had never paid him much attention save the nights she and Thom had attended royal parties and they'd laughed about him behind their hands, appalled at such drunken and lecherous behaviour.

'In addition,' said Mickey, ignoring her expression, 'I've done what I could for your friends but there was nothing to be done about the boy. Evander, was it? He killed a man and that's a fact. He's to be executed shortly. The woman will join Nate in the work force for a period of two years before being shipped back to the Southern Lands. The girl will be given to a home in Brantryne and will have some hope at a future. I assured the King that she was simpleminded and knew nothing of the crimes and he has agreed to pardon her fully.'

Tears sprang to Kitty's eyes at his words. 'But Daddy, Evander –'

'It's done, there's nothing else to do.'

'But –'

'Hush,' her father ordered. 'That's enough. I've done what I could and that's that. You will accept your punishment and bear it with grace. Do not disgrace me. I have saved your life and saved your worthless friends to what extent I could. Shut your mouth and be grateful.'

Kitty swallowed. 'C-can I see him? Please? Just let me say goodbye and tell him about his sisters.'

Her father raised an eyebrow. He did not seem much inclined to agree, but after a few moments of tense silence, he put his glass down and nodded. 'Fine. Come with me.'

The walk back down the corridor was horrible. Kitty could not stop crying, although she managed to do it silently. She thought of

Evander – sweet, loyal, wonderful Evander who had never done anything but protect his family and his friends. How she would ever explain it to Zoe and Tove, she had no idea.

They walked outside into a small courtyard covered in snow. There, chained to a pole and shivering, was Evander. Not caring that twenty armed guards were watching her, Kitty dashed forwards, colliding with her friend. Solid, confident, beautiful Evander had never seemed small to her. Until now.

'Kitty?' He opened a swollen eye. 'Kitty, what's going on?'

'I'm sorry,' she sobbed, hugging him tightly. 'I'm so, so sorry.'

Evander leaned against her, blood ebbing from his lips and nose and eyebrows. He had been beaten within an inch of his life, and the wheezing sound he made with every breath told her that he had most likely punctured a lung.

'What's going on, Kitty?' he said again.

'I tried to stop this,' she said, taking off her coat and wrapping it around his freezing shoulders. She suddenly felt intensely cold; she didn't care. All she could see was Evander and how truly helpless she was in this world. 'I begged my father to ask the King to spare your life, but he refused. I'm so, so sorry.'

Evander shook his head. 'I never even hoped,' he grunted. 'What about Zoe? Tove? Nate? They're not out here. Are they ... have they ...?'

'They're going to live,' she said. 'Zoe's got two years of labour and Tove's going to a girls' school. They're going to live, I swear.'

'Thank God,' he said. 'Thank God. And Nate?'

'The King's sleeping with his mother, so he got off, too,' she said into his ear, not wanting anyone to overhear her words. 'My father says that because they have evidence of you killing a man there's nothing to be done. I tried, Ev. I really did.'

'I believe you.' He did not seem scared. That almost made it worse. 'Am I to die now, then?'

Kitty nodded, unable to answer.

'Will you do something for me? Promise me one thing and I'll die easily.'

'Of course. Anything.'

Evander smiled. 'Once this is over, once they are out of holding, will you look after them? We never told you just how bad things got out there, and I know the workforce isn't kind. Don't let them live horrible lives. I couldn't rest if I knew they were resigned to such a fate. Promise me that.'

'I swear,' she said, hugging him tightly, ignoring the fierce cold that was numbing her knees and threatening to break her like glass. 'I swear.'

'Thank you.'

'You're the brother I always wanted,' she cried. 'I really wanted to go to the Outlands with you.'

Evander's dark eyes filled with tears and his breath hitched. 'I did too. More than I've ever wanted anything.'

Kitty swallowed hard. 'Will you tell Thom I love him when you see him?'

'I will,' said Evander. 'And tell my sisters the same.'

'I swear.'

He pressed his forehead against hers. 'God protect you, Kitty.'

'And you.' Tears spilled from her eyes and she tightened her grip around him. They stayed on the ground until her father called her name.

'It's time,' he said. 'Let's go.'

'Wait,' she said, scrambling to her feet. 'Daddy, at least make it quick. Please. I don't want him to go like this. What about poison? Just let him die in peace.'

Her father sighed heavily. 'Your heart's too soft. This isn't the place for you.'

'He's my friend.'

'Apologies,' her father said, and to his credit he looked like he actually meant it, but he waved his hands and two guards moved from their posts to stand on either side of her. 'Take her up to my office,' he ordered. 'She's not to watch.'

'Daddy!' She tried to yank her arms away from the grip of the guards, but it was impossible. It was like trying to rip away from stone. She wished desperately that she was stronger as she was dragged away from Evander's hunched form, so small and terribly alone in the snowy courtyard.

She was sure, looking back, that she imagined the sound of him screaming, because there was no way for sound to echo through those solid walls.

First Thom and now Evander.

In the hours that followed, Kitty was aware of very little.

She felt stupidly dazed and no matter how hard she tried, she couldn't stopping thinking of Evander. His final words played over and over in her head until she felt like she was losing her mind.

When Mickey returned, he announced that the hover was waiting for them and it was time to go home. 'Put that cloak on,' he added, gesturing to one of the black cloaks on the door. 'It's cold outside and you're a horrible sight.'

'Daddy?'

'Yes?'

'I want to see Nate.'

Mickey shook his head. 'You're bound to Lord Gabriel now, Catherine. It's time for you to accept your duties.'

'Just let me see him. Please.' Kitty bowed her head in subservience. It was a gesture reserved only for extreme begging, and most only used it before royalty, but it was a mannerism of Anais, and she hoped it would appeal to her father. 'Please just let me see him.'

'You can see him,' said Mickey at length. 'But you are forbidden to speak to him.'

Kitty followed her father out of the office hurriedly, her heart pounding. He took her down a side passage that led to a capture centre. Inside, a dozen or so screens flashed images from the grounds of the prison. Mickey pointed to one of the screens. 'There.'

Kitty stepped forwards. It was Nate. He was on the ground of his cell, curled tightly in a ball. There was something silver in his hand that glinted when he twitched, but she couldn't make out what it was. He seemed to be bloody, although she couldn't tell if it was his or a guard's, dried or fresh. Her stomach tightened as she watched him and without registering her own actions, she reached out and touched his face on the screen.

Nate has good reason to fear those buildings. He experienced nothing but cruelty within their walls.

Thom's urgent parting words replayed in her head. So many nights during Nate's stint in prison had seen Thom awake, soaked in sweat, eyes wild, *knowing* – knowing something was wrong and unable to do anything about it. How he had eventually bartered his way into Redwater when not even Cecily could, Kitty had never learned. If the bargains he had had to make were anything like the ones she was having to make now, she had no desire to ever learn what he'd been forced to do.

She had known him to be dead for months now, but he still seemed so present. Perhaps that was due to Nate – Nate, who could have been his twin. Nate, who refused to believe he was dead and clung to an ever maddening hope that Thom had escaped the guards somehow and was waiting in the Outlands. She hoped he would keep believing it. He needed to believe in something.

'Enough,' said Mickey. 'You've seen him. We're leaving.'

The flight home was silent and uncomfortable. Kitty found it impossible to quash the ever-growing sense of powerlessness and depression that was threatening to suffocate her. She closed her eyes for most of the ride, and only opened them when she felt the hover begin its descent.

It didn't even occur to her how strange it was being in her childhood home after so long away until her mother ran out and embraced her. Kitty hated her for it. Hated her father for his cruelty, her mother for welcoming her home as if nothing had happened. As if Thom had not been murdered, as if Evander's body wasn't still warm with life, as if Nate and Zoe and Tove weren't still imprisoned, alone, far from her.

'Thank God, you're home!' her mother cried. 'I've been so worried! Are you well? You look so thin, Catherine! Come inside, let's get you some food. There's so much to be done. I'm so pleased.'

Kitty followed her mother automatically. It was strange, not being happy to see her own family. She couldn't be. Kitty ached for her friends, for Nate, and her thoughts were so consumed with their fate that she hardly gave a thought to her own. Distantly she remembered what her father had said about Complementation and the future, and she found that she hardly cared. The only thing she hoped was that the others were all right.

Her mother made her a large meal that she barely touched, moving the food around her plate, having all but forgotten how to eat, and by the evening, she excused herself to her old bedroom, collapsing onto the bed, unable to move.

She dreamed of the bright green field again, although this time Nate was not there. The field and sky stretched on for eternity all around her, and she dropped to the ground, weeping in the safety of her mind.

One of the only things she could still control.

For the first weeks of her return to her old life, Kitty was visited daily by bodymen who took her bloods, her temperature, her pulse; they made notes of everything and asked her the exact extent of her illness and what all she had undergone whilst infected. They wanted to know what she ate, if and when she was sick, to what extent Nate had been able to heal her, and whether she noticed any enhancements or only detrimental side-effects. She told them as much as she dared, answering questions abstractly and without flourish or extensive detail, and kept the rest to herself. When asked direct questions, she replied numbly, distantly, and did not fight or run or argue. She was not forthcoming or inquisitive.

The months she had spent on the road with Nate and the others felt personal, even more so now that they were gone and she didn't know if she was ever going to see them again; the loss of Evander affected her more than she would have thought, and for days on end she could neither sleep nor eat. Terrible thoughts and daydreams about where the others were, what was being done to them, plagued her mind for hours on end, and as time went on, she started to wonder how much of her thoughts were memory, and how much was conjecture or simply fear, and discerning reality from fantasy became a constant struggle. It was the arrival of the designers, dress-makers, caterers, florists, capturists and planners that forced sudden awareness upon her. A gathering resignation towards her future settled upon her, and she spent her days staring out the window, dreaming of the Outlands and reuniting with her friends, of escaping the Kingdom forever.

The winter days of Anais had once been such a wonderful time. She would go skating with Thom after class, go to the winter festivals with her friends, see the latest reel or take a carriage ride through the streets, hauled jauntily along by pit ponies. Now the winter seemed soulless and wretched, and her thoughts returned always to the prison, and the strange dreams she had that were only ever in a bright green field.

Her binding ceremony to Lord Gabriel drew closer every day, and Kitty tried hard not to think about it. In the wake of Thom's death, the thought of ever touching another human had been repugnant to her. After months at Nate's side, healing slowly and not without effort, Kitty now found that the idea of another's touch was not terrible, it was just the idea of Lord Gabriel's touch which made her want to kill herself.

Jaiani seemed to have no such reservations. Her mother spent every hour that Kitty was not being poked and prodded by bodymen discussing the ceremony. Her father was out of the house most days, no doubt arranging another innocent man's hanging or whipping, and Kitty was glad of his absence. Whilst her mother might natter away and chastise her for her attitude and bother her unendingly, she had never ordered someone's death or the destruction of an entire group of starving citizens. She had never, Kitty was certain, sanctioned or overlooked rape.

One of the things Kitty did notice, despite her dejection, was that no one mentioned Thom. No one brought up his death or the reasons surrounding it. No one enquired as to whether or not she was all right or if she had grieved. No one save the bodymen asked her any personal questions at all, and there was a notable skirting of discussion when it came to Nate and what had occurred on the road.

Whether she had her father or Nate's mother to thank for the lack of interrogations, Kitty never bothered to find out, but eventually the bodymen declared that she carried no trace of disease or transferrable contagion, although her blood would forever play host to the mutant genes that had wormed their way inside of her, and they, too, left her alone.

In the weeks that followed, she lost herself in daydreams and contemplations and musings, and by the time her binding day came calling, she had almost convinced herself that reality was in her mind, rather than in the world around her.

The day of the ceremony was a grand day, bright and sunny, without a cloud in the sky. Almost warm for the winter months. One of those days that was deceptively perfect when it had absolutely no right to be. As if the weather itself had a sarcastic sense of humour and enjoyed mockery. Rainy on the days which ought to be the happiest, sunny on the days where rain and wind would more aptly echo the mood.

After a month under the unending and intrusive scrutiny of her mother and father, Kitty was all but marched from their home in Anais into the waiting hover and from there to Kingscote where the ceremony would be held. It was rather a formal palace, built in King Franklin's honour just after the war. A blockish and ominous design more akin to a prison than one of the most popular places for bindings, ceremonies, parties and games.

Kingscote was tucked into a corner of the city, adjacent to the River Crow, downstream from the prison and the Diseases Department, and all the places Kitty now harboured fervent desire to burn to the ground.

Everyone who held the King's favour, or her father's favour, everyone who wanted position and power, everyone she had ever known or loved or feared, and a thousand people she had never seen before in her life, attended her Complementation to Lord Gabriel. So many people and yet even their vast, pulsating mass did not seem to fill the hall as they ought to have. The room was so cold and empty that no amount of inhabitants could make it feel cosy or welcoming.

She was dressed in a beautiful maroon gown with golden flowers adorning the waist and ending halfway down one side of the skirt; the black tattoos of binding stained her wrists and the side of her face.

It was surreal to see her reflection. She did not recognise herself. Her father's emblem, clear on her mother's face, was a hawk, and now adorned Lord Gabriel, who had removed the tattoo from his previous binding after his Complement's death. It now marked her.

As she stared in the mirror, ignoring the seamstress and face-painter, doing her utmost not to communicate with any of them, Kitty appraised the hawk now flying from the corner of her eye to the middle of her cheek. She ought to have hated it. She hated Lord Gabriel already and she had barely spoken to him once, yet every time she looked at it she thought of Nate, and it was the thought of his fate which kept her standing.

Kitty had already determined that once she was Complemented she would use the Lord's extensive wealth and power to find out where exactly Nate, Tove and Zoe had been sent and make certain they were being treated well. She just had to make sure she had the resolve to get through the ceremony.

'Mistress, do you want your hair up or down?' enquired the stylist, showing her several different options in captures. 'You ought to choose. It is your binding day after all.'

Kitty shrugged. 'I don't care.'

The stylist, a young man with wild green hair and black eyes, looked baffled. 'But Mistress! You must be excited! The amount of guests – the *King* is here.'

'I don't care,' she said again, feeling more tired than she ever had whilst on the run. 'Just do whatever you want.'

'Very well,' said the stylist, looking thoroughly putout.

Kitty looked back at her reflection and said nothing. Her thoughts were a thousand leagues away, and she had no intention of paying attention to this ridiculous affair. Lord Gabriel was a lecherous old man. It was a wretched punishment for any woman, let alone one that had had such great prospects once. Thom was surely rolling over in his grave at the thought of her binding with someone so heinous. Anyone was better, but perhaps that was why her punishment was so light. Even the King knew that Gabriel was loathed by the entire population.

When her dress was done and her feet adorned in jewels – no shoes were worn at the ceremony – and her hair was pinned back from one side of her face, cascading down her opposite shoulder, the workers announced they had finished.

'All the people in the Kingdom will love you,' said Freya, the face-painter.

Kitty raised an eyebrow. 'What?'

'The broadcasters are here,' she replied. 'The King has ordered that the ceremony be shown on every screen in the Kingdom.'

Kitty's jaw dropped. 'He's what?'

'You didn't know? It's been all over the news, Mistress! The whole Kingdom is waiting with bated breath to see your Complementation.'

'Oh excellent,' said Kitty. 'Just what I've always wanted.'

'It's perfectly fine to be nervous,' said Freya cajolingly. 'Anyone would be. But don't worry, dear, you look beautiful.'

'I'm not worried. I'm furious.'

Before Freya could say anything else, the door opened and the last person Kitty had ever expected to see walked in.

'Ciara!' Kitty all but flung herself at her old friend.

Ciara held her close, her grip almost as tight. 'I'm so sorry, Cat,' she whispered. 'I'm so, so sorry about Thom. I would have done something if I could.' To the workers behind Kitty, she said loudly, 'I will wait with Lady Catherine. All of you – out.'

Without protest, the workers left the room, closing the door behind them. Ciara took Kitty's hand and led her over to the sofa. 'Oh, Cat. What happened?' Ciara's hair was cut close to her head, giving her a sharper look than the last time Kitty had seen her. Her eyes were as wide and genuine as ever. She was also noticeably pregnant, her belly swelling in front of her breasts, giving her a motherly air which Kitty thought suited her well.

'How much time do we have?'

Ciara looked out the small timekeeper that hung from her neck. 'About an hour until the ceremony starts.'

'How'd you even know about it?'

'Your mother invited me,' said Ciara, sticking out her tongue. 'I think she knew you might need a friend.'

'I do,' said Kitty. The overwhelming urge to tell someone, anyone, everything that had happened, finally took over, and she relayed everything to Ciara, telling her even about Archie and all the horrors that had transpired. The only thing she didn't mention, was the one thing she would never tell anyone – that Nate had killed Archie. All the rest she told her best friend, holding Ciara's hands and feeling far more stable than she had in the weeks that had passed since she had been separated from her friends in Redwater. When she got to the part about Evander, she felt her throat close and her heartbeat quicken, and Ciara had to guess what had happened as Kitty tried not to choke.

By the time she had finished, her makeup was well and truly ruined, and Ciara retrieved the paint from the table, drying Kitty's tears with a cloth before beginning to fix the mess. 'I can't believe it,' she said, smearing the paint over Kitty's cheeks with except flicks. 'I'm so sorry, Cat. About Thom and Nate and your friend – Evander? Was that it?'

'Yeah,' croaked Kitty. 'Evander. Tove. Zoe.'

'They sound wonderful.'

'They are. I miss them.'

'You miss him,' said Ciara knowingly.

'I never thought I would. How strange is that?'

Ciara shrugged. 'It's not so strange. I can't imagine going through that much with Adil.'

'How is bound life?' Kitty gestured to her stomach. 'Good, I assume?'

'It could be worse,' said Ciara. 'Adil's happy in the countryside. But we're not friends. Not in the way you were with Thom. We're still formal, even now.'

Kitty pursed her lips. 'I still can't believe your parents wouldn't let you come with us to study. Adil could have as well. Then you would have known him a bit better before you Complemented.'

'No,' said Ciara, shaking her head sadly. 'I don't think we would ever have become friends. We're too different. Nothing we say is of interest to the other. The only thing we have in common is the children, and even then I think we both know that we're only doing our duty to King Markas.'

The population was dwindling so quickly that any couple who had more than three children was given money from the Crown, encouragement to have more. If a couple had six, they were given a free house and their income was doubled for an entire year. Many families had used the system to raise their position in society. It was the only sure way to rise through the ranks. Anything else was next to impossible. Kitty was infinitely glad that Lord Gabriel was as high in society as one could go. She had no intention of giving him three or more children. She had no intention of giving him one.

'How do you do it?' she asked.

Ciara raised an eyebrow. 'Do what?'

'Have sex with him when you don't like him?'

'I close my eyes and pretend I'm somewhere else,' said Ciara. 'With someone else. Margot or Rose.'

'Do you still see them?'

'Sometimes. When I'm not too busy with the children.'

'Once this whole bloody thing is finished with, I'll come and stay with you,' Kitty offered. 'If you want? I don't want to live with this wretch for long if I can help it, and it's as good an excuse as any. We can keep each other company.'

Ciara's eyes lit up with delight. 'Really? Oh, yes, please do. I'm so bored out there, you've no idea.'

The two women embraced until Ciara announced that she had to use the toilet and disappeared into the other room. Even pregnant, Ciara was still tall and beautiful. She had always been the more beautiful of the two of them, something that had once driven Kitty mad with jealousy, but now she was glad of. Ciara's loveliness supplemented her selflessness, and it was impossible to still be envious of her. Kitty pulled her legs into her body and wrapped her arms around them, resting her chin on her knees. If one thing had gone slightly differently, she would be in this room, preparing to Complement Thom, happy and ignorant.

A knock at the door startled her, and she looked up to see her mother walk in.

'You look beautiful,' she said. 'Absolutely beautiful, Catherine.'

Kitty merely nodded.

Jaiani sat down across from her with a furrowed brow, looking every bit the elegant Complement of the King's right-hand. Her mother had always been the most beautiful woman in the room, the most collected and controlled. She struck fear into the hearts of more people than her father, if that was even possible, and Kitty had always been more intimidated by her than she had been of Mickey.

'Catherine, you brought this whole mess upon yourself,' her mother chided gently. 'Your father was able to save your life, and a life as the King's niece is hardly something to fret over. You should be grateful. Yet you look like you're going to your death.'

'Forgive me,' said Kitty. 'I don't see this as a gift.'

'You're alive.'

'Evander isn't.'

Jaiani clenched her jaw and shook her head. 'Was it Nathanial who encouraged this attitude? What am I asking – of course it was.

Catherine, Nathanial is exactly where he belongs. It was by the good grace of your father that he even lives.'

Kitty snorted. 'Yeah, that's what I call King Markas fucking Cecily: "good grace". You should tell him that later. I'm sure he'll find it as funny as I do.'

The slap caught her off guard, and Kitty reeled away from her mother, stunned. 'Don't you ever speak such lies again, young lady,' her mother warned. 'You will be the daughter I raised and do your duty to your Crown and Council. That is life.'

Ciara chose that moment to return, surprise etched all over her beautiful face as she sensed the tension between mother and daughter. 'I think it's time,' she said softly. 'Shall I walk back with you, Jaiani?'

'That would be lovely, Ciara, thank you,' said Jaiani, standing and refusing to look at her daughter as she added, 'I hope you remember what I said, Catherine. Do not disgrace this family.'

'No,' said Kitty as the door shut behind them. 'We wouldn't want that.'

There was a bottle of alcohol on the table; one of the workers had brought it in as a gift. Kitty opened it hurriedly, forcing the foul tasting liquid past her lips even as her stomach threatened to turn against her, rebelling against the strong substance. When she set it down, a deep warmth was spreading through her veins and her sight was fast becoming hazy. She drank another few gulps until she was certain that she would not care about the next several hours.

When the escorts finally came for her, each man and woman dressed in gold and dark green, Kitty had felt numb enough to move. She took the arm of the one of the male escorts, Gabriel's cousin of some distance, and was impressed that she was able to walk without falling. The cousin grinned at her as they made their way down the corridor.

'Drunk?'

'Not nearly enough.'

He leaned close conspiratorially. 'Gabriel's rarely sober. I doubt he'll even notice.'

'Wonderful.'

'Can't believe he finally got someone,' said the cousin. 'Sorry it had to be you.'

'Why?'

'I'd not wish him on the cruellest woman in the world,' he said. 'And I certainly wouldn't wish him on someone as pretty as you.'

Kitty gave him a weak smile. 'Just tell me there's going to be enough drink to make me not care.'

'That I can guarantee.' They had reached the doors to the great hall. The cousin released her and bowed low. 'Good luck. I'll see you at the feast.'

'Bring the drink,' she whispered.

With a hearty laugh, he assumed his place behind her, beside a short girl with bright blonde hair and invisible eyebrows.

Kitty turned to face forwards and steeled herself for what was about to come. The doors opened and she was almost blinded by the light that burst forth. It was a huge room, with light coming from the glass ceiling. More than a thousand guests filled the seats up to the podium. Great baskets of spilling flowers were hung from the walls, filling the room with strong smells. She caught sight of a few faces that she recognised. She saw Ciara and Adil seated to her left, and was glad of Ciara's reassuring smile. Blaise Roman, the man Nate thought of as a best friend, nodded sombrely to her, his mouth a thin line of commiseration. A few seats away she caught sight of Nadia Tam, standing beside her Complement. And then, nearer to the front, Cecily and Hamish Anteros.

Lord Gabriel stood in front of the officiator. Kitty had never been so repelled by anyone before. He had burst veins in his cheeks and nose from too many years of drinking, and there was hair sticking out of his ears and nose. A bad smell, like mould, emanated from him, almost choking her.

The huge broadcast at the front of the room showed a close-up of their faces, and Kitty couldn't understand how anyone watching the ceremony could presume this to be a joyous affair. Perhaps that was the punishment, the warning to the rest of the Kingdom – this is what happens to the daughter of the King's second when she breaks the law. See how much she hates it. Imagine how terrible your punishment would be.

The moment the ceremony ended and they were announced, Kitty turned away from him. Most kissed or hugged at the end of the ceremony, depending on how well they knew each other, but it was not required, and she had no intention of touching him.

The King, who had been sitting in the very front, approached them. He was an old man now. Born to King Franklin's second Complement when the first King was almost to the end of his days, and having survived the first wave of the Plague just as her father and Lord Gabriel had, King Markas had a strange air of wisdom and knowing about him that was disconcerting. It was clear that he had been handsome once, and for all that he had done, Kitty had to admit that he didn't appear evil. Perhaps that was why so many followed him.

'A truly blessed union,' said the King. 'I could not be more pleased for you, nephew. What a lovely Complement you now have at your side.'

Gabriel smacked her rear. 'She's a fine thing.'

Kitty's face went hot with rage and she had to bite her lip so hard that she tasted blood just to keep from punching him.

'Shall I escort the Lady to the feast?' The King held out his arm and Kitty had no choice but to take it. 'Why don't you walk the Queen, nephew?'

Without waiting for Gabriel's response, King Markas led Kitty away with a firm grip, the great crowd parting before them, each bowing once to the King as he passed by. As they stepped out of the hall and into the corridor, the King looked down at her.

'You should look more happy, Lady Catherine,' he advised. 'It is your Complementation day. And to think, you almost had no days left.'

A chill spread through Kitty's body, as if she had just plunged into ice. 'What makes you think I am not happy, Your Majesty?'

'I am old. I am not blind.' He stopped and turned to face her. Only then did Kitty realise that they were alone save for the guards. 'Do you think it is your good fortune that you are alive today? You play a very dangerous game.'

'I don't play any games,' she snapped. 'The whole thing was a great bloody accident. The man who ought to've been my Complement is dead and the man who saved my life is now slaving away in the a workforce somewhere because we were trying to find a cure to your illness.'

The King's lip curled. 'Yes, I know the little lie you told your father. Continue to spin it. Any hint of dissention reaches my ears, and not even your new Complement can save you.'

'I'm not lying!' It was so strange – arguing with the King. 'Do you know what Serum 23 does to a person? Have you any idea what it was your father had manufactured? Nate Anteros was rotting away before my eyes. Any touch from another human being sent us both into unimaginable pain. You think I'm lying?'

'Careful, child,' he warned. 'You are very close to losing the life I have granted you out of gratitude towards your father.'

Kitty closed her mouth, panting through her nose.

'Good,' he said. 'You may yet learn your place. Whatever it was that you and your friend stumbled across in Nitoib, I do not care. This is why history is so dangerous, child. It gives people clues to things they have no ability to comprehend.'

'You had Thomas Anteros executed for trying to save my life,' she hissed through gritted teeth, unable to stop herself.

The King grabbed her and slammed her against the wall, his hand closing tightly around her neck. 'I had Thomas Anteros executed for breaking into the most restricted of buildings and searching through the historical databases. I admire your spirit, child, but I warn you that it will be your undoing. I granted your father this one gift because he has done more for me than anyone else in this Kingdom. But you, *Lady Catherine*, are owed nothing, not even your worthless life. Step outside the bounds of your place once more and you will not only return to Redwater, you will be joined by Nathanial Anteros and the two Southern brats your father saved. Do – not – test – me.'

His grip on her neck was so tight that she was starting to see stars. He released her and she buckled, gasping. It wasn't the threat to her own life that struck her, but the threat to Nate's once again. She wondered if the King had ever done anything without threats and fear. But then, she supposed, he would not have been so powerful. Was there no other way to win the hearts and obedience of millions without frightening them into submission? Had there ever been a time before this one where people did not fear for their lives at every turn?

'I do not hold my Kingdom together through rebellions and strife because I am kind and forgiving, my dear,' he continued. 'I hold my Kingdom because nobody else can. I will not have my authority doubted because two children decided to go for an evening stroll through the mountains, which, if you recall, are out of bounds and completely off limits. You're lucky you're not in more trouble.'

He held out his hand pointedly, and after a moment she took it. He wrenched her ungallantly into an upright position.

'Now, shall we go to your feast? I do believe my nephew is waiting.'

Kitty said nothing else as he led her down the corridor and into the dining hall.

The tables were laden heavily with food, all but groaning under the weight. Roast beef, sauced beef, diced and fried and grilled beef; roast chicken, baked chicken, chicken soup and chicken stripes in ten different coloured sauces; pork, lamb, deer, fowl, hare, horse, dog, turkey and a few other types of meat she couldn't identify; grilled vegetables, fifteen different types of salad, some potato, some rice, some egg; mountains of bread with different seeds, grains and wheat of several different colours; bowls of steaming soups and chowders and stews; ice sculptures every few feet in impressively carved shapes – there was a horse, a lion, a hawk, a fish, a sword, a boat – all surrounded by pitchers of beer, wine, juice, water, and several other unidentifiable liquids. There were meat pies, fruit pies and vegetable pies, each with impressive designs in the crust; dumplings, chips, roast potatoes and mashed potatoes; jellies and puddings and custards; and near the front, a cake that was taller than Kitty herself, covered with chocolate and vanilla icing, so impeccably done that Kitty was almost sad to know it would be carved into and devoured later.

Everyone bowed as the King entered, but the moment he left her side, more people than she had ever seen approached her to give their congratulations and wish her many children and a long and healthy binding. Kitty barely heard any of them. She thanked them distractedly and tried to make her way towards the nearest table with alcohol, wanting desperately to get drunk enough so as to forget her own name.

She reached the table after almost twenty minutes of trying to part the endless crowd. She picked up a few of the pitchers, smelling curiously. One of the clear ones, the smell so strong it almost bowled her over, she recognised and her chest tightened. Cisco. She poured herself a large glass and took a large gulp. It tasted like Talon. It tasted like Nate.

Kitty choked at the thought, not knowing where it had come from. The sudden, desperate ache in her heart made her take another sip, closing her eyes and remembering the beautiful town and their time there.

She drank. And drank. And drank.

She didn't remember eating anything, and she certainly didn't remember leaving the dining hall, but she became very aware when she was suddenly in a strange bedroom being undressed by one of the maidservants. She went cold all over and gripped tightly to the nightdress that was hanging loosely from her shoulders in place of her gown.

The door at the other end of the room opened and Gabriel stumbled in, food down his front and eyes bleary. Kitty looked at him in disgust. 'Sleep in another room,' she said. 'I don't want you near me.'

Gabriel stared at her drunkenly. 'Excuse me?'

'You heard what I said – I didn't stutter. Get. Out.'

'You're my Complement,' he said, moving towards her.

'So I must live with you,' she said. 'I don't have to enjoy you. And I certainly don't have to sleep with you.'

Gabriel lunged at her. Despite her own drunkenness, she suddenly felt very aware and managed to dodge out of the way. The maidservant looked between them awkwardly, not knowing whether to linger or leave.

'I will not be made a fool of,' he warned.

'And I will not be made a prize of,' she retorted. Gabriel was not a tall man, but he was larger than she, and she had the same horrible feeling from him that she had got from Archie. It made her stomach twist uncontrollably. 'I was promised to another and if you for one moment think you are on par with him, you're an idiot. I will stand beside you in public if I must, but do not presume you own me in private. It is against the law to force me into your bed, and you know that well, being the lawmaker's nephew. Now kindly leave.'

Gabriel gaped at her. 'You little whore.'

'Oh, that's very good, insult the woman forced to bind with you. Not only do you embarrass yourself with your drunken stupidity – you know you're the laughing stock of the Kingdom, don't you? – you only hurt your case by insulting me. Get out.'

'You should be happy to be bound to me,' he hissed. 'I'm the highest man in society you could have ensnared. Any woman would be lucky to have me.'

'I'd rather have a rat.'

She was unprepared for his fist. He hit her hard, right in the stomach. He started to undress, and she slammed her fist as hard as she could into his groin. He cursed violently and clutched his crotch. She scrambled away, gasping for breath, her stomach hurting so much that she thought she was going to be sick.

'Touch me again and you'll die painfully,' she said.

'Are you threatening me?'

'Yes.'

They glared at each other for almost a minute before he turned and stormed out of the door, slamming it with such a *bang* it caused the painting on the wall to fall off, crashing dramatically to the floor. If she hadn't been so scared, Kitty would have laughed at the absurdity. Instead she allowed the maidservant to help her to her feet and walk her over to the bed.

'You shouldn't have angered him so much,' said the woman softly. 'He's not one to forget, Lord Gabriel.'

'I don't care,' said Kitty. 'Just so long as he keeps away from me.'

'He won't do that, either.' The woman brushed a loose strand of hair back from Kitty's face and shook her head. 'You should have just let him have you. Then he would have grown bored and moved on to the next one. Nothing is ever of interest to Gabriel except when he can't have it.'

Kitty's lip curled. 'I am not afraid.'

'You'd be a lot safer.'

After the maidservant left and Kitty had double-checked that the doors were firmly locked, she collapsed onto the bed, bone tired and terrified, and entirely unable to sleep. She closed her eyes and tried to think of Thom. Memories of him had so often been her refuge. She remembered back to when they decided to take a boat trip and it started raining. Thom's hover wouldn't start and they had conn'd Nate to come and pick them up. And then suddenly she was thinking of Nate and her heart began to race.

She remembered him as he once was, with dark, curly red hair that danced in every direction, a ginger beard that was always unkempt, strong arms and wicked grey eyes alight with mischief. At the time, she had been so annoyed with his music, his conversation, his entire being. Now she thought of how he had teased them for not checking the forecast and she smiled to herself. The memory of him giving her a dry shirt to wear that she had thought smelled bad at the time – and now would have loved to have wrapped around her – made her feel almost better.

Clenching her eyes shut, she clung desperately to the image of him, and fell asleep replaying their old conversations in her mind.

The next morning dawned bright and grey, a fresh layer of snow on the ground. Kitty bundled herself tightly in warm clothes and left the bedroom.

A large crowd gathered to send them off, though Kitty dearly wished they wouldn't. Gabriel had come down to breakfast that morning, so angry that she wouldn't have been surprised to see smoke coming out of his ears, but he had said nothing to her parents or the King and Queen about their night apart, although Kitty assumed that was more to save face for himself rather than for her. If the King had sensed any tension, he seemed to put it down to the fact that Kitty hated the entire situation, rather than that she had rejected Gabriel, and he gave her no lingering looks of deadly promise, for which Kitty was glad. Her stomach was a dark purple colour, her neck similarly bruised, and she really wasn't in the humour to deal with either of them.

Ciara hugged her tightly as they waited on the side of the road beside the thrumming hover, promising to come and visit her in the next couple of weeks, and wishing her luck with a pointed look on her face. Kitty kissed her on the cheek, looked at her parents once, and clambered inside. She was too angry at them to say anything. For his part, her father had spent the morning talking to Gabriel with obvious disdain, seemingly appalled by the man's entire existence. Her mother was as friendly and charming as if she'd just had a new son, and Kitty was furious about it.

It was going to be a long flight to Lord Gabriel's palace in the countryside near the border of Redland. She had seen captures of the estate a few weeks before and it looked large enough to get lost on, with wide open fields and forests. As long as Gabriel kept his distance from her, she thought it might not be too terrible. At least the scenery would be beautiful.

Kitty curled up in the seat across from Gabriel and stared resolutely out the window, not wanting to look at him. He still smelt noxious and she opened the window, preferring frostbite to death by mouldy asphyxiation.

'Shut the window,' he snapped. 'It's freezing.'

'Take a bath and I will,' she retorted.

Gabriel's chubby hands balled into fists. 'No wonder the King had to beg me to take you. No one would ever want you.'

Kitty let out a bark of laughter and sneered at him. 'Many have wanted. Don't be so presumptuous because I'm not impressed by you. It may have worked on others, but I'm not easy, nor am I desperate. I'm here solely because I have to be. Nothing more. If you made more of an effort, perhaps I could tolerate you. As it is, you are a foul smelling, foul tempered, foul man, and I have no desire to remain in your presence longer than I have to. So do us both a favour and leave me be.'

It was clear that he had more to say, but Kitty looked back out the window and refused to acknowledge him for the rest of the journey. When they stopped at an inn that evening, she booked into her own room and charged it to her father's account. She had a feeling that her father would stay quiet and accept the charge.

She slept poorly.

The second day of travelling passed much like the first – in complete and uncomfortable silence. They did not stop the second night, instead flying straight on until the early hours of the morning. The stars were bright and beautiful when they finally pulled to a stop in front of the palace, the moon full and foreboding, almost yellow against the blackness. A footman ran out and opened the door for Lord Gabriel, who stormed past him and waddled as quickly as he could up the steps and into his palace, disappearing from view.

'Prepare a separate room for me,' said Kitty as she stepped out of the hover and pulled her woollen cloak around her shoulders to ward off the cold. 'As far from Lord Gabriel as can be managed.'

The housekeeper, who had joined her at the top of the stairs, was surprised. 'But every room in the house is cold, Lady Catherine. It will not be comfortable.'

'Neither would sleeping near my Complement,' she said. 'Your furthest room, please.'

'As you wish.'

She followed the housekeeper, who introduced herself as Magda, up two storeys of winding stairs and into another wing of the great manor. It was desperately cold, and she could see her breath billowing around her but the room Magda led her to was large and beautiful, and once the fire was lit and the heaters turned on full, it felt cosy enough. Kitty sat on a fat chintz chair and drew her legs into her chest.

The servants brought up her luggage, a few of them giving her curious looks, but not one spoke to her. It was incredibly lonely.

She stared at the dancing flames in the fire, flames so similar to the ones that had lit up the grove, keeping them warm as Evander told his stories and Nate kept her warm and Tove smiled at her and Zoe sang softly, ever on guard, ever protective of them all. Kitty's chest ached and she wondered, not for the first time, if one could die from the agony of memory.

When the last of her bags were brought in, Magda came over and sat beside her. 'Is there anything else you need, my Lady?'

'Call me Kitty,' she said softly. 'I'm not a lady. That's not me.'

'But you are.'

Kitty looked over at her. 'Please.'

'Kitty,' she agreed at last. 'Do you need anything else?'

'A computer,' she said.

'There's a spare in the study,' said Magda. 'I'll have one of the servants bring it up to you.'

'Thank you.' Kitty smiled at her. 'Oh, and one more thing.'

'Yes?'

'Do the doors lock from the inside?'

Magda raised an eyebrow curiously. 'Yes. And you can deadbolt the door as well.'

Those few words gave her more relief than anything else had in the last couple of days, and Kitty thanked her gratefully.

Light was beginning to filter through the window, making the place feel less sinister than it had when she first entered. She sat on the window seat, comfortable with multiple pillows and a thick blanket, and watched as the sunrise shone down upon the immense gardens, fields and forests of the property, covered in a layer of beautiful snow and looking far more spectacular than anything she could have imagined. The thin computer that Magda had brought her rested lightly on her lap, and she accessed the network without difficulty.

She almost choked when the first thing she saw on the news page was her own face, scowling back at her. There was a long article published the day before about her binding to Lord Gabriel.

Dumbfounded, she read the article, mouth open.

> *Well-wishers and members of the royal family filled the halls of Kingscote yesterday evening for the Complementation ceremony of Lord Gabriel, nephew to King Markas and widower of Lady Gloria, to Catherine Taenia, daughter of Mickey and Jaiani Taenia.*
>
> *Catherine Taenia made headlines in recent months for absconding with convicted criminal Nathanial Anteros after the death of her original Complement, Thomas Anteros, who was executed shortly after breaking into the Building of Historical Records. Per reports,*

Taenia did not know the extent of criminal activity going on at the time and was manipulated by Anteros into believing that she had no other choice. The binding to Lord Gabriel is believed to be proof that Taenia has once again returned to the King's favour and is believed to be welcomed back in most circles.

Although her original inclination to work as a mathematics teacher in Cutta has since become obsolete due to her associations, she fairs better than Nathanial Anteros, who has since been sent to work in the criminal camps in the west. He is sentenced to five years' hard labour, after which time he is expected to re-join his parents, Cecily and Hamish Anteros, in their home in Cutta. Known favourites of the King and Queen, the Anteros family was able to convince His Majesty to spare the life of their only remaining son who will inherit the family fortune one day despite his criminal record.

For her part, Catherine Taenia painted a beautiful picture at the binding, seen below wearing a Yann Follett original gown. The ceremony began at precisely five o'clock, unhindered by the heavy bouts of snow that have plagued Anais in recent months.

Escorted by cousins and family members, Taenia and Lord Gabriel exchanged their vows in front of an awestruck crowd numbering almost fifteen hundred strong. Although noticeably reserved, Taenia cut an incredibly elegant figure, putting to rest all rumours of her immaturity and flightiness that her adventures in recent months have lent supposed credence to.

Lord Gabriel, a well-known womaniser throughout his previous binding, made headlines a month ago when he pledged that he had calmed down following the death of his Complement from the Bite, and would be a far different man to his young Complement than he had been to the late Lady Gloria. Whether or not this pledge will hold credence has yet to be seen as the couple left almost immediately for Timberview Palace where they are expected to remain.

Alona Tolstoy, spokesperson for the Crown, has said that His Majesty awaits news of a child in upcoming months. Medical testing has already shown Taenia's fertility to be of no concern, and the King has said they expect at least six children.

Annoyed, Kitty exited the page and went to the criminal profiling site. It had been set up in the first years of King Markas' reign. Every criminal was recorded, their capture displayed, their location given, their crimes there for the world to see. It was meant to be shaming and informative, but Kitty knew few people who actively used it. The criminals that weren't executed were always sent to the work camps, so there was nothing to know most of the time.

She found Nate's profile instantly and there was a nervous fluttering in her chest when his capture appeared. It had been taken recently, she could tell from how thin he was. His full beard was longer than it had been when last she'd seen him and his hair was starting to return.

His crimes took up several paragraphs, going into great detail, but she knew them already and didn't bother to read through them. After a minute's scanning, her eyes found his location – Argon Basin, Redland.

She let out a shaking breath she hadn't known she was holding. Argon Basin was a ways away, but it wasn't the worst place in the world, and it was better than some of the places he could have been sent to.

The profile told her that he was to be working there until the city was completed. It would be a long while, and she hated to think of him slaving away in the freezing weather, but at least she had proof that he was alive.

A weight she hadn't even known she was carrying lifted from her shoulders. Keeping the page open, she pulled up another and typed in Zoe's name.

The capture of Zoe was heart-breaking. Her hair had been shaved off and there was a fading bruise on her cheek. Her eyes looked hollow. She knew about Evander, then. There was a look to that kind of loss, and Kitty knew it instantly. Zoe was listed as working in Nesrol, Redland, several hundred kilometres south of Argon Basin. Kitty's heart sank. She'd been hoping that Nate and Zoe would be together, for moral support if nothing else.

'At least you're alive,' she whispered to the screen. Keeping both pages up, not wanting to lose the images of her friends and the printed assertion that they were both still alive, Kitty searched through the girls' schools in Brantryne and after almost an hour of flicking through captures, found Tove.

The girl looked thinner and sadder than Kitty had ever seen her, but she was dressed well and attempting a smile for the capture. Kitty leaned back against the wall, hands trembling over the keyboard, allowing the relief to sink in. They were all still alive. Her father hadn't lied to her.

It was only then that she realised she had no faith in her parents anymore, not even her father. She could barely remember being the woman who was pledged to Thom, saw her parents for lunch every weekend, and had a future with a good position and uncomplicated prospects.

A sudden thought occurred to her and she looked at the date at the top of the page.

She had been twenty-two for weeks now and hadn't even realised it. Nate's words floated back to her from the boat.

You should have a proper birthday, darling. After everything we've been through, it's the least we could do.

The words left a hollow feeling in her chest and her hands balled into fists.

It was late afternoon before Kitty left her perch on the window seat, feeling worlds better than she had that morning, reassured with the knowledge that at least her friends were safe and alive. She took a bath, scrubbing the wrist tattoos as hard as she could just to see if she could get them to come off. It was pointless endeavour, but she felt better for having tried. It was still so strange to see the tattoo on her face every time she caught a glimpse of her reflection in the mirror, and every time she saw it, she was filled with a mixture of opposing emotions – an ache for Nate and an almost overwhelming hatred for Gabriel.

To bide time before going to find something to eat for dinner, she cut her nails and dried her hair meticulously and then braided it firmly into a plait so that none of the wayward strands would annoy her. She dressed in soft house boots, and at last left her room, plucking up the courage it would take to face Gabriel if she happened to run into him again.

Timberview Palace was a gorgeous manor that had been built during the Last War as a refuge for King Franklin. When the war ended, it remained in the family and Lady Beatrice, King Markas' sister, was given residency there. Gabriel and his siblings had been born in the palace, but it bore the marks of his mother's touch and had a rare elegance that Kitty was certain Gabriel had never once tried to emulate.

She wandered down the marble stairs, gazing at the various portraits and captures on the walls, not really paying attention to them. At the bottom of the stairs, she found Magda busy dusting, and walked over.

'Where's the kitchen?' she said awkwardly.

'Dinner will be ready shortly,' said Magda. 'Do you want me to show you to the dining room?'

Kitty shook her head. 'I'll just eat in my room.'

'Lord Gabriel has requested your presence,' said Magda. 'I don't think he would take kindly to your absence.'

Not sure of just how much she could get away with before Lord Gabriel snapped altogether, Kitty gave in and followed Magda to the dining hall. The large room housed a long table. Garish candelabras and chandeliers that were powered by the great solar panels on the roof, lit the room brightly. It was clinically white, and the statues in the corner were of strange, mutated creatures that Kitty hated almost instantly. Gabriel was already seated at the table, his eyes narrowing as she entered.

'So you've decided to join me,' he observed. 'Have you decided to fulfil your other duties as my Complement?'

Kitty found herself instantly regretting her decision to come. She sat down at the opposite end of the table and crossed her arms. 'Hardly. I was told you wanted my presence, so I've come. That's the extent of it.'

'Your father clearly did not discipline you properly in your youth,' he said, taking a sip of dark red wine. 'A pity. Such a beautiful creature should not have such a sharp tongue.'

'Go fuck yourself.'

Lord Gabriel's brow furrowed, and he pursed his lips as he appraised her. 'What do you think the King would say if I informed him of your attitude?'

He was trying to frighten her, Kitty was well aware of that. Nate's words rang in her ears. *Don't let them see your fear.* She swallowed. 'I've no doubt he would be displeased,' she said. 'But you won't say anything.'

'Won't I?'

'And admit that your Complement finds you repugnant? I doubt it.'

Whether her words actually offended him, she had no idea. He chuckled darkly and set his glass down. 'It is your duty as a citizen to provide the Kingdom with children.'

Magda entered at that moment, two other servants following her, and great platters of food were placed on the table.

Kitty's wine glass was filled to the brim and she drained the glass and refilled it before the servants had even left. Rubbing her forehead, she met Gabriel's beady eyes. 'I will outlive you,' she said bluntly. 'My next Complement will be the father of my children.'

She had always wanted children with Thom. A family. She no longer ached for that as she once had, but for some reason when she imagined children, she imagined them looking the same. The straight Anteros' nose, striking eyes, proud and strong.

They looked nothing like Gabriel, that much was certain.

Gabriel snorted. 'You think you're that sought after? A criminal and belligerent who is widely believed to have whored herself out to Nathanial Anteros? No one wants you. No one will. I'm the only one who would have you, and that was a favour to my beloved uncle.'

Kitty sneered at him. 'And if I did fuck Nate Anteros?'

It worked. Gabriel had been trying to hurt her with his words yet it was clear he had not truly believed them; no one really did. Criminals were widely believed to be diseased degenerates who should never be touched, and her words cast a shadow over his face. Yet he recovered himself quickly and shrugged. 'I have been with many women who have been with many men. What do I care? I require an heir and you shall provide me with one.'

'I won't.'

'You will, or I will see to it that Anteros is sent to Perry for the rest of his sentence – should he last that long.'

Kitty froze. The Perry Mines were notorious for their terrible conditions. Located in the far north of Cutta, only the poorest of citizens and indentured convicts worked there without choice, and most died in their first two years of labour. The mines were deeply unstable. If the cave-ins, rock slides, fumes or radiation didn't kill you, the mutant animals, violent workers and riots certainly would. No one had ever survived there for more than a few years. Nate was as safe as possible in Argon Basin, but he had no favours left and she doubted even the King's infatuation with Cecily would prevent him from sending Nate to such a place. If anything, he'd be delighted at the chance to have one more way to punish them.

It was evident from his expression that Gabriel believed he had won.

Kitty drained the last of the wine and glared at her untouched plate of food. Did she have any choice? Had she not agreed to this because it was the only option? She had meant it when she swore up and down to her father that she would do anything to keep Nate and the others alive. Somehow she had never thought it would get this far. Her mind had never allowed her to imagine such a grim fate. She had felt some semblance of power in those moments, bargaining for the others.

Kitty appraised Gabriel, a sneer curling her lip, wondering what it would be like to kill him the way Nate had killed Archie. She was astonished by how much the prospect appealed to her. Such thoughts would have horrified her months ago. She imagined stabbing him, poisoning him, strangling him, smothering him, each image more graphic than the last.

She took another gulp of wine, mulling over her options, hating each and every one of them. Could she play him? Use him to her advantage as Thom would have done? She wasn't sure. Even pretending to acquiesce to his request sounded repugnant. Her stomach turned and she wished she didn't feel so afraid.

She said nothing to him for the rest of the night, and disappeared to her bedroom, bolting the door behind her, not sure if there was a solution, or if she would have to admit defeat. The thought of touching Gabriel made her want to tear her skin off; bile rose in her throat and she walked over to the window, breathing deeply through her nose, trying not to panic.

Eventually, the anger and helplessness left her exhausted, and she stared up at the moon, a heavy blanket wrapped around her shoulders, and thought of Nate. Days of travel separated them, and the might of Crown and Council, but as Kitty stared at the moon, choking on bitterness and regret, she found that she wanted nothing more than to steal his strength and tear the world apart, hurting everyone who had ever damaged or imprisoned them.

She thought of the last few months and how very differently her life had turned out to be. Six months ago she had dreamed of a life with Thom; two months ago she had wanted to be in the Outlands with Nate, Evander, Zoe and Tove. Now she wondered idly if death would bring her peace, if she would see Thom again.

She looked down at the grounds below and wondered if it would hurt, falling so far and landing on the ground, thinking of nothing but impact and blackness.

Kitty made a face and sighed, leaning her head back against the wall. A small voice in the back of her mind kept whispering to wait. A soft, deep voice, refined by years of elite education and somewhat lilted. The sort of voice that should narrate a reel or sing a melody. There was an undeniable comfort to the voice, and she closed her eyes, listening to the faint whisper of memory.

When she finally fell asleep, she dreamed of a bright green field with endless hills where the wind was like the last grasp of warmth before an oncoming thunderstorm. Walking towards her was a tall, broad-shouldered figure with hair like fire, and dark eyes once storm grey now reddened to maroon; inhuman, mutated, lovely eyes. He was smiling broadly, whole and strong once more, and Kitty felt a surge of relief.

If she was only ever to have one kind of dream, she wanted it to be of him.

finis

Made in the USA
Las Vegas, NV
12 July 2022

51428941R10166